SONS
OF WAR 2
SAINTS

OTHER BOOKS BY NICHOLAS SANSBURY SMITH

SONS OF WAR 2
SAINTS

NICHOLAS SANSBURY SMITH

BLACK STONE
PUBLISHING

Printed in the United States of America
Originally published in hardcover by Blackstone Publishing in 2020

First paperback edition: 2021
ISBN 978-1-66501-994-1
Fiction / Science Fiction / Apocalyptic & Post-Apocalyptic

1 3 5 7 9 10 8 6 4 2

CIP data for this book is available
from the Library of Congress

Blackstone Publishing
31 Mistletoe Rd.
Ashland, OR 97520

www.BlackstonePublishing.com

To all of those brave souls on the front lines of the COVID pandemic: doctors, nurses, paramedics, scientists, police officers, firefighters, soldiers, grocery store clerks, delivery drivers, cooks, etc. Thank you for your service, sacrifice, and selflessness.

"To win in life, a man must have a plan to conquer a mountain."

—Don Antonio Moretti

"If we stoop to the level of our enemies, we risk becoming evil ourselves."

—Lieutenant Zed Marks

-1-

The Four Diamonds public housing complexes in Ascot Hills Park reminded Vinny Moretti of his home in Naples, a place he had fled long ago. And now it seemed he had come full circle, back to where he started, in a crime-infested slum.

There was one major difference between then and now. Unlike the trash-strewn *bassifondi* of Naples, the all-new Four Diamonds were not rundown shitholes—not yet. But the crime rate was rising by the day.

"Reminds me of home," Vinny mused as he pulled his BMW into a parking lot.

"Give it a year," said Daniel "Doberman" Pedretti. "You won't be able to tell 'em apart."

Barking dogs, thumping bass, and shouts greeted Vinny and his closest friend and associate as they opened their doors. Only one of the four diamond-shaped structures was open. The government had gotten the building up quickly to help with the refugee crisis, and the others would open over the next few months.

Vinny made sure he had the tank locked to

discourage thieves from siphoning gas. Most of these vehicles were empty, and when people did use them, they brought the gas out of their apartments in red plastic containers.

The early-winter breeze cooled his face as he and Doberman walked through the maze of run-down vehicles. The wind wasn't bad today, and the threat of toxic dust blowing in from around the city was minimal. On the drive in, Vinny had checked the city signs for today's air quality. All but one read "moderate," and almost no one he saw had a dust mask on.

Still, he could almost taste the chemicals in the air. Nearly six months after the Second Civil War ended, and the city was still reeling from the nukes detonated in California. The bombs had created long-lasting health concerns.

On the walk across the parking lot, Vinny decided to put on his mask. Doberman, a borderline hypochondriac, already had his on.

The clank and rumble of heavy equipment carried across the construction site. Most of the earthmovers, cranes, and bulldozers were American, but the Chinese and Japanese contractors who won the bid on the project had brought their own workers.

Fences blocked off the other three diamond-shaped complexes. A small army of workers was finishing up the exterior of one, while two cranes tilted up the concrete walls for the next.

Over the construction noises came the *vroom* of motorcycles and scooters as a posse of young men came tearing around a corner. Laughing and cheering, the gang sped on by.

Vinny and Doberman crossed the street to a new park, built on the south side of the open complex. The whine of two-cycle engines faded into the heavy thump of amplified bass.

A group of teenagers had set out an old-school boom box at a skate park nearby. Hip-hop blared from the speakers as they honed their skills on their boards.

It was Saturday, not that it mattered. None of these kids were in school or college during the week. All educational institutions had shut down for the year. They were rumored to be reopening next spring, but Vinny wasn't betting on it.

In the meantime, the kids did what they were doing now, or they went to the beach to screw around. Boredom, as Vinny knew from experience, bred trouble, even for the younger kids playing on the new swing sets and blue slides.

This place wasn't just for swinging and sliding and skateboarding—it was a selling ground for the Morettis.

Today, Vinny and Doberman were here to meet with the dealer in charge. They were dressed down, trying to blend in, not wanting to draw attention. And except for the slicked-back hair, they were almost pulling it off.

Being Italian made them a target for enemies in other areas of the city, but Vinny wasn't worried about that here. Everyone knew that the Four Diamonds were Moretti turf.

And thanks to the deal his uncle, Don Antonio, had made with Chief Stone of the LAPD, cops rarely set foot here—unless they were trying to get a piece of the action. But that didn't mean undercover cops weren't waiting in the wings, ready to take the Moretti family down the moment the deal with Chief Stone crumbled.

Looking out across the flow of people coming and going, Vinny had a feeling one of them was out there, perhaps even living right here. He shook off the suspicion and walked around the playground.

The laughter of teenagers and children was a reprieve, but by midafternoon the junkies would be feeling the chimp on their back and prowling for their next fix. Any parents who actually gave a shit about their kids had them inside, where it was safe.

Vinny stopped to watch two younger boys kicking a soccer ball.

"That was us a decade ago," Vinny said.

"What?" Doberman was busy watching some young girls gossiping on the stoop of a side entrance to the open building.

A middle-aged woman, probably the mother of one of the girls, shouted from a balcony on the fifth floor. She went back to watering the potted plants on the small deck. Most of the residents grew what they could to help compensate for the lack of rations. Every radish, tomato, and lettuce leaf counted, no matter how meager.

The government had done a good job getting the buildings up, but the city was responsible for feeding these people, and Mayor Buren was having a hell of a time. Produce from Mexico and South America was helping, and proximity to the border helped, but the aid coming in from other countries wasn't enough.

Vinny kept walking, noticing people who could easily be fellow Neapolitans. Through his eyes, they were innocents with families—people just trying to survive in a dangerous, upended world. But to his father and his uncle, these people were customers, and business was again on fire. People paid in whatever currency they had: silver, gold, jewelry, guns, even the greatly devalued US dollar.

One of the first customers of the morning staggered out of a building and put a hand above his eyes against the glare of the sun. Wearing shorts, flip-flops, and a torn T-shirt, the man headed for the street corner.

Vinny and Doberman approached the same corner, where a Moretti employee stood watch under a light pole. The ten-year-old kid with a backward baseball cap saw them and whistled to a boy across the street, who took off running.

Vinny didn't like some of the strategies his family used, but he had to admit, his uncle had vision. He was always two steps ahead of his enemies and the police.

"Yo!" shouted a voice.

A man in a denim jacket and faded jeans waited for a car to pass, then hurried across a street. Curly black hair hung over his ears.

"'Sup, Lorenzo?" Vinny said.

"Hey, hey, my friends," Lorenzo said, raising his arms. "What brings you to the Kingdom of Heaven this morning?"

"Doing the rounds," Vinny said. He gave the man a homie handshake, and Doberman did the same.

"How are things here?" Vinny asked.

"Ah, good, good," Lorenzo said. "We're blowing through everything you guys give me, and the Vegas are keeping their distance. Cops, too."

Vinny looked down the street at another car passing by.

"Good," said Doberman. "We have enough problems with so many of these bums not paying."

Lorenzo snorted. "It's getting worse, and I don't have enough men to hunt down what we're owed."

"We're working on that," Vinny said.

Doberman suddenly stepped away, and Vinny's hand instinctively went to his pistol. He relaxed when he saw the kind features of Raffaello Tursi, one of his father and Don Antonio's most loyal and trusted friends.

He held the hand of a fair-skinned woman with freckles and red hair.

Seeing the old-country Moretti soldier and the American woman together the first time had been a shock to them all, but Raff was finally getting married, and Vinny was happy for him. Of all the soldiers and associates over the years, he had always treated Vinny with kindness and respect.

Since that fateful day in Naples when Vinny lost his mom and half his family in an ambush, Raff had looked after everyone. Now he mostly served as a special bodyguard to Vinny's Aunt Lucia and younger cousin Marco.

Raff raised a hand as he walked over. "Vin, Daniel," he said politely. "You guys remember my fiancée, Crystal, right?"

"Good to see you," Vinny said.

Doberman nodded.

Crystal nodded back, her freckled face blushing as Lorenzo gave her the elevator eyes. Raff noticed, but he didn't react by throwing a punch, as some in his position might.

Vinny often thought Raff would have made a good teacher, psychotherapist, or maybe even a cop—definitely not a gangster. Carmine, Frankie, Yellowtail, Lino, Christopher, and Antonio—all the other made men in the Moretti organization—fit the part, but not Raff.

Another whistle distracted them, and Lorenzo jogged over to the kid with the backward baseball cap.

"I'll see you later," Raff said with a warm smile. "Got to get to the compound before your uncle starts wondering where I've been."

"Don't worry, he's happy for you," Vinny said.

They left, and Vinny walked over to Lorenzo. "What's up?" he asked.

Lorenzo looked at the top of the ten-story building. "Follow me. We might have trouble."

He led Vinny and Doberman through the building's front entrance, into a hallway with overflowing wastebaskets. The new cheap carpet already smelled like a broken sewer line.

For a new building, this place was going downhill fast, and the Moretti family had a lot to do with it. Three junkies were curled up on the tile floor, sleeping off the night. One of them stirred as Vinny passed. He reached up toward Lorenzo.

"Hey, man, you got—"

Lorenzo kicked his hand away. "You still haven't paid for your last fix, asshole. I'll be back for you later."

He opened a door to a stairwell and motioned for Vinny and Doberman. The concrete walls were already marked with graffiti and colorful paintings. He admired some of it on the way up to the tenth floor.

Lorenzo opened the exit door to the blinding glow of the sun. Vinny put his sunglasses on and stepped onto the roof. Rows of wooden beds were set up, the sprouts of pole beans and carrots already pushing up through the dirt.

Long tarps were rolled up at the railings, waiting to protect the crops from dust storms and acid rain. Among the rows was another type of farm—banks of solar panels angled toward the sun, absorbing the energy to help power the building when the city shut the grid down.

Lorenzo took Vinny and Doberman past the panels and the residents tending their crops, to the north side of the roof.

The sound of motorcycles below grew louder, but this time it wasn't just some teenagers screwing around. At least a dozen new motorcycles were parked on a street framed by construction zones.

Two bikers blasted down the road on their crotch rockets.

"Yamazakis," Vinny said.

"Yup," Lorenzo said. "I told them I have no problem selling them our shit, but they need to keep their fucking bikes out of here. It's bad for business."

"You sure they aren't selling our shit to our own retail customers?" Doberman asked.

Lorenzo cursed in two languages, but Vinny just shrugged. That didn't bother him. What bothered him was that the Yamazakis didn't have their own turf.

His uncle had feared that the construction projects

would bring other crime organizations and gangs from around the world. The Yamazakis were one of them. From what Vinny knew, they had fled political upheaval and fighting in Japan to seek refuge in Los Angeles, much as his own family had done.

"Want me to send some guys to deal with 'em?" Lorenzo asked.

"Nah, I'll do it," Vinny said.

With Doberman, he set off walking toward the bikers.

"You sure this is a good idea?" Doberman asked.

"They won't touch us here," Vinny said.

"I've got a few of my guys on the way just in case," Lorenzo said, trying to keep up. He was out of shape, and he smoked. Not a good combination.

Vinny slowed as they approached the bikers.

The street was abandoned, and the only people in sight besides the Yamazakis were construction workers on the other side of the fences. Most of them were busy working, but a few had stepped up to watch the racing and fancy moves.

Vinny wasn't impressed.

"Which one of you is Isao!" he shouted.

A dozen full-coverage helmets turned in his direction. Several men hopped off their bikes, but none approached.

"You just going to stare, or what?" Vinny asked.

Lorenzo and Doberman stepped up to his side.

A muscular guy in black pants and a tight-fitting red jacket took off his helmet. He was almost a foot taller than Vinny, probably even taller than Doberman. Two bikers followed him. He stopped a few feet away.

"You're Isao?" Vinny asked.

"I am. And you must be Vinny Moretti." He spoke perfect, virtually unaccented English.

Vinny cocked one brow, and Isao beamed a handsome grin of white, straight teeth.

"I like to know my enemies and my friends," Isao said. "The question is, Which are you?"

"Do you realize where the fuck you are?" Vinny asked, taking a step forward.

Both of Isao's men also took a step, and Doberman and Lorenzo mirrored them.

"We're just having a little fun on our bikes," Isao said.

He gave the towers a fleeting glance, and Vinny caught the greed in his eyes. In that moment, he knew what Isao wanted—exactly what his uncle had feared.

And in the same moment, Vinny knew he would have to kill this man.

The people living here wouldn't rat him out, but the Japanese construction workers might.

In his peripheral vision, he saw that more of them had stepped up to watch. It would take a second, maybe two, to reach behind his back, draw the Glock, and put a bullet in Isao's handsome face. But he didn't trust the workers.

"Have your fun somewhere else," Vinny said. "I won't tell you again."

"We buy from you," Isao said, his tone deepening to almost a growl. "You're telling us you don't want our business?"

"I'm telling you you're not welcome here anymore," Vinny said.

Isao's lip curled, and he inched closer to Vinny.

"Watch it," Doberman said.

The rumble of older bikes rose in the background. Vinny didn't need to turn to see that Moretti associates were on their way.

But Isao did. He looked over Vinny's shoulder, sizing up the numbers. Then he smiled again and nodded at Vinny.

"I'll be seeing you, Vinny Moretti," he said.

Isao walked back to the bikes with his men. They hopped on and sped away.

"Assholes," Lorenzo said.

"Keep an eye on them," Vinny said. "Don Antonio was right. The Vegas aren't our only enemies."

Ronaldo Salvatore looked out at a sky the color of a dead fish. He had seen more gray skies than blue over the past six months. It could have been much worse. The short but devastating civil war had raged across the country, ending in nuclear fires that leveled several American capital cities, including Sacramento.

Although the radioactive ash had stopped raining down long ago, the ravaged terrain and droughts had transformed parts of California into a wasteland. Wildfires burned through dry forests, dumping smoke into the sky. Much of the Angeles National Forest was nothing but black stumps and white ash.

Ronaldo pulled his breathing apparatus over his mouth and nose to protect his lungs from the toxic smoke that hung in the air. It was getting worse by the day as more of the hills around Los Angeles burned.

Charred trees lined both sides of Highway 39 as the tan pickup traveled farther away from the Pasadena border walls. He sat in the passenger seat, bored.

"Chaplain" William Bettis gripped the wheel, and Callum "Tooth" McCloud lounged in the back seat.

Now that the Marine Corps and the United States Army had been disbanded, the three men worked for the Los Angeles County Sheriff's Department. Having his brothers in arms with him at least made the hostile conditions bearable.

The men had been through a lot in the past few years, from the battlefields in the Afghan mountains to the wild streets of Los Angeles. They all had aged considerably. Even fresh-faced Tooth had a few gray hairs popping up in his ginger goatee.

For the last part of the windy drive, silence filled the cab—nothing but the low hum of the V-8 engine and the crunch of rocks under the off-road tires. The team should have been nearing the end of a twelve-hour shift that started at four in the morning, but they wouldn't be going home anytime soon. Dispatch had called in a drone sighting of suspected traffickers.

Tooth nodded off in the back seat again only to be woken up by his own snoring. He sighed and blinked, looked out the window, then relaxed.

Bettis kept focused on the road. So did Ronaldo. They were looking for three vehicles: a pickup and two SUVs, all black, heading southwest. The highway was a main artery for refugees headed to the processing centers on the border of Los Angeles. It was also the thoroughfare used by traffickers of all sorts of commodities. The big three were always drugs, automatic weapons, and humans.

Ronaldo flexed his right fist. His daughter was one of thousands kidnapped and sold off by crime organizations and dirty cops. His heart ached at the thought that came a thousand times a day when he was awake and filled his nightmares when he slept.

But he *would* find her.

Every time his team got a call, Ronaldo wondered whether this was it. Would they find Monica in the back of some shitty pickup truck or inside a van that smelled of urine and feces? But with every day that passed, the chances of that happening dwindled.

She's still alive, he promised himself. *And she's waiting for you to find her.*

Ronaldo wasn't the only one looking. His best friend, Marine Staff Sergeant Zed Marks, was now a lieutenant in the LAPD, where his personal priority, even above battling the crime families and stopping the rampant trafficking, was to bring Monica home—assuming she was even still in Los Angeles.

Now, more than six months after she was taken, she could be anywhere. Ronaldo tried not to think about the worst case and focused on the mission.

"We should have intercepted them by now," he said. "Get back to dispatch and see where that drone is."

Bettis picked up the radio handset from the dashboard.

The dispatcher had a scratchy voice, and she sounded annoyed. "Last sighting was at mile marker fifteen," she replied.

"Copy that," Bettis said. He put the receiver back, and Ronaldo unfolded the map.

"We're about two miles from that marker," Ronaldo said. "Chances are, they pulled off on a side road to wait for dark. Not a bad move now that they're close to the city. Probably planning on ditching the vehicles and going in on foot so they don't have to queue up for entry."

"So, we can go home now?" Tooth asked. He poked his head up between the front seats. His breath reeked like a pond full of dead minnows.

"No," Ronaldo said. He looked right. "Take that road."

Tooth groaned, and Bettis steered off the highway and onto a dusty road into the foothills. A small copse of trees had survived in a cleft below a bluff, protected from the wind that had swept embers across the rest of the canopy.

That cluster of trees was like Los Angeles, one of the only major cities in California to survive the crippling civil war. But like the city, the trees weren't spared entirely. They were infected with a blight that caused their leaves to wither and fall in rustling brown piles. A disease festered in the city as well.

While the LAPD had won the war against the major street gangs, something worse had risen in the wake of Chief Diamond's assassination. After removing the one man standing in their way, crime families had clawed their way to the top of the food chain in the void the gangs had left behind. Seeing the same opportunity, new criminal organizations had come from other countries, seeking to seize turf in the aftermath of the apocalypse.

The pickup jolted up a hill. Ronaldo pulled his mask down and wiped the sweat off his face, guts sinking as he glanced out the window. There wasn't much of a shoulder on the passenger side, with probably five hundred feet of air between them and the bottom of the ravine.

A dry creek bed snaked through the canyon. Ronaldo spotted bones of a large animal, maybe a deer or a calf, lying on the rocky bank.

Not much was left in this part of the county. And every day, while good people watched their lives go up in cinders, the crime families grew stronger from their misery.

The remnants of the Norteño Mafia, now under the banner of the Vega and López families, were one of the most powerful. But old-school Neapolitan mafiosi had also grabbed a piece of the pie, with the Moretti family coming out on top. The Russians had cut out a sliver under the leadership of Sergei Nevsky, a Cold War gangster with blood as frosty as Siberian vodka in January.

There were others, too: the Boai family from China and the Yamazakis from Japan.

All these families and syndicates were adding more territory, and more cops to their payrolls, while the good guys like Lieutenant Marks and Ronaldo's son, Dominic, lost ground and saw their resources sucked dry.

"Yeah, girl," Tooth mumbled.

Ronaldo looked in the back seat just as Tooth jerked awake.

"Dude, you have been talking in your sleep a lot lately," Ronaldo said.

Tooth shook his head, disoriented. He turned to the window and saw the terrain. Then he rubbed his eyes and sat up straighter. "Man, I was having a dream about my favorite ex-girlfriend."

"We don't want to know, man," Bettis said. "We don't even want to *suspect.*"

Tooth's lips parted in a grin, flashing the prominent upper incisors that earned him his moniker. "I forget you're a prude, Monsignor."

"And I forget you're a—"

"Watch out!" Ronaldo shouted.

As they rounded a corner, Bettis slammed on the brakes, jerking to a stop in front of a badly shot-up silver SUV blocking the road. The seat belt stopped Ronaldo from slamming into the dashboard. He clicked out of it before the truck had stopped. Then he put his mask back on and grabbed his M4A1.

"On me," he said.

As Ronaldo jumped out, Tooth stumbled out the back and Bettis came up on the other side. In front of them was a silver Ford Explorer riddled with bullet holes.

Ronaldo flashed hand signals, and the men fanned out, checking the forest left of the road, and the bluffs above, for hostiles.

It appeared that whoever had shot up the SUV was long gone, but they had left several victims behind.

Ronaldo came around to the front passenger side, where a man was slumped against the dash, his back spotted with blood from multiple gunshot wounds. A touch confirmed he had been dead for a while.

"I got a live one," Tooth called out.

The injured man lay in the grass at the edge of the road, perilously close to the railing that had snapped in half.

A pickup truck had gone over the other side and stopped halfway down the slope.

"Bettis, with me," Ronaldo said. "Tooth, you help this guy."

Tread marks carved down the slope, the dislodged rocks and chewed-up vegetation providing a path that Ronaldo followed carefully. He stepped down at an angle, left boot first, rifle in both hands.

The pickup had smashed into a boulder halfway down the hill. Bullet holes perforated the tailgate, and all the windows were shattered. Ronaldo gave Bettis a hand signal and shouldered his rifle.

They took different sides. Ronaldo opened the rear passenger door. Little cubes of safety glass littered the empty seats.

"Over here," Bettis said.

Ronaldo joined him and saw a stuffed animal on the driver's-side floor. He reached in and picked up a furry dog with tattered ears.

It affirmed what they had suspected: the traffickers likely had kids with them—young ones.

"Where the hell did they go?" Bettis asked.

"I don't know, but someone must have rescued them and killed the fuckers that . . ."

Something in the creek bed below had caught Ronaldo's eye.

Ronaldo brought up the combat sight on his rifle and scanned the area. Three naked bodies lay near the dry shoreline. Their ankles and wrists were bound. He pushed the scope away when he saw the wounds.

"Up here!" shouted Tooth.

He stood near the smashed guardrail, waving his arms.

"Come on," Ronaldo said to Bettis.

They scrambled back up the ravine and followed Tooth back to the injured man. Tooth had propped him up against the shot-up Explorer and given him water.

"We gotta get this guy to a hospital," Tooth said. He looked shaken—a rare sight.

"No," the man mumbled. "My daughter . . . my wife . . ."

He licked his cracked lips and pointed.

Ronaldo followed his finger to the guardrail.

"Did you find them?" the man asked.

The realization hit Ronaldo hard. His wife was one of the dead bodies at the bottom of the ravine. And his daughter . . .

The same fate as Monica.

While the man begged them to find his family, Ronaldo waved his men over.

"They're refugees who were trying to make it to the walls," Tooth said. "The traffickers must have hit them and snatched the kids."

Ronaldo looked at the bluffs in the distance.

"Someone's hunting on these roads," he said. "And we're going to find them."

* * *

The sleek black BMW M7 pulled up on a hill overlooking a sprawling construction site. Gravel crunched under the expensive machine's tires.

Darkness carpeted the landscape as the horizon swallowed the last glow of sunset. The LED headlights adjusted, firing on and illuminating a fence with a No Trespassing sign.

Lino De Caro rubbed the gold hoop in his ear. "We're here, Don Antonio," he said.

Lino pulled off and killed the engine, then got out to open the passenger door. Antonio Moretti's Gucci loafers stepped out onto the wet gravel.

He pulled on the cuffs of the black Gucci suit, also new. Not entirely practical, but expensive suits were tradition, and he wasn't going to break tradition just because the world had gone to shit. If anything, this was the time to show the world who was in charge. He

buttoned the middle button to conceal the P320 SIG
Sauer holstered inside his waistband.

Storm clouds rolled over the skyline as Christopher, his younger brother, got out and joined him.
They gazed out at a lucrative part of their kingdom: the
Four Diamonds public housing complexes at what had
been Ascot Hills Park.

Two of the city blocks built in a diamond pattern
were lit up. The city was still working to get the power
grid back on, so the bulk of the complexes' power came
from the solar and wind farms that Mayor Buren had
promised six months ago.

When at capacity, the diamond-shaped complexes
would house over fifty thousand people. These structures looked modern on the outside, with a brick facade
and solar roof panels. But the insides were slapped together fast, with the cheapest materials. Fifty-dollar
toilets with plastic seats, one coat of paint throughout,
and the cheapest appliances. They were slums by design.
Antonio had seen plenty of them in his life, not only in
the Middle East while serving in Italy's Fourth Alpini
Regiment, but also in Naples, where he had grown up.

If Antonio had to guess, these new buildings would
be run down and overflowing their capacity within two
years. Not much of a guess, though, what with a fractured government in charge that didn't know shit about
how to rebuild a country.

The buildings were a "gift" to help the city deal
with war refugees, but the real gift was to the Moretti
family. This would be their biggest selling grounds now
that Antonio had flushed out the gangs by sparking
a war between the cops and his rivals. And by killing

Chief Diamond, he had ensured that the new LAPD ranks would remain corrupt.

A smile crossed Don Antonio Moretti's face. He had more than earned his place on this hill overlooking the slums, and this was only the beginning of the empire he was planning. Soon he would be king of the entire city and, eventually, the whole West Coast.

"Almost done," said Christopher. "The other two complexes open in a few weeks."

Antonio looked at his younger brother. His longish goatee was streaked with gray, which also flecked the sides of his thick hair.

"What are you thinking?" Christopher asked.

"I think you should never doubt me again. When we first came here, you said none of this was possible, remember?"

Christopher nodded ruefully. "I'm sorry, broth—"

"Don't talk," Antonio said. He grabbed his brother by the scruff of the neck. Then he tightened his grip and brought his face close, so they were inches apart.

"We have money, guns, and power," Antonio said. "But family is the most important of them all. When you can't trust your family, you have nothing. "Don't you *ever* forget that."

"I won't, and I do trust you."

"I know."

Antonio let go of his brother as gravel crunched behind them.

A black Mercedes SUV pulled up, bringing four more men who had been with Antonio and Christopher since the massacre that nearly wiped their family out almost nine years earlier.

Frankie Trentino and Carmine Barese got out. They wore leather coats and had their hair slicked back. They both lit cigarettes—back to old habits they had kicked after coming to Los Angeles.

Trails of smoke rose into the air behind them as they joined Antonio and Christopher. The other two men, Raffaello Tursi and Zachary "Yellowtail" Moretti, held small submachine guns.

They had several more rifles in the cars—and grenades, too, if they needed them.

Wherever Antonio went, he came prepared for battle. The war wasn't over until he was king, and he had plenty of enemies to conquer before the throne was his.

"Looks like more acid rain," Frankie said.

"At least the air quality isn't bad tonight," Christopher said. "'Cept for you guys, sucking on them cigarettes."

"I'd go for a cigar if you got one," Carmine replied. His English was getting much better, and judging by his eyes, he wasn't doing any of the company product. That was good. And ever since Carmine had blown off part of Chief Diamond's head, Antonio remembered why he'd made the soldier a captain.

Frankie cracked his neck from side to side. "So remind me," he said, "what did we drive out here for?"

"We'll find out soon," Antonio said. "In the meantime, enjoy the view."

"Who would have thought the apocalypse would make us rich men?" Carmine said.

"I gotta admit, I had my doubts," Frankie said.

"I still don't like working with the cops," Carmine grumbled.

Frankie nodded.

Antonio felt his blood pressure rising. He needed to have the same trust talk he'd had with Christopher, but Frankie must have sensed it.

"Most of the cops are as crooked as a hooker taking it in the *culo*," Frankie said with a grin. "And so far, it's working to our advantage."

Carmine shrugged, and Antonio let it go. His blood was already boiling from another problem far bigger than whatever Carmine and Frankie thought of his plan to work with local law enforcement.

"We're selling more drugs than we can bring in," Antonio said, "but it's attracting a lot of attention. That's why we're here. The Vegas aren't the only family I'm worried about, as you already know."

"I'm getting close to finding Esteban," Frankie said. "Miguel, too."

Antonio thought about the power struggle between the Vegas and the López family, who had entered an alliance not long after the Norteño Mafia dissolved. The two families had absorbed the Zetas, MS-13, Florencia 13, the Latin Kings, the Sureños, and every other shitbag who cared about drug money more than about old oaths and the tattoos that branded their flesh.

"Speaking of the pigs," Christopher said.

In the distance, blue and red lights glowed from several police cruisers that had parked on the road bordering one of the open complexes. Within a few minutes, an entire street was filled with flashing police strobes. Antonio could see emergency crews walking over the border, but the cops stayed behind the line, watching.

Headlights approaching from behind made

Antonio turn, reaching for his gun. Then the LED beams flicked off, and he saw a third car, an older-model black BMW. His nephew Vinny got out with his tall, tattooed friend, Doberman.

"About time," Christopher grumbled. He walked over to his son, but Antonio stayed where he was, waiting patiently to hear what had happened.

Vinny, sporting a fresh gentleman's cut, hurried over with a duffel bag. He dropped it in the dirt in front of the gathered men.

"The fuck is this?" Carmine asked.

Doberman, holding another bag, stepped up next to Vinny but didn't say a word.

"Open it," Antonio said.

Vinny bent down and unzipped the bag, then pulled out two bricks of cocaine and held them up.

"This is all that's left of our last haul," he said.

"What do you mean?" Carmine said. "That's it?"

"And this is all that's left of our dealer Lorenzo." Doberman gently lowered his bag to the ground and opened it. Inside was a head with curly black hair. The eyes were missing.

"Esteban Vega, that son of a poxed whore," Frankie grumbled.

Antonio bent down and fished out one of the arms. He had seen plenty of disassembled body parts in his time—that didn't bother him—but his was different.

"This wasn't the Vegas," he said. Holding up the arm in the moonlight, he gave his men a view of the cut. "This was done by a samurai sword."

"I should have killed Isao instead of just telling him to fuck off," Vinny said. "We got to hit back hard.

This time they took our product, but next time they'll be back for our turf."

Antonio was curious and let him keep talking.

"We've got to set an example," Vinny continued. "Do something to make them never mess with us again. I say we kidnap one of them and send him back to Isao in a barrel of acid."

Antonio smiled. He liked his nephew's enthusiasm, but the boy was still young and had no idea how to respond to an attack like this.

"Killing ten of them won't set an example," Antonio said. "It will start a war."

"So we don't hit back at all?" Vinny asked, taken aback.

"Oh, we'll hit them, all right," Antonio replied, "but not your way."

A smirk crossed Carmine's scarred face—probably feeling nostalgic about some of the tricks they had learned back in Naples.

"Let me do this," Vinny said eagerly. "Lorenzo was my friend."

Antonio scrutinized his nephew, unsure that he was ready for the challenge. In this new world, they couldn't make a single mistake. They had to be lions, and his nephew was still just a pup.

"Chrissy and I will deal with this," Antonio said. "You just make sure the shipments that come to the port get to their location safely, got it?"

Vinny hesitated a beat, then nodded.

"Leave these wannabe samurais to me and Don Antonio," Christopher said. "When we're done with them, they'll be swimming their asses back to Japan."

-3-

"Man, I miss the days of Spotify," said Andre "Moose" Clarke. He flipped through the radio stations on the police cruiser's dashboard. Pickings were slim for listeners in Los Angeles: one news station that reported the constant trickle of information coming in from across the fractured country, one that played the top 100 from before the Billboard charts vanished, and a third station, now playing the Beach Boys.

"Surf music? *Really?*" Dominic Salvatore reached over from the passenger seat and turned it to rap. An old-school remix featuring Doctor Dre and Tupac boomed from the crackling speakers.

"Now, that's what I'm talking about, baby," Moose said. He moved his massive shoulders side to side, snapped his fingers to the beat. "My man, Tupac."

It was good to see his friend happy. Losing both parents and a promising career as an actor, and another as a professional soccer player, had put Moose through the wringer.

Everyone had lost someone in the war. For Dom, it was his sister.

His spirits sank at the thought, and Moose must have noticed.

"Okay, bro?" He turned his head, his sculpted antler-shaped dreadlocks scraping on the cruiser's low headliner.

"Yeah, I'm good," Dom lied. He listened to the song's now-ironic words about California knowing how to party. Once, maybe it had, but that was far from the current reality. Most people with the means had fled the city, to the Midwest or the Southeast, where radiation-free zones were attracting families looking to work on farms and in factories.

Dom wasn't one of them. He wasn't leaving until he found his sister.

"Let me welcome everybody to the Wild Wild West." Moose rapped the lyrics, using one hand to mimic the beat.

"Ain't that the truth," Dom said.

Moose slowed to let several people jaywalk across the street to the Saint Francis Medical Center in Lynwood. A line of people with radiation poisoning and other ailments snaked out of the lobby. Most of them wore masks and goggles, though some had only scarfs covering their faces, and nothing over their eyes. Not that they hadn't been warned. All across the city, signs cautioned everyone to protect their eyes and lungs.

Dom wore a Chinese-made breathing apparatus when he was outside. It was wrapped around his neck now since the windows were up. The device was well made, with a filter that had to be changed only once a week. The Chinese had mastered the technology after decades of serious air pollution in their major cities.

This wasn't just smog, though. There was still radioactive contamination, too, especially outside the walls.

Many refugees who had come in from bordering cities and states were afflicted with radiation poisoning. No doubt, some were in the line that now wrapped around a parking lot of tents.

"Jesus," Dom said. Medical centers all over town were hanging on by a whisker, trying to keep the starving, diseased population alive while aid trickled in from other countries and the most unlikely donors.

"Ironic that Antonio Moretti is the biggest financial supporter of Saint Francis," Dom muttered. "Although I guess we shouldn't be surprised."

"Nope, gotta keep the customers alive," Moose replied.

"Whatever helps him sleep at night."

"I don't think that scumbag has a hard time sleeping. Most sociopaths don't."

Dom sighed. That was what separated the good guys from the bad guys. If you could murder another human being and still sleep like a baby at night, you had a tarnished soul. Dom wasn't sure about this, but he hadn't slept a full night since he first killed a man in self-defense.

Even now the thought sent a chill through him.

He had killed more since that night, many with the rifle now propped against his seat. The M1A SOCOM 16 was almost always within reach, and even now, at three a.m., he was ready and alert as the cruiser crossed

Central Avenue into Compton. The city had been no-torious for violence even before the collapse.

Storm clouds blocked out the moon, but the way was lit by burning trash barrels outside an aban-doned elementary school turned into a flophouse for junkies.

They passed a burned-out Jack in the Box. Dom's mouth watered. After MMA training, he would hit that place and eat two double cheeseburgers. He could almost smell them cooking. The phantom scent made his stomach growl.

Odd, the things Dom missed from the old world. Only six months had passed since the government col-lapsed, and not even a year since the global economy tanked, but it all seemed like the distant past.

Gone were his dreams of going to college, buying a house, and traveling the world. All the luxuries he had taken for granted had also dried up: a shower every day, electricity, internet.

But he was alive and had clean water and food to keep him hunting for his little sister and the demons who had taken her.

Dom's belly growled loud enough for Moose to look over.

"You want something to eat?" he asked. "I packed a few sandwiches back there."

"Know what? I do," Dom replied. As he reached behind him, the radio crackled. Gunshots at the Angel Pyramids.

"Vega territory," Moose grumbled. "Great. We're an hour from shift being up."

"Doubt they'll send us there, man," Dom said. He

grabbed a sandwich and wolfed it down while his partner and best friend steered down another street.

The drive back to the station in Downey would take another hour if they covered their whole beat, but Moose pulled over and found a parking lot. With gas so limited, they often would find a safe place with good vantages and kill the engine.

But the radio crackled again.

"Officer down at the corner of Twenty-Ninth and Vine Street," said the dispatcher. "Requesting all units in the vicinity."

Moose mashed the pedal as Dom grabbed the radio off the dash. "Unit nineteen responding," he said.

The tires squealed as Moose pulled out of the empty lot. Speeding toward Highway 105, other squad cars joined them, lights flashing.

Moose glanced over. "Your vest tight?"

"Always, brother," Dom said, patting his chest.

The highway gave them a view of inner Compton, or what the LAPD called "No-Man's Land." The Vegas controlled most of this area, too, and normally, when the gangs started shooting each other, the police let them fight it out. But tonight, one of their brothers had been caught in the cross fire.

The cruiser's engine groaned.

"She needs a tune-up, man," Moose said. "Shit, I keep telling the mechanics, but nobody does shit. Just wait until it breaks down on us."

Dom dreaded the thought. Cops already had a target on their back. A lone cruiser in No-Man's Land was a death sentence. They had just found three cops hanging from a bridge not far from the interstate a week earlier. Their crime: not taking bribes.

It wasn't the crooked cops who were in danger; it was the good ones.

Dom took a swig from his water bottle as the radio sounded again. This time, the dispatcher reported multiple officers down at the same location.

"What in the hell is going on?" Dom muttered.

Three more cruisers joined them on the interstate. Seven raced in a line, their headlights spearing through the haze. They pulled off on Crenshaw and raced toward Inglewood.

Heart pounding, Dom prepared for more violence.

At times like this, he always thought of his family. His mother was back at their apartment, probably lying next to his father, staring at the ceiling, worrying about their little girl.

Dom hated seeing his mom in such rough shape, but at least his dad was with her tonight. Ronaldo had gotten off not long after Dom set off for his shift. It was tough not seeing his dad much, but they both were doing their part to find Monica and save the city.

Although nights like tonight, it felt like pissing on a house fire.

Dom saw the flashing lights ahead.

"This looks like an F-five shitstorm," Moose said.

He turned at Crenshaw and Century Boulevard for their first view of the Angel Pyramids. The six new public housing buildings were lit up like Vegas on New Year's Eve.

Moose followed the other cars to an overpass that gave them a view of the scene. Muzzle flashes came from multiple windows of a building across the street from the Hollywood Park Casino.

This wasn't a skirmish—it was a battle royal.

Four police cruisers and an unmarked car were parked in front of a building off West Century Boulevard. If Dom had to guess, the cruisers had responded to the gunfire but had been ambushed.

Across the road were public housing units, their floors stacked like Mayan pyramids. Hundreds of civilians were on the grass, watching from a distance.

"Get back!" Dom shouted out the window.

Moose parked behind a dozen other cruisers and emergency vehicles a block from the scene. He and Dom jumped out and ran through the maze of cars and trucks.

A patrol sergeant with a Kevlar helmet and an old-school M16 was barking orders at a group of rookie cops who had beat them there. Palm trees and a parking lot of broken-down vehicles separated them from the abandoned apartment buildings across from the Pyramids.

"We've got ten officers pinned down!" shouted the patrol sergeant. "Take up position in the parking lot and lay down covering fire so we can get the wounded out!"

"Why not send in an armored vehicle?" asked a female officer.

"You see any armored vehicles around here, shithead?" the sergeant replied.

The man looked to Dom and Moose, but Dom didn't wait for orders. He took off running across the parking lot, keeping low. Moose did his best to hunch over, but he was huge and made an easy target.

Gunfire zipped in their direction, shattering a minivan window.

"Down, down!" Dom said.

He got behind a sedan and crouched there with Moose. The other officers fanned out, taking position across the center of the lot. Dom and Moose had been in situations like this, but he still wasn't used to bullets flying inches away from his flesh.

"Keep your damn head down," Dom said. "I'm going to have a look."

He inched up behind the car and glanced over. Bullets punched through the back doors. A tire hissed, and more glass shattered.

Moose scrambled for cover behind another car, and Dom followed. The woman who had asked the question earlier was there, trembling with a pistol clutched to her chest, eyes wide with fear.

"Stay down, and don't draw attention to us . . ." Dom looked at her name tag. "Julia, you listening to me?"

She managed a nod.

Dom waited a few moments before taking another look at the building. No bullets were hitting the vehicle. He scanned the side of the building with his binoculars.

Muzzle flashes came from windows on the third, fourth, and fifth floors. There was also movement on the roof: two men carrying what looked like an M240.

"I've got at least ten shooters, all with auto weapons, one fifty-cal," he reported.

"And I got this hunk-of-shit M4 that freezes up worse than a zit-faced kid on a first date," Moose grumbled.

Gunfire cracked from the cops making their way toward the street where the officers were pinned. The dozen-plus men and women drew the attention of the *sicarios* in the windows.

Dom pushed the scope back up to his eye and zoomed in on the rooftop. The men with the .50 were setting up, their tattooed necks illuminated in the moonlight. Most of these guys were former Latin Kings or MS-13, mortal enemies who had given up their differences for a piece of the pie after the war.

Dom never found it easy to take a life, but it was easier when the perps were trying to kill good cops. Lining up the sights, he pulled the trigger once, twice, three times. Both men on the .50 went down. He aimed at a muzzle flash coming from the fourth-floor window.

Two trigger pulls, and the flashes ceased. But his position was compromised. He hunkered down as gunfire pounded the vehicle from another location.

Moose grabbed Julia and shielded her with his body as bullets perforated the hood.

"Stay here and cover me," Dom said.

Moose nodded.

Dom ran for another car and checked the firing zone. No bullets chased him this time, but he still waited before propping his rifle up. He found a target within seconds and took it out with a shot to the chest.

Then Dom bolted for another vehicle as rounds slammed the car he had fired from seconds earlier. Nine bullets remained in his magazine, and he used two to take down a fifth sicario.

Moose provided covering fire, allowing Dom to get even closer to the street. By the time he got to the end of the parking lot, Dom had taken down six shooters and had two bullets left.

Dom hid behind one tree, while Julia and Moose took up position behind another. Dom could see the silhouettes of shooters behind the missing windows.

He counted six, which meant more sicarios had joined the fray. Several continued firing at the cops in the street. Dom glanced around the tree for a look.

Red and blue lights flashed over the scene of crumpled bodies. A young officer was on the ground behind a cruiser, holding his leg and crying out in pain. Four other cops weren't moving at all. A sixth crawled away from a vehicle, toward the curb.

"Stay put!" Dom shouted.

The man reached up, only to have fingers blown off.

Dom squeezed off his last two rounds. The casings flew away as he hunkered down.

"Moose, grab that guy!" he yelled while changing his magazine. "Julia, you cover him with me!"

Moose handed Julia his M4.

"Now!" Dom shouted. She hesitated, and then rose to her feet to fire while Moose ran out into the street. Return fire forced her down, but Dom kept firing, moving the scope from window to window.

Bullets ricocheted off the concrete, catching Moose out. He dragged the wounded cop back to a cruiser for shelter.

"Stay where you are, Moose!" Dom shouted. He looked to Julia. "When I tell you, shoot at the fourth floor, third window from the left, okay? There are two snipers there."

She nodded.

Dom crouched into position. The other cops making their way across the parking lot were firing and attracting some of the fire, but he knew it wouldn't be enough. As soon as he moved, gunfire would follow, and he couldn't keep getting lucky. Eventually, a bullet would find him.

Another wounded cop cried out, this one from the parking lot. Dom watched in horror as the guy took multiple rounds to the chest, jerking with each impact.

Dom gritted his teeth. So much pointless death.

Bullets slammed into the tree he was hiding behind. A shout followed—something in Spanish. Perhaps a taunt to get him to move.

"Dom!" Moose yelled. "I'm gonna run for it!"

"NO!" Dom shouted back.

In the parking lot, another officer went down with a bullet to the leg. He tried to find cover behind a car, but several rounds caught him first.

Dom closed his eyes, then looked to Julia.

"Get ready," he said.

She nodded back, clutching the M4.

They couldn't wait another second. He stood, still protected by the tree, and readied his rifle.

He bolted away to draw fire while Julia kept shooting. Something hot hit his left leg. He went down on the dirt and rolled behind a bus-stop bench.

When he looked back to the tree, Julia had fallen and wasn't moving.

"Jesus, no," Dom groaned. He checked for Moose. The big guy was still hiding behind the cruiser with the gravely wounded officer. Bullets continued to riddle the car's roof and sides.

The cop car was shot to hell, windows shattered, tires flat. Dom's leg felt as if it had caught fire. Blood dripped from his pant cuff, but for all that, it looked as though the bullet had just nicked him.

He got up on his other knee to fire, only to be pushed back down by rounds chipping away at the concrete bench. Panting, he crawled in the dirt to another tree.

Over the pop of gunfire came another sound: a diesel engine rumbling in the distance. Dom sneaked a look as two armored vehicles sped toward the embattled cruisers.

"Oh, hell yes!" Dom said.

He got up and fired, and a shooter fell out of a window and smacked onto the sidewalk.

The doors of the trucks opened, disgorging officers in full armor with automatic weapons. They surged around the vehicles, shoulder firing as they advanced into the building.

Dom limped away from the bench as muzzle flashes lit the upper floors. One by one, the strike team was clearing out the sicarios with methodical precision.

"Moose!" Dom said. The big guy was carrying the injured officer over to the trees where Julia had fallen.

Dom got down and turned her gently onto her back. A touch to her neck confirmed what he knew. Her lifeless eyes stared up at the clouds.

Emergency crews were searching for the wounded, but they couldn't do anything for her now. Dom closed her eyelids.

She hadn't stood a chance. Sent in with a Glock and a vest that couldn't stop a high-velocity round. Julia was another good cop, killed by the vermin overtaking the city.

"You're hit," Moose said.

Dom got to his feet and looked down. "Just a scratch."

"Still should have someone look at it."

"Later, bro, I'm good," Dom said firmly.

Two armored strike team officers walked out of the building, practically carrying a squirming shirtless man covered in tattoos. Symbols of MS-13 were inked into his neck and torso.

"Andre, that you, bro?" boomed a voice.

One of the armored cops trotted up to Dom and Moose. He took off his helmet and grinned.

Dom recognized those pearly whites right away. It was Ray Clarke, Andre's brother.

"Wasn't expecting to see you here, kid brother," Ray said.

"You're a little late," Moose said.

Ray frowned. "Got held up."

He gave Moose a hug and then patted Dom on the shoulder.

"How's it, Dommie boy?" Ray asked.

Dom just glared. How could he be so chill at a scene of such carnage?

"What do you mean, you 'got held up'?" Moose asked.

"Red tape, bullshit," Ray said with a shrug.

Dom new exactly the kind of red tape he was referring to. Chief Stone had a deal with the Vega brothers and had probably delayed sending in the troops until there was no other option.

"Rat fucker," Dom muttered.

"What did you say?" Ray said. He inched up closer to Dom.

Moose stepped between them. "Whoa, whoa, guys. Take it easy."

"Wasn't talking to you, Ray," Dom said.

Ray eased back. "Best go get some fresh air, brah, if you can't handle this shit," he said.

Moose looked to Dom. "Go have your leg looked at, please, Dom."

Dom limped away, his heart breaking as a medic laid a sheet over Julia.

Tonight was another reminder of what they were up against. It wasn't just the powerful crime families. It was the crooked cops in their employ—men and women who had sworn the same oath he did to protect the City of Angels.

And Dom was starting to wonder what side Ray was really on.

-4-

Vinny Moretti sat on the hood of his BMW, looking out over the ocean at Long Beach. He wore black jeans and a light jacket to keep warm in the cool breeze. This was the first winter since the end of the war, but it was still warmer in Southern California than in most of the country. For those living in the Midwest and along the East Coast, freezing to death was a real possibility. That was on top of the threat of disease, famine, and violence.

The canopy of palm trees shifted in the breeze as the sun peeked above the city skyline, spreading a warm purple glow over the horizon. This was the first time in a week that airborne dust didn't blur the sun.

There was no need for a mask this morning. The freshest sea air the city had known in weeks filled Vinny's lungs, and the sun's warmth prickled across his five o'clock shadow.

Vinny basked in the glow, happy to be alive after another night of violence had rocked the Angel Pyramids and the Four Diamonds.

News reports were streaming in over the radio

playing in his car, but he mostly ignored the announcer. He had already heard the stories about an unfortunate event between a dirty cop and a sicario associated with the López family. Probably a former MS-13 or Latin King, Vinny thought. Those guys weren't known for their patience, and sometimes the cops got too greedy taking their cut.

He didn't know the particulars, but the shoot-out had left five officers dead or wounded. This time the López family had gone too far and would face severe repercussions.

It was good for the Morettis, though. The weaker the Lópezes were, the weaker the Vega brothers would be. And once their alliance crumbled, the Morettis would be able to swoop in and take over the Angel Pyramids, adding some prime real estate to their growing empire.

Something on the radio caught Vinny's ear. "*Ten LAPD officers have been confirmed dead,*" said the newscaster.

Just like that, the number had doubled. It made him wonder how many more sunrises he was going to see.

Ever since Vinny took the oath of omertà, he had known that his days could be numbered. This line of business was not one in which most men lived into middle age, let alone grew old. Carmine, Frankie, Antonio, and his dad were anomalies, but they weren't old men yet.

The business wasn't just terribly dangerous. It also lacked ethics—something Vinny struggled with every day. The spot where he had deceived Carly Sarcone wasn't far from here. He still thought of her now and again—and her father, Enzo.

He was one of the men who had betrayed Vinny's family in Naples almost a decade ago, resulting in the death of his mother. She had taken a bullet that would have killed young Vinny, giving her life for his. And with Enzo's death, Vinny had finally gotten his revenge.

Vinny took another drink of coffee, recalling the moment. As the sun inched higher, he relived the past. From the Basilica in Naples to his journey to America and his rise to being a made man in the Moretti family.

Sirens keened in the distance, masking the radio, as three cruisers raced down the street behind him. The familiar wail had become the theme music for the city.

Hearing the rattle of an old dirt bike, Vinny turned to see his best friend and business partner, Doberman.

"Man, what a piece of crap," Vinny muttered under his breath.

Doberman hopped off the ancient Yamaha Enduro. He wore jeans, sneakers, and a leather jacket. He took off his helmet, revealing a skullcap of short black hair.

"Sorry, Vin, had a long night," Doberman said. "Remember that broad—"

"Jenny?"

"No, she was two weeks ago, I'm talking about Leslie."

Vinny shrugged. "I can't keep track of them all."

"You should spend more time with the ladies and less time out here."

"I do just fine with the ladies," Vinny said. "But you don't get to see a sunrise like this every day."

"Yeah . . ." Doberman pulled sunglasses out of his coat pocket and put them on to look at the ocean. "Ready to go?"

"I've been ready," Vinny said.

He got into his BMW and drove away from the beach, entering light traffic on the way to the Port of Long Beach. Several ships were berthed at the wharf while cranes noisily lifted away containers filled with supplies, aid, and on one ship, drugs.

The Marine Corps had guarded this place during the war, but now with the military all but disbanded, rent-a-cops protected the shipments. Most of the hired muscle turned a blind eye to what came in. They were here only to keep people from stealing cargo.

Vinny had several of the security guys on his payroll. So far, they had done a good job. It was when the Moretti product left the port that it was really at risk.

He drove behind warehouses on the eastern side of the port. A few minutes later, Doberman hopped a curb on his bike and skidded to a stop beside the BMW. He took off his visorless helmet again, grimacing.

"Dude, I just swallowed a fucking horsefly," he grumped. "This thing blows."

"If you hustle harder, maybe you'll make enough to buy a car."

"Dude, I hustle damn hard all day every day, and I like this bike. I can go anywhere on it. I just don't like bugs for breakfast."

"Get a helmet that covers your face," Vinny said. "Or don't rap when you ride."

Doberman had to laugh.

On foot, they cut through an alley between warehouses, skirting heaps of trash and a few rats still out and about. Diesel valves clattered in the distance as two semis pulled away with containers on their beds. Cranes and forklifts loaded other trucks.

The longshoremen were busy this morning, unloading ships that had arrived overnight. He waited for a forklift to drive by and then set off with Doberman to the docks.

Their destination was an Italian ship they called the *Goomah*. She was docked on Pier 18. Three garbage trucks waited in the road framed by the piers. One was filled with trash—a decoy just in case an honest cop wanted to take a look.

The door to one of the green trucks opened, and a large Latino man hopped down. He pulled his sagging pants up and walked over, silver chain swinging, open shirt reeking of body odor that Vinny could smell over the bouquet of garbage and dead fish.

"Mikey," Vinny said. "Sorry to keep you and your crew waiting."

"Not a problem, 'cause you pay us by the hour," Mikey said.

Vinny frowned. It wasn't just Mikey he had to pay today. The dockhands unloading the ship were going to need their cut, and so were the rent-a-cops watching from a distance.

Mikey raised a grimy hand and motioned for his men to back the trucks up. The rumble of the old engines filled the morning as they moved into position.

Vinny checked for any watchful eyes.

This wasn't the first shipment they had unloaded in broad daylight. The deal with Mikey worked flawlessly. Using his garbage trucks to move the product away from the port was the perfect disguise. No one seemed to notice a thing.

"Let's get this shit loaded up fast," Vinny said.

Mikey glanced over.

"Since you're by the hour and all, right?" Vinny said.

"*Sí, amigo,*" Mikey said with a wide, yellow grin.

Four of his men hopped out and walked across to a gangplank for the *Goomah*. The merchant vessel had come straight from Columbia, where Javier González and his brother Diego ran a thriving drug operation specializing in cocaine, marijuana, and hybrid opioids.

Now, with so many people in chronic pain, the opioids were the hottest thing in the city. Mikey's crew unloaded them from the ship in garbage bags. Vinny watched them carefully, making sure none of the men fished anything out of the bags. They took them to the back of the trucks and tossed them in.

Vinny followed the men back up the ramp to the deck to meet with their contact, Chuy. The fortysomething man with long hair, a dark beard, and a blue mole centered between his eyebrows was smoking a cigarette near the port gunwale.

"Watch Mikey's guys," Vinny said to Doberman.

"Gotcha, bro."

Vinny crossed the deck. *"Hola, Chuy."*

Turning, Chuy threw a hand up. "Vin, how you doin', man?" he said in his thick Latino accent.

They embraced and then shook hands.

"Good to see you, Chuy," Vinny said. "How are things in Colombia? Better than the States, yes?"

Chuy scratched at his beard and half shrugged.

"Things are not good, my friend," he replied. "The

government has been raiding our fields more often and asking for more and more money to protect us. I'm afraid this shipment is light."

"Light?" It had seemed like fewer bags. "How light?"

"Only half what you ordered. Don't worry, your full payment will go toward the next shipment."

"*Half?* You've got to be shitting me," Vinny said. "When's the other half coming?"

Chuy pulled another cigarette out, a joint this time. His hands shook as he shielded it from the breeze and lit it.

"Well?" Vinny asked.

"Two weeks, but there's going to be an extra ten percent tariff, so you will need to pay that in addition to what you have paid."

"Tariff?" Vinny's eyes went cold, though his blood was aboil. "You're *taxing* us? This isn't a governmental deal, and Javier already raised the fee once."

"I'm sorry, but things are bad, Vin. You got to understand, I'm just the messenger."

"And I'm the nephew of Don Antonio Moretti," Vinny said. "He's not going to be happy about this, and while I can't speak for him, I'll give you this much of a heads-up: it might be time for us to look for a new supplier."

Chuy took a deep breath, exhaled, then took a hit. "I'll do what I can to get you the best price, okay, my friend?"

Vinny paused, considering his next words. If the shipment was light, he couldn't do anything about it right now.

"I'll see you in two weeks," Vinny said. He turned and left Chuy to smoke his joint.

Doberman waited by the gangplank, arms folded across his chest.

"They done?" Vinny asked.

"Yeah, all loaded up."

Vinny pulled his mask up over his face as he went back to the garbage trucks. He paid off the two rent-a-cops and a dockhand who marked the shipment as trash. Then he walked over to Mikey's truck.

Mikey looked Vinny up and down and said, "Want a ride?"

Vinny could smell the trash even through his mask. He thought about saying no, but he didn't want to take an eye off this shipment, especially since it was half what they had ordered.

"Hop on," Mikey said.

Vinny and Doberman each grabbed a handle and stepped up. The trucks fired up, rumbling with their precious cargo tucked in the back. Holding his breath, Vinny tried to keep it in for the short ride to his car and Doberman's bike in the parking lot. From there, they followed the convoy of garbage trucks onto the highway.

Bulging clouds rolled over horizon, swallowing the sun and shading the fractured metropolis in shades of rust. He should have known the weather wouldn't last.

As he drove, Vinny thought about what he was going to tell his uncle and father when he got back to the compound. They were already low on product, and a shortage was going to put the brakes on their expansion.

The whine of motorcycles snapped him from his thoughts. He checked his rearview mirror. Four crotch rockets sped up behind him. They were a variety of bright colors, and the riders were decked out in leather outfits and shaded helmets.

He gulped when he saw the samurai swords sheathed over their backs.

The Yamazaki clan.

Vinny cursed and reached into his jacket for his Glock.

The bikes zoomed closer, flanking him on both sides. None of the riders reached for their swords, but he kept his gun out. Doberman was just ahead on the Enduro, looking over his shoulder, gun in his left hand.

The rider on the driver's side wore a tight red leather jacket. He pointed at Vinny, then traced a finger across his neck. It was Isao, and this was Vinny's chance to take him down despite his uncle's orders.

Vinny rolled down the window and aimed the pistol as Isao suddenly accelerated, roaring past Doberman and cutting in front of the garbage trucks.

The other motorcycles followed.

Vinny put the pistol on his lap and wiped the sweat from his brow. His heart was pounding, but not because he feared Isao.

He feared his uncle. Don Antonio would not be happy about the light drug shipment, the new tax, and, worst of all, that Vinny's scheme for protecting the shipments had failed.

The Yamazaki clan knew how they moved their product.

* * *

"How's Elena doing?" asked Lieutenant Zed Marks.

Ronaldo had his running shoe up on a bench in

the locker room of the gym. It was the one place he still got to see his best friend and former squad mate. Tooth and Bettis were also here today, changing out of their uniforms into shorts and T-shirts.

"How do you think she's doing, man?" Ronaldo asked. "We've made no headway in finding Monica."

Marks rummaged in his locker, calm as always. He had grown a thick mustache and cut his hair short around the edges, hiding the grays. and he had lost so much weight that his ribs were showing on his bare chest.

He pulled his head out of the locker. "The city is tearing itself apart," he said. "We lost ten men the other night at the Angel Pyramids. I'm doing everything I can to find her and bring her home, but the city is falling to pieces."

"I heard about that, man," Tooth said while admiring himself in the mirror. "What the hell happened?"

Bettis walked over to listen.

"I can't say," Marks said. "But I'm sure you can guess."

"Dirty cop makes dumb-shit move against asshole gangbanger with no soul, shoot-out reliably ensues, and cops get slaughtered," said Tooth.

"Dominic was there," Ronaldo said. "Got nicked by a bullet. Sounds like Moose was almost killed, too."

"What? You didn't tell us that, man," Bettis said. "They okay?"

"Yeah, they're both fine," Ronaldo said. He turned back to Marks.

"Like I said, I'm doing everything I can," Marks said. "Following every lead, checking every report of trafficking, and through it all . . ." He lowered his voice.

"I'm giving you classified intel that could get me in deep shit with Chief Stone."

"Fuck Chief Stone," Ronaldo snapped.

Marks looked to Bettis and Tooth. "Give us a minute, guys?"

The two deputies left the locker room, and Marks went and checked the second row of lockers. He returned with an angry frown.

"You're lucky no one's in here," Marks said. "Do you know how fucked I would be if Chief Stone found out you said that and I *didn't* break your jaw?"

"Eh," Ronaldo said while lacing up his other shoe. He took a moment to look at the photos he had taped inside his locker: pictures of Tooth, Bettis, Marks, and Ronaldo from their deployment overseas, and at a barbecue back home.

Those days seemed so long ago.

Marks put on his T-shirt that said, "*All it takes is all you got*"—a Marine Corps motto. "This city isn't the only thing crumbling, Ronaldo," he said. "Case you haven't noticed, the entire country is coming apart at the seams. The federal Executive Council is picking cities to give aid to, and right now we're in the top tier."

"Yeah, I know," Ronaldo said. "The energy-efficient desalination technology from Japan, the new public housing, and the wind and solar farms are great, but none of that is going to bring back my girl, and it's not helping us fight the crime families, either."

Marks moved his lips to speak, but Ronaldo kept talking.

"We need more cops with better pay—a group of men and women who don't take bribes and are focused on restoring order in this city and clearing out the corruption . . ." Ronaldo let his words trail off, then decided to finish his sentence. "You know the buck stops, as they say, at Chief Pay-to-Play's desk."

Marks sighed. "You aren't making my life any easier," he said. "You know my hands are tied, but you're welcome to leave the Sheriff's Department and come join me in the fight against the crime families."

"I have a better chance finding Monica as a deputy, not a street cop." Ronaldo's head dropped. "It just all seems so damn hopeless."

He swallowed hard. Every time he thought of Monica and what she could be going through out there, he felt sick to his stomach. He sat on the bench. The thought of working out no longer appealed to him.

"I wasn't going to say anything, but there's something you should know," Marks said.

Ronaldo looked up, filled with equal parts dread and hope.

"I don't want to get your hopes up, but I got some fresh intel. Before I tell you, though, I need a promise you won't get in the way of the operation."

"Operation?"

"Promise me," Marks said.

Ronaldo got to his feet.

"I can't do that. If you know where Monica might be, I'm not leaving it to some cops that may or may not be crooked."

"My men aren't crooked," Marks snapped back.

"You sure about that?"

"You're not making this easy, Ronaldo."

"Neither are you, man."

Ronaldo backed away as Marks walked over to the other lockers. He lowered his head and scratched his brow, then turned back to Ronaldo. For a moment, they stared at each other, neither man wavering.

"If I tell you and you fuck it up, I could lose my job. Then you lose your one resource besides Dominic in the LAPD."

"I won't fuck it up."

"I should have just told you after the fact, but if something went bad and Monica was there, I'd never forgive myself, and you wouldn't, either."

"You're right, so tell me." Ronaldo didn't back down an inch, and it worked.

"There's some apartment buildings on Seal Beach Road that we've been watching."

"Seal Beach Road. Why does that sound familiar?" Ronaldo choked on the realization. "That's by Los Alamitos, or what's left of it."

"Yup, the perfect place to hide, but also a dangerous place from the radiation levels," Marks said. "Our detectives have identified trucks frequenting those buildings. They snapped some pictures."

Marks went back to his locker as the door to the locker room opened. Two men walked inside, laughing and drenched in sweat. They went to the other side of the lockers to change.

"Show me," Ronaldo said.

Marks opened his locker and took a manila folder from his backpack.

The showers switched on, voices echoing off the tiles.

Marks opened the folder, and Ronaldo bent down for a look. In the first photo, men wearing black ski masks and carrying guns were escorting groups of teen-agers and some kids from an apartment building.

The door to the locker room opened again, and Tooth poked his head in, showing off his famous inci-sors in a grin. "The fuck you two doing? Thought we were going to shoot some hoops today."

"Give us a minute," Marks said.

Bettis pulled Tooth away, and the door clicked shut.

Ronaldo went back to looking through the pictures. There were dozens, and he went through them one by one. None provided any clue who the men were. They could be part of a crime family, gangbangers, or just ban-dits trying to make a buck in the new black market.

Whatever—they were all going to die.

"We have to hit them before they move," Ron-aldo said.

"Don't worry, I've got teams watching. This seems to be temporary housing before they get sold off. We're trying to figure out where the main hub is. If we can determine that, then we can bring this organization down and save a lot of lives."

Ronaldo stared at the pictures, searching for his Monica even though he knew Marks would have told him if she were here.

"When are these teams going to make a move, and who's leading the operation?"

"Tonight. And me," Marks said.

Ronaldo glanced up.

"Soon as the sun goes down, but you have to promise me you won't interfere."

One of the showers clicked off, and a police offi-cer Ronaldo recognized walked around the corner in a towel. Ronaldo turned his back to shield Marks as he put the photos back in his locker.

"Promise me, Salvatore," he said.

"Fine, but I need a promise, too."

"What's that?"

"Bring Dom with you. I want him there. Otherwise, I'm going."

Marks let out a low sigh. "I was afraid you'd say that."

-5-

The Commerce Hotel and Casino had been under renovation since Antonio Moretti took it over during the war. It had changed drastically since then. He still vividly remembered the fighter jet's delta wing that had blown off and lodged in the side of the building. Removing that was a son of a bitch.

Overall, he had sunk two million dollars' worth of silver and gold into repairs, security upgrades, bulletproofing of apartment windows, and landscaping.

Inside, the hotel still looked like a resort, but from the outside it looked like a fortress. It even had a checkpoint with an M240 machine gun to stop any vehicle that might try to make a run at the fifteen-foot-high steel gates.

Since the acquisition, Antonio had hired crews to tear up much of the parking lot and lay down sod. He walked on the grass now, hand in hand with his wife. The dust storms and airborne toxins made growing plants and flowers difficult, but the weather would eventually clear.

For now, he had purchased three greenhouses to

grow the flora that would eventually be planted on the grounds. The greenhouses were erected at the eastern edge of the property, tucked in the lee of a wall to protect them from the weather.

Another storm was about to hit the city. The wind howled, and bulging dark clouds rolled over the southern edge of Los Angeles.

"Maybe we should go inside," Lucia said.

Antonio watched the rust-colored storm front barreling toward them. The sight was commonplace, but spending time with his wife wasn't, and a little bluster wasn't going to stop him from taking her to the greenhouses.

"Antonio, did you hear me?" she asked.

He pulled on her hand, giving his answer as he led her toward the three glass structures.

Soldiers wearing black fatigues, breathing masks, and goggles patrolled the grounds, keeping a respectful distance. Walls topped with razor wire rose above the men, forming a border that sealed off the small paradise from the hell world that surrounded it. While Antonio didn't love the look, he cared much more about his family than aesthetics. Besides, the inside of the compound was gorgeous.

He crossed a stone courtyard with a fountain. Statues of Roman soldiers surrounded the patio, their swords pointed at the storm. The art was shipped in from Italy weeks ago, after the cash started rolling in from the opening of the Four Diamonds.

The wind picked up, blasting him and Lucia. Antonio looked at the skyline again and continued to the greenhouse, where he opened the door for his wife.

She stepped inside, pulling down her mask to reveal deep-red lipstick.

"Angela," Lucia said with a smile.

Angela De Caro, younger sister of Lino De Caro, turned from her task of watering plants with a hose.

"Ciao," she said with a grin. The attractive young woman with dark hair and a pretty face reminded Antonio of his wife when she was in her twenties. Angela had arrived with the shipment of statues and other art from Italy, and her presence made Lino happier than Antonio had seen him in years.

Lucia spoke to Angela in Italian, telling her that a storm was coming and she could finish her work later. But Angela insisted on staying if Lucia and Antonio were going to be here.

Antonio walked down the aisles, breathing in the scents of flowers growing in the humid air. He cupped his hands behind his back, admiring life that would shrivel and die outside the safety of their controlled environment. He gazed at the bed of orange and yellow tree poppies. Among his favorites, they reminded him of springtime in the hills surrounding Naples.

The greenhouse door opened, and Antonio gestured for Lucia to join him. Yellowtail walked inside. He pulled down his mask and pushed his goggles up, flattening his blond Mohawk.

"Don Antonio," he said, panting. "Vinny's back from the port and needs to talk to you in your office about something urgent."

"I'll be right there," he said.

Yellowtail hesitated in front of the door.

This must be urgent indeed, Antonio thought. He plucked a yellow poppy and tucked it in Lucia's hair.

"My beautiful queen," he said.

Her brow went up. "Not a queen yet," she said. "You still have to take out the Vega brothers."

"Soon, my love."

He led her out of the greenhouse, and Angela followed. Yellowtail jogged across the lawn, keeping his head down as a gust swept grit over the grounds.

When they got inside, Marco was waiting in the lobby with his cousin.

"Dad," he said. "Can I—"

"Not now," Antonio said.

"Come here, baby," Lucia said.

Antonio clenched his jaw. They had to stop treating their son like a child or he would never grow into a man. And in this new world, only the strongest men survived.

One of the strongest was just ahead. Yellowtail's tank top revealed bullet scars. He had been shot five times in the past year.

Antonio got in the elevator with his soldier, not bothering to ask him what was wrong.

Two guards holding MP5s waited outside the double doors. They pushed them open, and Antonio stepped onto the new Persian rug over the floor of Italian marble. New paintings hung in expensive frames, but he didn't stop to admire them.

Christopher, Vinny, Doberman, Raff, and Lino were sitting around the war table near the recently installed bulletproof windows.

They all got up as Antonio entered. He went to his desk, poured a glass of wine, and sipped. "Speak," he said.

Doberman looked at Vinny.

"Don Antonio, I have bad news," Vinny said.

"Javier González and his brother Diego have had problems with the government raiding their fields and taking more of a cut."

"They want more, the greedy motherfuckers," Christopher hissed.

Antonio silenced his brother with a look, then nodded for Vinny to continue.

"They're taxing us ten percent on the next shipment, which is the second half of the one we already paid for," Vinny said. "The first half has been delivered to Carmine and Frankie at the warehouse, for distribution."

"Half?" Antonio said. He felt the rage bubble up inside him, and the wineglass in his hand shattered. Dark pinot noir pooled on the marble tiles, dotted with drips of his blood.

Yellowtail rushed over, but Antonio waved him back.

"Go get something to clean that up with," he ordered.

The soldier retreated to the bar, and Antonio pulled a small shard of glass out of his palm. Then another. His finger was also cut, but his anger overwhelmed the pain.

His men all remained standing at the table, trying not to stare. Even Christopher, who had experienced a lifetime of his brother's volatile temper, seemed nervous.

Antonio looked at his nephew, who ran a nervous hand over his hairline, foreshadowing more news.

"What else?" Antonio asked.

This time, Vinny did look away to his dad.

"Don't look at your father," Antonio said. "You tell *me*."

"I'm sorry, Don Antonio, but the Yamazakis cased me and Doberman this morning. They saw the garbage trucks."

Vinny lowered his hand. "Four of their soldiers

followed us from the port. One of them pointed at me, then took off."

"They threatened Vinny's life," Christopher said. "We got to deal with these needle-dicked rice burners, and not just by sending a message. We got to wipe them out entirely."

Antonio took a rag from Yellowtail and wrapped his hand. Then he walked over to his window to watch the storm surging across the city.

His brother was right. Complete annihilation was the only option.

"Christopher, put a team together," Antonio said. "We hit them before the next shipment."

* * *

A group of cops in black fatigues stood across the dimly lit warehouse from Dom and Moose. The two partners were awaiting orders while Lieutenant Marks and a sergeant spoke at a table in the front of the room. The other officers stood around checking weapons and gear.

A couple of the hardened cops glanced at Dom and Moose, probably curious about their presence. Dom was equally curious about them. All he knew about this strike team was that they reported directly to Marks. He didn't know any of them personally besides Marks and Camilla Santiago.

She hung out by a stack of supply crates with two other female officers and a male. A simple nod was all Dom had gotten from her so far. Maybe she didn't want to mingle with the new guys.

"You got any idea why we're here?" Moose whispered.

Dom shook his head, though he prayed they had found his sister and he was going to be part of the mission to bring her home. But Dom also knew that hope was a dangerous thing.

The thought of his sister made Dom's muscles twitch. He had finally calmed down after the shootout two nights ago at the Angel Pyramids, where he had watched multiple cops get gunned down, including timid young Julia. Now he was feeling the high and the low of violence.

He had a bad feeling they were going to experience more of it tonight. But if that meant bringing his sister home, he would happily tear out hearts with his bare hands and swim through a river of blood.

A mental image surfaced: his father covered in blood after raiders attacked them in the Angeles National Forest.

"Let's get started," Marks said.

Dom and Moose walked to the front of the room. They had already changed into black fatigues and were given black masks, but they still hadn't been assigned new weapons like the other cops, who carried M4A1s and submachine guns of various models.

That was fine with Dom. He preferred his M1A anyway.

"All right, listen up," Marks said. "First off, this is Officer Dominic Salvatore and Officer Andre Clarke. They will be joining us tonight on Operation Castaway. This raid will take us to an apartment complex just west of Los Alamitos. Before any of you ask, you won't be there long enough to worry about radiation exposure, but you're free to wear rad gear if you'd like."

Several cops exchanged looks. Camilla glanced back at Dom, her eyes meeting his for a moment before she turned away. The shared moment reminded him how much he cared about her. They had bonded during the night of hell, when Moose almost died.

"This is our target," said Sergeant Frank Willows. The muscular young man with a neatly trimmed beard went to a map hung on an easel. "I'm taking Alpha Team in on the east side, and Lieutenant Marks will take Bravo on the west side."

Dom studied the map of the apartment complex. There were three buildings, all five stories tall. They were headed to the middle one, third floor.

"We expect at least ten hostiles, maybe more, equipped with fully automatic rifles," he continued.

"The objective is to free prisoners," Marks said. "There are fifteen teenagers, and a few younger than that, so I don't need to tell you how sensitive this mission is."

Dom's heart skipped. He was right: this was about Monica. He wondered whether his dad knew.

If he did, he'd be here.

This was up to Dom, and if Monica was in there, he would do whatever it took to bring her out alive. Then he was going to kill every one of the bastards who took her.

Marks continued the briefing, explaining the delicate insertion. Several snipers would be positioned across the street to take out hostiles on the rooftop or perimeter of the target building. The strike team would then enter with night vision and flash-bangs.

"It's risky, but we have no choice," Marks said.

"We take them either now or when they move, and I'd rather do it at night, when most of the hostiles are probably sleeping or fatigued."

Camilla again looked to Dom. There was fear in her eyes, but it wasn't about the men they would face. Dom knew her better than that. She worried that an innocent like Monica might be hurt.

Dom felt the lump of fear in his gut, too, but he wouldn't let it overwhelm him. He had to be strong for Monica.

"All right, get to your assigned teams; finish your gear and weapon checks," Willows said. "We move out in fifteen."

Marks walked away from the table and through the departing cops, toward Moose and Dom.

"Dominic," he said. "Let's talk for a minute."

Dom followed him to the back of the room, where three black Suburbans and a black Toyota pickup waited to take them to the target.

"I'm sorry I didn't get a chance to talk to you before, but things have been nuts," Marks said. "I'm sure you can guess that your dad wanted you here."

"No, I figured he didn't know." Dom hesitated, then asked, "Why's he not coming?"

"He's not a cop."

"Yeah, but . . ."

Marks changed the subject. "Your leg feeling okay?" he asked.

Dom nodded. "It's just a scratch. Do you really think Monica could be at the target?"

"I have no idea, but this is the biggest group of kids we've located yet, so it's a possibility."

He put a hand on Dom's shoulder. "If she is, you have to be prepared."

"I know." Sucking in a deep breath, he thought of what that meant. He had tried to keep the horrible images out of his mind, but he knew deep down that his sister had experienced hell and that it would show. Now it was time to pull her from it and start her recovery.

"You sure you're up for this?" Marks asked.

"Yes sir."

Marks held his gaze a moment, then dropped his hand. "You and Moose are with me."

"Okay, sir."

Marks got into the passenger seat of a Chevy Suburban, and Dom climbed in the back with Moose. Camilla loaded into the other one, a mask over her face.

These were the best of the best. The uncorrupted cops who were still trying to save the city. Dom hoped to be part of the team someday, for more than one mission.

The warehouse doors opened, and the convoy pulled out into the storm. Grit sandblasted the vehicles as they turned onto Orangewood Avenue in Anaheim. For two days straight, the city had been pounded with bad weather, but that wasn't going to stop them tonight.

Dom sat stuffed between Moose and another cop, who stared ahead. The drive from Anaheim to Los Alamitos would take ten or fifteen minutes—plenty of time to think about what they would find in these apartments.

It also gave him time to think about his mom and dad. He hoped they were together at home.

"We're going to bring Monica home," Moose whispered.

"I know."

The Suburban jolted over a pothole in the road. Then another. They were driving west, just south of Angel Stadium. The upper walls were moonlit, though darkness enshrouded most of the empty parking lot.

"I never was an Angels fan," said the cop next to Moose.

"Me, neither," he replied. "Always liked the Dodgers, myself."

"I'd do just about anything to see another game, but I don't think that's gonna happen anytime soon," the cop said. "Probably more likely to see gladiator gangbangers fighting to the death."

Moose chuckled. "Would save us some trouble. I'd sure pay to see that."

Dom tuned out the conversation as he grew more anxious by the minute. By the time they closed in on Los Alamitos, his heart pounded from anxiety.

"Get ready," Marks said.

They passed the former military base on the north side, and Dom had to lean over for a glimpse of the fences erected around the base. Radiation warning signs were posted every few yards, but industrial lights illuminated a work site where bulldozers and earthmovers were running at full tilt.

Dom had heard the rumors they were going to build a prison here.

He turned back to the front of the vehicle. The other officers dialed in their night-vision goggles and made final preparations.

"Everyone on me to the target," Marks said.

Dom wasn't surprised that the lieutenant was taking point. Marks had always put himself in danger before his men.

The pickup truck leading the convoy pulled into a parking lot, and Dom's Suburban sped past. The other two SUVs followed close behind; then the four vehicles split up.

Dom's halted.

"Go, go, go!" Marks said.

Dom hopped out and followed Bravo Team to the west entrance. He didn't see any hostiles outside, nor did he hear the soft crack of suppressed sniper shots.

Marks was first to the door. He gave the "execute" signal to another officer, who, instead of kicking the door down, simply opened it and pushed it inward.

An unlocked door, no hostiles outside—this was easier than Dom had thought it would be. He followed the team into a hallway that reeked of urine and mold. A stairwell took them to the second floor, where Marks gave the all clear from a landing.

They made their way to the third floor and moved at combat intervals into an empty hallway. At the other end of the hall, more officers arrived to flank.

Most of the doors were open, exposing empty rooms covered in trash, clothes, and plastic buckets. Only two of the doors were closed.

The same cop who had opened the door outside went for the first door, but Marks held up a hand to stop him.

Dom sensed it, too. Something was off. There were no guards, and he doubted they were all sleeping inside.

He readied his rifle, sensing an ambush.

Marks pointed at one of the open doors across the hall. Two officers shouldered their weapons and cautiously entered the room.

They emerged a moment later, one of them holding a child-size backpack.

Marks then gave the order to kick open the other two doors. Officers smashed them in and stormed inside.

Dom and Moose were the third and fourth into the room on the left side of the hallway. The filthy carpeted room was furnished with a single couch. Shades were drawn over the windows, and blankets and pillows were strewn about.

"Son of a bitch," Marks said.

"Where are they?" Dom asked, though he already knew the answer.

What didn't make sense was why the lookouts hadn't notified Marks. Unless those lookouts were dead.

Dom concealed his anger and disappointment, trying to keep cool and professional even though he wanted to punch a wall.

Sergeant Willows walked over and spoke in a hushed voice to Marks while Dom hung out with Moose near the stairwell.

"I'm sorry, Dom," Moose said quietly.

Another officer walked over. Judging by size, it was Camilla.

"Sorry, Dom," she said, patting him on the shoulder.

With a hand signal, Marks gave the order to head back outside. The teams parted, leaving the way they had come in.

Dom sulked as he walked down the stairs, wondering whether Monica had walked up and down the very same grubby steps.

He gritted his teeth, trying to manage his anger and not lose hope.

She was out there somewhere, and eventually he would find her. But right now he just wanted to know what the hell had happened to this operation.

He hurried outside. Five of the other officers were already there, walking toward the SUVs and the truck. Dom paused on the sidewalk to look across the street, where the snipers were supposed to be positioned with the other lookouts.

Had something happened to them?

Dom glanced over to Marks and Willows, who had just exited from the building. A bright glare flashed in his periphery, and the ground rumbled. It all happened so fast, he could only flinch before the two men in front slammed into him, along with a wave of scorching heat.

He hit the ground on his side, getting a sideways view of the pickup as it dropped back to the ground in a flaming heap. Someone grabbed him and dragged him away from the inferno.

Screaming came over the ringing in his ears, but Dom couldn't make out the words.

Moose picked him up and brought him inside, setting him against a wall.

"Dom!" he yelled. "Dom, are you okay?"

Dom blinked and looked over as more officers were carried into the hallway.

It was obvious what had happened on this operation. They got set up, and the explosion was a warning.

Next time, there would be no warning. Next time, they would all be dead.

-6-

The morning after Vinny broke the bad news to his uncle and his father about the González brothers and the Yamazaki clan, he had to go see Captain Carmine Barese.

In some ways, Vinny feared Carmine more than his uncle. At least Don Antonio showed him some respect and didn't make fun of him and Doberman in front of the other guys.

Things had actually gotten worse since Vinny was made. Carmine still seemed to see him as his errand boy. But it was the sly comments about his and Doberman's sexual orientation that were really starting to piss Vinny off.

Doberman stopped at the chain-link fence surrounding the drug warehouse that Carmine managed. They had come in the back way to avoid drawing attention.

"You go first," Doberman said.

He held the snipped links back for Vinny to duck under. Then Vinny did the same for his friend. With their breathing masks on and sunglasses covering their eyes, they made their way across the cracked dirt behind a row of businesses—the hub of the Moretti drug empire.

Antonio had moved it three times in the past six months. This time, it was in a warehouse next to a block of self-storage units.

Strategically, the location was perfect. Vinny could see the Long Beach Freeway and the Los Angeles River, which they had used for night shipments. It was almost halfway between the Port of Long Beach and the Moretti compound at the former Commerce Hotel.

He had helped scout out the location a few months ago. The only negative was the distance from the Four Diamonds. It was a long drive from here to move the product, and with the Yamazakis onto them, it was more dangerous than ever.

Pushing his sunglasses back into his hair, Vinny crossed the parking lot. Several guards were standing inside the walled-off grounds, wearing breathing masks. A German shepherd was chained up next to a broken-down school bus. The dog knew his scent and didn't bark, but it did give Doberman a glance before sitting back on its haunches.

Vinny walked around a pile of scrap metal to the back door of the building. Lowering his breathing mask, he stepped inside and took in a breath of steamy air. It was hot as hell in the hallway.

"'Sup, Vin?" said the guard holding sentry.

He simply nodded at the man and continued with Doberman to another door, which opened to a garage once used to train mechanics. Where beater cars had been, there was a single garbage truck and a pickup that belonged to Vito.

The room was as hot as a sauna and reeked like a landfill on a hot day.

Vinny put his mask back on, preferring the sweat over the horrific smell. He crossed the room, which was divided up by stations. At the first row of tables, shirtless workers mixed cocaine in kitchen blenders.

Supervising them was Vito. He wore a white wife-beater undershirt stained yellow around the armpits and neck. His gut hung over his shorts, adding to his slobbish appearance.

"Not like that, shithead!" Vito said, smacking one of the workers in the back of the head. A female worker pointed at Vinny and Doberman approaching, distracting him. He turned toward them, raising his jiggling, hairy arms.

"Ah, Vin and his guard dog," he said, mimicking a barking sound.

"How's it going?" Doberman asked.

"How do you think it's going?" Vito pointed at the garbage truck. "Do these things really have to stink so fucking bad? Why can't they clean 'em first?"

"Because they're supposed to look—and smell—the part," Vinny said. "You ever seen a *clean* garbage truck?"

Vito frowned. "Nah."

"Hey, you two cocksuckers, up here!" a voice yelled.

Vinny craned his neck toward a second floor of offices, where Carmine leaned over the railing, a wide grin on his droopy face. He stood and gestured for them to join him in his office.

Vito led the way across the factory floor, where sweating workers slaved away in the heat, counting pills, cutting cocaine, weighing product, bagging and tagging. The entire process ran like clockwork.

Guards monitored the workers, walking down the aisles to watch their every move. It was a well-honed process that the Moretti family had learned long before they came to the United States.

When they got to the second-floor balcony, Carmine was back in his office. He sat behind his desk, feet up, hands behind his head. Frankie stood in the shadowed corner, arms folded over his chest, back to the wall, chewing on a matchstick. He brushed his long hair back and nodded at Vinny and Doberman in turn.

"So, Javier and Diego González decided to be assholes, huh?" Carmine said.

Vinny explained the situation, bracing for more shit. Some days, he really hated being the messenger. But it was worse when the recipients were master assholes.

"We have to be careful moving this shipment to the Four Diamonds," he said. "The Yamazaki clan is onto us."

"So we can finally get rid of these ass-scented garbage trucks?" Vito asked.

Carmine took his feet off his desk and sat up straight. His nostrils flared, which implied he was about to give Vinny some major shit, but instead he shrugged and pushed himself up.

"We got the first of the shipment just about ready to go," he said. "Guess we'll need some extra security."

Frankie lowered his arms and walked away from the wall. "When are we responding to what happened to Lorenzo?"

Vinny opened his mouth but froze at the sound of his father's deep voice.

"Soon," Christopher said behind them.

Doberman and Vinny moved out of the doorway to let him inside. The smell of cigar smoke drifted off his suit and silver tie that complemented the steel gray in his goatee.

"Sorry I'm late," he said. "Got caught up back at the compound."

Carmine gestured to one of the chairs in front of his desk, but Christopher declined.

"I'm here to make sure our product gets to the Four Diamonds," he said. "Vinny, I'm pulling you off the street until we deal with the Yamazakis."

"What!" Vinny gasped.

"They know your face," Christopher said. "I'm not going to risk them ambushing you. Doberman, you make sure Vinny listens, got it?"

"Yes sir," Doberman replied.

Vinny swallowed his anger. He hated being treated like a kid. He was a made-fucking-man now! Not a goddamn kid like his cousin Marco.

"And our response?" Frankie asked again.

"We're working out the details," Christopher said, "but we're hitting the Yamazakis before next shipment. In the meantime, we got to protect what we got. Carmine, Frankie, I'll need both of you, so be ready."

"What about me?" Vito asked.

Christopher shook his head.

"Too fucking fat, *grasso*," Carmine said, then chuckled.

Vinny couldn't hold back a laugh.

Vito did not appear amused. "You stick me in this fucking pressure cooker that smells like a dead rat's asshole and have me mixing coke all day, every day," he snapped. "Least you could do is let me kill some of the fucking assholes that are stealing the product I make for you."

Christopher waited a moment, then said, "You done?"

"No," Vito said.

"Then forget about coming with us to the Four Diamonds today to deliver this shipment," Christopher said.

Vito turned to look out the window, then straightened his back. "Sorry. I'm done."

Several chuckles broke out.

"Let's get moving," Christopher said. "I want to get this shit on the streets. We've got bills to pay."

He led the way back to the factory floor, where Yellowtail and Lino stood with Raff. All of them wore Kevlar vests over their suits and held submachine guns.

Raff tossed a gun to Christopher, who caught it in midair.

Carmine and Frankie hurried down the stairs with their M4s and body armor. The men gathered by a pickup truck and the Cadillac Escalade Christopher had parked on the other side of the garbage truck. No one seemed too bothered by the scent now.

Workers loaded up the rest of the product into the open back.

"Who's driving this shit heap?" Vito asked.

Christopher smirked. "You wanted to come, right?"

"Aw, hell," Vito said. He pumped his shotgun, then opened the door and hopped into the cab. One of his men got in on the passenger side.

Christopher got out his breathing mask and walked over to Vinny and Doberman. "Vinny, I'm sorry about this, but it's for your own good," he said. "I lost Greta, and I can't lose you, too."

"I know, but—"

"Doberman, remember what I said. Stay away from the Four Diamonds until we've dealt with the Yamazakis."

"We will, sir."

Vinny looked at his friend.

"Good luck," Doberman said to Christopher.

"Be careful," Vinny said.

Christopher put his mask on, went to the Escalade, and clicked a magazine into his submachine gun. Lino got in the driver's seat while Yellowtail and Raff got in the pickup.

"Let's go," Vinny said. He went outside with Doberman.

"Later, ass-fucks," Carmine called out.

Vinny snorted as Frankie and Carmine trotted over to a Mercedes SUV parked outside the building. Frankie pulled his hair back into a ponytail before getting in.

By the time Vinny and Doberman got to their car on the other side of the fence, the convoy was headed out. The garbage truck rumbled past on the street.

Vito honked the horn and then gave them the finger.

"Buncha goddamn assholes," Doberman muttered.

"Kids in adult bodies," Vinny replied. "Except for my dad and Antonio. And Lino, and Raff."

"Raff talks about as much as a fence post."

Vinny laughed. "He's a quiet, respectful man. Wish the others would take after him."

"Don't count on that."

"Here." Vinny tossed Doberman the keys to the BMW.

They took off in the opposite direction. He hated running from a fight, but this wasn't exactly running—it was an order.

At least the sun was out now. Vinny put his shades back on and relaxed in the leather seat on the drive back to the compound. As they drove, the last of the clouds rolled away, leaving the bluest sky Vinny had seen in a while.

"So what do you want to do now that we're on vacation?" Doberman asked.

Vinny cracked a half smile. "Beach, maybe?"

Doberman looked at the watch obscuring his tattoo sleeve.

"Too busy to hang, huh?" Vinny asked. "I get it, you got girls to see."

"Nah, man, it's just . . ." Doberman looked in the side mirror. "Dude . . ."

"What?"

"That black Audi's been following us for a while."

Vinny looked in the rearview mirror. "Make some space."

Doberman gunned the engine, speeding away.

The Audi sped up.

"We got a tail," Vinny said.

Doberman pulled out his piece, and Vinny reached for his.

"So much for the fucking beach," Vinny said.

Doberman took a right, then a left. But the Audi kept following them.

"Pull off here," Vinny said.

The car jolted into a parking lot overgrown with weeds.

"Get ready," Vinny said.

The Audi pulled in and slowed to a stop. The front door opened, but it wasn't a Yamazaki that got out.

A black man with shades walked over.

"That Ray?" Doberman asked.

Vinny rolled the window down as Detective Ray Clarke approached the passenger side.

"New car?" Vinny asked.

A shit-eating grin took over Ray's face. "Just got it," he said, pushing up his shades to take a look.

"Why you following us?" Vinny asked.

Ray took off his sunglasses and bent down to look inside the car.

"Came to let you know that you got more to worry about than the Vega brothers and Yamazakis right now," he said.

Vinny clenched up.

"Lots of cops been dyin' across the city," Ray said. "That deal between my boss and yours is on thin ice, my Sicilian friends."

"We're not Sicilian," Doberman reminded him.

"Italian, whatever," Ray replied.

"Our people aren't responsible for killing any cops, and you know that, Detective," Vinny said. "Maybe you should worry about keeping the Yamazakis off our turf, if you want to keep getting your cut."

Ray held up a hand. "Take it easy, Vin. I'm just passing on a message to you, which you can pass up the line. We're all just messengers, right?"

Vinny's eyes rolled. "Lately, yeah."

"Be careful out there," Ray said. He patted the door and straightened up, then hesitated. "Forgot to ask. You ever hear anything about that girl I asked you about?"

"Girl?"

"Monica Salvatore," Ray said. "She's the sister of a friend of mine. Been looking for her for a while now."

The name didn't ring a bell as being anyone Vinny knew, but he did remember Ray asking a while back.

"Nah," Vinny said.

"Just keep your ears open, okay?"

"Sure, but there's a lot of missing girls in this city, Detective Clarke."

* * *

"They knew we were coming," Dom said, taking off his body armor and tossing it on the floor in his room. "I'm sorry, Dad. I don't know what the hell happened, but—"

"Marks has a mole; that's what fucking happened," Ronaldo said. "God damn it, I should have been there."

He punched the wall in frustration, his fist breaking through with a *thunk* and a little puff of gypsum dust. There was little pain thanks to the anger that now never seemed to go away.

"Ron?" Elena called out. She rushed out of the kitchen and into the hallway, where he stood with his son. Still in her nightgown, she held a spatula in one hand.

"What did you do?" she gasped.

Ronaldo lowered his fist.

"It's nothing," he said. "Give us a minute, please."

She looked at Ronaldo, then to Dom, but held her ground.

"Is this about Monica?" she asked.

"No," her son and husband said in unison.

"Please," Ronaldo said again. "I need to talk to Dom."

Elena shook her head and walked away.

"I should have been there," he repeated. He looked at the hole in the drywall and wanted to pound it over and over. Closing his eyes, he took in a breath to release some of the pent-up tension.

"We don't even know that Monica was there," Dom said quietly.

"No, but she could have been," Ronaldo said. "And we lost the opportunity because of some corrupt asshole." He turned away and started toward his and Elena's bedroom.

"Where you going?"

"To get ready for patrol."

"I thought you don't have to be there for another few hours. We're having breakfast together."

"I'm going in early."

"Dad . . ." Dom followed him to the bedroom.

"We'll have dinner later this week," Ronaldo said.

"Dad, we should spend time with Mom for one meal, please. She isn't doing well." Dom kept his voice low, but Ronaldo heard every word.

"Please, Dad."

Ronaldo dropped his uniform on the bed. "Yeah . . . yeah, okay."

They went back to the living room to find Elena sitting on the couch, sobbing into her hands.

"Mom," Dom said, "everything's going to be okay."

She looked up. "You keep saying that, even though we have no idea where Monica is. All I do is sit here and think—think about where she is and what's happening to her, and all these horrible . . ."

Elena wrapped her arms around her body and rocked to and fro.

Dom went over to comfort his mother while Ronaldo just stood there. He didn't know what to do for his family anymore. Every day that passed, he felt further away from his son and his wife. If he didn't find Monica soon, he was going to lose his entire family.

He turned and went back to his bedroom.

"Dad," Dom called out. "I thought you said—"

"I have to get back to work!" Ronaldo said in almost a shout.

"Let him go," Elena said. "Even when he's here, he isn't."

Ronaldo stopped in the hallway to look over his shoulder. Elena shook in Dom's arms.

"Mom, it's going to be okay," he said. "I love you, and I promise we're doing everything we can to find Monica. We even had a lead."

She pulled away from Dom.

"A lead?" she said. Her eyes flitted to Ronaldo.

Dom looked to his father as well. "Can't we tell her?" he asked.

"You already did," Ronaldo said. "May as well just say the rest."

Elena's eyes widened. "Tell me."

"There was a raid on an apartment complex near Los Alamitos," Dom said. "I was on the mission with

Marks, but when we got there, the kids had all been moved."

"You think Monica was with them?" Elena asked.

"I don't know," Dom replied.

"Ronaldo?" she asked.

"I don't know, either," he replied. "Marks made me promise not to go."

"But you had Dom go?" she asked.

Ronaldo huffed with frustration. "Elena, I'm not a cop; Dom is. Marks said he wouldn't even tell me about the operation unless I agreed not to go, so I made him promise to include Dom on the operation instead."

Elena nodded once but didn't seem convinced.

"Either way, Marks's team is compromised," Ronaldo said. "Someone sold them out—let the traffickers know they were coming."

He left out the part about the bomb blowing up the pickup truck when the strike team went outside. And the two snipers they found tied up and gagged. From what Dom had heard, neither man knew who or what hit them. Rumor had it they were now off the task force for fear they'd been compromised.

"We *will* find her," Dom said. "We won't stop looking until we do."

Elena got up from the couch, and Dom gave her a hug.

"So can we have some breakfast now?" he said, looking at Ronaldo. "As a family?"

He hadn't eaten all day, but he had no appetite. If not for his promise to his son, he would have just gone off to work, running on empty again.

Elena went to the kitchen, turned the stove on,

and put a pan on the burner as Ronaldo walked over to the barred window.

Their apartment in eastern Downey was part of another government program that reminded Ronaldo of the Soviet Union. Everything was basically the same size, everyone had access to the same services, and everything was rationed, including electricity and water.

This morning, the gas was working but the lights weren't. That was typical for mornings, especially in the winter months. They were lucky to live in a region where they could survive without heat. Two-thirds of the country was not so lucky.

Elena cracked four of the eggs Ronaldo had brought home with the rations he received at the Sheriff's Department. Along with the rations Dom got, it was enough to keep them fed while most of the city went hungry.

Dom joined him at the window.

"These treaties Chief Stone made are at risk," he said quietly. "If more cops die, he won't keep his post."

"Good. I hope he falls down the stairs and breaks his neck," Ronaldo whispered back. "Guy's a coward."

"Dad, I was thinking. I'd like to join the strike team Marks commands . . . for good."

Ronaldo looked away from the window. He had considered asking Marks to look out for his son by adding him to the team, but it was even more dangerous than being a cop on the streets.

"Too risky," Ronaldo replied after the pause. "That bomb was a warning to Marks and his strike team to stay in their lane. This mole, whoever it is, if they know the identity of those men and women, every one of them is at risk of assassination."

"So much for face masks protecting our identities," Dom said.

"Yeah. You just keep doing what you're doing with Andre, okay?"

Dom shrugged. "Feels like we're pissing on a forest fire."

"I know, but remember what I told you—"

"Let's eat," Elena said. She carried a plate of scrambled eggs over to the table, and two pieces of toast—the last of their bread.

Dom reached for one, then withdrew his hand. "You guys eat. I'll be good."

"No," Ronaldo said. "You and Mom have them."

Elena shook her head. "I'm not even hungry."

"You have to eat," Ronaldo said. "Please."

She sat down and finally grabbed a piece of bread. They didn't have butter or jam to put on the toast, but they did have salt and pepper for the eggs.

Ronaldo ate slowly, trying to think of something to talk to his wife and son about. This was the first time they had eaten at the same table in weeks. Dom looked exhausted, and so did Elena.

But if he looked in the mirror, Ronaldo would see the same dark bags under his own eyes. He took a sip of watered-down coffee almost as bad as the battery acid they brewed at the FOB in Kandahar years ago.

"I heard schools are going to start opening again next year," Dom said. "That's good news."

"Maybe you could volunteer, Elena," Ronaldo

suggested. "You always did love teaching, and I'm sure they'll need teachers."

"Maybe when Monica comes home."

His wife still spoke as their child would show up at the front door, but if she knew what he and Dom had seen out there, she wouldn't be talking like that.

Ronaldo finished his eggs and got up.

"Thanks for breakfast, but I really should get going," he said. "We're headed outside the walls this afternoon, and I want to make sure the truck will get us there and back."

"You can't stay a few more minutes?" Dom asked.

Ronaldo answered by taking his dish to the sink and going to change into his uniform.

When he was ready to go, he came back to the kitchen to find Dom and Elena still at the table. They both looked at him with resentment.

"I can't just sit around . . . I'm sorry," Ronaldo said on his way to the door.

"You can't just sit around?" Elena called out. "Because that's *all* I do. I sit here and wait!"

Ronaldo knew it was wrong just to leave, but his patience was shot. He was giving everything in his search for Monica, and he couldn't stand to have drama at home.

Leaving was easier than arguing.

Both Dom and Elena stood and watched Ronaldo open the door. He realized then that he wasn't at risk of losing his family. He had lost them the day Monica was taken.

"I'm sorry," he said.

Four hours later, he was in the Humvee with Bettis

and Tooth, driving beyond the walls. This time, they were headed to Chino Hills State Park after reports of more traffickers camping there last night.

As Ronaldo put on his breathing mask and sped down the road, he felt relief and joy—feelings that no longer happened at home.

Out here, he was doing something to bring his little girl home. Out here, he still felt alive.

Almost two weeks later, Dom still didn't know what had happened the night of the failed raid outside Los Alamitos. He had come to work every day hoping for answers, but Marks wasn't talking, and things at home only got worse.

His parents had grown more distant, torn apart by resentment, guilt, and anger. The same emotions were eating Dom alive. Right before he left the apartment for work, Ronaldo had come home and gone straight to the bedroom. Elena was already there, sleeping away the afternoon.

Dom's heart hurt thinking about the pain his parents were going through. He shifted his thoughts back to tonight's briefing at LAPD Headquarters downtown.

The first hour was the same bullshit that Dom had listened to since he joined the force—mostly talk about how to "police" crime, not mitigate it or investigate things. But tonight, the most glaring difference in the briefing was the man giving it.

Lieutenant Best, one of Chief Stone's main lackies,

was at the podium. Standing in front of city maps and pictures of crime bosses, the sweating, pear-shaped lieutenant spoke as if he actually gave a shit.

Dom would have thought a twenty-two-year veteran of the LAPD would have the city's best interests at heart. Quite the opposite had occurred.

He suspected that Best was one of the rat fucks working with the crime organizations. Rumors of meetings with the Morettis had made their way through the LAPD ranks. But what really gave Best away was how he started the briefing.

"You're to stay away from the Four Diamonds unless given explicit orders," he said. "It's far too dangerous, and I don't want to lose any more of our brothers or sisters."

Dom would have laughed at the reasoning, but it wasn't funny. This wasn't about losing brothers or sisters. It was about breaking the deal Chief Stone had in place with Don Antonio Moretti. So instead of keeping drugs off the streets, officers like Dom and Moose had to stand on the sidelines and watch the city descend into hell.

A tsunami of drugs was coming in from all around the world. And with them, like sharks to blood in the water, came new crime organizations.

The fifty officers in the briefing listened in silence. Everyone seemed to have the same opinion about Best being a prick.

"We believe the Yamazaki clan is making a play for the turf at the Four Diamonds," Best continued. "Chief Stone's position is to let the Moretti family deal with this on their own."

"What about Mariana López?" asked an officer

at the front of the room. "We're just going to let her sicarios get away with what happened at the Angel Pyramids two weeks ago?"

"No," Best said. "That's why we're here tonight, if you'd have let me fucking finish."

Dom was suddenly attentive.

"Things are complicated, as you all know," said another voice.

Captain Gregory Baird strode in, his sleeves rolled up exposing tattoos of his old Army Ranger platoon.

Lieutenant Marks also stepped into the room, with Chief Stone. The chief walked up behind the podium, smoothing his graying handlebar mustache.

"Evening, everyone," he said. "I'll cut right to it. When the Norteño Mafia fractured, Esteban and Miguel Vega absorbed much of MS-13, the Sureños, the Latin Kings, Florencia Thirteen, and a dozen other gangs that I don't care to waste my breath on. Many of these animals were given an option: form a new organization or join the Vega family."

Stone grasped the edges of the wooden lectern. "In most cases, they all joined the Vega banner, but some of them decided to work for Mariana López."

Dom didn't know much about her aside from rumors that she slept with Miguel Vega and that she was part of the reason the two families hadn't fought an all-out war.

"Apparently, some of her people have gone off the reservation," Stone said, "and I'm giving the green light to take her out."

"Everyone in this room's going to be part of the task force that goes after her," Baird said in his deep, raspy voice. "Anyone discovered leaking information will not only lose their job, they will serve prison time."

Dom couldn't believe his ears. Things were actually changing, and not small things. The LAPD was going after one of the big fish, not just the sardines.

"With the López family taken out, we can work on taking down the real threat: Esteban Vega and his brother Miguel. And we will finally have justice for Chief Diamond."

Stone paused, looking down—probably for dramatic effect, Dom thought. Everyone knew that Stone hadn't cared much for his predecessor, and up until now he had taken a very different approach to running the police force.

"For now, you're all to report back to the streets, where I want you to hunt her down," Stone said. "Use any means possible to find her."

No one said a word.

"Dismissed," said the chief.

Dom waited in case Marks wanted to have a word with him, but the lieutenant marched out of the room with everyone else.

Moose and Dom went to the garage to do a final check on their cruiser, which continued to have mechanical problems.

"Hey, Dom!" a voice rang out in the echoey space.

Camilla Santiago jogged over, dressed in plain clothing today, with her partner, Alex Rodney. He wore clear-rimmed glasses and had a straggly beard. The hipster still looked as if he were living his old life as a software engineer in Silicon Valley.

Dom was surprised the guy had lasted this long.

"Hey, guys," Camilla said. "Where you headed to-night?"

Alex walked over, hands on his duty belt.

"How you doin'?" Moose asked him. He clapped Alex on the back, nearly knocking off his glasses.

"We're patrolling downtown tonight," Dom said. "How about you guys?"

"Same," said Camilla. "Want to tag-team?"

"Huh?" Moose asked.

"I mean head out together," she said. "Our cruiser is being worked on."

"Yeah, sure, but ours ain't working the best." Moose opened the door to the back seat and turned away from the car. "Damn, I cleaned it out yesterday."

"Smells like the junkie we had back there," Dom said. "He was pretty ripe."

"Lovely," Alex said. He gave Camilla an imploring look. "Why don't we just go get caught up on paper-work, Cam?"

"Because our job isn't to sit around, and because pa-perwork blows." She nodded at the back seat. "After you."

Alex brought up his breathing mask and scooted in.

"Where'd you find this nerd?" Moose muttered to Camilla.

Dom elbowed Moose in the side. "Mind your manners tonight, bro."

The four officers got into the cruiser and pulled out of the garage, following several other cars out into the dusty night. On the way to the interstate, Moose drove past the Staples Center and the LA Convention Center. Several police cars were parked outside to pro-tect the precious buildings and what was inside.

"If someone had told me the Staples Center would be turned into a factory farm, I woulda laughed my ass off," Moose said.

Dom couldn't quite believe it, either. Both buildings had become livestock factories run by the city. Tens of thousands of chickens were being processed every day.

"Mayor Buren is doing a heck of a job, negotiating that deal with Mexico to send us fresh produce we can't grow in our toxic soil," Alex said from the back seat.

Dom and Moose exchanged a glance but kept their thoughts to themselves. They drove by the Convention Center, where more officers patrolled. The next few blocks of downtown were always depressing. Filthy people pushed shopping carts full of everything they owned.

Six months ago, residents would have been hurrying home from their six and seven-figure jobs, texting on their cell phones about which parent was picking up Junior from the AP tutor. Now the focus was on staying alive.

Moose pulled onto Highway 110 and headed north toward Dodger Stadium. Against a fiery sunset, dozens of massive wind turbines turned slowly on the hills behind the stadium. It was one of many power-generating sites that the mayor had promised throughout the city.

"Mayor Buren's two-year goal is ambitious," Dom said. "I find it hard to believe these things will ever power the city, even with the solar farms."

"They will," Alex said. "I've done the math. It should be plenty of power on days when the sun is out and the wind is blowing."

"And when both things aren't happening?" Camilla asked.

"We go to backups," Alex said. He pushed his glasses up again. "It's actually a pretty good system."

Moose kept his eyes on the road but snickered under his breath.

The radio crackled with the first call of the evening: a car theft that turned into a high-speed chase. They were late to the party. By the time they got there, the thief had run the Ford Mustang head-on into a concrete barrier, ending his brief Grand Prix moment in spectacular fashion.

The next few hours, they responded to several calls of muggings and domestic violence in Lincoln Heights. At eight o'clock, the city was shadowed in darkness and things were heating up.

Moose pulled up to a house with a woman screaming on the front lawn, waving two bloody knives in the air. Camilla got out first and shined her flashlight at the woman. The front of her white shirt was drenched in blood.

"Please put the knives down. We're here to help you," Camilla said in her best soothing voice, which Dom didn't find all that soothing. He approached on the left side but kept his distance, one hand on the butt of his gun, the other raised nonthreateningly.

"Please drop the knives," he said.

"They took my husband!" she screamed. "They took him to the stars!"

She slashed at the sky.

Moose took a step into the yard. "Ma'am, who took your husband?" he asked.

"*They* did!" she yelled, pointing to the sky. "The aliens. They come every night, and this time they took him!"

Neighbors on the street walked over and spoke with Alex, who stood back at the cop car. He came over and whispered something to Camilla.

"Keep her busy," she said to Dom.

They went inside the house while Moose and Dom tried to talk the woman down.

It turned out the aliens hadn't taken her husband—maybe they didn't want him after she killed him, Dom thought. He wasn't surprised she had killed the guy. What did surprise him was how many times Moose had to tase her before she dropped the knives.

On the third shot, she finally let go.

"Goddamn meth," Moose whispered. He put the moaning woman in handcuffs and got her into an LAPD van. A half hour later, the medical examiner showed up and went inside.

As soon as they had written it up, the four officers were off to the next call. It, too, was drug related. A high-school-age boy had overdosed on opioids in a skate park. They were the first on the scene.

The kid's friends had circled around his body, which was crumpled next to a skateboard.

"Out of the way," Moose said.

Dom could tell by the shade of his skin that the kid was gone. A touch to his neck confirmed it.

"God damn," he said.

Camilla bent down next to him. "It's like a virus—gonna keep spreading until we find a cure."

Again the medical examiner came and took the body, and Dom and his team were back on the road. At ten o'clock, the dispatcher reported gunfire at the Four Diamonds housing block, just a mile away. Moose gunned it there but stopped a block away, where several police cars were parked, strobes flashing.

They got out and joined the other officers, keeping behind the cruisers to watch the gun battle from a distance. Camilla stepped up to Dom, keeping low.

"We got to just stand here and watch?" Moose asked.

"You heard the chief," Alex said.

Dom fished out his pocket binoculars and zoomed in. Two men who looked like Moretti guys were hiding behind a Mercedes. They both got up and fired shots at contacts across the road.

A tall olive-skinned man wearing a lot of ink also fired from behind a planter.

Two people were already down. One looked like a civilian caught in the cross fire.

"This is fucking bullshit!" Dom said. "There are tens of thousands of innocents in those buildings."

He walked around the car, but Camilla put a hand on his arm.

"Pick your battles, Dominic," she said.

He pulled out of her grip but froze at the sound of engines. Three bright-red motorcycles sped down the road toward the vehicle with the two men hiding behind it. The riders aimed Uzi submachine guns and strafed the car with bullets. Both Morettis crumpled to the pavement, but one crawled away only to be riddled with another burst of rounds.

The tall man with the tattoos strode out to fire when a fourth bike came screaming around the corner. The rider wore a tight red leather jacket and black pants. He raised a samurai sword and sped toward the tall Moretti man.

A fifth bike hopped a curb to flank him.

Both riders slashed him with their swords. For a moment, he just stood there, then he slumped to the concrete in a fetal position.

The Yamazakis sped away, probably with drugs they had just stolen—drugs that would kill people and drive others insane, like the woman they had encountered earlier tonight.

"I think I have a cure for that virus," Camilla said. "But it ain't gonna be pretty."

* * *

Antonio sat at the head of a long table in a ballroom of the former Commerce Hotel, drinking coffee and enjoying cannoli his chef had made fresh that day. The ingredients for cannoli and the pasta dinner they had earlier were hard to come by these days. But Antonio could buy pretty much anything.

All around him, his most trusted soldiers and confidants sat with their wives and girlfriends. All were in a good mood after indulging in luxuries rare in the postapocalyptic city. All were stuffed, and some were well on the way to being shit-faced.

Carmine had already unbuttoned his pants to let his gut out. He had his arm around his wife, Antonio's cousin Gia. Antonio never knew what she had seen in Carmine, but then again, he wasn't sure what Carmine saw in his cousin, either.

They were both mean, selfish people with substance

issues that Antonio had to monitor constantly. On the other hand, Carmine was the mastermind behind their successful drug operation—their cash cow—and the reason they could afford to have cannoli and pasta shipped in from Italy.

As long as Carmine didn't use their product, he would remain captain.

Two loyal soldiers, Yellowtail and Lino, both single, sat next to Carmine. They were comparing scars while they drank beer. Angela, seated by her brother Lino, was picking at her food and looking down.

It was obvious she missed the old country, but this was her home now, and she was safer here, especially with the news she had brought back from Naples. News that Antonio had yet to share with his brother.

He looked at Christopher, who didn't seem to have a care in the world. He was in his finest suit, drinking wine and smoking a cigar with Vinny. Both of them laughing about something Doberman had done yesterday at the port.

Antonio turned back to the conversation with Raff and his fiancée, Crystal, who sat to the left of Antonio and Lucia. Normally, he tried to get as far away from them as possible, and not because of Raff, who rarely spoke. It was his fiancée who seemed unable to stop talking.

Crystal hadn't paused except to breathe. Going on and on about this and that and shit that Antonio didn't give a flying fuck about. In a way, he felt bad for Raff and wondered whether his quiet old friend ever got a word in at home.

Lucia listened to Crystal talking about how much

she missed nail salons, the old-school kind. But he could see that his wife was ready for the evening to end. Antonio eyed the bottle of Montepulciano in front of them.

He would have loved to drink half of it, but he was stone sober tonight. He never drank when they had business to attend to, and if he was right, they would have some issues to mop up later in the evening.

He was right.

At eleven o'clock, Alan Rush, the former sergeant with AMP, opened the ballroom doors and motioned for Christopher. He got up and crossed the room, smoke trailing from the cigar in his hand.

Antonio took a drink of coffee and looked over to admire Lucia's beauty. Tonight, her dark hair hung down to her cleavage. She caught him looking, and her red lips parted in a sly smile.

"What did I tell you about staring, Antonio?" she murmured.

"That it's not polite," he replied. "Unless it's your bride."

Standing, he took her hand and kissed her.

"Don't wait up for me, my love," he said.

Her brow furrowed, the smile gone.

"Where are you going?" she asked.

Christopher walked back into the room. "Vinny, come with me," he said. "Antonio, we're ready."

The rest of the men got up, not knowing what was going on.

Only two of them knew what was happening outside, and that was the point.

"Enjoy your dessert and coffee," Antonio said.

"We've got a situation to attend to. Raff, if you wouldn't mind, come with me."

He and Raff walked out of the room, letting the ballroom doors slam behind them. A team, led by Rush, waited in the circular drive outside with a group of ten Moretti associates holding automatic rifles.

A small convoy of SUVs was parked behind the men, engines rumbling.

"Don Antonio," came the soft voice of Raff.

Antonio stopped. "You're in charge until I get back," he said.

"And Carmine?"

"Is drunk." Antonio patted Raff on the shoulder. "You can handle things."

Then he jumped into the Escalade with his brother and nephew. The interior had the rich smell of cigars, a scent Antonio had always loved. Christopher had smoked his almost down to the cherry. He rolled down the window and tossed it out.

The gate at the front of the compound opened, and the convoy rolled past the checkpoint, where two associates manned a machine-gun nest. Both men nodded and raised hands to wish them well.

Respect. There wasn't much Antonio valued more than loyalty and respect. And tonight was about ensuring that he would have it in the future.

Christopher led the convoy down streets that were deserted except for a few vehicles puttering by. Those who could afford gas generally stayed off the road at this time of night to avoid getting carjacked.

No one with half a brain would mess with the Moretti vehicles. They would hit safer targets, single cars or trucks without escorts. He knew because his own men hit trucks carrying shipments of produce all the time.

Part of the meal digesting in his gut was from a hijacked load.

But enemies like the Yamazaki clan had their eyes on his drugs and were brazen enough to hit him. And he knew exactly how he was going to deal with them.

"Someone want to tell me where we're going?" Vinny asked.

Christopher kept focused on the road, and Antonio remained silent as he checked the loads on two Heckler and Koch MP5 submachine guns. He handed them up to Vinny, and then passed the bulletproof vests.

"Where are we going?" Vinny asked. He turned to look in the back seat as Antonio took off his suit jacket and folded it neatly on the seat.

His nephew was a smart young man and figured it out as soon as they got on the interstate.

"The Four Diamonds?" he said. "Did the Yamazakis hit us again?"

"Relax," Christopher said.

Vinny grew more anxious, talking faster and breathing harder. "Doberman is there," he said. "If something happened to Doberman . . ."

Antonio put his vest on over his shirt. "Maybe we should have left you back at the compound," he said. "But your father thought you should be part of the plan to end the Yamazakis."

That made Vinny relax in his seat. He stared forward with his father, and Antonio did the same.

It wasn't long until they saw lights in the distance. Red and blue pulses lit up the dark streets.

Antonio leaned back out of reflex when a siren wailed behind them. The police cruiser shot by, easily doing a hundred.

Two more cop cars followed.

"Jesus," Vinny breathed.

"Don't worry," Christopher said. "They can't touch us."

Vinny shook his head. "You sure about that?"

"Why? What do you know?"

Antonio leaned forward. "You know something, Vin?"

"Detective Clarke told me and Doberman that our deal is at risk."

"He doesn't know shit, then," Antonio said. "I met with Chief Stone, and our deal is intact."

He decided to tell his nephew why, even though only Christopher knew the truth.

"What happened at the Angel Pyramids was us," he said. "We started that fight. Stone knew it and delayed sending cops."

"What!" Vinny said.

"It was unfortunate cops had to die, but now Mariana López has a target on her back, and that means the Vegas will lose one of their biggest allies."

Vinny looked to his father, but Christopher kept his eyes on the road. He took a gravel frontage road that ferried construction equipment to and from the Four Diamonds. Bulldozers, concrete trucks, and other vehicles sat parked along the shoulder. The four public housing complexes loomed in the distance.

They stopped outside a gate. One of the other men got out and opened it, and Christopher followed the vehicles to the nearest complex.

Vinny grabbed the door handle, ready to jump out.

"Patience," Antonio said. "You may be young, but you're not invincible like you may think."

The convoy parked along a road lined with palm trees, their fronds dancing wildly in the breeze. Antonio put his mask on, then motioned for the soldiers to follow him into the dark complex.

Judging by the lack of gunfire, the team was too late, and Antonio prayed his plan hadn't injured too many of his men.

Grading and sodding equipment stood about on the bare dirt around the building—finishing touches being made by the crews.

Antonio had been right about the effect the projects would have, drawing opportunists from around the world, just as Los Angeles had drawn his family.

Dust whipped through the site. Christopher took point and didn't stop until he got to a chain-link fence blocking off the street. From here, they had a view of the next diamond-shaped complex.

Rush walked over to Christopher and spoke quietly. Then they slipped through a gap in the fence. Antonio took care not to snag his shirt on the sharp snipped ends.

The next stretch of road was filled with civilians, all trying to get a look at what had happened. The wail of sirens filled the night.

Rush took point this time, crossing the street and making his way into a courtyard outside the pointed western end of the nearest complex. Antonio rarely came here, but tonight he must show his face to his men, to prove that their leader didn't hide.

But tonight, it seemed the fighting had already ended.

"Spread out and make sure there are no more threats," Antonio said to Rush. He handed his weapon over and took off his vest.

"What are you doing?" Christopher asked.

Proving I'm not afraid.

The soldiers who had accompanied them fanned out in the shadows while Antonio, Christopher, and Vinny walked toward the scene without their vests and weapons.

The first thing Antonio saw was a motorcycle down on the street, and the rider against a curb, blood pooling around his head. Then he saw the two more bodies behind a car.

Ambulances had already arrived, but the medics were working on other people.

"Daniel!" Vinny yelled.

He sprinted to Doberman, who lay on ground with two medics working on him.

Frankie was there, too, standing with a hand to his face. Several other associates stood guard, dressed in street clothes to blend in.

The three well-dressed Morettis stood out like a flame in the night, but Antonio didn't care. He had plenty of security here, and the Yamazakis were long gone.

Frankie walked over, still covering his eye, blood dripping down his face.

"Don Antonio," he said.

"You okay?"

A nod from Frankie. "We lost three men, and Doberman's in bad shape."

Vinny had bent down by his tall friend, who had multiple slash wounds across his body and face.

"Swords?" Antonio asked.

Another nod from Frankie. "Three guys ambushed him."

"Did they get the drugs like planned?" Antonio asked.

"Yes."

"Good," he said, slapping Frankie gently on his bloody face. "You did good tonight, my friend."

"You shouldn't be out in the open, Don Antonio. The cops are here." Frankie pointed with his chin, and Antonio turned to see several cruisers with officers standing behind them, rifles in hand.

The medics picked Doberman up in a stretcher and hauled him off toward the ambulance.

Vinny got up and walked back over to join them.

"Is he going to be okay?" Christopher asked.

"I . . . I don't know," Vinny replied. "He's lost a lot of blood."

Antonio waved at the cops in the distance.

Vinny put up a hand, but instead of waving, he gave them the bird.

The kid was starting to get it.

This was Moretti territory now, and if all continued to go as planned, the bugs trying to encroach on it would be squashed.

-8-

The Sheriff's Department truck crunched over the rocky fire road off the Angeles Crest Highway. Ronaldo sat behind the wheel, his mind awhirl with worry. He felt as though he had lost his entire family.

Usually, being outside the city helped him clear his mind and focus on bringing Monica home. But now there didn't seem to be much of a family to bring her home to, and that shook him badly.

Bettis, riding shotgun, could clearly sense his dread.

"If you want to talk, I'm all ears, my friend," he said.

"Thanks," Ronaldo replied. "Just some troubles at home, nothing new." He would have gone into more detail, but they had a fourth deputy with them to-day—a man named Jay Pierce, who was about the same age as Tooth and equally immature.

But Tooth was a fighter, and Pierce was not.

Ronaldo had severe reservations about a man who came with the reputation of being a pussy and was here just for the rations. He checked Pierce in the rear-view mirror. The man had caterpillar eyebrows over a crooked nose and thin lips, vaguely reminding Ronaldo of a Mexican eagle.

If he had wings, he probably would fly away from a fight, Ronaldo thought. But he was still willing to give the guy a chance, and today he would probably get one.

Ronaldo drove to a radio station that had been owned by the FAA in the San Gabriel Mountains. It was abandoned after the war and was probably being used by squatters. They had gotten the call to check it out after a Sheriff's Department drone spotted vehicles outside.

Ronaldo saw those vehicles now: an old Volkswagen van and a Volkswagen bug.

"Just some damn hippies," Bettis said with a chuckle.

"Doesn't mean they aren't armed," said Tooth.

"Keep your finger off the trigger," Ronaldo said, glancing into the rearview mirror. His eyes moved over. "You, too, Pierce."

Tooth laughed. "You ever even fired that thing?" He elbowed Pierce in the shoulder. Pierce didn't like that.

"Don't touch me, man," he whined.

"Knock the shit off," Bettis said, turning. His gaze shut both of them down.

Ronaldo pulled down a road around the station's perimeter fence. The vantage point gave them a view of both desert and mountains—normally a beautiful sight, but not today.

Heat lightning, odd in the winter months, slashed at the desert. Normally, there would be snow up here, but the last storm had melted days after it fell.

"Looks like we're going to get wet," Tooth said.

"Not for a while," Bettis replied. "It's slow-moving—assuming the weatherman is right."

Ronaldo grunted. "Lyin' sack of shit is never right, and with this weird weather, it's hard to say if it's going to rain, snow, or piss acid on us."

He parked on the east side of the radio station and grabbed his rifle.

"Stay frosty," he said, to Pierce more than anyone else.

The deputies got out of the truck and took up position behind it. There was no sign of anyone outside the building, but some clothing was soaking in plastic containers outside.

"See that?" Bettis said, pointing.

Ronaldo followed his finger. The Mountain High Resort, once a popular destination for skiers, stood on the peak next to the one where they now stood. The days of skiing were long gone, and the resort was shut down, the lifts idle and rusting.

Someone was up there, though.

Smoke chimneyed into the air. It wasn't thick enough to be a wildfire, which meant it had to be a campfire.

"Stupid fucks," Ronaldo said.

Everyone knew how dry it was, and that burning anything came with a heavy fine and jail time. But with prisons overfilling and people cold, no one seemed compelled to obey an unenforceable law.

"We'll check it out after this," Ronaldo said, stepping away from the pickup. He walked to the gate and pushed it open.

Rifle cradled, he went to the front door, where he saw a bloody footprint.

Out of instinct, he flashed hand signals for Pierce and Tooth to flank. Bettis came to the door with him, and he gave the nod to open it.

Like the gate, it was unlocked. Bettis twisted the knob, then pushed it open.

Ronaldo went inside, and even with his breathing mask on, he picked up a rancid smell. He motioned for Bettis to check the rooms to the right while Ronaldo went left. He stepped into an office that squatters had used as a bedroom. Sleeping bags, blankets, and pillows were bunched up on the ground, but no bodies.

Bettis stepped into the room. "You better see this," he said.

Ronaldo followed him to a bathroom and discovered a macabre scene. Bloodstains in the shape of a snow angel marked the tile floor.

"Come on," Ronaldo said.

They went back outside, where Tooth and Pierce were on watch.

"Well?" Tooth asked.

"All we found was blood," Bettis said.

"'Cause someone took these people, just like the people we found in that ravine a few weeks ago," Ronaldo said. "And if we're lucky, the people responsible are over there." He looked over at the peak where they had seen the smoke. "Let's go check it out."

"Don't you think we should call this in?" Pierce asked as they walked back to the truck.

"Not until we're sure," Ronaldo replied. "I don't want LT to bitch about burning through precious fuel if we take him on another wild-goose chase."

"Last time, Sheriff Benson even bitched us out," Tooth said.

Ronaldo stared at the horizon. As much as he wanted

the smoke to be from the traffickers who were hunting in Angeles National Forest, the chances were slim.

Still, he would do anything to find his daughter, even if it meant burning some gas and getting another ass-chewing from Sheriff Dale Benson. The cowboy was a maniac for following rules, and Ronaldo had already received several lectures.

Getting back on the interstate, Ronaldo gave the truck some juice and headed off toward the smoke. According to Bettis and the map he had out, it appeared to be coming from a peak beyond the ski lifts, called Blue Ridge.

"It's a campground," Bettis said.

"So it makes sense that people would be *camping* there, right?" Pierce said.

Tooth scowled at him. "Dude, how long you been a deputy? You don't seem to know shit from shoe polish out here."

"This is only the third time I've been sent beyond the walls."

Bettis pointed to the map and looked at Ronaldo. It took him a moment before realization set in. This was outside the boundary of their jurisdiction, and Bettis was trying to keep that from Pierce.

But it didn't matter if Pierce ratted them out, anyway. All it took was a drone flyover. And if that happened, he would be severely screwed.

Ronaldo shook his head, pissed off that they were saddled with this gutless rookie. Being a pussy out here could not only could get you killed; it could get your team killed.

As they made the winding drive up to Blue Ridge,

Ronaldo considered just telling Pierce to wait in the truck, but he knew that doing so could cause other problems.

The drive took them off road across a burned-over hillside. A slope of blackened trees jutted sharply out of the alpine terrain. A few patches of dirty brown snow, like scabs on burned flesh, had survived the heat.

"We scope the site out," Ronaldo said, "and if this does fit the profile for our raiders, we call it in and wait for backup."

Pierce nodded, but Bettis and Tooth just looked ahead.

There were several ways to get to the top of Blue Ridge, but Ronaldo took an old track mostly overgrown with weeds.

If there were hostiles, they would likely have spotters on the main road, but they probably didn't even know this one existed.

One of the defunct ski lifts was to the south, the chairs blowing slightly in the rising wind. Ronaldo lost sight of them as he drove into a section of forest that the flames had spared.

The denser cover limited his visibility. The engine growled up the steep path. At the top, he drove toward a closed gate with a bullet-riddled No Trespassing sign.

Someone, or something, darted away from the gate and into the forest.

"See that?" Bettis said.

Ronaldo pushed down harder on the pedal and kept both hands on the wheel as they jolted over the rocky ground.

"Hold on," he said.

"What are you doing?" Pierce said.

Ronaldo kept his foot down and slammed into the gate, breaking it open with the cow guard on the truck's grill.

The road curved around into an open area for camping, but he didn't see any tents or vehicles or any evidence of a campfire.

"You got eyes?" he asked Bettis.

"No," he replied, twisting and turning.

Ronaldo drove through the camp, searching the other open areas. Pierce suddenly shouted and pointed out his window.

"Over there, two SUVS!"

Ronaldo spotted them making a run for the other road.

"Tooth, get out and shoot their tires if you can get a shot on their way down the mountain," he said. "I'll come back for you later."

"You got it, boss." He jumped out, and Ronaldo floored it.

"Bettis, time to call for backup," Ronaldo said. "I got a feeling these are our guys."

Bettis picked up the receiver and radioed in the description of the vehicles while Ronaldo roared ahead. The two SUVs kicked up a rooster tail of dust that obscured the path to the road.

"Be careful!" Pierce yelled.

"Shut the fuck up!" Ronaldo shouted back.

The chase took them in a circle around the campground and toward the main road through the forest. Once they hit the blacktop, the dust wouldn't be a problem.

But they never made it there.

"WATCH OUT!" Pierce screamed—this time, for good reason.

A third vehicle, which Ronaldo hadn't seen, came from behind an abandoned building and slammed into the back of their pickup. Glass shattered on the right side, showering Bettis and Pierce.

The pickup spun, jerking Ronaldo left, right, and back again. Smoke and the scent of burning rubber filled his nostrils as the truck skidded to a stop.

Dazed but alert, Ronaldo grabbed the door handle and opened it. Then he undid his seat belt and fell out onto the dirt. He opened the back door to find Pierce unconscious, blood dripping down his head.

Bettis was moving in the front seat, but he, too, had hit his head. There wasn't anything Ronaldo could do for them now but try to keep them from being shot at.

No sooner had the thought occurred than bullets pounded the hood and shattered the windshield.

Ronaldo grabbed his pistol from its holster. He saw the shooter approaching the vehicle with an AK-47. But before Ronaldo could get off a shot, a gun muzzle pushed against the back of his head.

"Drop it, piggy," said a nasal voice.

Ronaldo considered his options. From what he could see, the vehicle that had hit them was an F250, and the man in camo fatigues with an AK-47 was the only hostile besides the guy behind Ronaldo. But even if he could take the guy holding the gun to his head, the guy with the AK would kill Bettis and probably Pierce.

He had no option but to hope these men wouldn't kill them. He dropped the pistol in the dirt.

"Smart move," said the man behind Ronaldo. "Now put your hands on your head and slowly turn around."

Taking a deep breath of filtered air, Ronaldo did as ordered. The man was wearing a mask, but his eyes were young. Probably about Dom's age.

"I don't like killing cops, but a lot of you fucks killed us during the war," the guy said. "My dad died by a rebel bullet. Now I'm curious. Were you in the war?"

Ronaldo nodded.

"Which side did you fight on?" the man asked, tilting his head.

Ronald knew that his answer would likely determine whether he lived or died, and he had no idea whether this guy had fought with AMP or the other side. Each side had called the other "rebels."

"Well?" the man said. He raised his rifle to Ronaldo's forehead.

A sharp crack made Ronaldo flinch, and in his peripheral vision, the man in front of their truck dropped. As the young man's eyes darted to his fallen comrade, Ronaldo's hand shot up and whipped the rifle barrel away from his head.

In several swift moves, he snapped the gunman's wrist, eased the weapon out of his hand, and smashed him in the face with it. The guy hit the ground holding his nose with his good hand.

Ronaldo pointed the gun down at the man. "Which side were *you* on, asshole?"

Tooth jogged over to check the guy he had shot. "Dead," he reported.

"What about those SUVs?" Ronaldo asked, not taking his eyes off the guy on the ground.

"Didn't get a shot, but I saw one of our trucks from the bluff. They will catch up to the bastards."

"You know what that means?" Ronaldo asked their new prisoner.

He gingerly touched his cut and broken nose, saying nothing.

"It *means* that I have plenty of time with you before backup arrives," Ronaldo said. "Not good news for you, I'm afraid."

Tooth was already checking Bettis, who had stumbled out of the vehicle.

"How's Pierce?" Ronaldo asked.

"Concussion, probs, but otherwise fine," Tooth called out.

Ronaldo jerked the barrel toward the prisoner's mask. "Off."

The wind was picking up, swirling dust through the camp. The guy coughed as soon as he removed his breathing apparatus.

"I'll make this simple," Ronaldo said. "You tell me where the people you've taken are, or where you sold them, or you'll be strung up on the radio tower where you killed those hippies."

"But . . ."

"Did I mention you're going to be naked and that I'll be sure to have you up there before *that* rolls in?" He indicated the darkening sky.

The guy, who looked to be in his twenties, smirked. "You can't do that; you're a cop."

"Look around, bucko," Ronaldo growled. "This is the Wild, Wild West. I do as I please, and it would please me to shoot your tiny nuts off."

He pointed the muzzle between the guy's legs and fired a few inches below his crotch.

"What the hell!" the prisoner screamed, scooting frantically backward.

"Tell me where you took those people, who you sold them to. I want to know everything."

"Fuck you."

This time, Ronaldo shot him through the calf.

The man howled in pain and reached down to grab the wound.

Ronaldo backed up and picked up his M1911. Then he handed the rifle to Tooth while the man squirmed in pain.

"Open your mouth," Ronaldo said.

He crouched next to the guy and forced the muzzle of the .45-caliber pistol into the man's mouth, chipping a tooth.

"Tell me, or you can end your worthless existence right here, right now, and I'll just ask the other guys we're about to catch." Ronaldo pulled back the hammer. "I'm okay with whatever you decide."

His captive's eyes widened and he murmured something.

"You going to tell me?"

The man nodded as vigorously as he could with a gun in his mouth.

Ronaldo withdrew the pistol and got to his feet as the guy sobbed.

Over the next few minutes, he spilled his guts, telling them about their little hunting operation in the Angeles National Forest. But it wasn't just his group. There were multiple crews, many of them former AMP soldiers, and all of them selling off the people they kidnapped to an organization known as the Shepherds.

"Take off your clothes," Ronaldo said when the man had finished.

He glanced up, tears making twin crooked lines down his sooty face. "But I just told you everything . . ."

"You told me you're an evil man," replied Ronaldo. "And to deal with evil men, I've got to act like one, too. Now take off your clothes, or I'll take off your nuts."

He pointed the pistol at groin level.

"Please . . ."

Ronaldo pulled the trigger, and dirt flew up between the man's thighs. Whimpering, he let go of his calf and started taking his pants off.

"Ronaldo," Bettis said, "let's bring him in."

"We will—after the storm."

"Salvatore," Tooth said. "I don't think this is a good idea."

Ronaldo turned toward his men. "I didn't put this up for a vote. I'm in charge, and this asshole deserves it."

"Hey!" Tooth yelled.

Ronaldo whirled as the young man pulled a pistol from his back and aimed it at Ronaldo.

A gunshot cracked, close enough that it hurt his ears, and he closed his eyes on reflex. When he opened them, the man was lying limp in the dirt, his pants halfway off.

"What the fuck," Tooth said.

Ronaldo turned to Bettis, but he wasn't the one with a raised gun. It was Pierce.

"There," he said to Tooth, lowering the M16. "I shot someone. You happy now?"

Pierce was the last man Ronaldo had expected to save his life. He checked the dead guy as the storm winds picked up, showering the bloody face with grit. Ronaldo put a finger to his neck and felt a light pulse.

He got up and jerked his chin at the truck. "Let's ride."

"What about him?" Bettis asked.

"Leave him for the storm."

-9-

An angry orange sky churned over Los Angeles. On the twilit street, a black BMW pushed through the dust storm, leaving the port. Behind the wheel, Vinny was doing his best to keep his eyes on the road and his mind on the mission of moving their newest shipment from the *Goomah* to the warehouse.

But his heart was back at the compound, where Doberman was still in critical condition from his wounds. Isao Yamazaki had almost killed him, and Vinny felt responsible. He should have killed the bastard when he had the chance. Twice now, he had passed up opportunities to take him out.

Now his best friend was fighting for his life because Vinny hadn't pulled the trigger.

He wanted to be by his friend's side, but Don Antonio had sent him to the port for the delivery, reversing his former orders.

Vinny understood the change. They had lost four associates last night in the Yamazakis' attack at the Four

Diamonds. They were short on manpower, and he was needed for this transfer.

He drove his BMW behind the garbage trucks driven by Mexican Mikey and his crew. In the passenger seat, Yellowtail nervously massaged his gold cross.

"This is either a really bad idea, or it's genius," he said.

"It's a good way to cover our trail, that's for sure," Vinny replied.

He peered into the flying dirt. Vinny was getting used to driving in the storms. But the wind was worse than normal, whipping grit, trash, and the occasional tumbleweed across the road. Visibility was maybe fifty feet.

He kept his distance from the last garbage truck in the convoy, just in case it had to brake.

Somewhere out there, his father drove an Escalade with Lino, Frankie, and Carmine. They were probably waiting on some overpass. It wasn't just them monitoring the shipment. Don Antonio had deployed six vehicles, filled with Moretti associates led by Rush, along the route.

That didn't inspire much confidence, though. Traveling on the freeway was dangerous even in good weather.

"I don't like this," Vinny admitted. "Brings back bad memories of the time the Vegas hit us on the highway. When Esteban almost killed Don Antonio."

"I remember," Yellowtail said. "That's why we're not taking the highway the entire way."

"Huh?"

"Get in front of the trucks and take the second exit," Yellowtail said.

Vinny pulled in front of the garbage trucks, and they followed him down the off-ramp. One of the trucks nearly clipped a stalled car on the shoulder.

"Where now?" Vinny said.

"Take your next right, then another right."

Vinny did as directed, and pulled through an open gate. Seconds later, he was driving down the sloping concrete bank of the Los Angeles River. Dry as a bone, the passage was like an empty superhighway.

He smiled at what had to be another brilliant plan by his uncle.

The trucks followed them onto the open path. It wasn't just clear of vehicles; it was mostly free of blowing dust.

Vinny felt his heart calming as they drove for several miles down the broad concrete ravine. All he had to do was get the shipment to the warehouse, and then he could go and watch over Doberman.

As they closed in on the location, he veered toward the on-ramp, but Yellowtail shook his head.

"Keep going straight," he said.

"What?"

"Just do it, Vin. And stop asking questions."

Vinny looked over at the ramp leading out of the riverbed. He glimpsed motion on the road above them to the right. At first, it was just a flash of red in the thick grit of the storm. Then he heard the high *vroom* of a two-stroke motorcycle.

Left of the road, more bikes pulled into view.

"Oh, shit," Vinny said.

They passed under a bridge, where multiple men on motorcycles looked down.

Vinny stomped the pedal, but Yellowtail held up a scarred hand. "Take it easy, Vin." Then he raised his SIG Sauer Rattler and rolled down the window. "Keep us steady so I can get a shot."

Ahead, several motorcycles raced down onto the concrete riverbed. Normally, Vinny wasn't afraid of a fight, but this one wasn't exactly even. Isao Yamazaki had brought his entire clan.

Twenty motorcycles converged on the riverbed. All the riders were armed with submachine guns or pistols, and they had swords over their backs.

"What do I do?" Vinny asked.

Yellowtail stared for a moment. The tough son of a bitch normally didn't show emotion, and that bothered Vinny even more.

He readied his gun, then looked over his shoulder.

A glance in the rearview mirror confirmed what he was looking at.

More bikes were following them.

"Stop," Yellowtail finally said. "Stop and kill the engine and keep your hands up."

"*What!*"

"Do it!" Yellowtail shouted.

He put his submachine gun down as Vinny slowed. The garbage trucks did the same thing, easing to a stop behind the car.

"Don't move," Yellowtail said.

The bikers zipped past without firing their weapons. They turned around and came back, circling the garbage trucks like mounted warriors attacking a wagon train.

All but one motorcycle stopped. The riders dismounted and raised their weapons.

Vinny swallowed hard when he saw the final bike driving toward them in the side mirror.

"Don't do anything stupid," Yellowtail said.

Vinny heard his cousin, but he would be passing up his third chance to end Isao right now. Gritting his teeth, he restrained himself.

Isao stopped, dismounted, and removed his helmet. He walked over to the side of the BMW and tapped on the window with the tip of the same sword that had slashed his best friend.

Vinny rolled it down.

"Get out," Isao said. He had that handsome grin again, but this time it was a bit cockier. The victor's smile.

And Vinny had the tight, impotent face of the vanquished.

"Out," Isao repeated.

Yellowtail nodded at Vinny to comply. They got out of the car. Mexican Mikey and his men also jumped down from the cabs. They dropped their weapons and raised their hands.

"The fuck's happening, Vin?" Mikey called out.

"Do what they say," Yellowtail instructed.

Isao gestured for Yellowtail to join him and Vinny.

"I bet you're regretting our little talk at the Four Diamonds, aren't you, Vinny Moretti?" Isao said.

Vinny didn't answer.

"You're making a big mistake," Yellowtail said.

Faster than Yellowtail could react, the sword flashed.

Vinny's heart caught as he looked over, expecting to see his cousin's head slide off his neck. Instead, the top half of his Mohawk fell onto the concrete.

"Speak again, and I'll take your head," Isao said.

Yellowtail's features tightened as Isao's men broke out laughing all around. But Isao just stared at Yellowtail.

"Yeah, I know, you want to take *my* head," Isao said. He looked to Vinny. "And so do you, since I cut your tall friend. How is he, by the way?"

"Alive," Vinny said.

That seemed to surprise Isao.

"Italians are tougher than I thought," he said.

Stepping away, he gestured for his men to open the backs of the trucks. The soldiers fanned out to get what they had come for.

Vinny searched the top of the riverbed for his uncle and father.

Where the hell were they? Had the Yamazakis somehow gotten to them first?

He got his answer the moment they opened the doors and climbed up onto the first two trucks. Gunfire rang out, making Vinny flinch.

Several Yamazakis fell off the garbage trucks. Others crumpled or staggered, gripping their wounds. One man crawled toward a truck, then pitched sideways as bone and brain spattered the ground.

Men in black fatigues jumped out of the garbage trucks. Isao shouted something in Japanese. Vinny grabbed him by the arm, and Yellowtail punched him in the face. But the muscular young clan leader fought free, slashing Vinny's palm as he withdrew his sword.

Backing away, Vinny clamped his hand over the gash. Isao had raised the sword to strike Yellowtail when a bullet punched into the top of his right shoulder.

He staggered backward, dropping the blade and reaching back to grip the wound. Then he turned and ran toward his bike. Gunshots slammed into the concrete as Moretti soldiers fired downward.

Vito, who had hopped out of one of the garbage trucks, pumped his shotgun and fired into one of the cabs, blasting the Yamazaki trying to drive away.

In another cab, a Yamazaki wearing a bright yellow shell managed to shoot one of the Morettis in the head before a dozen bullets stitched him from groin to ear. He fell out onto the concrete.

"Vinny!" shouted a familiar voice.

He spotted his father at the top of the riverbed with his men. Lino, Carmine, and Frankie were all there, picking off the Yamazakis who were scrambling for their bikes. Two of them managed to get back on their wheels and sped toward Isao, who also got on his.

Snapping out of the shock, Vinny reached behind his back and pulled out his Glock. Yellowtail suddenly tackled him as the three motorcycles screamed toward them.

Bullets struck a rider, knocking him off the bike, which hit the back of the BMW and flew over in a lazy arc.

Adrenaline flooded Vinny as he pushed himself up and grabbed his pistol. He ran to the fallen bike and picked it up, wincing from the pain in his slashed right hand. Then he jumped on, ignoring Yellowtail's shouts to stop.

Although this bike was much faster than the old Yamaha Enduro, Vinny was grateful that Doberman had taught him how to ride a few months ago.

Adrenaline and the desire to avenge his friend helped him keep control of the bike. He twisted the throttle and raced after Isao and the other Yamazaki soldier.

Raising his pistol in his injured hand, Vinny gritted his teeth and fired three shots at the other rider before hitting the rear tire. The man lost control, skidded, and flipped.

He pitchpoled into the concrete riverbed, his skull cracking open like an egg.

That got Isao's attention.

He turned and looked back at Vinny, then gunned his bike toward the highway.

"Fuck me," Vinny muttered, accelerating in pursuit.

His sunglasses flew off as he crested the ramp and the storm slammed into him.

Cursing some more, Vinny bent down to protect his face behind the bike's tiny racing windscreen. He nearly lost control as he turned in the wind, but managed to stay upright. Twisting the throttle felt like gripping a hot skillet handle.

The street was abandoned, and for good reason. The wind made it almost impossible to see through the flying grit and dust. He spotted the glaring Cyclops eye of Isao's brake light.

Vinny raised his pistol and fired several shots. None seemed to hit the bike or Isao, and he ducked back down behind the windscreen as particles of grit peppered his face. A piece stung his eye, and tears blurred his vision.

With only one eye open, Vinny considered giving up the chase. That notion passed with the next heartbeat, and he gave it more gas.

Closing in on Isao, Vinny popped off another three shots.

Isao changed lanes, and the brake light glowed red. Then it winked off.

Vinny braked and downshifted when he saw that Isao had slammed into the back of an abandoned vehicle. He sailed over the top and vanished in the blowing dirt.

The tires screeched as Vinny's bike wobbled and then toppled over. He hit the ground rolling, not far from where Isao's bike had gone airborne.

Vinny pushed himself up, another jolt of pain racing down his hand. His left leg burned where it had scraped the pavement. He limped over to the front of the car to find Isao crawling away.

Raising his pistol, Vinny fired a bullet in front of him, and Isao rolled onto his back.

"Who's regretting what now, bitch?" Vinny shouted.

Isao raised his hands. "I'm sorry!"

I'm sorry? Did this douche bag really think he could apologize his way out of a bullet to the head?

"My parents will pay you whatever you want for my life," Isao said. "Think about it. You'll be a rich man and won't have to risk your life ever again."

Vinny hesitated, but not because of the offer. He thought about what his uncle would tell him to do. Money was their lifeblood, the reason for their existence.

But money wouldn't absolve Isao for what he did to Doberman.

"You'll be rich," Isao said again, wincing as he tried to sit up. "We have gold. Lots of gold and silver, and—"

Vinny silenced him with a bullet to his collarbone.

Blood ran down the red leather jacket. Isao fell back, his handsome face contorted in pain.

"Please," he begged.

Vinny knelt down beside him.

"I'm sorry for what I did to your friend," Isao said.

Vinny rose to his feet, towering over the tall man, trying to decide what to do. He aimed the pistol at Isao's face, finger hovering over the trigger.

"Please, don't," Isao slurred. He shielded his face with his hand. "Don't shoot me, please. You'll be rich."

The sound of an approaching vehicle made Vinny look over his shoulder. A big black SUV emerged in the dust storm. Reinforcements had arrived.

"All the gold you could want," Isao said.

Vinny slowly lowered his pistol.

"I'll give you to my uncle and see what he wants to do with you," he said. "But I promise you . . ."

He clenched his jaw, knowing that if he passed up his third chance to kill this man, he might regret it forever. But reason won out over the burning anger coursing through his veins.

"I promise you, if my friend dies of his wounds, I'll cut you up and serve you as sushi to those parents who love you so much," Vinny said.

* * *

Antonio made love to his wife on the new couch she had begged him to import from Italy. It was the second one, after the first proved "not comfortable enough." This one, Lucia seemed to like, especially with her naked back against the expensive leather. He didn't care a fig about the fancy Italian couch, but he did enjoy breaking it in with her.

While they made love, Antonio's men were gunning down the Yamazakis halfway across the city. The storm beat against the bulletproof windows, moaning almost as loudly as his wife.

She rolled off and walked naked across the room to the wet bar.

"So," she said, holding a bottle of red up toward the window. A trickle of sweat ran down between her breasts. "You want to tell me what our soldiers are doing outside today, in *this*?" She looked at the raging dust storm outside.

"Dealing with bugs," Antonio said. "Worms."

"The Vega brothers?"

"No, but they will be dealt with soon."

He got up and took the glass she handed him. Then she opened the bottle and poured them each a glass.

"Cheers, my love," he said.

The glasses clinked together, and Antonio broke his rule of not drinking during business. It would be good for his pounding heart to relax a little.

They enjoyed half a glass each, and he dressed. His men would be back soon—victorious, he hoped, assuming his plan had gone well.

It was a good plan, and Antonio had a feeling the Yamazakis would take the bait. Christopher hadn't liked it at first, using Vinny as that bait. But in the end, he had agreed and sent his son with Yellowtail to deal with the pesky Yamazaki clan.

Antonio walked Lucia back to their room, where

Raff was sitting at a table playing chess with Marco. Raff had remained behind from the attack to help guard the compound. He had become more of a caretaker than a soldier, and Antonio was okay with that. There wasn't anyone he trusted with his family more than his loyal old friend.

Raff stood and Marco popped up as his parents entered.

"Dad, Mom, where have you been?" he asked.

"We had some business," Lucia said—not entirely a lie.

"Who's winning?" Antonio asked, walking over to the table.

Raff sat back down. "Marco is. He's getting better."

"Or you're getting worse," Marco said, grinning.

Antonio was happy to see his son engaging in a game that exercised his mind. It sure beat what he normally did with his friends. Once schools started again, he was going to have Marco in the best one available.

"Can I go outside after the storm is over?" Marco asked. "I want to play with my friends."

Lucia looked to Antonio.

"Soon," he said.

"Soon? That's what you keep saying, but this place . . ." Marco looked at the ornate crown molding and the gold chandelier, and the six-figure pieces of antique furniture. "It feels like a prison," he said. "I hate it here."

"Things will get better, my love," Lucia added.

"A *prison*?" Antonio said. Anger flared hot. "Do you know where I grew up?"

Marco looked puzzled, and Antonio realized he had never told him.

"Raff knows," Antonio said. "'Cause he grew up

with me in the slums, a place infested with rats, crime, and almost zero opportunity to rise out of poverty."

Lucia folded her arms over her chest—a clear signal that she didn't want him to tell the story of their upbringings. But their son *needed* to hear this.

Marco sulked. He had changed a lot in the past year, especially after Antonio took him out to see the refugee camps during the war. He had hoped it would jog his son's perspective on the new reality and inspire some gratitude, but apparently the kid needed another reminder.

"Raff, me, we each had only one pair of shoes, one shirt, and one pair of pants," Antonio said. "We didn't have food some days, and we always had to watch our backs."

"Why?" Marco asked.

"Because we were poor," Lucia said. "Your father is telling you this because he wants you to understand what it's like to be at the bottom, and how to appreciate what you have."

"I do . . . appreciate things," Marco said. "I just want to play with my friends."

Lucia glanced at Antonio with a concerned gaze. He felt his anger subside, but this conversation wasn't over.

"Come with me," he said to Marco.

His son followed him to the windows, where Antonio pulled back the drapes to look out over the city. Downtown was hardly visible, with only the tallest buildings poking out above the roiling dust.

"To win in life, a man must have a plan to conquer a mountain," Antonio said to his son. "Someday, you will have to make your own way and your own plan.

My father taught me this. He also taught me that to get the full view of the mountain you wish to conquer, you must first climb a hill."

Marco nodded as if he understood. In due time, he would.

"This city is my hill," Antonio said. "My father had one, too, in his prime, back in Naples. But he never had a mountain. And someday, I will. Someday, the West Coast will be ours. That is the mountain I still must climb."

He gave Marco a hug and then kissed Lucia on her cheek.

"I'll see you tonight," he said. "Raff, come with me."

Antonio left his family in the suite and went to the elevator. The ground floor of the casino was mostly empty, with only a few guards on duty. He crossed to the front entrance and looked to the driveway outside. More soldiers waited behind the glass doors for his men to return.

The gates opened a half hour later, and Christopher's Escalade skidded to a stop outside. By his driving, Antonio could tell they had injured with them. He just hoped it wasn't Vinny or any of his blood.

But if it was, they had taken a bullet for the cause. *An honor.*

The first person to hop out was Vinny. He had a bandaged hand and torn jeans but didn't appear seriously injured. He limped around the SUV, where Christopher and Lino emerged. Another relief.

Three vehicles screeched to a stop behind them. More injured men were carried inside, but these were all Moretti soldiers or associates.

Then, with Christopher and Lino's help, Frankie

pulled a man in a red leather jacket out of the Escalade.
"Isao Yamazaki," Antonio said aloud, trying to figure out
why they had brought an enemy back to the compound.

This had better be good.

Vinny was first to the lobby doors. The guards propped
them open, and he rushed toward Raff and Antonio.

"How's Doberman?" he asked.

An odd first question, considering the circum-
stances. Antonio had a better one.

"Why the fuck are you bringing that rat shit into
my home?"

Vinny looked over his shoulder, then back to Antonio.

"One word: gold," he answered.

Antonio arched a brow, his interest piqued.

Chaos reigned in the lobby as his men carried in
more wounded. They took them to the second floor,
where they had set up a hospital with stolen medical
equipment. Vinny beat them all there and was already
by Doberman's side.

Dr. Jameson, hired months ago, was directing
his two nurses to get the other beds ready. There were
only three others—not nearly enough for the wounded
being rushed from the vehicles.

Antonio walked over to Vinny and his young
friend, who was hooked up to oxygen and IVs. A bandage covered most of his face, and another was wrapped
around his chest, where Isao's katana had slashed him.

In an ironic twist, Christopher and Frankie got
Isao on the bed next to Doberman's. The Japanese gangster was unconscious, and judging by his jacket, he had
lost a lot of blood.

"Someone needs to explain to me why this maggot

gets a bed when we don't even have enough for our own men," Antonio said, his voice rising with anger. "Someone tell me why the FUCK he is even still alive!"

Vinny stiffened. "Don Antonio, he promised me that if I spared his life, his parents would pay gold to save him—enough gold to make it worth it. I thought the decision should yours to make, not mine."

Antonio studied his nephew, sitting at his best friend's bedside. A man fighting for his life because of the man next to them. It must have taken some serious restraint for Vinny not to kill Isao out there. And Antonio respected that.

He patted Vinny on the cheek. "You did the right thing, Vin," he said.

Christopher leaned next to Antonio and whispered the number of casualties in his ear. Only one had died, a man Antonio hardly knew. All the injured would survive.

He snapped his fingers at Dr. Jameson, who was treating Rush for a bullet wound to the arm. The former AMP soldier nodded at Antonio, who nodded back.

All in all, one hell of a successful day.

Antonio stepped up to examine Isao. His chest moved up and down slowly but evenly.

"Make sure this *piccolo stronzo* survives," he said. "You got that, Doc?"

Jameson moved from Rush to Isao. He checked the gunshot wounds while a nurse took his vitals.

Antonio scrutinized the doctor as he worked. In his forties, he had spent his career in emergency rooms— part of the reason Antonio hired him. The guy was used to severe trauma.

"Can you save him?" Antonio asked.

"I don't know," Jameson said. "I'll do my best, I promise."

"Save him, and I'll make you a wealthy man."

Jameson simply nodded and then went back to work.

Antonio gestured for Vinny and Christopher to follow him out of the room. Now that one threat was removed, he had to tell his soldiers the truth about another.

One by one, his most trusted confidants entered his office, which still smelled like sex and sweat.

"Have a seat," Antonio said.

Frankie, Carmine, Lino, Raff, Yellowtail, Christopher, and Vinny passed the couch and took seats at the war table.

"You all did good today," Antonio said. "Another enemy wiped out, and gold to compensate us for our losses—assuming our Japanese friend survives his wounds."

Carmine swept his sweat-slick hair back over his head. "Gold to buy more merchandise," he said, grinning. "I could use twice what he got in today's shipment—three times the weight once all of the Four Diamonds are open."

Antonio looked at Vinny, who stared at the floor, his thoughts no doubt on Doberman.

"That's part of the reason I called you here," Antonio said. "I want to make a new deal with a faction of the Sinaloa Cartel in Mexico. It's closer, cheaper, and higher quality."

Vinny kept his gaze on Doberman and didn't seem to be listening.

"I'm tasking you with this, Vinny," Antonio said loudly.

Vinny's eyes darted his way.

The other men didn't seem to understand the important task. It had been Christopher's idea to give his son the important job—something normally reserved for him or Antonio.

"You're probably wondering why Christopher and I aren't going, and I'll let him tell you," Antonio said.

Christopher cleared his throat.

"When Angela returned from Italy, she brought news with her," he said.

Everyone looked at Lino, her older brother. Antonio tried to gauge whether he knew the truth. There was no spark in his gaze, and no lie. She had kept this news from her brother.

"The Canavaros," Christopher said. "They have returned to Naples. The *bastardi* that killed my Greta and many of our family members. And now Don Antonio and I are returning to finish them off forever."

-10-

The worst of the storm had passed, leaving a blanket of fine brown powder on the ground. Every warning sign in the city flashed Severe Danger. The wind had stirred up radioactive material from Los Alamitos and other areas.

Going outside without a mask was a death sentence—maybe not today, but anyone who breathed the shit in would die before too long.

Dom had picked up a new mask at the station. He drove his cruiser with Moose, trying to make sure the refugees and homeless people stayed indoors. That was secondary to their other mission: keeping an eye out for whoever had slaughtered the Yamazakis hours ago in the dry bed of the Los Angeles River.

He drove on the Long Beach Freeway, knowing they wouldn't find jack shit. Whoever did it was long gone now. And even if they did find evidence, he doubted Chief Stone would do anything.

As far as Dom was concerned, the more dead gangbangers and gangsters, the better. They were all fighting for turf to sell their poison in the city. But he did care about the people addicted to that poison.

Many of them were so screwed up, they didn't know left from right.

Two ambulances shot by, probably with a cargo of victims of the toxic air. On days like this, Dom thought of his sister even more, hoping that wherever she was, she was at least indoors. It would be too much to hope for her safety, though. Monica would never be safe until she was home.

"You okay, bro?" Moose asked.

"Yeah."

"Don't lie, man. I can always tell when you're upset."

Dom hated to lay his problems on his best friend. Moose had lost his parents during the war, and he didn't sulk. He was still pretty much the same old friendly, caring guy with a smile for everyone.

But Dom felt himself changing. An anger he couldn't control was worming through his flesh and organs and into his bones like a cancer. At some point, it would consume him entirely, as it was already consuming his father and mother. They had always had their problems over the years, but the final spark of love had fizzled out. It seemed they both blamed each other for Monica.

A convoy of city trucks rolled by, their blades clanking on the concrete as they moved half a foot of dust off the roads. Another truck followed, spraying some sort of white stuff on the pavement.

Dom got off the freeway and drove over to Silverado Park on the west side of Long Beach. It was at the border of their normal jurisdiction, but he wanted to check it out for refugees and junkies camping outdoors.

Sure enough, several tents rippled in the wind on the baseball fields. He grabbed the receiver and turned on the loudspeaker.

"Where's the closest shelter?" he asked Moose.

Moose looked at his map and pointed to a church. Dom relayed the location through the speaker and told the campers they needed to move *now*. Only one person had emerged from a tent. The guy brushed at the air, then went back inside, zipping it shut.

"What ya gonna do?" Moose muttered.

Dom drove around the block and eased to a stop when Moose pointed out people in the skateboard park.

"You believe this?" he said.

"Those kids?" Dom asked. He turned the wipers on to clear the windshield. In the momentary clear view, he saw two kids. "Well, I'll be damned."

"Keep the engine on," Moose said. He opened his door and started off toward two boys standing in the skate park with their boards up.

"The hell you kids doing out here?" Moose asked through the open car window. "Did you not see the city signs flashing to get indoors?"

"We got our masks on," one of the kids replied.

"I don't care. It's not safe. Now, go home and get inside!" Moose yelled.

"Make me," said the smaller of the two.

"Happy to oblige."

He took a step forward and raised a hand. That did the trick. The kids took off on their boards.

Moose ran back to the car, then stopped, looking down the sidewalk. Dom followed his gaze to a woman sitting under a tree with a tarp over her and her kid. Neither of them was wearing a mask.

"Christ have mercy," Dom muttered.

He drove forward as Moose approached.

The woman pulled the tarp down, trying to hide, but Moose grabbed it and bent down. A few minutes later, with a promise of sandwiches, he had talked her and her preteen son into the back seat of the car.

Their clothing was full of dust, their faces dark with grime. They wolfed down the bread-and-cheese sandwiches. Moose tried to get them to speak, but the kid wouldn't say a word. His mother said only that they were homeless.

"I'm taking you to a shelter," Dom said.

"I already tried that," she said in a low voice. "They said they were out of beds."

"When's the last time you guys had something to eat?" Moose asked.

The boy looked up with big brown eyes.

"I don't remember," said the woman. "Maybe two days ago?"

Dom shook his head, his heart breaking. He drove them to the shelter and parked. This time, he got out of the car, locked it, and escorted them to the church doors.

A pastor opened it and looked at the police officers in turn before glancing over their shoulders.

"Make room," Moose said before the pastor could say a word.

Dom moved to the side and gestured for the mother and her son to go inside.

"I'll be back," Moose said. "They better still be here."

The pastor simply nodded and ushered the mom and her son into the safety of the nave.

The boy turned and spoke for the first time. "Thank you, mister."

Dom hurried back to the cruiser with Moose. As they approached, the city emergency sirens began their rising and falling wail.

Dom turned the radio to the weather station just in time for an update from Regina Díaz, who often reported the forecast. The former singer had turned to radio with her sexy voice that almost everyone recognized. It also got her a free pass for consistently getting the weather wrong.

"Hi, all you beautiful angels, this is Regina-a-a Día-a-az with yet another absolutely depressing report of alkaline dust and acid rain heading for our borders. Again. City officials are telling everyone to stay indoors and put plastic over the windows . . ."

Moose closed the vents in the dashboard. Then he checked the seal on his mask and gave Dom's a tug.

"Yours on tight?"

Dom nodded.

"We're getting an updated report on gang violence at the Los Angeles River . . ."

"Turn that up," Dom said.

"Assailants are unidentified at this point, and no witnesses were present, but we've been told this incident involved a motorcycle gang, with victims killed in what appears to be an ambush-style attack."

"You don't say," Dom said. He considered the implications again. With the Yamazakis out of the game, the Morettis had become even more powerful. Now they had free rein to sling their poison at the Four Diamonds.

Dom got back on the interstate, but instead of returning to their jurisdiction, he hit the southbound Long Beach Freeway. He pushed the pedal to the dusty floor, trying to outrun the storm as darkness draped the city.

"Whoa, easy, bro," Moose said. "Where you going?"

"Want to scope something out."

The car engine groaned, doing all it could.

"We don't want to get too far away from our beat with this rattletrap."

Dom turned on the fog lights, which helped penetrate the swirling dust across the road. Several vehicles were out—workers trying to get home.

"Dom, where we going?" Moose said, a hint of annoyance in his voice.

"Port of Long Beach. I want to see where the drugs are coming from."

"Dude, *why*?"

"Because maybe we can think of a way to stop it."

"Like how? You gonna nuke it? They'll just bring it in somewhere else."

The drive to the port really pissed Moose off. He protested several more times, but Dom managed to convince him it was worth checking out. This was the Russians' territory, but he didn't know of a single instance of Sergei Nevsky or any of his soldiers killing cops.

In size and strength, territory, and revenue, they were the weakest of the crime families, and the last thing they needed was problems with the LAPD.

Wind slammed the cruiser as they neared the ocean.

Dom got off the highway and took John S. Gibson Boulevard. The tires thumped over railroad tracks and then the cracked concrete of an abandoned parking lot. He shut off the lights and looked out across the harbor.

Under the glow of industrial lights, hundreds of containers waited for ground shipment. Several forklifts and cranes were still working in the storm.

Drugs weren't the only contraband coming in here. There were guns from other states—lots and lots of guns that weren't allowed through the walls into the city. Machine guns from the war, and other black-market weaponry, from grenades to rocket launchers.

Everyone was armed these days—in many cases, better than the police. Dom thought back to the M240 machine gun that the López sicarios had set up on the rooftop weeks ago. If he hadn't shot those assholes, they would have killed a lot of cops.

"This is where they're bringing death in," Dom whispered. "This is where we have to stop them."

"You're nuts, bro," said Moose. "Have I mentioned that recently? You've been on the hunt for Monica all this time, and now you also want to take on the crime families?"

Dom stared at the containers. "The crime families are the ones responsible, Andre."

The people who had taken his sister were financed by product coming in through the port. He might never find Monica, but that didn't mean he couldn't take down the organizations responsible for kidnapping her and trafficking thousands of other kids.

"Seen enough yet?" Moose asked.

Dom scanned the ships berthed at the wharf. Then he got out his notepad and started writing down the names.

"Dude, what's gotten up your—"

A bright light flashed the car, dazzling both of them. Dom reached for his pistol as a loudspeaker cracked, followed by familiar voice.

"Hello, boys," said Ray.

Dom and Moose slowly sat up as the light dimmed. A man approached on the passenger side. Both of them kept their hands on their guns as Moose rolled down the window, letting in a blast of grit.

"You're a long way from home," Ray said.

"What are you doing here, man?" Moose said. He opened the door and got out with Dom.

"I could ask you the same question."

"Were you following us?" Dom asked.

"I'm a detective, bro," Ray said. He patted Moose on the shoulder. "Mom, God rest her soul, always told me to be my brother's keeper."

"I don't need a keeper," Moose said.

"Me, neither," Dom added.

"Yeah, yeah. Thing is, ya do," Ray said. "You two dumb fucks are out of your jurisdiction, acting like Crockett and Tubbs."

Dom didn't find the comparison funny. It was just more of Ray being a prick.

"And you're acting like Denny Malone from *The Force*," Dom snapped back.

Ray scowled. "Who the fuck's that?"

"Never mind."

"Yeah, that's what I figured." Ray shook his head.

"You two need to stay in your lane and not do anything stupid. It's dangerous out here—more than you think."

The wind picked up, howling over their voices. Waves lapped the shore with kelp and dead fish.

Ray walked closer to Dom. "I know we've had our problems in the past, bro, but I like you, and I don't want to see you get killed, because that's exactly what'll happen if you go rogue."

"Why you lookin' at him?" Moose asked.

Ray turned back to his brother. "'Cause I know you play by the rules and Dom has always had a thing for pushing them."

And you don't? Dom thought. He resisted the urge to convey his true feelings. After all, this was Moose's brother. And now more than ever, Dom wondered exactly how far Ray himself was pushing the rules.

* * *

"We got to get these people inside," Bettis said. He opened the door to the small observation booth. The tower looked over the wall built at Pasadena's northern border with the Angeles National Forest, on Highway 2.

Ronaldo and Tooth finished putting on their breathing masks and goggles. They had been on wall duty most of the day, called off the road due to severe weather and toxin warnings.

"You got too big a heart, Chaplain," Tooth said. "You can't save everybody. Even God can't do that."

"What makes you think God has anything to do with who gets saved and who doesn't?" Ronaldo asked.

Tooth zipped his heavy brown deputy-sheriff jacket up to his chin but didn't answer.

"God gives us free will to do his bidding," Bettis said. "To save the innocent."

"And exterminate evil," Ronaldo said.

Marks didn't see things the same way, but Ronaldo had no problem using any tactics necessary to clear the filth from the earth. Throwing on his jacket, he prepared to face more evil men and women. He made sure the heavy, stifling hazard suit was secure. Then he walked out onto the platform of the wall blocking off the freeway.

Spotlights mounted to poles shone down on the twisting caravan of refugees awaiting entrance into Los Angeles County. There were dozens of vehicles in the convoy, and at least fifty people on foot. A few people had even come in on horses.

Some weren't dressed for the storm, leaving their bodies exposed to the toxic, radioactive dust in the air.

The deputies stationed here were usually prepared to vet refugees for entry during bad weather, but not this many at once. And with the storm increasing in size and strength, he didn't know what was going to happen.

Only Sheriff Benson could give the order to open the gates, and he wasn't here.

Bettis stepped up to the razor wire curled around the metal railing. "We've got to do something," he said.

The spotlights illuminated even more refugees streaming down the freeway.

"Where the heck are these people coming from?" Tooth asked.

"We're not the only location with refugees," said another deputy. "The eastern border at Chino Hills is flooded with them. Just heard it over the comms."

Ronaldo stared out over the freeway. If this was happening in other areas, it meant that something they didn't know about was happening far beyond their borders. Another city that had fallen into complete anarchy or had been taken over by raiders.

The implications put an icy lump in his gut.

Ronaldo turned to look out over the LA Sheriff's Department's forward operating base, but the boss hadn't arrived.

Only two pickup trucks were parked outside the mobile offices they used for screening refugees. Behind the trailers were rows of warehouses that had once been used to store all sorts of products.

Now they stored people—refugees waiting for housing assignments at the Four Diamonds, Angel Pyramids, and other public housing blocks. But they were packed full, with hardly enough room for the people already there.

For a moment, Ronaldo thought about just letting all these people in, but then he flashed on the monsters they had taken down on Blue Ridge. Those sociopaths were exactly the type he was trying to keep out, and there could very well be more traffickers down there, hiding amid the horde seeking refuge.

He continued down the platform, almost losing his hat in another blast of wind that peppered his visor with grit. Three deputies stood above the gate. One of them was Pierce. He had taken only a few days off after his head injury, which proved to be a mild concussion.

Ronaldo had been wrong about the younger man being a coward and owed him for saving his life.

"What we going to do with these people? Pierce asked.

"Good question," Ronaldo replied.

Over the rise and fall of the distant sirens came the authoritative voice of Lieutenant Hernández over the loudspeakers. The big Latino was inside a guard tower overlooking the gate.

"Get back in your vehicles!" Hernández ordered. "You will be processed in the order you came in."

The deputies around Ronaldo angled their rifles down at the vehicles to add weight to the lieutenant's words. Below them, a door opened, and two deputies on the ground led the family of five to the mobile command centers. The door was shut and locked behind them.

Horns honked, and people clamored to be let in.

Another gust of wind slammed into the deputies. Pierce returned to his enclosed guard tower with Hernández.

"We should get back inside, too," Tooth said.

"Yeah," Bettis said. "Nothing we can do up here but point our rifles, and these people are already scared. God will look over his flock. He has a plan for everything."

Ronaldo scanned the group, his eyes falling on women and children. He always had a hard time understanding how God could have a plan that involved killing so many people. How could a just God allow his daughter to be kidnapped and . . .

No. If God was up there watching over everyone, that's about all he was doing: watching.

But the chaplain was right about one thing. What most of these people needed was help, not more guns aimed at them. They were Americans, and although the war was over, there was still plenty of rage to go around after the atrocities of the past year.

He thought again of the man his team had killed on Blue Ridge. There could be more of them in the crowd below.

Ronaldo remained on the platform, watching over the road while Tooth returned to the guard tower. He pulled down his mask and took a drink of water as he looked out the glass window at Ronaldo.

Bettis stepped back outside.

"This is nuts," he said. "Can't we just let them in and put them in the shelters?"

"Protocol is to keep the gates locked during storms," Ronaldo said. "Because of what happened last month. You know that."

A memory of that day surfaced. Ronaldo and his team had stood on the same platform during another storm, when a desperate man with a sick wife decided to push ahead by driving onto the shoulder. He mowed down two refugees he couldn't see, then backed over another woman.

Ronaldo stared at the spot, where refugees on foot now huddled behind cars for shelter.

Not all of them.

A guy wearing a trench coat and a black mask dashed toward the gate. That got him a good look at the muzzle of Ronaldo's M4 rifle.

"STOP!" Ronaldo shouted.

Over the wind, the voice of Hernández boomed from the loudspeaker. "Back away from the gate!"

Ronaldo kept his gun on the man in the trench coat.

He could very well be the same kind of guy Pierce had shot on Blue Ridge. Or he could be a peace-loving former pot grower who just wanted a safe place to plant some bud.

As the storm intensified, several more people approached the gate. From what Ronaldo could see, almost all were adult males, and all were armed.

"Tooth, get your ass out here!" Ronaldo shouted. The radio on his vest crackled, but he couldn't make out the message over the howling wind. He kept his rifle pointed.

Tooth and Bettis moved up on his flanks, their rifles angled at the men crowding the heavy steel gate.

A truck peeled away from the convoy and took off, probably trying to find a different place to gain entry, or a place to ride out the storm. They would have a hard time finding either now.

"Back up!" Ronaldo shouted.

The guy with the trench coat looked up at him and raised his middle finger.

Ronaldo didn't care that the guy had flipped him off, but he was worried about the teenage kids who had gotten out of an ancient Dodge station wagon and were making their way to the gate. A girl and a boy, their faces enshrouded by scarves and goggles.

These two teenagers were basically the same age as his own kids, and they were pushing their way into danger.

"Get BACK!" Ronaldo shouted at the men pounding on the gate. Pierce had returned to the railing nearby and was also shouting with three more deputies.

The teenagers were almost to the gates now. Only two parked vehicles separated them.

"Gun," Pierce said.

Ronaldo saw it, too. One of the men below had pulled out a pistol.

"Drop the gun!" shouted Tooth.

The kids waved up at the platform now, distracting Ronaldo. He noticed that the guy with the trench coat had also pulled something out and was turning toward the kids.

Ronaldo lined up the sights, trying to get a look.

The crackling from the loudspeakers sounded almost like gunfire. It took him another beat to realize that it *was* gunfire. With only a second to react, he fired a burst into the man's back. He fell in front of the kids.

A second later, Tooth hit the platform, wailing in pain. His voice was silenced by the crack of automatic gunfire. Muzzle flashes burst from along the platform.

"Hold your fire!" Bettis shouted.

Ronaldo bent down to apply pressure on Tooth's wound.

"Stop firing!" Bettis screamed.

The gunfire ceased, the final empty casings clinking on the platform. In the respite came screams and shouts of horror from the road below.

Hernández stepped out of his guard booth, and the door slammed in the wind. He hurried to the railing and looked down, then put a hand on his head as if at a loss what to do.

When Ronaldo got up, he saw why.

All ten men outside the gate were down. Several women ran over to their fallen husbands, brothers, and sons. The two teenagers were kneeling beside the man

Ronaldo had shot. They looked up at him, and he saw what the guy had pulled out earlier.

It was a radio. Not a gun. A fucking radio.

Ronaldo nearly dropped his rifle. Had he just orphaned these kids?

"Lower your goddamn weapons!" Hernández boomed.

"They shot first," said one of the deputies.

"So you mow them all down?" Bettis asked. "There are kids down there!"

He turned to Ronaldo. "Why did you fire?"

"I thought I saw him pull a gun on those two . . ." Ronaldo's heart pounded, and stars broke before his vision. He was just trying to protect the kids—just trying to keep another innocent life from being destroyed.

"Guys, I'm bleeding bad," Tooth said.

Ronaldo snapped out of it to check the bullet wound. Blood had soaked through Tooth's jacket. By the time they got him inside the guard booth to the medical kit, a vortex of dust rolled in from the west. A convoy of sheriff trucks raced down the freeway, with ambulances close behind.

In the center of the convoy was a brown MRAP all-terrain vehicle with a skull in a cowboy hat painted on the door.

The Cowboy was now here.

"Bettis, stay with Tooth," Ronaldo said. "I'm going down."

Bettis stared at Ronaldo, clearly disturbed at what had just happened.

Ronaldo checked on Tooth again and then squeezed past him and Bettis. He hurried to the gate, where medics were already waiting to help the injured on the other side.

Sheriff Benson wore his trademark cowboy hat and boots with spurs. A more useless affectation Ronaldo couldn't imagine, unless it be chaps. A breathing mask covered his mustache as he talked to Hernández. With the protection of the wall, the wind wasn't as harsh, and Ronaldo could hear their conversation.

"Deploy the riot-control team to secure this site," Benson said. "I've got buses on the way for the civilians. We'll vet them later. For now, get 'em inside."

The sheriff and the lieutenant parted ways, and Hernández barked orders at the deputies. The gate began to clank open, and a group of ten men in riot gear moved outside with batons.

Sobbing women and kids clung to the bodies of their fallen loved ones. The teenagers were still with the man Ronaldo had shot. He let out a relieved sigh when he saw the guy reach up toward a medic.

"Salvatore!" barked a voice.

Sheriff Benson strode over. "I want to talk to you in the mobile unit."

Ronaldo caught Hernández looking at them. Had his lieutenant just pinned the whole thing on him?

Benson had started toward the mobile units when shouts erupted. Two of the deputies in riot gear were wrestling a gun away from one of the guys the deputies had shot.

They finally got him in cuffs and dragged him away. Hernández watched them go and then jogged back over to Benson and Ronaldo.

"You know that guy?" Benson asked the lieutenant.

"Yeah," Hernández said. "Been looking for that asshole for a month."

Benson nodded and turned to Ronaldo.

"After we clean up this mess, we can talk about what really happened here *and* at Blue Ridge," he said. "Then I'll decide if this is your final shift, Deputy Salvatore."

-11-

Vinny had sat by Doberman's side for the past three days straight. Watching his friend fight for his life while he himself could do nothing reminded him of the worst day of his life, when he had watched his mother gunned down in the basilica, helpless to do anything but watch.

But this time, there was indeed something he could have done. He could have killed Isao at the Four Diamonds three months ago, or on the highway after leaving the port the first time Isao's gang followed them, when Isao had threatened Vinny's life.

But both times, he had let the gangster live, and soon he would have to tell his friend why.

They had moved Doberman out of the critical-care rooms to his own apartment, a former luxury suite that hotel guests had once booked on their gambling trips to LA. It looked out over the new landscaping Don Antonio had spent a small fortune on. The storms had passed, and the horizon was clear.

But Doberman couldn't see any of it. He lay on his

back, IV lines hooked up to his tattooed arms to fight an infection in the gash that ran from his naval to his shoulder. Bandages covered his torso, chest, and most of his face.

A knock came on the door, and Vinny turned as Raff walked in. He walked over quietly and whispered, "How's he doin?"

"Not out of the woods yet, but he's off the oxygen," Vinny said. "The medicine and morphine has him knocked out—hasn't said much of anything yet."

"Glad he's doing better," Raff said.

Vinny nodded toward the other chair. "Have a seat."

"Thanks."

For a few minutes, they sat in silence as the sun dipped through the horizon, ending another day of violence in the city. Vinny had been mostly in the dark about what was going on outside the compound walls, but Raff gave a short update.

"That's not why you're here, is it?" Vinny asked.

"No," Raff said. "I'm here because Don Antonio wants me to go to Mexico with you, to make a deal with the new boss of the broken Sinaloa Cartel."

"But I thought Frankie or Carmine would—"

"Carmine is needed here to keep the operation running while your father and uncle are in Naples with Lino, and I'm not sure about Frankie yet."

"What about Yellowtail?"

"I haven't heard yet. He might come with us, but I doubt it. The trip to Italy is far more dangerous, and honestly I'm not sure . . ." Raff's words trailed off.

Vinny had never seen the man question orders. "It's okay, I understand," he said.

Raff nodded just as the door opened again.

Christopher walked in, wearing a suit. "Am I interrupting something?" he asked.

Vinny and Raff rose to their feet out of respect, and Raff motioned for Christopher to take his chair.

"I'm good." Christopher went to the window and folded his muscular arms over his chest. He had been hitting the weight room downstairs hard lately—his way of dealing with stress.

It was better than the bottle, anyway.

"Esteban and Miguel have just seized more turf in southern Los Angeles County, taking several prime areas from Sergei Nevsky," Christopher said. "The old Cold War gangster is losing ground, and rumor has it that the LAPD is about to take down Mariana López."

"Really?" Raff said. "If that's true, things are going to boil over sooner rather than later."

"And you're going to Italy on a revenge mission when the volcano is about to blow?" Vinny asked his father.

Christopher turned from the window and smoothed his already smooth goatee—something he often did when he was thinking. He narrowed his brows at Vinny.

"The Canavaros killed your mother, Vin."

"I know." Vinny looked back to Doberman. His chest had seemed to flatten, causing Vinny's heart to skip a beat. But then his friend took a sharp breath, and his chest resumed its rhythmic rise and fall.

"You should take a break, Vin," Raff said. "Head downstairs and get something to eat."

"And watch the transfer from a distance," Christopher

said. He looked out the window again. "The Yamazakis will be here in two hours to exchange their fortune for their golden child."

"I know; I'll be there," Vinny said.

"No, you won't," Christopher barked. "I said *from a distance*, because you're the one that shot him the second time, and we don't want any problems during this exchange."

Raff nodded in agreement. "Best to sit this out."

"I'm also the one that spared his life—and, in the end, saved it," Vinny reminded them.

"True enough, but Isao and his parents might not see it that way," Christopher said. "Besides, we have all hands on deck."

Vinny joined his father at the window. Multiple patrols walked the property, including the two new canine units they had brought to the compound.

Don Antonio continued to take his security very seriously.

"I'm headed back downstairs," Christopher said. "You coming, or what?"

Vinny nodded. "I'll be right there."

The other two men left, and Vinny sat back down by the bed. He didn't like leaving Doberman alone. For the first time, Vinny wished his best friend had a steady girlfriend. Then, at least, he would have someone to look after him.

"You're going to be okay, brother," Vinny said. He patted Doberman on his tattooed biceps and got up to walk away.

Doberman grabbed his wrist.

"Vin," he mumbled.

"Whoa, there you are, bro!" Vinny said excitedly. He leaned down close to the bed.

Doberman blinked several times, as if trying to focus his eyes. Then he reached up to the bandage on his face. He slowly ran a finger over it.

This was the most coherent Vinny had seen him in days.

"How bad is it?" Doberman asked. "My face . . ."

"I won't lie, 'cause I know you wouldn't lie to me," Vinny said. "You got cut bad, but the good news is, you won't lose your nose, and the blade missed your eyes."

"I don't really remember. I just remember . . ." Doberman's brows tried to bridge the narrow gap between them. "You kill him?"

"I . . ."

Vinny had thought about what he would say when the time was right—all the reasons he had spared Isao the third time. But now the words wouldn't come. There was only guilt.

"Vin, did you kill Isao?" Doberman repeated.

A knock on the door saved Vinny from the unpleasant truth.

Fran, the duty nurse, walked into the room. A tall twenty-five-year-old blonde with long legs, she would have turned Doberman's head on any other occasion. But he barely acknowledged her presence, locking his gaze back on Vinny after the briefest glance.

"Good to see you awake, Daniel," Fran said with a cheery smile. "How are you feeling?"

"I don't know. I'm waiting for my friend to tell me what happened to the guy that tried to make sushi out of me."

Vinny gave her a nod. "Come back in a bit," he said.

She smiled and shut the door behind her with a click.

"She's hot, right?" Vinny asked, stretching time while he thought what to say.

She was someone Doberman would have tried to bang, but with his wounds, he wouldn't be banging anyone for a while. And when he did heal, he was going to have some nasty scars.

Doberman's face contorted with pain, and he closed his eyes.

"Bro," Vinny said, gripping his hand. "Bro, you okay?"

"Fucking hurts."

"I'll go get Fran," Vinny said. He tried to pull away, but Doberman tightened his grip.

"No," Doberman said. "I want to know what happened to Isao."

"You need more painkillers, man. That's why you woke up, because they wore off."

"I don't need more fucking painkillers. I need to know what *happened*." There was rage in his voice that Vinny hadn't heard before.

He drew in a deep breath, afraid the truth would have Doberman climbing out of bed and trying to kill the bastard himself during the exchange.

"We ambushed the Yamazakis in the LA River a few days ago," Vinny finally said. He held up his bandaged right hand. "Isao got me, but I got him worse. Shot him in the collarbone and was about to put one in his dome, when he begged me to save his life. He promised a lot of gold from his parents."

Doberman listened, not saying a word.

"I left the decision to Don Antonio, and he spared

his life. The rest of his men are dead, though. We left them to rot in the riverbed."

Doberman still didn't speak.

"I should have killed him. I'm sorry, man, I'm so sorry."

"No."

"No?"

Doberman turned his head to the side, looking out the window, wincing again. "You did what you had to do. For the family. Someday, maybe I'll be a made man, too, and I'll get to make decisions instead of . . ."

The words made Vinny angry. His friend should already be a soldier. Doberman was full-blooded Italian and had proved his loyalty. But it would take more than getting sliced to earn his button, apparently.

"I think I know how that can happen," Vinny said.

Doberman looked back at him.

"I'm not sure when, but soon, I'm headed to Mexico with Raff, to negotiate a new deal with the boss of what's left of the Sinaloa Cartel. I can try to delay it until you're better, and you can come with us."

"I can go." Doberman tried to push himself up, grunting.

"Relax, man. You've got time to heal."

A car engine stopped outside, and Vinny knew that the time was about up. The Yamazakis were here.

He pulled out his Glock and placed it on the bedside table.

"What you doin?" Doberman asked.

"Leaving you a weapon."

"Thanks."

Vinny nodded, feeling another pang of guilt, this

time for lying. He wasn't leaving the gun so Doberman would have a weapon to defend himself. He was perfectly safe here. The biggest threat facing Doberman would be to get a woody when he realized how hot his nurse was.

No, Vinny left his gun so *he* wouldn't be tempted to finish Isao off during the exchange.

"I'll be back later," Vinny said. "Get some rest. I'll send Fran in for your meds."

"Thanks."

Vinny hesitated. "You're going to be okay, bro."

"Yeah."

Doberman rested his head back on the pillow, and Vinny took a minute to look at his friend. He was going to be okay; Vinny knew that now. He just hoped Doberman would forgive him for not killing Isao.

"I've got big plans for us," Vinny said. "We're the future of this family, brother. You've just got to trust me."

* * *

Antonio had invited Lucia for a rare glimpse into the darker side of his business, although this afternoon, it wasn't going to appear dark at all. He had considered bringing Marco, too, but the boy was too young for this. Besides, Lucia and Antonio had agreed that they didn't want this life for their son.

When schools opened back up, Marco would be enrolled, far away from all this.

He sat on the couch, playing on a tablet while their nanny fixed his lunch in the kitchen.

"We need to go," Antonio said, glancing at his gold Rolex Oyster.

"Almost ready," Lucia said as she finished putting on her diamond stud earrings.

Today, she wore black pants and a tiger-print blouse. The top buttons were open, revealing three gold necklaces, one with a 2.5-carat diamond stud.

She put on her heels next, hopping over to Marco on the way out of the room, with one foot still not quite in.

"Be good," she said.

Marco hardly looked up from the glow of his tablet as she kissed him on the head.

More interested in games than real life, Antonio thought.

He opened the door and led his wife onto the checkered carpet of the hallway, where Lino and Yellowtail waited in freshly pressed suits. They went to the elevator and stepped inside.

As the doors closed, Antonio reached for his wife's hand. He held it on the short ride to the casino floor.

The soldiers stepped out first to make sure the way was clear. Then they started across the spacious room that had been cleared of slot machines and was now furnished with couches and tables covered in beautiful floral arrangements.

None of the other family members were relaxing here today, and the workers were all out of sight preparing food, gardening, or tending to the ongoing renovations. The only people here were Moretti soldiers and associates.

Christopher stood with a group that included Rush. The former AMP sergeant was dressed in a black suit and had an earpiece in. If his injured arm was bothering him, no one would know it.

"We ready?" Antonio called out.

Rush and Christopher walked over. "The Yamazakis are outside, sir," Rush said, "and I'm waiting for confirmation from our scouts that there aren't any potential hostiles waiting outside our walls."

"That'd be the stupidest move ever, them trying something when we have their son," Christopher said.

Antonio agreed, but he was still making sure all security protocols were being scrupulously followed, especially since Lucia was present.

"Where is Isao?" she asked.

"He'll be brought down as soon as his parents show us the gold," Antonio said. "Why don't we have a seat. Lino, send a server over with some wine and olives."

"Yes sir," Lino said, hurrying off.

Antonio followed his wife to a section of plush leather couches. Yellowtail stood behind them with Raff, their eyes riveted to the lobby doors.

Though his eyesight was getting worse, Antonio could make out the two black Mercedes sedans with tinted windows. If he'd worn his glasses, he might be able to see the people getting out of the cars.

Moretti guards checked them for weapons before escorting them into the lobby. A dark-haired woman named Kara, whom Antonio had hired as a server, walked over with a silver tray and glasses of red wine.

Fifty workers were in the building now—only a small fraction of those who once worked here when this was an operating hotel. Every one of them had been personally and painstakingly vetted.

Kara smiled warmly as she put the glasses down.

"Mrs. Moretti," she said. "Mr. Moretti."

"Thank you, Kara," Lucia said.

"You're welcome, ma'am."

"Olives," Antonio said.

"Oh, I'm sorry. I was—"

"It's okay, we don't need them," Lucia said.

Antonio shrugged, and Kara walked away. In the interview, the young woman had reminded him a bit of his wife when she was younger. Kara was a hard worker who had lost her father at an early age. She was beautiful and kind, but there was one difference. The girl was absentminded, unlike Lucia, who never let a single detail go unnoticed.

"All clear," Christopher said. He signaled for Rush to let the Yamazakis inside. Lucia started to her feet, but Antonio put his hand gently on her arm and the tennis bracelet he had given her a few weeks ago.

"They stand for us," he said. "Not the other way around."

She sat back down and took a drink of wine.

Footsteps clicked on the new marble floor as a group of Moretti associates under Rush's command escorted three people over to the couches. As they got closer, Antonio got his first glance at the patriarch and matriarch of the Yamazaki clan.

Isao's parents looked to be in their sixties.

Daisuke Yamazaki was a thin man with a square jaw, sharp eyes, and thick black hair. His wife, Chizu, was slender and graceful. She wore a black dress, and her silver hair was up in a tight bun.

The third person had a muscular frame and a

gleaming shaved head. He carried two cases that looked quite heavy. This man was at least two decades younger than Daisuke. Probably a nephew, Antonio thought.

Christopher joined the group and guided the three Yamazakis to the couches. He gestured for them to sit across from Antonio and Lucia.

"Please," Antonio said, nodding.

Daisuke glared at Antonio, but there was something beyond the anger. Maybe envy, or perhaps simple curiosity. Chizu had nothing but hatred in her gaze, which she focused on Lucia.

The three Yamazakis finally took a seat when Lino and Yellowtail closed in, essentially forcing them down.

Antonio broke the ice. "Thank you for making the journey," he said. "I know it's dangerous driving these days. As you know, I'm Antonio Moretti, and this is my wife, Lucia."

"I am Daisuke. This is my wife, Chizu, and my nephew Mitsuo."

"Where is our son?" Chizu asked.

Daisuke shot his wife a look that silenced her. In some Italian families, the woman was also supposed to be seen and not heard, but Lucia was here as Antonio's equal, and he was proud to hear her speak up.

"Your son will be brought down once you show us the gold he promised," Lucia said.

"Isao made a fatal error and has brought great shame on our family," Daisuke grumbled. "This is our offering to restore honor to our name."

He gave Mitsuo a nod.

The younger man brought the cases over and placed them on a table in front of Antonio and Lucia. His jaw was clenched.

Antonio watched him cautiously, keeping his right hand close to the concealed subcompact pistol at his hip. His men had disarmed these three, but that didn't account for all the weapons. Fists and feet of a trained fighter could be just as deadly as a knife or gun if you knew how to use them. And judging by this young man's body, he was a warrior.

Mitsuo clicked the first case open, revealing a dozen gold bars. Then he did the same with the second case.

Lucia leaned forward, but Antonio kept his eye on Mitsuo even as he backed away from the cases.

"What we promised," Daisuke said.

"Now bring us our son," Chizu said.

Lucia smiled politely at the other woman, then snapped her fingers at Lino. "Bring Isao down," she said.

Mitsuo took a seat next to Chizu and Daisuke again, placing his hands on his knees, his back straight. Antonio found himself wondering how many men those rough hands had killed.

"Would you like something to drink while we wait?" Lucia asked. "We have wine and some sake."

Chizu's face contorted in anger, but then she raised her head, proud.

"I'm a mother, too," Lucia said. "My son isn't much younger than yours, and for what it's worth, I'm sorry for what happened to yours."

"He made a grave mistake attacking my family," Antonio said. He looked to Mitsuo, who seemed to be the real strength of this little trio.

"I know your kind," Antonio said. "But you won't kill me. Not today, not ever."

Mitsuo showed not a hint of emotion. Several Moretti soldiers took a step closer to the couches, and Yellowtail pulled out his pistol for everyone to see.

The moment of tension eased as Chizu shot up to look at the elevators. Antonio didn't bother turning. But he did notice a figure across the room, standing in the shadows of a corner alcove. It was Vinny, probably thinking about finishing Isao off.

But his nephew remained in the shadows as Isao's bed was rolled over the marble floor.

"We accept this exchange for your son's life," Antonio said. "May you all live in prosperity for the rest of your time in the City of Angels."

He rose to his feet, and Lucia followed suit.

Mitsuo remained behind while Daisuke and Chizu walked over to see Isao, who reached up with a hand.

"My son," Chizu murmured. "What have they done to you?"

Daisuke spoke in Japanese, silencing his wife again.

"After you," Antonio said to Mitsuo.

The Japanese man nodded politely and then followed his family with their armed escorts. Antonio watched them leave while Lucia bent down to the cases.

"Antonio, these are solid gold bars!" she said excitedly.

Vinny finally joined them. He looked down at the bars, then at the Yamazakis as they left the building. Antonio knew what his nephew was thinking: that the gold wasn't worth leaving Isao alive.

"How is Daniel?" Antonio asked.

"He's off oxygen and was awake earlier," Vinny said.

"Good. I'll make sure he is well compensated for what he has endured."

Lucia held one of the bars. "It's so heavy."

"Lino, take these to the vault," Antonio said. "I'll see you upstairs soon, my love."

Lucia put the bar back. "Where are you going?"

"With Vinny. We have some more business." He put his arm around his nephew's shoulder and guided him away from the lobby, to a side exit door.

Raff was already there.

"We all set?" Antonio asked.

"Yes sir," Raff replied.

Antonio opened the side door and stepped out into the cool afternoon just in time to see the Yamazakis leaving the compound through the open gate.

Lino, Christopher, and Yellowtail followed Antonio and his nephew outside with Raff. They all piled into the Cadillac Escalade sitting in the drive.

"Where are we going?" Vinny asked. "I didn't bring my gun."

"You won't need it," Antonio said.

Christopher drove through the open gate and took off into the streets. Bulldozers and construction equipment sat idle around mounds of debris from old buildings that Antonio had paid to demolish.

His vision for this area would take time, but when it was finished, the Moretti compound would be surrounded by green space and fields. Bit by bit, they were getting closer to that long-term goal.

Smoke rose into air around the next corner, and Christopher eased off the gas.

"What the hell . . .?" Vinny breathed.

A city plow truck had slammed into one of the Mercedes, pinning it against the wall of a building. The other Mercedes was stopped in the middle of the road, steam rising from the engine.

Bodies were crumpled on the asphalt, some of them still moving.

By the time the Escalade pulled up, only one Yamazaki was still on his feet, fighting.

Antonio wasn't surprised to see that it was Mitsuo. He staggered in the street, holding a short sword, blood leaking from multiple bullet wounds to his limbs and torso.

The Moretti soldiers got out of the SUV and formed a phalanx around Antonio and his nephew, just in case other hostiles remained.

They approached the scene of death cautiously.

Mitsuo grunted as he lunged with his sword at the closest Moretti associate, Rush. The former army sergeant backed away, and Christopher took his place, striking forward with a wooden baseball bat.

Mitsuo brought up his sword to deflect the blow, and Christopher swung again, hitting him in the back and knocking him to the street.

Isao lay nearby, still alive. He wept as he crawled toward the bodies of his parents.

"You never leave an enemy to come back and kill you," Antonio said, pulling a SIG Sauer P320 from the holster. He handed the gun to Vinny. "Finish what you started."

Vinny didn't hesitate. A gunshot rang out, then faded away under the rumble of diesel engines. Two garbage trucks came around the next corner and slowed to a stop.

Mikey the Mexican hopped down. This was his payback, too.

"Put the garbage in the trucks, and hurry," Antonio said.

Sirens sounded in the distance as they began to clear the road. Mitsuo pushed himself back up, then fell to one knee, glaring at Antonio.

Vinny handed the gun back to him.

"I told you that you won't kill me," Antonio said, raising the SIG.

Mitsuo did not shy away. He stared down the gun barrel of his own death and accepted the bullet with honor.

After Mitsuo had fallen, Antonio bent down and picked up the short sword. It would fit nicely in his collection.

As Mikey's crew finished loading the other bodies into the garbage trucks, Antonio waved them back from Mitsuo.

"Give this one the proper burial that a warrior deserves," he said.

"And the rest of them?" Mikey asked.

"Throw 'em in the landfill, where they belong."

-12-

Dom didn't feel like partying. In the old world, he wouldn't have been old enough to drink in this watering hole two blocks from the LAPD headquarters downtown. But times had changed. Not only were the neighboring buildings rubble, but most of the cops here were as young as he. Judging by the dour looks, most of them were drinking away their sorrows, trying to forget bad times or remember better ones.

Dom sat at the bar nursing a glass of whiskey, doing a little of both. He wasn't sure why Moose was drinking, but his friend was already on his third beer.

"Better slow down, or you're going to blow through your rations," Dom said.

Moose tipped his glass back, polishing off the beer. Then he wiped his lips. "We earned this, man."

After a seven-day stint that included several double shifts, they needed a break. But this wasn't exactly what Dom had had in mind, and he worried about his mom, back home by herself again.

Something was up with his father, too, and Dom

worried that it had to do with his job. Of course, Ronaldo denied anything was wrong.

"Cheer up, brah," Moose said. "You look like
someone killed your dog."

Dom shrugged and took a sip. Then he turned to
look out over the other booths, both near the bar and
in the next room. Most were occupied by cops and
their wives or girlfriends. But a few women and men
were on the prowl.

Considering the risk that came with this job, Dom
had no clue why anyone would want to date a cop, let
alone marry one.

"Where's Ray?" Dom asked. "I thought he was
going to meet us here."

"He's always late, man, you know that." Moose
slapped the bar, attracting the attention of the barmaid,
a redhead practically bursting out of her tight tank top.

She brought Moose his fourth, and he passed her a
coin. There were a few different ways to pay for things
now. Mostly you could spend the ration coins being
minted in Colorado, or, if it was all you had, cash,
which was so deflated it didn't buy much.

More and more, though, Dom saw the oldest
medium of commerce: barter, which was currently
being conducted down at the end of the bar. A pro was
giving a cop Dom didn't know a look at her assets. She
then whispered something into the man's ear—probably a description of her services.

No one else would bat an eye at the transaction,
but it made Dom think of his sister. He wondered
whether she was out in some crummy bar, doing the
same thing under some handler's watchful eye.

He drank half his glass to burn the dread into submission.

Moose slapped him on the back.

"Ray's here," he said.

Dom rotated in his stool as Ray strode in with a woman on each arm.

"Is he really wearing a fur coat?" Dom said.

Moose laughed, but Dom thought of the implications. No one making the pay of a detective first grade could afford a wrap like that. Either he had picked it up in a bust, or he was taking money from the crime families. Neither possibility was good, but Dom could live with the first. The second, maybe not . . .

He downed the rest of his whiskey and pushed back from the bar, heading for the other exit. He shouldn't even have come tonight.

"Dom, dude, where you going?" Moose called out.

"Home."

"Dommie boy, why you leaving?" Ray called out. "The party's just startin', baby!"

Dom halted, but not to talk to Ray. He spotted Camilla and three other people in a booth in the other room. It seemed she hadn't seen him yet.

A hand clasped Dom's shoulder. He looked down at the familiar gold lion's-head ring.

"Someone I'd like you and Andre to meet," Ray said. He nodded to the tan, blue-eyed young woman on his left.

"This is Alicia," he said. "Alicia, this is my bro Andre and his friend Dominic."

"Nice to meet you," she said, holding out her hand.

Moose enveloped it in his.

"How's it going?" Dom said.

Alicia smiled at him.

"This is my girl Yolanda," Alicia said, nodding to the dark-skinned woman on Ray's other arm. She also smiled at Dom, but smiled wider for Moose.

Moose beamed a huge smile back.

Ray clapped his hands. "Who's ready to drink?" He led them back toward the bar, but Dom stayed where he was until Moose gave him a motivating glare.

"Come on, dude," he growled.

Ray stopped at several booths to give palm slaps and exchange homie handshakes with other officers. Moose walked over, and Dom started to follow. He stopped at the sound of a soft female voice.

"Some of our brothers and sisters in blue are wearing Gucci belts and Cartier watches," it said. "Meanwhile, my old Nikes have holes in them."

Camilla stepped up next to Dom, twirling a straw in her Jack and Coke as she watched Ray.

"So, what are you doing here?" she asked. "Didn't think this was your scene."

"Oh, it's not, but you know Moose likes to have a good time. How about you?"

She looked over her shoulder at the booth where she had been sitting. Dom recognized her brother, Joaquín. With him were another guy and a girl.

"Double date," she said, rolling her eyes. "In other words, my bro's trying to set me up with his friend."

Dom was almost relieved to hear this. Not that he had a crush on Camilla, but he didn't want to see her with some douche, and the guy sitting by her brother had a blowout haircut and wore a shirt two sizes too small.

"Dommie boy!" Ray shouted from the bar. "Come have a shot with me. Bring your little firecracker."

Camilla grunted. "I really wish you'd put him on his back one of these days. I know you got it in you."

"I don't think that would go over too well with Moose."

"True, I suppose."

Camilla took a long sip through her straw, then sloshed the ice around and downed the rest.

"Want another?" Dom asked.

She shrugged. "Rather go to the bar than back to the table."

"If I have to deal with Ray tonight, I need more whiskey."

Camilla arched a brow and studied him. "You a mean drunk, Dom? Or a nice one?"

"I don't really know."

"I'm a combo," she said with a wink.

"Good to know."

They went to the bar, where Moose wrapped Camilla in a hug. Then he introduced her to Alicia and Yolanda.

Dom hung back, watching the rest of the room. There were a lot of guns in here and a lot of young people like him, who weren't used to drinking a lot. In his experience, alcohol, big egos, and guns rarely mixed well.

"Let's get a booth," Ray said. He picked up six shot glasses and brought them over to a booth occupied by three cops still in uniform.

"Up," Ray said.

"What?" replied one of the guys.

"Get *up*," Ray said again. "This is my booth."

The three men exchanged looks. The biggest one, a white guy who looked like a power lifter, rose to his feet. "Bro, we were here first, and"—he made a show of examining the table—"I don't see your name on a reservation sign."

"Do you even know my name, shithead? 'Cause if you did, I think you'd get the *fuck* out of here," Ray said through clenched teeth.

"That's Detective Clarke," said one of the other cops.

"Everyone knows this is where I sit, 'cept for you three shits," Ray said.

Dom wanted to say something, but he knew that it would just make the situation worse.

"How about you guys go to the bar?" Camilla suggested. "I'll buy you a round of shots."

"I don't want to go to the bar," said the standing cop. "I don't care if you're a detective, either. You're not my CO."

Ray's face tightened, and Dom stepped between them. "Let's just settle down," he said.

Moose also stepped up.

The other two guys scooted out of the booth. "Come on, Jimbo," said one. "Let's go to the bar."

Jimbo stared, the heavy scent of cheap gin on his breath. This wasn't going to end well, Dom thought, preparing to put someone in a choke hold.

Jimbo's eyes flitted to the entrance. The loud bar quieted, and all heads turned to see what had changed the vibe so suddenly.

Lieutenant Best walked in with two officers carrying assault rifles.

"Doubt they're here to have a drink," Camilla said.

"We need all hands back at HQ, ASAP," Best said. "There's been an attack on an LAPD convoy."

"So much for some R&R," Moose grumbled.

* * *

Ronaldo knew that he was losing it. Every time he saw a girl Monica's age, he felt the desperate hope that it was her. And each time, another bit of his heart broke off when he discovered that it wasn't. Soon, he would have nothing left but an empty cavern in his chest.

His grief had driven him close to the edge, caused him to make mistakes, and threatened what little was left of his family. Now it also threatened his job.

Bettis drove him across town with Tooth in their assigned pickup truck to the central sheriff's station. A full investigation had been launched into what happened at Blue Ridge and, two days ago, at the border wall.

Ronaldo had no idea what awaited him at the meeting, only that it would be nothing good. He had shot an unarmed man in an event that led to a massacre at the wall.

"It'll be okay," Bettis said, glancing over. He could always sense when Ronaldo was distraught. Ronaldo loved the guy, but he missed Marks. Marks could always talk him off a ledge. When he and Elena had almost thrown in the towel, it was Marks who reminded him that the marriage was worth fighting for.

When Ronaldo had killed two young Taliban in a roadside attack in Afghanistan, it was Marks who helped him deal with the aftermath when Ronaldo couldn't sleep for a month straight, each night waking to the image of the fourteen-year-old kid he had killed that day.

And it was Marks who had helped him get through the Second Civil War.

"The guy you shot at the wall is going to be okay," Bettis said. "You should be happy about that."

"I am."

From what Ronaldo knew about the guy, he was the father of the two teenagers who had stormed the wall. The man had been in the military, which explained the body armor under his jacket and also why he had a radio.

"Doesn't anyone care about the fact *I* got shot?" Tooth said from the back seat. "My arm is killing me today."

"You're fine," Bettis said. "Stop complaining."

"*Fine?* I'm lucky to be alive, man!"

Ronaldo couldn't help but snicker at Tooth's melodramatic exaggeration.

"The bullet grazed you," he said.

Tooth shook his head and looked out the window. "You guys are corndog dicks. Burned corndog dicks without mustard."

"What does that even mean?" Bettis asked.

"No clue," Ronaldo replied.

"No ketchup, either," Tooth added. He pinched his fingers together and muttered. "Just two small burned corndog dicks."

Ronaldo chuckled, but they drove the rest of the way in silence. It wasn't long before they reached the sheriff's station downtown at the Hall of Justice. The looming building was the last place Ronaldo wanted to be this morning.

Bettis parked and killed the engine. "Stay calm today, brother, and I think you'll be fine."

"I'm calm," Ronaldo said.

"Seriously, man," Tooth said. "You're here because you have—"

Ronaldo got out of the truck, cutting Tooth off. He didn't want to hear anything about his temper—or anything else, really.

They went to a desk, where an admin took his name. A half hour later, an older deputy in uniform walked into the lobby and directed them to follow him up a stairwell.

But instead of leading them to a court, the guy led them to the fifth floor. Tooth and Bettis were instructed to sit in chairs in the tiny lobby outside the Sheriff's Administrative Offices.

"This way," said the deputy.

Ronaldo walked down a carpeted hallway to a closed door. The man knocked and opened it.

"Deputy Salvatore is here," he said.

"Bring him in," came the response.

The deputy gave Ronaldo a quick up-and-down look, then propped the door open.

Ronaldo walked into an office with a postapocalyptic view of downtown Los Angeles. Sitting behind the desk was Sheriff Benson. But he wasn't alone.

A man stood up from a chair facing the desk and turned toward Ronaldo.

"*Marks?*" Ronaldo said.

"Good to see you, brother," Marks said. He walked

over and gave Ronaldo a hug. "I didn't think we'd be meeting under these conditions, but here we are."

"Conditions?" Ronaldo said.

Benson gestured to the other chair in front of his desk. "Have a seat, Deputy Salvatore."

Ronaldo sat, looking around the office. Photos of hunting and fishing trips hung from the walls. Benson had taken some trophies over the years: a rhino, a black bear, and the biggest buck Ronaldo had ever seen.

There were also pictures of his service in the Gulf War. Benson wasn't a marine, but he was a veteran, and Ronaldo had hoped that might count for something when deciding whether he got to keep his badge.

"I'm not a man to beat around the bush, Salvatore," Benson said. "If you were anyone else, anyone at all, I'd have you kicked to the curb."

The sheriff scratched at his acne-scarred neck.

"You're a war hero, but this is a new war we're fighting, and I need men I can trust on the front lines. Not only did you go out of jurisdiction at Blue Ridge, but you stripped that trafficker naked and slung him up on a pole, in a storm."

"I'm sorry, sir. I did so because—"

"Look, I get it," Benson said. "You lost your daughter and you were punishing that evil bastard for what happened to her, but that shit does not fly in my department. We are not bandits."

"Yes, sir."

Marks looked over. "I warned you about this."

"I can turn a blind eye to Blue Ridge," Benson said. "But what happened at our border is another story. Those refugees—some of them were fleeing from places that have experienced some terrible evil."

He leaned forward, eyes fixed on Ronaldo as if on prey that he was hunting.

"While there were certainly some assholes in that caravan, you shot a man who did not pose an imminent threat to you or anyone else, and it led to a firefight that left ten people dead."

"That's not how it appeared, and someone shot at us first, sir."

"Stop calling me 'sir,' God damn it."

"Yes, Sheriff."

Benson sighed and stood up. He looked out the window at downtown. "There," he said, pointing. "That is a battleground that Lieutenant Marks and the LAPD are in the fight to save. Did you hear what happened last night?"

"No," Ronaldo said.

"A group of heavily armed sicarios that we believe are affiliated with Mariana López hit an armored transport of LAPD cops," Marks said. "This is classified information and is not being shared outside the force. The ten officers were kidnapped, and we still don't know their whereabouts."

"Christ," Ronaldo said.

"The armored transport was full of military-grade weapons that were to be distributed among our ranks," Marks said. "We believe Mariana took them so she can fight back, now that she knows she has a target on her back."

Benson scratched his neck again, and Ronaldo decided that it must be a nervous tic.

"The war never ended," Benson said. "It just became something else. And my department and the LAPD are outgunned and outnumbered."

"It's more than that," Marks said. "Corruption has become a stage-five cancer. Almost impossible to remove."

"That's why I need men I can trust." Benson lowered his hand. "If you want to stay a deputy, your job is to protect the walls, secure our borders, and make sure refugees aren't hurt on their way here."

"I will, Sheriff."

"I need assurance you will follow protocols."

"I will," Ronaldo said.

"We're the good guys, brother," Marks said. "If we stoop to the level of our enemies, we risk becoming evil ourselves."

Ronaldo held his tongue. Neither his old friend nor the sheriff saw things his way, and that was why they were going to lose the city if they stuck to the old way of doing things.

Still, he didn't want to lose his job, and he didn't want to be a cop. He still believed the best way to find his daughter was by looking for her out there.

"Lieutenant Hernández doesn't like you. He thinks you are dangerous to yourself and to others," Benson said. "He doesn't want you under his command. But I've ordered him to give you a second chance. You can thank Lieutenant Marks for that. He vouched for you."

Ronaldo nodded at Marks, who nodded back.

"He even suggested adding you to a new team I'm putting together," Benson added.

"Team?"

Benson sat back down at his desk. "To go after the Shepherds," he said. "The guy Pierce shot on Blue Ridge wasn't the only one who spoke of them. His buddies gave us plenty of intel during an intensive interrogation."

"We believe the Shepherds are an organization beyond our walls that is trafficking people to and from Los Angeles," Marks said. "I will be working hand in hand with Sheriff Benson to locate and bury the bastards."

"I'm in," Ronaldo said.

"Not so fast," Benson said. "I mentioned rules and protocols, and this new team will be breaking a very important one. It will be leaving our jurisdiction and going far beyond our borders."

"This means you will be away from Dom and Elena for an extended time," Marks said. "And it's a bloody, dangerous mission."

"It's also a damn good chance to find where Monica was taken," Ronaldo said.

Marks nodded.

"I'm in, Sheriff," Ronaldo said. "I won't let you down, I swear."

"I'll be right back." Marks got out of his chair and walked over to the door.

Benson leaned back in his chair, stretching his back.

A few minutes later, Marks returned with Tooth and Bettis.

They seemed just as confused as Ronaldo had been about why they were here, though they did seem happy to see Marks and an office, instead of a courtroom.

"How do you feel about a trip?" Marks asked.

Tooth winced. "What kind of trip?"

"This is classified information," Marks said. He

explained the task force and its mission to find and eliminate the Shepherds.

"I'll go where Ronaldo goes," Bettis said.

Tooth sighed. "Then to the desert it is, I guess."

"Good, it's settled," Benson said. "I knew I could count on marines."

"We'll find the Shepherds, and we'll eradicate every last one of those vermin," Ronaldo said.

"Sure you don't want to join the Desert Snakes again?" Tooth asked Marks.

"I miss you guys, but my duty is to the city now," Marks replied.

"I understand," Bettis said.

"Oh, one last thing," Benson said. "Hernández is in charge of this task force. You three will report directly to him in the field. He can be a dick sometimes, but you can trust him."

Ronaldo would be the judge of that, but he still gave a nod.

"Good," Benson said. "That'll be all. Good luck."

Marks shook Benson's hand and then left with Ronaldo and the other men. They didn't speak until they got to the parking lot.

"You're a lucky man, brother," Marks said. "Benson was ready to shit-can you."

"Thanks for sticking out your neck for me. I appreciate it."

"You know I'd do anything for you," Marks replied, "but now you need to do something for me." He put a hand on Ronaldo's shoulder. "You need a break, man, a few days off. Some time to decompress. Go spend some time with Elena and Dom. I'll keep looking for Monica."

"No, I'm good, really. I *need* to work."

Marks sighed. "Just promise me you'll change your tactics."

"Fair enough. Promise *me* something."

"What's that?"

"Take Dom under your wing. I want him assigned to your team, where you can watch him and look after him."

"I thought we decided not—"

"Things have changed," Ronaldo said. "I don't trust anyone in the LAPD but you."

They stopped outside the Desert Snakes' pickup. "Okay, but you've got to promise me you'll be smart out there."

"I promise," Ronaldo said. He looked his best friend in the eye, hoping he wouldn't see the lie.

Of course, it wasn't *all* a lie. He did plan on changing his tactics out there, just not for the better.

The Desert Snakes were going on a hunting trip to catch and kill monsters. And to do that, Ronaldo would have to become one.

-13-

A figure stood in the open doorway to Vinny's bedroom. Moonlight streamed through the window, but the person there remained in the shadows, just out of the faint glow.

"Dad, is that you?" Vinny asked.

He reached for the gun he kept on his nightstand, but it was gone.

Moaning came from the doorway.

Sitting up, Vinny suddenly couldn't move. He strained to make out a muscular shape. He tried to speak again, but the words wouldn't form. His breath caught in his chest.

The doorway suddenly filled with light from a flaming sword. The burning glow illuminated the figure of a man Vinny had killed.

Isao Yamazaki raised his fiery blade above the bullet hole Vinny had put in his forehead.

"Vinny Moretti, you broke your word," he said. "Your honor is gone, and now I shall send you to hell forever!"

He charged, slashing Vinny across the chest with the burning blade. Fire burst across the deep gash and spread over his body.

Unable to move or even scream, Vinny looked down in horror as his flesh darkened and then melted away from his bones.

Isao stepped back from the bed, lowering the sword, and was gone.

No! Vinny tried to scream.

He jerked awake, gasping for air. Sweat drenched the sheet wound around his naked chest.

Just a dream, Vinny. Just another damn dream.

He slowed his breath and rested his head back on the pillow. A month had passed since the Moretti family wiped out the Yamazakis. A month since Vinny had broken his word to Isao and blown his brains out on the pavement.

Killing had become a part of his life, and ghosts of the dead were starting to haunt him.

Three nights in a row, he had woken from nightmares. Tonight was the first time Isao had visited him. Last night, another enemy had tormented him in his sleep.

All of them came with the same message: that he would burn in hell.

Vinny got out of bed and went to the bathroom to take a piss. Then he splashed cold water on his face. It was four thirty in the morning, but he knew that if he went back to bed he would just lie there, and he had to get up at six anyway.

He thought about going to see Doberman, but his friend needed sleep more than Vinny did. After a month of difficult recovery, Doberman had lost much of his muscle mass from weeks of being bedridden, and an infection had set him back twice.

Vinny sat back on his bed and looked out the window. Most of the city was dark but for a few lights in the distance. And though he couldn't see it, there was a new light out at the Four Diamonds, where a third housing complex had opened a few days ago.

The deep voice of his father startled Vinny. "Can't sleep again?"

Christopher stood in the open doorway, holding a mug.

"I made coffee if you want some."

"Cool," Vinny said. He got up and went to the kitchen of the remodeled apartment he shared with his father in the Moretti compound. Christopher poured him a cup.

"You guys have your travel plans for Italy yet?" Vinny asked him.

"Not yet. Not after that stunt Mariana López and her shitbags pulled on the LAPD. Your uncle thinks they're planning something, and he's worried about leaving our families without proper protection."

Everyone knew where the Moretti family hung their hats at night. The compound was secure but not impenetrable. With enough men, the Vega brothers and their ally Mariana López could cause some major damage and maybe even break through the defenses.

But the Morettis also knew where the Vega brothers were holed up at the Angel Pyramids. So far, Antonio hadn't committed forces to take the men. Too risky, Vinny thought. They would lose more men than they could afford.

Christopher poured wine in his coffee and mixed it with a spoon.

"You?" he asked.

Vinny shook his head. "Nah, I'm good."

"This is a tradition."

"Not one I'm going to carry on, no offense."

"Your mom loved red wine in her coffee," Christopher said. He brought the cup to his lips, then paused.

Vinny tried to remember her mixing wine in her coffee. But with every passing year, his memories of his mom grew more distant. He was even having a hard time recalling the sound of her voice. At least, he had pictures.

"Come have a seat."

Christopher went to their two couches facing a mounted TV that they never used.

"I'm worried about you, Vin," he said. "You've been through a lot in the past year and a half. More than most men deal with in a lifetime."

"Not any different from going to war like you and Antonio did at my age."

"Yeah, but at least in war there are rules. Our enemies now are savages."

Vinny didn't disagree. "What do you want me to do?" he asked.

Christopher put his mug down. "I want you to stay in Mexico for a while when you go, until it's safe to come back here. Until we can deal with the Vegas."

"Stay in Mexico?"

"I don't want to lose you, Vin," he said. "We dealt with the Yamazakis, but the Vegas will kill you the first chance they get. I won't let Don Antonio use you as bait again."

There was anger in his father's voice, and he sensed a rift between the two elders of the family. But it was not his place to broach the subject, even in private with his dad.

"You are the future of this family," Christopher said. "Someday, your uncle and I will be nothing but bones."

"But why do I have to stay down there? I barely even know any Spanish."

"For your own good."

"How do you know it will be safer and that the Gonzálezes won't come after us once we sever ties?"

Christopher smirked and leaned back on the couch, putting his muscular arms up on the back. "Don't worry about that. Your uncle and I have already made a contingency plan."

Vinny hated it when his dad foreshadowed things but kept them from him.

"So when do I go?"

"Soon as Doberman is ready," Christopher said. "He's a loyal friend, and I trust you two will look after each other."

That made Vinny feel a little better.

Sand blasted against the window, distracting them.

Vinny got up and pulled back the drape. Several cars had parked below. Carmine, Frankie, and other Moretti soldiers jumped out with their weapons. Vito was with them, and he walked back to let someone out of one of the vehicles.

Don Antonio got out, pulled on his cuffs, and walked toward the entrance.

Normally, Vinny wouldn't have batted an eye at the

soldiers and Carmine pulling up at this time, but why was his uncle out there? He almost never left the compound.

He glanced at his Rolex. It was five in the morning. "What's Don Antonio doing?" he asked.

"What?" Christopher asked.

"Frankie, Carmine, Vito, and Don Antonio just pulled up."

"Don't worry about it," Christopher said. "We need to get ready for the port."

Vinny returned to his room and put on jeans, sneakers, and a hoodie that concealed his body armor. Then he grabbed his Glock and followed his father downstairs to the convoy.

Something was off. The usual guys weren't coming today. It was just his dad, Lino, and some soldiers who piled into another vehicle.

By the time they reached the Port of Long Beach, the sun was peeking over the horizon. Vinny rode with Christopher and Lino, who seemed even more tired than Vinny and his dad.

"Rough night?" Christopher asked him.

Lino pulled sunglasses down from his bald head to his eyes.

"You could say that," he said. "My sister hates it here, and I'm starting to wonder if she should have stayed in Naples."

"I miss home, too," Christopher said. "Always will. But she'll get used to this place. We all have."

Vinny had hated it here when he first arrived, but this finally did feel like home. And now he was being sent to Mexico. A place he had never set foot—a place that seemed every bit as dangerous as here.

He lost himself in his thoughts during the tedious work of preparing for the next shipment at the Port. It was ten in the morning by the time they finally pulled into Ascot Hills.

"What's the sheriff doing here?" Christopher said.

Vinny rubbed the sleep from his eyes. On the street outside the southern entrance to the diamond-shaped complex, four Sheriff's Department pickup trucks were parked. Beside them was an MRAP all-terrain vehicle with a skull in a cowboy hat painted on the side.

And they weren't alone. A line of yellow school buses had parked in the street. People carrying bags and suitcases streamed out of the last bus and walked in single file toward the entrance, where deputies stood guard.

Lino pushed his sunglasses up on his head as Christopher drove slowly by.

"Future customers," Lino said.

Christopher smiled. "Hope we got enough goods to keep up with the demand. But that's where you come in, Vin."

Vinny nodded. Once again he was tasked with an important job for his family.

In the past year, he had committed unspeakable crimes. If he had known this was what it meant to be a Moretti, he might never have signed up.

One thing was certain, though: there was no taking back his sins. Someday, maybe soon, he would see Isao and the other men he had killed, in the place they all were destined to go.

* * *

Elena sat on the couch, staring out the window. The swollen bags under her eyes made her look like Dom after a bad night at the Octagon.

He finished putting on his uniform and sat down beside her.

"Mom," he said quietly.

She didn't seem to notice he was there.

"Mom," he said again. He touched her arm, and she jumped as if he had touched her with a hot spatula.

"Mom, it's just me, Dom."

She stared at him and then returned her gaze to the window.

"Monica is out there," Elena said. "I know she is. I feel it in my bones."

"Mom . . ."

"Go," she said. "Go find her."

"Mom, please, I want to talk to you."

"I don't want to talk until you find her." A tear rolled down her cheek.

"Mom, I'm trying my hardest, and so is Dad."

Dom wanted to wait for his father to get home, but then he would be late for his shift, and tonight was important. He wasn't sure what was going down, but he and Moose had been called to HQ downtown, and Dom guessed it had to do with Mariana López. All intel had been kept under wraps for fear of leaks.

"I love you, Mom, and I'm sorry," he said.

"I love you, too," she said in almost a whisper.

Dom gave her a hug, afraid that if he didn't, he might never get the chance again.

As he walked to Downey Station, he braced for another night like the one that had almost killed Moose.

The battle against F-13 had taken the lives of too many good men and women in blue, marines, and soldiers.

And tonight, if they were indeed going after Mariana, the same thing could happen. F-13 had broken during that key battle for the city, but the rats had scattered, and many regrouped under her banner.

When Dom got to Downey Station, Moose was waiting outside his vehicle.

"'Sup, bro?" he said.

"Nothing, man. Just worried about my mom."

Moose put a hand on his shoulder. "She's a strong woman, like my mom was. She'll be okay."

Dom wished he believed the last part, but he was starting to have his doubts.

At LAPD HQ downtown, a sergeant instructed them to get into an unmarked van. Inside, they put on black fatigues and stuffed their uniforms in a duffel.

Three hours after their shift started, the van stopped and the back door opened. Dom was greeted with a bejeweled sky above a warehouse he didn't recognize.

Something big was going down, and the top secret location confirmed it.

A plainclothes cop outside the building motioned for them, and Dom walked inside with Moose. He saw the task force reporting to Lieutenant Marks—the same men and women who had been on the failed raid outside Los Alamitos. Dom wondered again whether his father had arranged this, but he wasn't going to ask questions. He was proud to be part of this elite team.

Camilla was already here, also in black fatigues. Dom nodded to her and looked around the room at the other officers.

He wondered whether Marks had rooted out the rat who gave the traffickers a heads-up weeks earlier. Not knowing made Dom leery of pretty much everyone here.

The cops in the cold warehouse certainly didn't look like traitors. Many were former soldiers and marines like his father. The dress code seemed to specify body ink, beards, and shaved heads.

Marks was at the front of the room. He pulled pictures from a folder, looking at them for a moment. Then he whistled for everyone's attention.

"Let's get started," Marks said. "As many of you know, Mariana López attacked our armored convoy the other night, kidnapping ten officers and stealing the cargo—military-grade weapons. We finally found the bodies."

He held up a photo.

"I'm showing you this because if anyone in the room is thinking of being a rat, just remember what she did to your brothers and sisters."

Now it made sense to Dom why the rest of the fifty officers from the first briefing weren't here. So many cops were on the gangs' payroll, they couldn't be trusted. That told Dom that Marks *had* found the rat in this group.

"This was Cecil Francisco, a twenty-five-year-old officer with a wife and baby at home," Marks said, holding another photo out.

Dom couldn't make out the image very well, but he was glad for that. The mutilated body was half covered by garbage in a landfill.

"This was Jenny Williams, a twenty-nine-year-old former medical student who joined up after the war,"

Marks said. "They were all found in the dump after being tortured."

He put the pictures away and then closed the folder, keeping his palm on it as if trying to hold back an evil jinni.

"Tonight, we will avenge them," he said. "Chief Stone has given us the green light to take out Mariana López, and this task force has the honor."

Marks finally took his palm off the folder. "We're told there should be light resistance, but I'm not expecting her to go down without a fight."

He didn't reveal the location of the raid, or anything else. While Dom understood the reasoning, he didn't like going in without knowing much of what to expect.

A sergeant walked over to Marks and whispered something.

"This is it," Marks said. "Time to take this she-devil down."

Dom and Moose pulled ski masks over their faces with the rest of the officers.

Marks came over to them.

"I don't think it needs saying, but you are to tell no one about this task force," he said. He looked hard at Moose. "Not even your brother."

"Understood, sir," Moose replied.

"I won't say a word," Dom said. "And thank you for trusting in us."

Marks held his gaze, then nodded. "Welcome to the team. This is your chance to change the city."

He walked away with the rest of the officers to a convoy of four black SUVs, where they were given vehicle assignments. Dom and Moose got into a Ford Explorer with three other officers.

Once the flush of pride at being selected for the team passed, Dom tried to figure out where they were. He wasn't familiar with this part of the city but finally saw Highway 105. The convoy drove west toward the ocean.

The vehicles turned off the interstate and pulled onto Crenshaw Boulevard a few minutes later. Dom readied his M1A SOCOM 16. They were heading to the Angel Pyramids.

"Breathing masks are optional but recommended tonight," said the cop driving the Explorer.

Dom fastened his breather over his ski mask. Then he checked over his shoulder. The other two vehicles weren't following.

"They turned off a few streets back," Moose said.

Dom wondered whether this twist was due to not trusting everyone with the intel, or whether they were going to two different locations at the Angel Pyramids.

"Get ready," the driver said.

Dom saw the lead SUV—Marks's—just ahead.

Both SUVs sped up as they neared the turnoff for the Angel Pyramids, but instead of getting off, they drove right past.

They kept driving north into a burned-out residential neighborhood on the east side of Inglewood Park Cemetery. The radio crackled, and the cop riding shotgun answered.

"Copy that. On our way," he said.

Moose looked over at Dom, the whites of his eyes showing through the holes in the face mask. The two SUVs slowed as they approached the cemetery's northern edge.

This was their location?

Dom scanned the dark field of graves, seeing no one. The driver then turned off into a parking lot adjacent to a block of houses.

"Let's move," he said.

Everyone piled out of the Explorer and ran over to the other SUV, where Marks was waiting.

"Okay, listen up," he said quietly. "Mariana is here visiting the grave of her brother. We have a small window to take her down, so we need to move fast."

"Five hostiles in the park, maybe more patrolling," said the sergeant.

"Everyone, on me," Marks said. "Keep low, move fast, and let's take this evil broad down."

"Fuck yeah," growled an officer even bigger than Moose.

Marks took off running through the parking lot. The group moved around a grove of trees and through another parking lot, concealed by a row of tile-roofed buildings.

The team had almost a full view of the graveyard now. Wind whistled through the trees, stirring up grit and dust over the eternal homes of the deceased. Dom hated graveyards, hated the idea of fighting in one even more.

He kept low, rifle up, scanning for hostiles with his new EOTECH XPS2 holographic sight. The officers fanned out among the graves around him.

Marks motioned toward a cluster of trees obstructing the view into the middle of the cemetery. The team joined him there and hunkered down, waiting for orders.

He signaled Dom, Moose, and five other cops to go left. The rest of the group went right with Marks.

As Dom moved away from the tree cover, he spotted the first contact.

A man wearing a tank top, watch cap, and baggy pants walked down a sidewalk. Two more walked behind him, each holding a weapon.

They weren't holding sentry, he realized. They were following a group of people through the maze of graves.

Mariana was already leaving.

Dom cursed and hurried after them, leading his group. They prowled silently among the tombstones, stalking their prey. One of the sicarios turned and tilted his head. He went down with a suppressed shot to the neck.

Two more of Mariana's guards turned, and both went down.

Dom centered his red laser dot on her head just as she turned to look.

An eerie silence passed over the cemetery, like a short truce, before automatic gunfire shattered the peace. He was forced down as rounds punched into the dirt and chipped a monument he ducked behind.

Moose opened fire behind a headstone that barely hid his massive frame.

"I'll cover you," Dom said. He got up and fired while Moose moved to another location. The sicarios didn't run after their leader as Dom had expected.

The crazy bastards ran toward the officers in a bum rush, screaming and firing.

Muzzle flashes came from the west of the cemetery, where more sicarios had lain in wait. Dom aimed at a flash and fired, then ran in that direction using trees and graves for cover.

Being the closest, only Dom saw Mariana taking

off. Even Moose was starting to head toward a group of six hostiles who had engaged Marks and his team.

Dom peered around the grave to see Mariana running for a parking lot where several cars waited. He rose slightly and fired at the guards accompanying her, taking down one of three.

The other two stopped and returned fire. Bullets slammed into the headstone just as Dom rolled away. He crouched behind another grave, then got up and ran.

"Dom, I'm with you!" cried a familiar voice.

He spotted Camilla to his right. It was just the two of them. Mariana was almost to the parking lot now. One of the cars purred to life, its headlights spearing the darkness.

Dom looked for the other two vehicles of the convoy, hoping they would show up and flank, but the road to the cemetery was empty.

"Cover me," he said.

Camilla nodded and got up to fire a burst while he sprinted through the darkness, guided by the moon and stars.

Using the darkness as cover, he ran until he almost reached the parking lot. Mariana opened a car door and hopped inside.

Dom stood and fired off the rest of his magazine as the car peeled away. The back window shattered, and a tire popped, but it kept going toward East Florence Avenue. If she got to the main road, he would have no way to stop them.

Ejecting the magazine, Dom grabbed another and slapped it in. He aimed again, said a prayer under his breath, and squeezed the trigger.

One of the bullets found another tire, and the car jerked to a stop.

Then he cradled his gun and ran. Camilla caught up to him, running by his side.

Across the cemetery, they heard pistols popping, followed by the chatter of automatic fire, with sporadic shouting between the gunshots.

Side by side with Camilla, Dom ran toward the car, ignoring the other battle. Mariana still hadn't exited from the vehicle, but he doubted she was dead.

"Careful," Dom said.

Not a heartbeat later, a muzzle flash came from the back of the car. Dom aimed and squeezed off a shot at the figure that had popped up.

Mariana, or whoever it was, ducked down, and Dom kept running until he realized that Camilla wasn't with him. He halted and looked for her.

"Go," she moaned, gripping her side.

Dom looked back to the car and saw that Mariana had gotten out and was limping toward the road. He aimed his rifle, but the vehicle blocked his shot.

"Go get her," Camilla mumbled. She winced in pain.

Conflicted, Dom lowered his rifle and ran back to her. Crouching down, he helped her roll over.

"Move your hand," he said.

He used his palm to apply pressure, eliciting a grunt of pain.

"You're going to be okay," he said. "Just breathe."

"Fucking bitch shot me."

Several officers, including Marks, ran over, and Dom pointed to where he had seen Mariana last. They took off running while someone else got down to help Dom.

Thirty minutes later, the park was filled with flashing lights. Dom had helped carry Camilla into the back of an ambulance, and with her secure, he had joined Marks at East Florence Street.

"Nice shooting, Dominic," Marks said.

They watched as medics worked on Mariana in the back of an ambulance. But they weren't the only ones watching.

A Cadillac Escalade slowed, and the passenger window rolled down as Marks clapped Dom on his back and walked away. Dom stared at the man in the passenger seat.

He had seen the man only in pictures, but Dom knew without a doubt that it was Antonio Moretti.

-14-

"Easiest bitch to get rid of in my life," Antonio said.

Christopher smirked as they drove away from the cemetery, leaving the flashing lights behind them. With Mariana out of the picture, the Vegas had lost their biggest ally, opening the door for the next stage of Antonio's plan.

He considered that plan as they drove past the landfill where his men had dumped the bodies of the dead cops. Christopher looked out the window but didn't say a word.

Neither man liked what they had done to frame Mariana. To like it, they would have to be soulless men.

Maybe we are soulless, Antonio thought. But this was war, and in war innocents died.

In the back seat, Frankie and Carmine stared at the dump. The two soldiers had taken part in the mission that ambushed the convoy of officers, stole their weapons, and killed them all.

Mutilating the cops had been Antonio's idea. He had to make it look like Mariana's work, and like the

Yamazakis, she had a call sign: teeth marks on their dead enemies' skin. Nothing that Frankie and Carmine couldn't handle. The two old-school gangsters had seen worse in their day, and that was precisely why Antonio had given them the morbid task.

Antonio shook away the memories.

"You're sure about Mexico?" Christopher said. "It's not going to be easy. I fear we can't trust the new *patrón* of the Sinaloa Cartel."

Antonio shared his brother's concern. After all, the Vegas were the remnants of the Gulf Cartel, sworn enemies of the Sinaloa. And while many loyalties had changed over the past decade, some never would.

"Eduardo Nina and Esteban Vega are mortal enemies," Antonio said. "Trust me when I say a deal with Nina is in his best interest if he wants to control the flow of drugs here."

Antonio glanced over at his younger brother. He was worried about his only son, and Antonio understood that. If he were sending Marco to a foreign country, he would be worried, too. But Marco wasn't Vinny.

"I would not send Vin into harm's way," Antonio said. "Besides, he's proved himself to be smart and he's a good fighter." He waved a finger. "But there is one thing he has yet to prove to me."

Christopher took his eyes off the road for an instant.

"He needs to learn to make deals," Antonio said. "We're growing older, and while we have started to build an empire—and we will finish that task—it'll be up to Vinny and the younger men to keep it going when we're gone."

"That's what I don't get. Our cash cow is drugs, and if Vinny does screw up a new deal, we're—"

Antonio clicked his tongue, *tsk, tsk*. "You think I would really leave us that exposed?"

Christopher thought on it a beat, then shook his head.

"The arrangement with Javier and Diego González will remain in place while Vinny is in Mexico negotiating," Antonio said. "And if I'm needed, so be it."

"True."

"Take a right here," Antonio said.

Christopher turned. "This isn't a good idea," he said.

Antonio looked at the Angel Pyramids in the distance—the territory of their main enemy. The wannabe narco king lurked in the public housing blocks, protected by a growing army of fierce, loyal sicarios.

"Seeing where our enemies sleep at night has always been your thing," Christopher said. "I don't get why you like it. Is it the adrenaline?"

"No."

"Then why?"

"Take us closer," Antonio said.

"Brother . . ."

"Do it."

Frankie and Carmine both got out their guns but didn't say a word.

As they pulled up to the abandoned streets surrounding the southern end of the Angel Pyramids, Antonio envisioned what Esteban and Miguel were doing inside. From what he had heard, they lived like Levantine pashas, with harem girls feeding them peeled grapes and lines of cocaine.

"Park over there," Antonio said.

Christopher drove behind the burned-out shell of

a McDonald's franchise. Several cars stood with their axles on cinder blocks, the wheels long gone. A group of teenage boys sat on the hoods, smoking joints.

A tall kid jumped off when he saw their car.

The Angel Pyramids towered behind him.

"This is a bad idea," Christopher said.

"It's necessary," Antonio said. "Keep the car on. Frankie and Carmine, with me."

They got out of the car while Christopher fumed behind the wheel.

"The fuck you doin', homie?" shouted the lanky kid.

His friends followed him over, each trying to look harder than the next. Decked out in jerseys, baggy pants, and cheap bling, they were typical teenage wannabe gangbangers.

But they weren't hardened gangsters, so he wasn't worried.

Frankie and Carmine stepped up next to Antonio, arms folded casually, one hand gripping a shoulder-holstered piece.

"I asked you a question, you guinea motherfucker," said the lead kid.

"You want to make some cash?" Antonio said calmly. "I got a job for you—an easy one."

The kid strode up, holding out his palms to his friends. Two of them held up knives, and one twirled a bat.

"You might wanna back the fuck up," Frankie said, the matchstick wobbling between his lips.

Carmine scanned the parking lot to make sure they weren't being flanked.

"I asked you a question," Antonio said. He remained polite, because disrespect to these puffed-up little shits would only cause problems. He could take insults, especially when it worked to his benefit.

"I'm always down to make cash, homes," the kid said, "but there ain't no easy jobs these days, so don't play me for a fool."

"Fuck that, brah, why work with a dago?" said a pimple-faced white kid with a shaved head.

Frankie's hand moved inside his sport jacket, but Antonio froze him with a glance.

"Watch your tongue, or I'll rip it from your rotten mouth and feed it to you," Frankie snarled.

The white kid backed away, mumbling.

Antonio reached into his suit pocket and pulled out a note. "All you got to do is deliver this to Esteban Vega," he said. "And give him this coin."

The tall kid walked up and tilted his head. He was in the moonlight now, the glow illuminating the silver chain around his neck. Just another boy who would probably die before he reached adulthood.

"Do it, and then go to the Four Diamonds and tell them I sent you," Antonio said. "You will be paid in cash or drugs, whichever you desire."

"Fuck, mon," said one of the other teenagers, a Jamaican with a colorful knit Rasta cap. "Don't do it, fam. Ain't ah good idea to be dealin' wid dis bomboclaat."

"How can I trust you?" asked the tall kid.

"I'm the one that has to trust *you*," Antonio said. "That's what men do in business. So the question is, are you a businessman or a wannabe?"

"I'm all 'bout the Benjamins, homes."

"Good. Then do this and get paid," Antonio said. He handed out the note and the coin, and the kid walked away, jerking his head for his friends to follow. They looked over their shoulders a few times before taking off toward the Pyramids.

"Let's go," Antonio said.

Frankie and Carmine got back into the Escalade, and Christopher sped away in silence. No one spoke until they got back to the freeway.

"What the fuck was that?" Christopher asked. "You going to keep this plan of yours from me, too?"

Antonio didn't like his brother's tone, but he understood it. Christopher was on edge about Vinny going to Mexico and about their own trip to Naples, the place where Christopher and his son had lost the most important person in their lives: Greta.

"So you're not going to tell me, then?" Christopher said.

Antonio grunted. "I passed along a note for Esteban Vega, proposing what I'd like to call a truce."

Christopher tilted his head as if he hadn't heard correctly.

"It's a cease-fire, not peace," Antonio said. "When we come back from Naples, the war will start again, and he won't even know we were gone."

An airliner screamed toward the one of the repaired tarmacs as they approached Los Angeles International Airport. An entire concourse had been bombed to rubble in the war, and a third of the runways were cratered and unusable.

Antonio looked to the back seat.

"Carmine, you're in charge while we're away," he said. "Can I trust you?"

"Of course, Don Antonio."

Antonio held his gaze for a few beats, scrutinizing him. From what he could tell, Carmine had eased off the booze and hadn't touched the powder since their little talk a few months earlier.

"Good," he said at last.

Christopher took a frontage road to the private side of the airport. Several hangars had survived the war and still housed multimillion-dollar jets once owned by the rich and famous. Some of the charter companies were still flying, and Don Antonio had booked one for their trip to Italy.

When they pulled up, Lucia and Marco were waiting with Vinny outside the hangar. Raff was there, too, standing guard with Lino and Yellowtail, watching the runway and surrounding area for threats.

Frankie got their bags from the back of the Escalade.

"Dad, I want to come," Marco said.

"Someday," Antonio said. "But this is a business trip."

Lucia looked at him with a worried gaze.

"It'll be okay," he reassured her. "I love you, *mia sposa*, and I will be home before you know it."

They embraced, and he gave her a long kiss. Then he put a hand on Marco's shoulder. "Look after your mom, and be good."

"I will, Dad," Marco replied.

Vinny and Christopher hugged, and he gave his boy a good pat on the back.

"I wish I was going with you," Vinny said. "To avenge Mom."

"Of course you do, but you have an important mission."

"I'll get it done."

"I know you will."

Frankie started up the ramp into the private jet, carrying their bags. Their families watched from the tarmac. Antonio felt odd leaving them for the first time since they arrived in this country, but it was time to go home again and do this one thing.

"You ready for this?" Christopher asked Antonio.

"I've been ready since the day we left."

* * *

"This isn't goodbye," Ronaldo said. "I'll be back, and God willing, I will have Monica with me."

Elena held his gaze. He saw strength in her dark eyes today—something that had been absent over the past few months. Ronaldo was relieved to see some fight left in his wife. She would need to be strong while he was away.

Dom, who had just gotten home from the hospital, walked into the living room, his face contorted to hold back a yawn. He had narrated what happened during the firefight with Mariana López's crew at the cemetery.

"So Camilla's going to be okay?" Ronaldo asked.

"Yeah. I talked to the doc, and he said she'll be just fine, but she could need another surgery, depending on the results of the first one."

"Poor girl," Elena said. "She has always been so sweet."

"She's lucky the bullet missed her spleen," Ronaldo said.

He went to his son and gave him a hug.

"I want you to know how proud I am of you."

"I love you, too, Dad."

Ronaldo held his boy for a few extra moments, grateful that Marks had agreed to look after him and his friends. But Camilla's being shot was a vivid reminder of how dangerous the task force was, even under Marks's watch.

"Take care of your mom," Ronaldo said. "And, Elena, take care of Dom while I'm gone."

She nodded, and Ronaldo gave her a kiss on the forehead.

"Be careful," Dom said.

"Always." Ronaldo walked out the door as he had so many times before, leaving his family to do his duty. This time would be different, though. If he found Monica, this would be the last time he ever left them. He would give up the life of a warrior and find another way to make a living, even if it was scraping up seagull shit at the port.

Ronaldo opened the door and turned to look at what remained of his family, one last time, before stepping outside. As he walked into the cool morning, a tear crept down his face. It rarely happened, but this morning emotions seemed to get the better of him.

By the time he drove to the meeting point for his new mission, his face was dry and his heart was pounding. He was ready to head to the wastes.

The meetup location Ronaldo had been given on his last wall shift took him to the garage of an old fire station about a mile from the border. He entered through a side door.

An MRAP all-terrain vehicle and a Humvee were parked inside the dusty garage. Both were in serious need of a wash—in other words, perfectly camou-flaged. Dents from bullets, probably fired during the war, marred the doors of both armored vehicles. The M-ATV had a cracked windshield but appeared in decent shape aside from paint and windows.

Ronaldo walked around the vehicles to see Sam Hernández, the hulking lieutenant who would lead the team. He had his back turned and was checking a clip-board against crates of supplies. Pierce stood reading a manual of some sort.

Tooth and Bettis were doing an inventory of their rucksacks. The packs were stuffed with clothes and gear for a month in the new suck, the high desert bordering the Angeles National Forest.

"You're late," Hernández said, his broad back still turned.

"Had to say goodbye to my family," Ronaldo said.

"I got one, too." Hernández turned. "Could have used some help going over our supplies, but that's mostly done now."

"You're welcome," Tooth said.

Hernández grunted. "So you're a smartass, too?"

"He means well, but yeah, he is," Bettis said.

The lieutenant gave a snort. "And we got a sarcas-tic priest, too?"

"Chaplain," Bettis said. "And no, I'm not sarcastic."

"Look, we all got to work together," Ronaldo said, "and we all respect your authority. So maybe we can cut the shit, okay?"

Hernández looked in his direction and shrugged. "Respect is earned, Salvatore, and you got some work to do if you want any of mine."

The dig got under his skin, which was probably the point, but Ronaldo brushed it off. The real enemies were out there, and this was his chance to find them.

"What do you need help with?" Ronaldo asked Hernández.

"Pack the M-ATV with these crates."

"You got it." Ronaldo opened the back hatch, revealing a dusty space with gear already stuffed inside.

"That's home now, so treat it like one," Hernández said. "Actually, why don't you scrub it down really good before you load up. We'll be driving both vehicles, but this baby is going to be our shelter when the sky pisses acid, farts dust, and shits radioactive fallout on us."

Tooth chuckled.

"Are you sure this thing's ready?" Pierce asked.

"It's been cleared by the department mechanics," Hernández replied.

"Why am I not reassured?" Pierce groaned.

Ronaldo found some cleaning supplies and started in with Tooth and Bettis. For the next hour, they cleaned the floor, bulkheads, and headliner until it practically shone. When they finished, they started loading up the crates.

"Careful with those drones," Pierce said. "We don't got spare parts for me to fix them if something happens."

Ronaldo set the crates down carefully inside, and Pierce helped load up the rest. Together, the men secured the load, then stepped away to have a look.

"We're going to need some paint," Tooth said. "Got to get the Desert Snakes logo back on here."

"I was thinking the same thing," Ronaldo said.

"You guys take the Humvee," Hernández said. "I'll drive the M-ATV with Pierce."

Ronaldo got behind the wheel and pulled out of the garage. The streets were mostly empty on the drive to the wall. No one seemed interested in going outside on this chilly overcast morning.

The two vehicles slowed as they approached the main gate. A group of deputies in hazard gear stood outside, braving the elements to process refugees.

The massive steel gate opened, revealing a group of people waiting on the other side of the freeway. A deputy raised a gloved fist to Ronaldo as if to say "good luck."

"We'll need it," Ronaldo muttered.

He drove slowly through the open gate as the refugees waiting on the other side made a path. The faces turned as the vehicles passed them by.

"Poor bastards," Tooth said. "They went through hell getting here."

"Now we're heading into the hell they left," Bettis said.

Ronaldo followed Hernández up the twisty highway into the mountains. The drive through Angeles National Forest was like a purgatory between the relative sanctuary of Los Angeles and the unholy horrors of what lay in the desert wastes beyond.

The marines-turned-deputies had seen much evil in the past year and in their military service before that, but Ronaldo didn't know whether he was prepared for what awaited them out here. Ready or not, it was time to leave the task of searching for Monica in Los Angeles to his best friend and his son.

He wouldn't admit it aloud, but Ronaldo doubted she was even still there. That was another reason he had jumped at the mission. In his mind, finding the Shepherds was the only way to find Monica.

The deserted road twisted through the mountains. Ronaldo sprayed the dusty windshield and hit the wipers. Blue Ridge came into focus in the distance. The events that happened there had almost cost his life and then his job.

He owed Pierce for his life, and Marks for raking his job out of the fire. And he had a feeling that by the time this mission was over, he would repay both debts.

The Humvee crested a hill, giving them a view of the valley north of the mountains. Dark clouds crept across the skyline. Not what this area needed—the acid would likely do more harm than good to any plants that had survived this long.

"This is the farthest we've been," Bettis said.

The two trucks headed down Angeles Crest Highway, into the valley of a river that had all but dried up. Hernández took them to Mountain Top Junction and Highway 138. Then they took Interstate 15 toward the cities of Hesperia and Victorville. Not another car or truck drove on the freeway.

And Ronaldo quickly saw why.

The sprawl of destruction before them looked as if a tornado had roared through the area.

"I can't believe this," Tooth said. "Looks like a nuke went off."

Bettis crossed himself and bowed his head.

The high desert had always been barren, but now it did indeed look like pictures of Sacramento after the nuclear detonation. Former green spaces were charred.

The entire town of Victorville appeared not to have a single roof or intact window.

Entire city blocks had burned to the foundations. The wildfires that ravaged the forest had spread, consuming even the Joshua trees and cholla cactus and leaving a landscape of rust-colored ash.

Los Angeles was lucky. Though it had been hit by dust and wind, the mountains had protected the city from the brunt of the storms.

Grit pecked at the windshield as they took Interstate 15 through Victorville toward Barstow. Hernández pulled off the highway and took a dirt road out into what appeared to be the middle of nowhere.

"Where the hell's he going?" Tooth asked.

"Good question," Bettis replied. He reached for the radio on the dashboard just as Hernández halted.

Ronaldo slowed and drove up beside the M-ATV. Another quick scan revealed nothing but sand, sage, and ash across the flat, sere terrain.

"Masks on," Ronaldo said. He secured his and pulled the goggles over his eyes. Then he got out of the vehicle and walked over to the M-ATV.

Hernández was behind the wheel, studying a map. He opened the door and stepped outside, still looking at the map.

"What are we doing out here?" Ronaldo asked.

"Checking something." Hernández's map was marked with small red circles. "Grab a shovel," he said.

Ronaldo walked to the M-ATV and opened it up, cursing under his breath. Not even an hour into their mission, and he was being treated like a ditch digger. He pulled out a shovel and joined Hernández and the other men.

"Pierce, Tooth, stay here and watch the trucks," said the lieutenant. "Keep alert. There could be hostiles in the area."

"Where are you going?" Tooth asked.

"You guys are full of questions," Hernández growled. "How about you just do as you're told?"

He tucked the map away and pulled out a GPS as he started walking. Bettis shrugged and set off with his rifle cradled. Slinging his weapon, Ronaldo carried the shovel in one hand and his pistol in the other, just in case.

They hiked a few minutes until they came to a drop-off. A steep embankment led to another long, rolling stretch of desert. Multiple sets of tracks, all big and treaded, like something a tank would leave behind, scarred the earth.

"There," Hernández said, pointing at a long mound of raised earth. "Go dig."

Ronaldo went over with the shovel. His mind whirred with questions, but his best guess was he was about to uncover stolen weapons or military equipment, maybe even a vehicle.

He started digging in the center of the mound, which was about four feet high. On the third stroke, the shovel hit something hard. It wasn't metal.

Bettis and Hernández stepped up and looked down as Ronaldo began shoveling dirt off whatever he had hit. Another careful scoop, and a long bone came to light. It was attached to human foot bones.

"What the hell!"

Ronaldo stumbled back, dropping the shovel as the top of the mound slid down one side and ran over his boots, exposing not one corpse but three. Not much remained—mostly just bones and hair and some torn clothing.

Hernández bent down to take a look, and Bettis crossed himself again.

"Guess our scouts were right," said the lieutenant. "This is a mass grave."

Ronaldo was too shaken to speak. Looking down the length of the mound, he realized that the tracks were left by bulldozers covering a massive crime.

"I guess we know why these parts are empty," Hernández said. "Both cities are ghost towns. Did you guys—"

Ronaldo grabbed the big man by the arm and spun him around.

"Those are people!" he shouted. "Innocent people who were just trying to stay alive!"

Hernández yanked his arm free. "Stand the fuck down, Salvatore," he growled.

Bettis put a hand on Ronaldo's back. "Calm down," he said.

"Jesus!" shouted a voice.

They all turned to see Pierce and Tooth standing behind them. Pierce started coughing, then lifted up his mask and vomited into the dirt.

"I gave you orders," Hernández said. "What the fuck are you doing here?"

"Yeah, no shit," Tooth snapped back. "But there's someone coming on the freeway, and they don't look too friendly."

Yellowtail slumped over to the gunwale, looking green about the gills. His recently shortened Mohawk fluttered in the wind like an injured bird. It was midafternoon, and the sun blazed in a cloudless sky.

"God damn it," he grumbled, wiping his mouth. "Why couldn't we have taken a plane?"

Vinny felt bad for his cousin, but he didn't understand how such a tough son of a bitch could not handle a twenty-four-hour boat ride.

"We'll be there tonight," Raff said.

"Just as well be a week," Yellowtail said.

"How about something to eat?" Vinny asked. "Maybe that'll help."

Yellowtail put his hand on his stomach as if he might puke again, then followed Vinny and Raff back toward their Jeep. The ferry was packed full of vehicles and people leaving Los Angeles for Mexico and South America.

At first, Vinny hadn't liked the idea of traveling by boat, either, but private planes were hard to come by, and it would have been impossible to bring automatic weapons aboard. His uncle and father had paid a small fortune to take a private jet to Italy, and they still weren't allowed to bring their rifles. When they got to Naples, they would purchase the weapons they needed to take out the Canavaros. For Vinny and crew, that wasn't an option.

But the ability to bring their own weapons wasn't the only reason Vinny had taken a boat. He and the other three Moretti men were doing their best to blend in.

Secrecy was paramount to their mission.

The other reason for the boat ride was the convenience of driving their own vehicle off the ferry instead of trying to find one when they got to Puerto Vallarta. The rusted Jeep Wrangler with a stick shift was nothing like the German luxury cars Vinny was used to driving, but it was exactly what they needed when they traveled to meet their contacts in the mountains.

Doberman rested in the rear passenger seat with the door open, soaking up the rays. He angled the mirrored lenses on his gold aviators toward Vinny.

"'Sup, bro?" Vinny asked.

Doberman shrugged.

He wasn't wearing the large glasses just to block the sun. The bandages were gone, but the wounds on his face still looked scary.

Vinny stepped over to the rail. Waves slapped against the ferry's hull. He took in a breath of fresh salt air—the cleanest he had breathed in months. Not having to wear a mask was freeing.

The heat was nice, too. Vinny wiped the sweat from his brow as Yellowtail stepped up with a jar of olives. He twisted off the lid but just stared at the contents.

"I got the shits, too," he muttered. "This is so fucked up. I shoulda gone to Naples."

"There's nothing there for me anymore," Raff said.

"Hey, Vin, can I talk to you?" Doberman said, getting out of the Jeep.

They left the vehicle under the supervision of Raff and Yellowtail. Not that anybody could steal it on a ferry, but they did have a lot of weapons, gear, and a down payment in gold bars. Yamazaki gold.

Other people had brought their wealth with them, too, but some were less subtle. Vinny had spotted a family in the passenger cabin earlier. The middle-aged man and his younger wife had their two young children with them.

They wore their finest clothes and held Gucci bags stuffed full of valuables and so much worthless cash they didn't zip. They were so dumb Vinny almost felt bad for them.

A hundred passengers were on the ferry, traveling to Mexico or points south for a new life. Some probably owned properties there and had finally given up on things in the USA getting back to normal anytime soon. Chances were they would find their vacation properties occupied by squatters. It wasn't just the United States going to shit. The entire world had crumbled.

Vinny scrutinized everyone he and Doberman passed. Most of the passengers were sitting in their cars with the windows down, but some had crowded into the cabin in the bow.

It was standing room only, and most of the windows were open to the breeze. Two uniformed security guards stood on the deck outside the hatch. Another, holding a scoped rifle, stood outside the command center above the passenger cabin.

Vinny spotted the family with the Gucci bags through the windows. The man was standing, and his wife was sitting with their daughter on her lap. The boy was curled up asleep on another seat.

Doberman went to the railing on the starboard side of the ferry. A few cars were parked nearby, but they were empty, and the guards were too far away to hear anything.

"I want you to know something," Doberman said. "I don't blame you for what happened to me, but I'm not stupid, man."

"I know you're not, brah."

"Then don't try and sell me on how we're the future of this family, like you did back when I was in that hospital bed. This . . ." Doberman lifted his glasses up. Raised scars ran in a diagonal line from his cheek, over his nose, and up his forehead.

"*This* means I'll never get made," Doberman said. "You're the future of this family. I'm just going to be the sidekick, and saying otherwise is bullshit, brah."

Vinny didn't shy away from his friend's awful scars. "Dude, you watched *Scarface*, didn't you?" he said. "Tony Montana rose to the top, man, and he did it by squashing cockroaches like the Vegas. That's all we've got to do to solidify our place in the kingdom of angels."

Doberman cracked a half grin at Vinny's accent, but his lips returned to a frown.

"You got a shitty Cuban accent, you know that?" Doberman said.

Vinny spat over the rail, into the ferry's bow wave.

Then he turned to his friend until they were almost face to face. "Brother," he said, "you're not my sidekick. You're my partner, and I waited for you to heal because I want you here by my side for this deal."

Doberman put his glasses back on.

"You're also my best friend, and I will make sure you get what's owed to you," Vinny said. He reached out and gave him a thump on the back. "You've been through a lot, but it'll be worth it, I promise."

Doberman pushed his glasses up again, but this time not to show off his scars. Squinting, he peered out to sea.

Vinny followed his eyes. A boat was approaching from the east. Two boats.

A third showed up on the horizon, all speedboats, thumping fast over the water on an intercept course with the ferry.

"Fuck, that looks like trouble," Doberman said. "Better get back to the Jeep."

The guards shouted for everyone to stay calm as people noticed the speedboats approaching. As Vinny ran through the maze of vehicles, he glimpsed the men on the boats. All of them wore face masks, and not because of the air quality.

These were modern-day pirates. The ferry had its own security, but the nerdy-looking rent-a-cops would probably jump overboard at the first shot fired.

By the time Vinny got back to the Jeep, Yellowtail already had a sawed-off Mossberg, and Raff had two Glocks on the passenger seat.

Since they were the senior soldiers, Vinny looked to them for orders.

"Should I get the M4s out from under the Jeep?" Doberman asked.

Yellowtail grunted and watched the boats closing in. The men on the pursuit craft carried what appeared to be automatic rifles. One even had a mounted M240 machine gun.

"Those guys are packing some major firepower," Vinny said.

Raff stroked his chin. "We're way outnumbered."

"God damn it, I gotta take a dump again," Yellowtail said.

"Clench your ass and tell me what to do," Vinny said. "Those guys are going to be here in two minutes."

"I say we play it cool," Raff said. "Chances are good they will take what they want and go. And the gold is hidden. They'll never find it."

"And our weapons?" Doberman asked.

"Let them try and take mine," Yellowtail said. He slipped the sawed-off Mossberg under his windbreaker and zipped it up. Then he undid his gold cross and went around the Jeep to hide it along with his watch, pausing to wince and grip his belly.

The lead boat sped away from the other two to cut the ferry off. Vinny looked to the command center and saw one of the crew members with binoculars.

When the captain didn't slow, the pirate with the M240 fired tracer rounds across the bow.

That did the trick.

The ferry's engines groaned and fell silent. A speedboat approached the stern while the other two kept their distance.

A man in the speedboat at the stern raised a bullhorn.

"Everyone with a weapon, place it on the deck!" he shouted. "Follow our simple instructions, and no one will get hurt."

"Fuck that," Yellowtail said.

The three guards on the ferry lowered their rifles and put them on the deck as Vinny had known they would.

"Pussies," Doberman said.

"Who's this clown?" Yellowtail said.

A shirtless man wearing a skull bandanna over his face, and a bandolier of bullets over his ballistic vest took the bullhorn.

"Good afternoon, ladies and gentleman!" he shouted in what sounded like a brusque English accent. "My name is William Gentry, and we're here to make sure you get safely to your destination. First, though, we're going to need every valuable on board."

He lowered the speaker and pointed with his other hand at the bow of the ferry. One of his men threw a rope and then jumped aboard to tether the speedboat.

"Everyone gather in the center of the deck with your loot, and we will be on our merry way. Thank you for your cooperation."

He lowered the speaker again, then brought it back up. "If we see any weapons, we will shoot you all, like fish in a barrel."

The guy laughed as he tossed the bullhorn back to one of his crew.

Normally, Vinny could handle a sarcastic asshole, but this flamboyant fuck was really rubbing him the wrong way. Still, he would rather not get into a firefight before they reached Mexico.

The ferry captain emerged on the platform outside

the command center with his own bullhorn and instructed the passengers to listen to these men. Then his guards and crew began herding passengers toward the center of the deck.

Vinny wondered whether they were in on the haul.

"We're going to have to give them something," Raff said.

Yellowtail gripped his gut as it growled. "Jeesuss," he mumbled. "Doberman, give 'em some coins and your watch or some shit."

"Fuck that. You give 'em your watch," Doberman protested.

"What did you say?" Yellowtail snapped.

"Guys, we got bigger problems," Vinny said. He took his watch off and nodded at Doberman. "Do it."

Raff opened the back of the Jeep and took out a few items to hand over. By the time they walked over to the frightened crowd, Gentry's men had his boat tethered to the ferry, and a boarding party of ten had come aboard.

Most of them looked like hard-asses, Vinny thought—maybe even former AMP soldiers or mercenaries.

The rest of their comrades stayed on the two speedboats bobbing in the water, with their rifles aimed at the ferry.

While a few of the pirates sifted through bags and loaded up valuables from the gathered passengers, Gentry and two others walked around, eyeing everyone.

A hulking guy with ropy muscles pushed an equally strong-looking passenger onto the deck. They held the young man at gunpoint while the other pirates searched his backpack.

Two of his friends, wearing tank tops that showed

off their muscular torsos, stood by, looking testy. They looked like frat boys on spring break.

"Just do as they say," said the ferry captain.

Gentry pulled his skull mask down around his neck. He had a dark beard, cut short, and a mole under his eye. He moved on with his guards and stopped in front of the guy with the Gucci bags.

With a nod, Gentry instructed his men to take the bags. They ripped them apart, tossing clothes and dumping out bricks of money onto the deck. The man cringed, but he remained calm and whispered something to his wife when she started crying.

Gentry didn't seem satisfied. He grabbed the guy and yanked him from his family, holding him by the neck. Both kids and the wife cried out.

"Where's the rest of it?" Gentry said, ignoring them. His light, bantering tone was suddenly all business. "Where's the rest of your shit?"

"That's it," the man said. "That's all we have."

"Bullshit. You think I'm stupid? Where's your car?"

"We don't have one," the man said.

Gentry looked to his wife.

"Fine, guess I'll take her instead." He pushed the man away and grabbed for the woman.

"Let her go!" the man wailed. He reached out to grab Gentry—much braver than Vinny had expected.

The man's fingers got about an inch from Gentry's face when a gunshot rang out.

A divot of hair, flesh, and bone flew off the top of his head. He sank to the deck as screams rose from all around. The wife, however, was mute, frozen in shock.

Vinny had seen plenty of death in the past year,

but this rocked him. He looked to Yellowtail for orders, but his cousin shook his head subtly. They were to do what Raff said: play it cool.

Gentry let go of the woman, and she dropped to her knees beside her dead husband. Both kids burst into tears.

Vinny considered reaching for his gun and blowing Gentry's head off right now, but that would cause a bloodbath. He knew now that the pirates weren't messing around, and if a fight broke out, a lot of people were going to die.

Like fish in a barrel.

Gentry turned to Yellowtail.

"And how about you fine gentlemen?" he said. "You got something for me?"

Raff handed over a bag of coins, and Vinny and Doberman gave their watches.

"Rolexes. Nice!" Gentry said. He looked to Doberman. "Nice shades, too. I'll take those."

Doberman reached up, hesitated, then pulled them off.

"Oh, God *damn*, what the hell happened to you?" Gentry said, tilting his head. "You look like you had the world's worst plastic surgeon. You're even worse off than the brave lad on the deck."

Several of his men chuckled.

Vinny clenched his jaw.

"He's alive," someone said.

The guy who had taken a round to the skull squirmed.

Gentry turned from Doberman to look. Then he broke into a laugh. "Full of surprises, aren't we, you rich asshole."

"Yeah, you could say that," Vinny said. He had pulled his Glock without thinking and had it aimed at the back of Gentry's head.

"Tell your men to drop their weapons, and get the fuck off the boat," Vinny said. "Try anything, and no plastic surgeon in the world will be able to fix you."

Yellowtail had pulled out his sawed-off shotgun, and Raff had both pistols leveled at the two guards with the pirate leader. Doberman moved to disarm them all.

Gentry raised his hands above his head. "Easy now, partners."

Vinny pressed the gun so hard, it pushed the back strap of the goggles up, and Gentry fell silent.

"Tell you what, you can even have my watch—something to remember me by. But get off the ferry *now*," Vinny hissed.

Gentry didn't say anything at first. A moment of palpable tension passed, all eyes on the pirate and the young *norteamericano*.

Then Gentry nodded at the men with him, and Doberman took their rifles.

"Hey, shit birds, make yourselves useful," Yellowtail called out to the security guards. The captain ran over with the three guards and took the weapons.

Within five minutes, they had disarmed all the pirates on board, and the guys on the speedboats had lowered their guns.

Still, Vinny couldn't just leave them with those guns and working boats.

He walked with Gentry toward the one tethered to the stern. The passengers watched him, and some even pointed guns at the speedboats.

When the pirates were all rounded up in the stern with Gentry, Vinny told him to turn around.

"Tell your goons to throw their weapons in the water," he said.

Gentry flexed his jaw.

"Do it," Vinny said, pressing the Glock to his neck.

"Throw your weapons overboard!" Vinny called out.

At first, no one did anything.

"Do it," Yellowtail said. "Or it'll be like 'shooting fish in a barrel,' I think was the expression."

Gentry swore softly. "You're a dead man," he said.

"Don't test me," Vinny said. "Tell your men to drop their weapons, or I swear on the Holy Father I'll put a moonroof in your skull."

"Throw 'em overboard!" Gentry shouted after a short pause.

Guns splashed into the water.

"Okay, get on the boat, get the fuck out of here, and don't come back," Vinny said.

When all the pirates but Gentry were back aboard the speedboat, Vinny told him to stop.

"Change of plans," he said. "I'll take that watch back, and everything else you took from these people."

"You little shit," Gentry snarled, "I'm going . . ."

Vinny pushed the Glock's muzzle back in the Englishman's face. "You're going to what?"

"I'll remember your face, and especially yours," Gentry said, eyeing Doberman. "A scarred greaseball can't be that hard to find these days."

The pirates tossed the bags of goods back onto the ferry, and one of them turned on the engine. Then they pulled away, with Gentry staring at Vinny the entire time.

"Have fun swimming, assholes!" Yellowtail shouted. He raised a confiscated M16 and blasted the speedboat's motor. Doberman and Raff did the same to the other boats.

"Get us out of here," Vinny said to the ferry captain.

The older man didn't hesitate and hurried back to the command center. His security guards and several newly armed passengers kept their weapons trained on the pirates in their useless boats.

Vinny walked back to the Jeep as the passengers applauded and cheered.

But when he saw the man in a pool of blood with his sobbing family, any sense of joy vanished. A woman, perhaps a doctor, knelt by the man's side while his wife clutched his hand and his children wailed.

Vinny wanted to turn around and kill all the pirates so they could never do this again. But he didn't want to draw that kind of attention right now.

By the time they reached Puerto Vallarta, the man with the Gucci bags was dead.

-16-

Dom looked at the moon and wondered whether his father was out in the wastes somewhere looking up at it, too. He still hadn't heard a word about how the Desert Snakes were doing out there, and he didn't expect to anytime soon.

"Want to stop by and see Cam at the hospital tonight after our shift?" Moose asked.

"Yeah, for sure."

"Knowing Cam, she's probably trying to escape."

Dom chuckled. He and Moose sat in their new black unmarked car, waiting for the next emergency call. He prayed his father, sister, and mother and Camilla were okay, but he knew they were all hurting. He was hurting, too, and hoped to take some of that pain out on some assholes tonight. When the call came in about a cage-fighting ring outside the Angel Pyramids, he grinned.

A second report came in—one of a "major" player potentially being present.

"Punch it," Dom said to Moose.

The car squealed out of the parking lot and onto the highway. Now that they had proved themselves on several missions, Marks had pulled them off beat duty and assigned them to his task force.

It felt good to be working with a man who wasn't corrupt. Someone he could trust, whom he had always respected.

Dom had earned Marks's confidence by fighting F-13 in the main battle for the city, and in all the battles since then, including the one that brought down Mariana López.

Being part of the task force was an honor, but it also gave him the best chance of finding Monica if she was still in the city.

He picked up the radio again.

"Proceed with caution," said the dispatcher. "Multiple high-level targets in the area. Consider them extremely dangerous. Confirm it's them, and wait for backup before engaging."

"Copy that."

Dom couldn't believe their luck. First Mariana López, now a top-level Vega?

"You really think Esteban or Miguel left the Angel Pyramids?" Moose asked.

"I doubt it, but you never know. There's a rumor going around about a cease-fire between Moretti and Esteban."

Moose floored it. This Dodge Challenger was a race car compared to the beater Crown Vic they had been driving for the past few months.

Dom pulled out a map to look for the location. The building was an old shopping center on the eastern edge of the Angel Pyramids. No surprise that crime families had taken over the abandoned buildings to house their illegal activities.

Some of them, like the Vegas, did their crimes right out in the open, unconcerned about the police because, usually, the police did nothing.

But tonight the Vegas were going to experience cops of a different kind.

Moose slowed as he approached the zone. Cars on cinder blocks, some of them stripped down to the chassis, lined the street.

People loitered on the corners, smoking joints and drinking from bags. A group of kids no older than ten hung out in a park. In places like this, many children were orphans or being raised by a single parent or grandparent. It wasn't a shock to see them out, even at midnight.

Several faces turned at the growl of the Challenger's engine. There were plenty of muscle cars left in the slums, but most belonged to gangsters who could afford the gasoline.

"Park somewhere discreet if you can," Dom said.

The other undercover officers on the way would be doing the same thing. Moose found a block of houses burned to the foundations. A few on the next block were still standing. One even had a garage.

He pulled inside and killed the engine.

Tonight, their uniforms were jeans and T-shirts. Dom had a tattered Yankees baseball cap.

He opened the trunk, and they donned their ballistic vests. After throwing on jackets and adding their breathing masks, he and Moose each concealed a pistol in a waistband holster and strapped another to their ankle. They checked their radios.

Moose pulled the garage door down manually, and they set off into the night. Fires burned in trash barrels, sending shadows playing across streets and parks. Palm trees swayed in the wind over camps where people slept in tents.

Most of the people living out here were straight-up junkies with nowhere else to go. The Angel Pyramids were now at full capacity, and the Four Diamonds were almost there. The city continued to build public housing, but it had more people than it could manage, and with refugees coming in every day, resources were maxed out.

Power to this area had been cut, leaving only the moon and a few barrel fires to guide Dom and Moose toward the shopping center.

A flashback to the night of the F-13 battle surfaced in Dom's mind—the night Moose had almost died, the night Ronaldo and the Desert Snakes had come to the rescue.

Tonight, Dom and Moose had a chance to exterminate more rats from the city streets. He tried not to think about how many rats there were—killing the ones at the top was the best way to liberate Los Angeles.

A crashing behind them made Dom spin and reach for his pistol. He relaxed when he saw the source of the noise. In the darkness, a homeless woman had steered her shopping cart too close to the curb. It had fallen over, dumping her worldly belongings in the gutter.

Dom would have stopped to help her, but they were burning time.

He and Moose trotted around a corner, passing another area hit hard during the war. In the center of the road, chunks of pavement surrounded a deep bomb crater. They took the sidewalk along a fenced-off park that was nothing but dirt, a melted plastic slide, and a jungle gym.

More teenagers hung out on the corner ahead, around a charred car being used as a firepit. Flames flickered out of the open trunk.

Two of the kids started walking toward Dom and Moose.

"I'll handle this," Moose said.

In the glow from the fire, Dom saw they were just kids, not even teenagers. One was a tall Latino, the other a buff black kid.

"'Sup, homies?" Moose said.

"What you want?" asked the Latino kid.

"Just passin' through," Moose replied.

"You gots to buy some food if you want through," said the black kid. He stepped up in a pair of spotless Air Jordans, arms folded over his muscular chest.

"Maybe on our way home," Moose said. "Now, get out of the way."

"Fuck you." The Latino kid pulled out a knife. "You buy food, or you go around."

Thirty minutes had passed since they took the call over the radio, and every second gave the targets more time to escape.

But Dom didn't want to make a scene, so he did something he had never done before. He bought some cocaine.

During the transaction, his radio chirped, and he subtly shut it off. The kid with the Jordans eyed him but didn't say a word.

Moose didn't speak, either, until they got to the next block.

"What the fuck you thinkin', man?" he asked.

"That we're running out of time. But looks like we're here."

An audience had congregated outside the shopping center. Moose and Dom hurried across the road and melted into the crowd.

Synthesizer bass boomed from inside the building.

Most of the people here were in their twenties and thirties, but there were a few forty- and fifty-year-olds dressed like narcos. That didn't make them narcos, though. Dom searched the outside crowd for anyone matching photos of the Vega leadership.

Seeing none, he approached the front entrance of a cubical six-story building. The former business's sign was gone, replaced by colorful skull masks—the symbol of the Vegas.

Two neckless guards sat on stools outside the entrance, checking IDs to keep out enemies and cops. But they didn't appear to be patting anyone down for weapons.

Dom decided to stash the radio and the Kevlar before they entered. They went into an alley and stuffed the gear under a storm drain grating.

"You sure about this?" Moose asked.

"Safer without a vest than with, if we get caught."

They went back to the front entrance and let the guards look over their fake IDs. Then they paid their silver dollar to get inside.

Subwoofers thumped from across the room, shaking the packed floor. The entire center of the building had been gutted after the war, and the ceiling was gone, providing a natural moonroof.

Balconies packed with noisy drinking, smoking patrons surrounded each floor. As Moose carved a path, Dom got a better view of what they were cheering at.

In cages hung from chains, topless Hispanic women gyrated suggestively. Some looked far too young to be here. But the women weren't what the spectators were cheering at.

The sight of two large fighting cages stopped Dom in his tracks.

In one, a fight was under way. He and Moose waded through the crowd to get closer.

Overhead, the girls did tricks on poles and shook their *chichis*. Dom looked past them at a group of men leaning against the railing on the third-floor balcony.

A tall guy with a cowboy hat moved in front of him, blocking the view. Dom tried to squeeze back up but bumped into another man, who was tilting back a beer. It spilled down his shirt.

"Sorry," Dom said.

"Fuck you, *ese*!" the man yelled. He looked ready to swing, when Moose stepped up.

"Here, have another on me," he said, taking a coin from his pocket.

The drunk guy took it and looked bleary-eyed up at Moose, looming a foot over his head.

"*No hay problema, maestro*," the man said, staggering back.

Shouting rang out around the cage as one of the fighters kicked the other in the head with an audible crack.

Two men walked inside the cage and dragged the unconscious guy out. The victor, a ripped Latino with a soul patch, raised two ink-covered arms, pumping his fists and chanting, "Vega! Vega! Vega!" Rattlesnake tattoos coiled around each leg, the heads inked onto the tops of his feet.

The crowd repeated the chant. Soon the only people not chanting or pumping fists were the guys on the third floor. But Dom still couldn't see their faces in the shadows.

He needed a better vantage point to confirm who was here, before calling the rest of the task force to what could end up as a brutal shoot-out.

Crossing the floor, Dom could see an announcer with a bow tie enter the cage. He grabbed the victor's hand and raised it in the air.

"Enri-i-i-i-ique-e-e-e 'the Rattlesnake' Baca wins yet another match by knockout!" shouted the announcer. "He now faces Joshua . . ." Lowering the microphone, he shouted to someone outside the cage, then brought the mike back up. "Joshua Gi-i-i-ilmo-o-o-ore."

The crowd booed and shouted slurs as a muscular white guy in green camo shorts walked into the cage. A Marine Corps eagle-and-anchor symbol covered a right biceps the size of a grapefruit.

Dom followed Moose through the enthusiastic crowd for a better look at the balconies. The bell rang, and Joshua came out swinging.

Enrique pulled his head back, avoiding the first jab, countering with a rapid series of kicks that struck Joshua in the chest, then the side, then the back.

The crowd went wild.

Dom finally got a better view of the balconies and spotted a guy with a cowboy hat, surrounded by muscle. Another man, with spiked hair, watched from the safety of the balcony as Enrique scored multiple kicks to the marine's body, the head of the rattlesnake hitting him over and over.

Blood dripped from an open cut on Joshua's face. He traded a punch at the air for a kick in the face. Dazed, the marine swung a massive haymaker, which his nimbler opponent ducked.

Moose grabbed Dom by the arm and leaned down.

"Bro, I think that's Miguel Vega," he said. "Third floor, four o'clock."

Dom checked as discreetly as he could. The Vega narcos were here, and not just Miguel. He would bet anything that Miguel's brother, Esteban, was up there, too.

He and Moose had two options: run and get the radio, or split up and keep an eye on these guys before they could escape to their castle.

Dom had decided to split up, when someone grabbed him from behind and spun him. Two muscular guards grabbed him by the arms. Another two already had Moose. The goons yanked Dom off his feet and carried him across the floor. The crowd parted to let them through.

Within a minute, the men had Dom and Moose out in the alley and tossed them to the ground. Boots pressed their backs down while they were searched.

Dom saw cowboy boots—and a pair of Air Jordans he recognized.

He didn't need to see a face to know that it was

the kid he had bought the "food" from. The little fuckers had ratted him out after hearing the radio crackle. Dom was relieved he had left the radios and Kevlar vests outside.

"You fuckers cops?" someone asked in a thick Mexican accent.

Dom couldn't see him and wasn't sure how to answer. Being a cop could save their lives. It could also get them killed.

"Nah," Moose said. "Just here to watch the fights, man."

The guards bent down and disarmed them both, then told them to turn over.

Dom rolled to his back as someone kicked him in the diaphragm, knocking the air from his lungs. They did the same to Moose.

Another shoe hit Dom in the mouth, splitting his lip. Tasting blood, he looked over at Moose. Maybe it was time to fight back and fuck some of these guys up.

Guttural barking put that idea to rest.

The alley door opened, and two pit bulls strained against the leashes held by their burly handlers. They snapped and snarled at Dom and Moose, one of them coming so close Dom could feel its hot breath.

Amid the animal noises, he heard the clink of spurs. He kept his gaze down, not wanting another kick to the face.

"My men tell me you two boys are cops," said a new voice in a thick Mexican accent.

"Your boys are mistaken," Moose said.

"We're not cops," Dom said. "I'm a fighter. Thought I could make some coin here."

Moose looked over at him, but Dom kept his gaze

on the spurred boots. The person wearing them bent down, and Dom glanced up.

A middle-aged Mexican man took off his cowboy hat to reveal a pockmarked face. Gold chains gleamed below the collar of his gold-patterned black shirt. He grabbed the silver belt buckle on his designer jeans and leaned down.

Not a single cop on the force had seen Esteban Vega this close.

Dom wiped the blood off his lips.

"Our *chicos* said they heard a radio on you," Esteban said.

"They heard wrong," Dom said. "We don't have radios."

Esteban looked back at his muscle heads, and one of them spoke in Spanish.

If they had found the radios, Dom and Moose were about to have a very bad last day on earth.

Esteban stood and motioned the kid with the Air Jordans over. Esteban put a hand on his shoulder.

"You sure you heard a radio on them?"

The kid seemed less sure now.

Esteban clicked his tongue twice, then pushed the kid away and paced in front of Moose and Dom.

"If you two are cops, then you've broken a cardinal rule," he said. *"Son muy estúpidos."*

"We're not cops," Dom repeated. The boot on his back pressed down, making it difficult to breathe.

"Maybe you are; maybe you aren't," Esteban said. "But the only way you're getting out of here alive is by fighting. Turn over."

Dom turned over and braced for another beating.

But instead, Esteban reached down to help him up. The other bodyguards helped Moose up.

"You want to go home tonight?" Esteban asked.

Dom nodded.

"Then you must fight."

"Okay," Dom said. "The Rattlesnake?"

"No," Esteban said. He grinned, exposing several gold crowns. His eyes flitted to Moose. "You fight your amigo."

Dom and Moose exchanged a glance.

"If you can beat this guy, then you can face the Rattlesnake," Esteban said.

"Come on, man, I don't want to fight my friend," Moose said.

That got him a kick in the back.

"You want to go home with your head? Then you fight, *ese*." Esteban hissed the words.

Dom looked again at Moose, who gave a reluctant nod.

Esteban smirked and motioned his dog handlers back. The pit bulls went down on their haunches, tongues hanging out of their saggy lips.

Dom pushed himself up, drooling blood. He was already hurt, and so was Moose, but what Dom planned to do wouldn't inflict too much pain on his buddy.

And it just might save their lives.

"Put up your hands," Dom said.

"Seriously, bro, I don't want to hurt you."

"You're the one that's gonna get hurt," Dom said. "Now, put 'em up."

Moose raised his hands. "Fine, if that's the way you want to play it." Striding forward, he threw a jab at Dom's head.

Dom evaded it easily and danced around his friend. A swift kick to the back sent Moose lurching toward the pit bulls, who snapped the air.

That got a few laughs from the guards.

Moose arched his back and then turned with his fists up.

"Dude, I really don't want to . . ." he began, when Dom kicked him in the back of the knee.

But Moose didn't go down as Dom expected. Instead, he threw a hook that caught Dom in the ear. It hurt, but not as bad as a punch to the nose would have.

He faded back, out of Moose's long reach, and began circling again.

Moose threw another punch, and Dom moved to the side, then kicked the back of the same knee. That did the trick.

Moose yelped in pain and went down on his other knee.

Dom wasted no time wrapping Moose up in a choke hold and arm guard. The Vega men shouted as Dom cut off his best friend's air supply.

Esteban stood stroking his chin, looking down with an expression of childlike curiosity.

When Moose finally tapped, Dom let him go and rolled away. He leaned down to make sure Moose was okay. The big guy was on his back, chest heaving, a hand to his throat.

Dom reached down and patted him on the shoulder. "You good?"

Moose grunted.

"Impressive," Esteban said.

"Something like that." Dom wiped blood from his ear. Then he helped a wobbly Moose to his feet.

"Our guns," Dom said.

"You'll get them in a moment," Esteban said.

"*Patrón*," one of his men said. "You really letting . . ."

Esteban narrowed his eyes at Dom. "Come back here in a week from tonight, and you'll get your chance at the Rattlesnake," he said. "If you beat him—and that's a big if—you'll win some real *dinero*, hombre."

Antonio felt drugged from the jet lag, but he was too excited to be tired, and not just because he was home for the first time in almost a decade.

He was here to finish something that he and his brother had been longing to do for all those years. They would soon get their revenge on men who had taken almost everything from them.

Lino sat at the window of their safe house, a shabby apartment looking out over the slums in Scampia, Naples. The grimy carpet, stained walls, and tattered furniture didn't bother Antonio. This place felt more like home than his new compound in Los Angeles.

The shouts of neighbors through the thin walls, and the smells of sweat and urine didn't bother him one bit. It reminded him of his youth. As bad as his childhood had been in some ways, this was where he had come from, and he felt the glow of nostalgia.

He walked into the bedroom, where Christopher snored on a mattress.

"Wake up," Antonio said.

Christopher sat up, rubbing his eyes. "Already? I just laid down . . ."

"Three hours ago," Antonio said.

He tossed his brother a jacket. The temperature was even colder here than in Los Angeles, and it was raining today. But the clothes weren't just to keep them warm and dry.

Their new outfits would make them harder for spies or enemies to spot.

Once they were dressed, the brothers joined Lino in the living room, where their pistols, coins, and valuables lay arranged on a table. Italy's economy had also tanked, but the country was still functioning, and they would be able to buy whatever they wanted with the gold and silver they had brought with them.

"As soon as we leave this room, everything changes," Antonio said. "We speak Italian only, and we keep our heads down. There will be people out there who might still recognize us—people who could sell us out to the Canavaros."

Antonio switched to Italian. It was odd speaking in his first language after all this time, but it was like driving a stick shift—something you never forgot—and he got right back into gear.

He thought back to everything Lino's sister, Angela, had told them. She hadn't heard much—only that Don Roberto Canavaro had returned to Naples with his retired uncle Pietro and a small group of loyal men to restart the business after Lino and Yellowtail killed most of their crew.

It was Pietro that Christopher was after. The old patriarch was believed to have been behind the order to hit the Moretti family. Roberto had merely helped carry it out.

"We don't know where they are right now or how many soldiers they have," Antonio said. "But with the help of our contacts, we'll find them, and then we will kill them. And after that, we will return to Los Angeles and kill Esteban and Miguel Vega."

He picked up his SIG Sauer P320 and chambered a round. Then he released the magazine, added one to replace the chambered round, and slapped the magazine back into the grip.

"Let's go," he said.

Christopher opened the door, and Lino led the way to their next stop, eyes scanning every person they passed on the exterior walkway that took them to a stairwell.

Antonio mostly looked at the older people—people who might have known him many years ago. But that was unlikely. The safe house was five miles from their old stomping grounds, and their contact here, a man nicknamed Diamante, had assured Christopher that this was safe from the Canavaros.

Lino stopped on the sidewalk and looked over the parking lot where they had parked their car, an early-2000s four-door BMW with a cracked bumper and a missing hubcap.

He motioned that the way was clear, and they got into the clunker.

Lino drove from the slums to the heart of Naples. Soon, they saw Castel Sant'Elmo, the fourteenth-century fortress and former prison that looked out over the historic center of the city.

Lino drove up a winding cobblestone road as pedestrians with umbrellas moved out of the way.

Antonio finally spotted their first stop, the little church of Santa Maria dei Sette Dolori. Rome had a much bigger and better-known version, but this place was important to him. Not because he was a religious man, but because this was where he had gone to mass with Christopher and their parents when they were just boys.

Lino parked on a side street. Just as he killed the engine, the rain stopped. Antonio got out of the car and looked to the sky. The sun was trying to burn through the gray clouds.

A sign, Antonio thought.

He wasn't a superstitious man, but he did believe in destiny, and this was where his parents had started to instill in him values that stayed with him today. To work hard, believe in something, and never give up, like Christ, even if it meant giving your life.

In those ways, he had a lot in common with the Son of God, even though, in other ways, they couldn't be more different.

Lino opened the wooden doors and peered inside the church. Then he gave a nod and stood guard while Christopher and Antonio went inside the nave.

Three people sat in pews, their heads bowed in prayer.

Antonio took the back row with Christopher, and they, too, got down on their knees. While Christopher's lips moved silently in prayer, Antonio remembered the parents who had brought him here, and his uncle, gunned down in the basilica of San Paolo Maggiore.

Antonio closed his eyes and prayed.

I don't know if you hear me, Lord, and maybe it would be best if you didn't. Because I'm not here to praise you. I'm here for revenge, and I ask, if you believe in justice, that you guide my hand in taking the lives of the men who took so much from my family. Even if you don't help me, I swear that I will fulfill this part of my destiny.

He looked up and crossed his chest. For a few minutes, he remained on his knees, remembering the times he had come here with his parents, dreading each time. Now he would give just about anything to be here with his parents once again.

Christopher crossed his chest and nodded.

They got up and walked down the nave to drop coins into a basket. A priest who looked about as old as the building, with hair as gray as the day's sky, sat in a chair. Antonio nodded at the old man and put another coin in the basket.

Then he left, stopping only to dip his finger in holy water.

Lino fired up the car and drove them toward one of the most beautiful bays in all Italy. The sun finally broke through, gracing them as they drove down a steep street with a rainbow glowing over its far end.

Antonio admired the architecture of the narrow streets, and the simple life the Neapolitan people led: the clothing strung between balconies; the old men smoking hand-rolled cigarettes and drinking espresso; teenage girls in short skirts, and the teenage boys chasing them as he had once chased Lucia.

In so many ways, Naples hadn't changed much in the past decade. Unlike most of the world, it hadn't been destroyed by war lately. And the economy here had already sucked before the global markets collapsed. His people were fighters, used to scraping by. And that was why he was winning the fight for Los Angeles.

As if in answer to his thoughts, he saw the Giuseppe Garibaldi monument commanding the center of the town's square. The Italian patriot was someone Antonio had always looked up to and related with, and not because they were both soldiers.

Garibaldi had helped bring unification to Italy by some of the same guerrilla tactics that Antonio was using to build his empire in Los Angeles.

Antonio looked away from the statue as they approached their destination. By the time they pulled up outside a century-old building downtown, the clouds had all but rolled away, leaving Naples bathed in a golden afternoon glow.

"This is it," Lino said, looking up at the four-story stone building. A man in a black coat with slicked-back hair and a raptor's beak for a nose stood outside, smoking a cigarette.

"That's Diamante," Christopher said.

Lino turned off the engine and got out to talk to the man. Then he turned and waved for Christopher and Antonio. They got out of the car, stepping into puddles of rainwater.

The man opened the door, then introduced himself with a smile. Diamonds sparkled from both his upper front teeth. Not small ones, either—these were at least half a carat each. Diamante's teeth took grills to an entirely new level.

He reached out, and Antonio shook his hand. Not a strong shake, but not weak, either. Antonio would need more to go on before deciding whether he could trust this man.

"Follow me," Diamante said.

Antonio and Christopher exchanged a glance and then followed. The marble hallway was framed with flaking gold crown molding. Diamante stopped outside a security-gated door, pulled a key from his coat, and opened it.

"Down here," he said.

They went down a dark stairwell that reeked of cigar smoke. At the bottom, a steel door with a metal-shuttered eye slot blocked off the basement.

Diamante knocked twice, and the shutter slid open. The eye on the other side looked at each of them in turn. A lock clicked, then another, and the door creaked open.

The brothers followed Diamante into a dark space lit by shaded lamps on empty card tables. Across the room, three men sat around a card table, smoking cigars.

Antonio didn't like that. These men were his age, and while he didn't recognize any, he had instructed Christopher and Lino to make sure they had complete secrecy.

"Don't worry," Diamante said, sensing his anxiety. "They are friends."

Antonio didn't make eye contact with anyone and kept his hands in the coat pockets as he crossed the room to another door. This one opened to a hallway with several more doors.

Diamante unlocked one and swung it open.

"What you asked for," he said.

Antonio stepped into a room the size of a walk-in

closet, filled with racks of guns. They were older models, not the new M4A1s he had gotten from Rush during the war, but he could make them work.

Lino grabbed an Uzi, and Christopher picked up a sawed-off shotgun, turning it from side to side.

"We're back in business," Christopher said.

"Who are those men?" Antonio asked Diamante.

"Locals. They play cards here once a week."

"Where are they from?"

Diamante explained that they were good men who lived across the city. All of them had retired from business positions in real estate and construction. Most of what he said helped reassure Antonio as they loaded up the weapons and ammunition into black duffel bags.

Christopher finished and zipped up the bags. The sound masked the growling of Antonio's stomach. He was ready for something to eat, something local that he hadn't had in a long time.

As they passed the three men playing cards, a voice called out.

"Lino," one of them said in Italian. "Lino De Caro, is that you?"

Lino stopped to look at the shaded features of the bald man who rose from his seat.

"I thought that was you, old—"

Antonio pulled out his pistol and shot him through the head before the guy could finish his sentence. Gore spattered the wall behind him.

The other two guys put their hands up, but that didn't save them. They fell beside their friend, with holes in their skulls.

"What the hell!" Diamante screamed. He ran over, stopped, threw up his hands, and then looked to Antonio, who pointed the gun at his face.

"I thought my brother made it clear that our visit was to be secret," Antonio said. "This"—he waved his gun—"was not that."

Diamante put his hands up. "*Mi dispiace.* I'm sorry . . . I'm so sorry."

Antonio kept the gun trained on him as Lino walked over to look at the guy who had called his name.

"Who is he?" Christopher asked.

"A friend of my father's, I think," Lino said.

"Was," Antonio said. "We can't trust anyone now."

He lowered the gun to Diamante's chest.

"Please, I meant no problems," he stammered. "It won't happen again. I beg you, don't shoot me. I will get you the Canavaros."

"We need him," Christopher said.

Antonio grimaced. He didn't trust the guy, but his brother was right. They did need him.

For now.

He lowered his gun, and Diamante heaved a sigh of relief.

"Anyone else hungry?" Antonio asked, holstering the gun. "I'm starving."

* * *

Ronaldo and the Desert Snakes had spent the past few days combing the all-but-deserted city of Barstow for the Humvee that Tooth had seen pull off the interstate not far from the mass grave. Its occupants had sat inside the vehicle, observing the team for a few minutes before speeding away.

It could have been a random group, but Hernández didn't seem to think so. Ronaldo wasn't sure what to think. The city was on Route 15, the same road he used to take with Elena on weekends when they had a sitter for Dom and Monica. That was when the kids were much younger, so long ago that Ronaldo could hardly remember.

The view hadn't changed much out in the open stretches of highway outside town, but the city reminded him of Fallujah, Iraq. Many of the residential areas were burned to the ground, along with a local school.

Hernández seemed to think the occupants of the Humvee were responsible for the devastation and the mass grave, but he wasn't saying much, and Ronaldo was getting bored in their hideout—a ransacked shop that had sold "quality" meats. Like many of the other grocery stores, gas stations, and the local Walmart, the place was a mess. Most everything worth anything was long gone.

That state of abandonment was partly why Hernández had chosen the location as a hideout. Also, it was on the edge of town, which gave them a better vantage point. It was the first decision Ronaldo actually agreed with the lieutenant on.

But he was still furious at being kept in the dark about the mass grave, and he wasn't happy not knowing what Hernández knew about that Humvee. If this was what they could expect for the entire mission, finding the Shepherds was going to be a chore in hell.

The mass murder was horrific, but the mission

wasn't to track down those responsible—unless they were the Shepherds, which Ronaldo doubted. He kept his mouth shut, following orders and trying not to rock the boat too much.

At dusk, he climbed up onto the roof, where Tooth was scoping the city with his binoculars.

"See anything?" Ronaldo asked.

"Negative," Tooth replied.

Ronaldo walked to the rear of the building, where they had parked their two vehicles. Both were hidden under tarps and protected from view by white brick walls.

Bettis was sitting in a lawn chair, watching over them with Pierce, while Hernández was inside planning their next move.

With a sigh, Ronaldo got down on one knee beside Tooth.

"This is fucking bullshit, boss," Tooth grumbled.

Ronaldo smirked. "Glad to know I'm not the only one thinking that."

"What the hell are we even doing in this shithole, and why won't the LT tell us?"

"He must have his reasons, but my guess is, he doesn't trust me."

They sat for another hour, until the sun became a streak of molten lava on the horizon and then hardened into darkness.

"Hey," Pierce said from the ladder. "The lieutenant has new orders."

"'Bout damn time," Tooth said.

He followed Ronaldo over to the ladder and back into the building. They found Hernández in the filthy office, hunched over a metal desk with maps draped across the surface.

The creaky chair turned as his team entered. Then he spat tobacco juice from a plug he had found into a plastic bottle.

"Tonight, we're doing recon in several areas, on foot," Hernández said. "I have reason to believe that the animals that killed and buried those people are still here. Our job is to find them."

Ronaldo bit his cheek, resisting the urge to ask a burning question.

"Salvatore, you're with me," Hernández said. "Bettis and Pierce will check out several other targets I've marked, and McCloud, you'll stay on the roof."

"I've been on that stinking roof all day," Tooth groaned.

Hernández looked at him. "You got the most important job: watching our rides," he said. "If you don't want it, I'll give it to Bettis."

"Want to switch, priest man?" Tooth asked.

"I don't care, honestly."

"Pierce, you're with me, bro," Tooth said, grinning. "If that's okay with you, LT."

Hernández gave a vague nod.

"Great," Pierce muttered.

The lieutenant went over the different locations on the map and then handed it to Tooth. "Soon as it's dark, we head out," he said.

Ronaldo went back to his gear and made sure his M4A1 rifle was ready to go. He had stripped and cleaned it earlier in the day. Next, he checked his "four eyes" night-vision goggles.

Darkness fell over Barstow as he made his final preparations.

"Radio silence unless someone approaches," Hernández said to Bettis. "And radio silence for the rest of us unless you spot that Humvee or anything else that looks military."

"Military?" Ronaldo asked. "You got reason to suspect these were former AMP soldiers?"

"They did take over the Marine Corps Logistics Base for a few months before we drove 'em out," Tooth said.

Hernández looked at them in turn but didn't say a word, merely pointing with his chin at the exit.

"I'll watch your six," Bettis said. "Good luck and be safe." He grabbed the sniper rifle, and the other four men went out the back door.

"See you in a few hours," Hernández said. "Good hunting."

Pierce and Tooth jogged toward several blocks of cookie-cutter houses. White roofing shingles, uprooted by the recent windstorms, lay strewn about the yards and driveways. Hernández led Ronaldo toward the Montara Elementary School. They cut through the campus's burned-down buildings.

Ronaldo kept alert, scanning for hostiles in what was effectively a ghost town. In two days, he had seen almost no one still living out here. On the drive before they found their hideout, he had spotted a kid behind an apartment window, pulling back the drape to watch them pass by. A woman pulled it shut as the boy raised his hand to wave.

An old man working on a car engine was the second

person. Besides that, there were only a few others, and roadworthy vehicles were almost nonexistent. Nearly all moving cars were on the freeways, in armed convoys that the motorists hired to get them safely through the lawless wastes.

The first few blocks away from the station, Ronaldo followed the lieutenant in silence. As the desert night set in and the crickets and katydids started up, he felt his paranoid side getting the upper hand, wondering why the lieutenant had teamed with him instead of someone else. Probably to keep an eye on him.

But there could be other, more sinister, reasons.

He shook away the thought. No way in hell would the guy would try to off him with Bettis and Tooth out here.

Ronaldo decided to break the silence as they walked toward the neighborhood where he had seen the kid and the woman behind the window.

"You thought about asking any civvies about that black Humvee?" he asked.

Hernández halted. "We're not cops," he said, "and canvassing here is like asking to get a face full of buckshot. But by all means, go for it." He motioned down a side street.

Ronaldo kept walking. He trusted that Hernández knew what he was doing. But being out here in the dark as the temperature dropped had him on edge.

A barking dog prompted both men to take cover behind an abandoned car. A second dog joined in. Ronaldo tried to home in on the barking. It didn't seem to be coming from the direction Tooth and Pierce had gone.

A gunshot shattered the silence, and the barking stopped.

"Where the hell did that come from?" Hernández asked.

Ronaldo pointed as the echo faded away. The crickets resumed their chirring.

Hernández and Ronaldo continued to their target along Highway 40, an abandoned office and storage yard for the California Department of Transportation. When they arrived, Ronaldo saw why the lieutenant had wanted to check this place.

In the open yard were dump trucks and two bulldozers—the sort of equipment that could be used to dig and cover a mass grave.

"You thinkin' whoever buried those people used one of these?" he asked.

"Bingo."

Ronaldo didn't mention that this was police work—something Hernández didn't think they were doing. He dialed in the binoculars to check the offices for the glow of candles or electric lights. But there was no sound of a generator engine, and everything was dark, including the garages.

"Let's go," Hernández said.

"Did you see someone?"

"No, but there's something I want to check out."

Keeping in combat interval, the two deputies entered the yard through a cut chain-link fence. Hernández seemed to know exactly where he was going.

He went into one of the warehouses and then directed them toward a bucket truck that was used to fix light poles and power lines. Looking up, Ronaldo saw a noose still hanging from the bucket.

"The hell is going on?" Ronaldo asked.

"You really don't got a clue, do you, man?" Hernández said.

"Try me."

"Okay, tough guy." The big body turned to face Ronaldo. "The farther we go, the darker shit is going to get," he growled. "You didn't listen to the stories of the refugees like I did. That mass grave is just the beginning of the horrors we're going to see if we survive long enough."

Ronaldo stepped closer so they were almost chin to chin. "Do you have any idea what I saw here, or overseas during the wars? I'm not some virgin dumbass like Pierce, and if you actually started working with me instead of being an asshole, maybe, just maybe, I could help more."

Hernández seemed to consider this for a moment. "You're a cowboy, Salvatore," he said at last, "and just because you've seen some shit doesn't mean you've seen everything."

"You're right, but that doesn't mean you don't need me."

"I *need* you to listen to orders," Hernández said. "Sheriff Benson's job is to protect our border, and whoever killed those people is a direct threat to Los Angeles if they're still out here. There could also be a link to the Shepherds."

Ronaldo eased back a notch, scratching at his jaw.

"The reason I didn't tell you is because I believe whoever is responsible isn't former AMP," Hernández said. "I think it's former *marines*, but I can't be certain."

"What!" Ronaldo shook his head. "No possible way, man. Marines would never . . ."

"Really? 'Cause even a few randos could have done that, and you and I both know there have been some batshit-crazy marines that did some unspeakable shit overseas, so why not back here?"

Ronaldo couldn't deny it, but he couldn't pan the Marine Corps because of a few bad apples any more than one could give up on law enforcement over a few bad cops.

"If they are marines, when we find 'em I'm going to—"

"You'll do what I tell you to do," Hernández said. "You got that?"

Ronaldo nodded.

"I want to hear you say it."

"I'll do what you order, LT," Ronaldo said.

"Good. Time to get to our next stop, then."

They took off for a part of the town Ronaldo hadn't seen yet. When they arrived, Tooth and Pierce were waiting in a ditch. Both men got up but kept to the side of the road, looking east.

At first, Ronaldo didn't see what they were looking at, but then he followed the angle of their NVGs to a light pole. Something was hanging from it.

Not something. Someone.

Around the chest was a cardboard sign. Ronaldo zoomed in, but the writing was in Spanish.

"Anyone know what that says?" Tooth asked. "LT?"

Hernández looked down his rifle scope. "It's a Mexican proverb."

"So what's it mean?" Ronaldo asked.

Hernández lowered his rifle and said, "They tried to bury us, but they didn't know we were seeds."

"What the hell's that mean?" Tooth asked.

"I don't know, but it's probably connected to the cartel."

"The *cartel* hung that guy up and buried all those people?" Pierce asked.

"I've wondered if they're affiliated with the Shepherds," Ronaldo said. "Question is, Which faction?"

Ronaldo didn't know the details—only that the Vegas were all that remained of the Gulf Cartel and that many of the Sinaloas had fled south of the border. It was also possible the Shepherds were MS-13 or 18th Street, the Mexican Mafia, or a combination, just as the Vega family had become.

He checked the bloated and decomposing corpse. The kill was fairly recent—at least three days, but inside a week—which meant whoever did it may still be around.

"Let's get back to Bettis," Hernández said. "I've got one more place I want to check out tonight, and we're going to need the vehicles."

Ronaldo had a feeling they were heading to the Marine Corps Logistics Base. He also got the feeling it was key to all this. But if Hernández was right about this being the work of former marines, then he wasn't sure the LT or Pierce was up for what awaited them there. They were deputies—not even soldiers, and definitely not marines.

Ronaldo hoped to God it was the cartel's work, because if not, it would be on him, Tooth, and Bettis to do something they had never thought they would have to do: kill a fellow Devil Dog.

-18-

Vinny pulled the tail off a coconut shrimp and dipped the rest in pineapple sauce. They were delicious, and he was starving.

Yellowtail had his appetite back, too. He pushed his plate of discarded tails away and reached over for a shrimp, but Vinny pulled the plate away.

"Dude . . ."

"Come on, Vin, I need my nourishment," Yellowtail said.

Vinny sighed. "Whatever."

Yellowtail smiled and took three.

Across from them, Raff and Doberman sat facing the ocean. Both men were keeping a close eye on their Jeep, parked on the street next to the restaurant. Vinny was also keeping an eye on the boardwalk.

After their adventure getting here, he was on edge and keeping alert for any signs of trouble.

Raff also seemed uptight. He hadn't touched his *tacos al pastor* and was now staring out at the bay as if in a trance. The surf lapped higher on the sand, moving slowly up toward their table.

The warm breeze rustled their clothing as the sun sank into the Pacific. This beautiful city on the ocean, with its lush mountain backdrop, reminded Vinny of Italy. The locals were kind and hardworking, much like the people he remembered in Naples.

An attentive waiter with a big smile walked over to check on them. "More palomas?" he asked in English.

"*Sí, por favor*," Vinny said.

They hadn't eaten this well in days, and one more drink would help calm his nerves. They were watered down, anyway.

"Raff, better eat something, man," Yellowtail said. "But hey, if you're not going to, I can help with one of those tacos."

"Sure," Raff said.

"Not hungry?" Vinny asked.

Raff turned away from the pleasant ocean view. "I was just thinking about Don Antonio, Christopher, and Lino, wondering if they are looking at the Bay of Naples right now."

"Probably," Yellowtail said around a mouthful of taco. "Damn, these are *dope*."

Doberman pulled out his cell phone and looked at it.

"Get any reception yet?" Vinny asked.

"Nah."

"So how the hell are we going to find these dudes if we can't get a text or call?" Yellowtail asked.

Vinny wasn't sure. He had expected their phones to have some signal here. The city had decent infrastructure, and the problem wasn't the carrier.

"We still have time," Raff said, "but if Doberman doesn't get a signal in the next hour, we'll have to head into the mountains."

The waiter brought more drinks, and Vinny took a paloma. Raff stuck with water. He got up to look at their Jeep as two kids approached. But both youngsters kept going and ran down the beach to the surf.

There were a few other tables of people eating on the beach tonight. Tourists mostly: Americans, probably some Canadians, and Latin Americans. Not many, though. That wasn't a huge surprise. Most countries were reeling from the shattered global economy and the violence that followed. But there were still people who had money and the means to protect it. Vinny had seen a man and woman with a heavy security entourage following them down the boardwalk a few hours ago.

There was also a large police presence in the Malecón area, which made up a large section of the city's historic downtown. But it wasn't just the cops keeping the locals and the few tourists safe. A convoy of military trucks with masked soldiers had driven past the port when they arrived. And they had seen other soldiers patrolling in all areas of the city.

Vinny took a slug of his paloma as a group of college-age Mexican girls walked past, barefoot, sandals in hand, short dresses showing off their tanned legs.

Doberman looked away—something Vinny had seen him doing more often lately. Months ago, he would have been out of his chair and chasing those lovelies down the beach.

That made Vinny think of Carly Sarcone and the ruse they had pulled on her. He felt a twinge of guilt and considered asking for something stronger than watered-down tequila. But shots of the straight stuff would only make things worse.

"We're running out of time," Raff said, looking at his watch. "Let's head into the mountains and try to get a phone signal there."

Yellowtail finished off his beer and paid the bill. The walk to the Jeep was short, but Vinny looked over his shoulder twice to make sure they weren't being followed.

Raff got behind the wheel, and Yellowtail rode shotgun. The old Jeep coughed as Raff steered onto a cobblestone road. The clay tile roofs and the stone architecture of the churches and other old buildings also reminded Vinny of Naples.

The view changed as they climbed into the foothills of Conchas Chinas. Hotel resorts rose through the thick canopy of tropical hardwoods in the affluent southern part of Puerto Vallarta.

Farther up in the hills, the resorts and lavish estates gave way to shacks of corrugated metal and tar paper. Chickens scratched and squawked on the shoulder of the road, and a bent old man pulled a donkey with a rope halter.

The diesel engine of a military truck growled around the next corner, and Raff gave it a wide berth on the narrow roadway. In the back were a dozen soldiers, their faces covered with masks—and not because of the air quality, which was surprisingly good.

These men were still at war with an old enemy: the cartel—probably the same people Vinny was here to meet.

He tried to relax as they drove out of the last out-skirts of the city and into the mountains. The views over the ocean were spectacular. Fishing boats trying to beat the sunset motored back to the harbor with the day's catch.

Behind the Jeep puttered rusty cars and trucks, bringing workers back to their humble homes after long shifts at the resorts tucked away in hidden coves along the shore.

"Got a signal yet?" Raff asked Doberman.

He shook his head. "Nothing."

Raff pulled off on a winding dirt road that appeared to lead toward three radio towers. A trail of dust followed them.

At the top, Doberman sat up straighter. "I got some bars. Now let's see if I got any messages."

Vinny looked over at the burner phone they had used to set up the contact. Several messages popped on the screen. Doberman clicked on one.

"Got a message to meet them at nine o'clock."

"Where?"

"Place called Sayulita," Doberman said.

Vinny pulled out the map and cursed. The beach town was a good hour in the opposite direction, and they had to go through jungle to get there. He checked his watch: just after seven o'clock.

"We can make it if you drive fast, Raff," Vinny said.

Yellowtail gripped his gut and reached for the car door.

"Dude, what's wrong?" Vinny asked.

Yellowtail flung open the door and heaved into bushes.

"Jesus Christ, not again," Doberman said.

Yellowtail wiped his mouth off, muttering oaths in English and Italian.

"Get it all out, because it's a long drive," Vinny said.

Yellowtail heaved again, and Raff turned around and drove back the way they had come.

They sped through the city and out toward Nuevo Vallarta, where the newer hotels hugged the shore. Multimillion-dollar buildings, only half complete, reached toward the last rays of sun.

By the time they reached the jungle, it was completely dark. Roadside stands, closed for the day, offered guavas, bananas, and other produce from the little jungle farms.

A dusty old bus drove past, a string of cars and pickups in tow. Vinny felt better seeing there was still vehicular traffic out here. An empty road would have made him feel like a target.

Vinny thought back to the ferry ride. The pirates were part of a growing violent trend across the world. There would be plenty of people on these roads, watching for anything that looked like an easy take. Even a rusted old Jeep Wrangler might look tempting to some.

He pulled out his gun, feeling better with it on his lap.

Almost an hour later, they reached the turnoff for Sayulita. The old signs showed a picture of a beach with cocktails and umbrellas. They passed a soccer field and an old amphitheater, then another small farm with cattle behind barbed wire.

"Take that turn," Vinny told Raff.

They drove through the coastal town, passing

locals on dirt bikes and four-wheelers. The road dust was bad, but Vinny didn't mind. In the moonlight, ocean beaches stretched as far as he could see.

Mansions and resorts rose out of the thick canopy covering the hills. This was a little hidden paradise.

Three more turns, and they were at an old cemetery near the ocean.

"This is it," he said.

Raff kept the Jeep running but shut off the lights. An old woman walked down the dirt road with a huge bouquet of white lilies in her hand. She passed them by without even looking at the vehicle.

She stopped at a large headstone and placed the flowers at the base, then lit candles. In the glow, Vinny read the engraving: *García Valdez 1945–2014.* Her husband, he supposed.

More candles flickered at other graves across the cemetery. Vinny looked over his shoulder at an imposing crypt. A large photo of a young beauty queen with a white sash across her chest leaned against the pale stone.

Lights snaked up the road.

Two pickup trucks worked their way up the trail into the cemetery. A third vehicle, which looked like an old UPS truck, hung back. The trucks parked on the edge of the grounds, and all the doors opened, disgorging at least ten men.

"Must be them," Raff said.

The Sinaloa sicarios walked over, all of them holding guns. Several powerful flashlight beams hit the Jeep, so that Vinny had to put a hand to his face. A man walked over to the front of the car and tapped the window.

"Out of the car, *ese*," he said in decent English.

Vinny opened the door. The woman at the grave stood and looked at the man.

"*Fuera, vieja,*" the man said to her. "Beat it."

She took a step forward, then must have seen the guns. Muttering under her breath in Spanish, she walked away.

"Which one of you *pendejos* is Vinny Moretti?" the man asked.

Vinny had enough Spanish to recognize this as an insult. And he suddenly felt stupid for not being more prepared.

"I'm Vinny. Which one of you is Sebastián?" He didn't know the guy's last name, but that was the contact Christopher had set up for them. And he hadn't anticipated these guys being assholes.

He started to wonder whether these were even the right guys.

"I'm Sebastián."

All but one of the flashlights shut off, and a man swaggered forward. He wore a red bandanna and loose clothing. He stepped up closer, and Vinny saw the dark eyes and weathered face of a man who had worked the fields for most of his life. That made judging his age difficult, as did his rough smoker's voice.

Sebastián looked at Raff, Yellowtail, Doberman, then back to Vinny.

"Welcome to Mexico," he said, raising arms adorned with tattoos and leather bracelets. "You're about to get a taste of some of the best drugs *en el mundo*."

He chuckled and lowered his arms.

"But first I need you to hand over your keys and then bow your heads."

Vinny looked to Raff.

"The fuck?" Yellowtail said.

"Don't worry about your Jeep," Sebastián said. "We will take good care of it, and the hoods are for your own good."

Yellowtail looked to Raff, but Vinny was in charge, and this was his decision.

"Do it," he said.

Raff gave a nod, and Sebastián's comrades surrounded them.

Vinny tried not to resist as the black hood dropped over his face. As he was pushed toward one of the pickups, he wondered whether he was ever coming out of this jungle.

* * *

Camilla was eating Jell-O when Dom arrived in the isolated hospital ward.

"Wow, that shit still exists?" he asked.

She smiled—not the full dazzling experience, but enough to make her dimples show.

"It's not bad, either," Camilla said. "But I'm ready to get the hell out of here."

"You got shot in the stomach," said Dom. "You're lucky you can eat at all."

She set the spoon on the tray. "So, you gonna tell me why you look like you should be here instead of me?"

Dom had forgotten his bruised face and bandaged ear.

"What's the other guy look like?" she asked.

As if in answer, Moose walked in.

"Damn. You too?" Camilla said.

"Long story," Dom said.

"Dom beat me up," Moose said. "Won fair and square."

"Wait . . ." Camilla looked at each of them again. Her brow rose. "You're shitting me, right?"

"Like I said, long story."

"I'm not going anywhere, obviously, so please, enlighten me."

Dom pulled a chair to her bedside and, in a low voice, explained everything that had happened, including Marks's order not to tell anyone outside the task force.

"Esteban Vega? The *real* one?" she practically shouted. "You're lucky he didn't kill you both."

Dom put a finger to his lips. "We don't know who's listening."

"Right. Sorry."

Moose checked out the window for the police officer posted on the floor.

"We're good," he said. "Guy's down the hall."

"I don't trust any of 'em," Camilla said. "Good thing they don't know I'm a cop."

"Yeah . . ." Dom didn't trust the cops guarding this floor, either, but at least they were in the dark about who she was. Marks had made sure of that. To keep the cops under his command alive, secrecy was paramount.

"If Mariana López's people knew you were here, they'd send an army to kill you," Moose said.

"Someone tell me that bitch is going to jail for life," Camilla said.

"Problem isn't putting her in jail; it's keeping her there," Dom replied.

"True," Camilla said. "We're going to need a bigger prison to hold all the assholes."

She forced down a bite of something that looked like mashed potatoes, and grimaced. "Almost as bad as prison food."

"Any idea when you are getting out?" Moose asked.

"Doctor said I need some rehab first, but I'll do my best to get out of it. I don't want to miss the takedown of the Vegas. When's it going to happen?"

"Marks is setting it up. It'll come down when I debut in their fighting ring."

"Dom, you're serious?"

Moose had the same concerned look.

"It'll be fine," Dom said. "I can handle myself, and it's our best shot at taking down Esteban—"

A knock came, and a nurse cracked the door. "Camilla Santiago?" he asked.

"That's me."

The nurse stepped in the room. "I'm Jake, and I'll be taking over for Andrea."

"Why? Where'd she go?" Camilla asked.

"She's not feeling well. But don't worry, I'll take great care of you."

He smiled as he crossed over to her bed and checked her IV line. His forearm was tattooed with ocean waves.

The nurse eyed Dom, then Moose.

"You want us to leave?" Dom asked.

"No, you're okay. Just got a few things to check."

Dom waited for Jake to finish his rounds. When he left, Camilla said, "I really liked Andrea. Weird that she just went home. She didn't seem sick."

Moose closed the door again.

"Oh, well, if you guys are going to stay a few more minutes, will you turn the radio on?" Camilla said. "I want to hear the news."

Dom went to the windowsill. "Local or wide?" he asked.

"Wide."

He selected a station in Tucson and watched the parking lot as the news trickled in.

"Want some?" Camilla asked.

Moose was looking at her tray of food.

"I am kinda hungry, to be honest," he said.

She passed the tray over. "Knock yourself out."

Dom rolled his eyes.

The Tucson announcer came on. "*Refugees from the Midwest and Northeast continue to flood Florida in search of sanctuary,*" he said. "*Local authorities say the border is being shut down for an undisclosed time.*"

Florida, like the other Gulf states, was taking in a lot of refugees from areas hit hard during the war, and Dom wasn't surprised they were closing their borders.

"Saint Paul," Camilla said.

Dom turned the dial. This time, the announcer was an older woman. She must have been in the business for some time, judging by her calm demeanor when reporting devastating news.

"*Chicago has been declared a dead zone, and refugees are now being sent to the following sanctuary cities, which are equipped with medical staff for treating radiation exposure.*"

Dom didn't recognize most of the cities, but almost all were in Iowa, Nebraska, Wisconsin, and Minnesota.

A bit of a surprise, since the grain belt had gotten some fallout during the war. But only time would tell whether next year's crop was affected.

He changed to a local station as an ambulance screamed up to the ER outside. The name "Palmdale" jerked Dom's attention back to the broadcast.

"Hi, all you beautiful angels. This is Regina Diaz with news from beyond the walls." The former singer's normally peppy voice was dull this morning.

"Palmdale has been added to the growing list of cities that travelers are advised to avoid," she said. *"We have unconfirmed reports of sheriff's deputies killed there."*

Dom froze up, and Moose walked over to the windowsill. Camilla sat up straighter in her bed. "Oh, no," she said.

"I doubt that's your—"

"Quiet," Dom said, cutting Moose off.

"The Sheriff's Department has not confirmed this report, but refugees from Palmdale have been flooding LA's northern border."

Dom leaned against the wall, feeling defeated.

Moose put a hand on his shoulder. "I'm sure your dad's okay."

"Really? Because it sounds like a war zone out there."

"He's survived other war zones," Camilla said.

Dom tried not to show his emotion. "We better go," he said, putting a hand on her arm. "Feel better. You'll be out of here in no time."

"You're leaving?"

"We got work to do."

She sighed. "Come and see me again soon. I'm bored as hell in here."

As they left, Camilla's brother, Joaquín, came down the hall.

"Hey, Dominic," he said with a big smile. "How's my sis?"

"'Sup, man? She's doing pretty good," Dom said. He exchanged a homie handshake with Joaquín and then went to the nurses' station. He was worried about his dad but also about Camilla.

When the nurse didn't look up, Dom tapped the Formica to get her attention. He discreetly pulled out his badge and slipped it across, then pulled it back before she could read the name.

"I want to see your current roster of nurses," he said.

She frowned and then dug through some paperwork on the desk.

Dom went over the list. "How long has Jake worked here?"

"Years," said the receptionist. "Why? Is he in some sort of trouble?"

"No." Dom walked over to Moose, feeling better about the situation until they passed the officer posted there. He was sitting in a chair, reading an old magazine, and didn't even look up.

Dom would have slapped him on the back of the head if he weren't undercover. The guy was useless. If any López allies found out Camilla's identity, she was a sitting duck.

The radio under Moose's coat crackled in the garage stairwell. It was Marks, and they were needed at the Angel Pyramids, where a gang shoot-out at the farmers' market had left civilians dead.

Dom and Moose ran to the Challenger.

The radio chirped as soon as Dom started the car. Like the news earlier, none of the reports coming in were good.

A riot at a food stand in Compton, a coordinated robbery at the port by masked men who killed two workers, another large group of refugees at a border entry, and worst of all, the gunfight at the Angel Pyramids farmers' market.

Dom and Moose grabbed their SWAT gear from the trunk, changed, and put on their masks.

A chain of flashing lights surrounded the blocks south of the Angel Pyramids. Dom parked behind an ambulance that was being loaded with two injured civilians.

He kept his face covered with the black mask. Today's air quality wasn't bad enough to require his breathing apparatus. And instead of goggles, he wore sunglasses.

Carrying his M1A SOCOM 16, Dom worked his way through the maze of vehicles to get to the front lines: an open-air market in the courtyards of apartment buildings bordering the Angel Pyramids.

The empty stands were filled with vegetables grown on balconies and rooftops, and fruit from Mexico. Smashed tomatoes and avocados littered the concrete outside a stall where a body still lay facedown.

Four bloody bullet holes dotted the back of a man still holding a head of cauliflower.

Police stood around the corpses. Dom counted five, including two women. Then he saw the body of a child.

He lowered his head, overcome with grief as he continued to the staging area inside an abandoned bank. SWAT snipers had set up on rooftops across the street, and an assault team was hunkered down in a parking lot.

Another team stood by, and two armored vehicles were parked on the street.

Inside the bank, Lieutenant Marks had set up a command center. He was on the radio when Dom and Moose got there.

"Where do you want us?" Dom asked.

"Here," Marks replied. "Can't risk you getting hurt, and we got plenty of firepower if negotiations with these assholes go bad."

Dom looked out the window at the building the Lópezes were holed up in.

"They got two of ours up there, plus a few civilians," Marks said. "They want to exchange them for Mariana."

Marks pulled Dom aside while they awaited Chief Stone's orders.

"You hear about the sheriff's convoy hit outside the walls?" Marks asked.

"Yeah. Was it . . ."

"I don't think so," Marks said. "From what I was told, the Desert Snakes didn't head toward Palmdale. Try not to worry. Your dad can handle whatever they find out there."

Dom nodded, though he felt frozen.

"They said if we don't give up Mariana, they'll kill the first hostage in ten minutes," announced a sergeant across the room.

Marks went over to the window and looked through binoculars. "My God, they have one of ours on the roof."

Dom and Moose joined him.

Two hostages, a woman and a cop, were standing near the ledge, hands tied behind them.

"Shit," Marks muttered.

The side door swung open, and a masked cop burst inside. "Sir, we've got unknown vehicles heading our way."

Dom rushed outside to the sound of diesel engines and shouting. City trucks repainted red sped down the left side of the road. More came on the right, their beds filled with sicarios.

Four SUVs and several pickups with mounted machine guns followed the trucks.

"Back! Back!" Marks shouted.

The officers in the parking lot changed positions to aim at the approaching vehicles, and so did the snipers. But Dom could see they were vastly outnumbered.

"Holy shit," Moose said.

The SWAT officers made a run for it, but the trucks were already closing in. They slammed into the cruisers on the street, pushing them up onto the curbs with rusted plows used months earlier to clear the roads.

But instead of opening fire on the running cops, the gunners pointed their weapons at the building the López sicarios were holed up in.

Ducking behind a wall with a group of other officers, Dom watched what had to be Vega soldiers form a perimeter around the building.

A tall, thin man with a bullhorn got out of a Cadillac sporting gold rims and skinny tires. He looked familiar, and Dom realized he had seen him at the fight in the cemetery.

"What's he saying?" Moose asked.

Another officer translated. "Esteban Vega has ordered you all to put down your weapons, release the hostages, and give up. Do this, and you will live. If you refuse, you will endure a fate far worse than death."

Dom looked to Marks, who had stood up to watch. One by one, the other officers and SWAT teams got up, looking amazed.

"What did Camilla say about needing a bigger prison?" Moose asked.

It took only a few minutes for the López soldiers to give up. A group came outside with their hands up. Next came the hostages, who were led across the street, where officers waited to herd them safely away.

Marks went out to talk to the Vega soldier, and Dom listened.

"A gift from Esteban to Chief Stone," said the sicario. "Now, get off our turf and don't come back, or next time, there will be blood."

Dom couldn't believe his eyes as the López soldiers were loaded up without incident and shipped off to join their leader, Mariana, in jail.

"The enemy of your enemy is your friend," Marks said to Dom. "Hope your dad realizes that someday."

As Dom and Moose headed back to the car, an orange skyline threatened Los Angeles with yet another dust storm. It was worse beyond the walls, and as Dom drove away, he couldn't help but wonder whether his dad was still out there.

-19-

Dust storms swept across the desert landscape for most of the day. Ronaldo's team stayed holed up in the ransacked convenience store, waiting for the wind to die and darkness to fall.

Last night, they had taken the Humvee out and discovered yet another grisly scene, on the road to the Marine Corps Logistics Base. Bodies were hung from poles on the side of the road, their flesh shriveled, eyes plucked out by crows.

Hernández had returned to their hideout after that—he had enough to call in to Sheriff Benson and ask for backup.

But so far, they hadn't heard a peep from command.

Waiting was always hard. But it was especially hard now, when Ronaldo wanted to be out looking for his daughter. Still, maybe something on that base would give them a clue to where the Shepherds were.

Or maybe they are *the Shepherds.*

An hour later, the storm died and Ronaldo climbed

the roof with the sniper rifle. A blanket of dust covered the roads and sidewalks like dirty snow.

Just after dusk, Hernández joined him on the roof.

"Got news, Salvatore."

"We got backup?"

"Negative. Backup isn't coming."

"Come again?"

"We lost an entire team—hit by raiders yesterday, about thirty miles north of here on Fourteen, near Palmdale."

"Jesus. How . . ."

"I told you what it's like out here," Hernández said. "Bloodthirsty bandits everywhere."

"So what's that mean for us?"

Hernández scratched the back of his neck and studied the horizon.

"It means this is on us," he finally said. "We go into the base tonight and figure out what we're dealing with."

Ronaldo nodded.

"And, Salvatore," Hernández said, "you better fucking listen to orders."

"I will. You have my word."

A few hours later, the team was geared up and preparing to move out. The plan was simple: park the M-ATV about a mile from the base, then go in on foot to look around.

This time, they would stay together.

Ronaldo liked the plan, though he wasn't sure they had enough firepower to win a big fight.

He drove with the headlights off, using his NVGs to see. Once they got through town, they crossed Highway 40, then another road, to a section of town with few houses. It was supposed to keep them from being spotted, but the dirt roads kicked up dust that showed even in the dark.

Ronaldo drove to the last dwelling, a largish triplex with solar panels and an aboveground pool. The tan dirt of the front yard was littered with trash and junk.

"Park here," Hernández said. "We'll do the rest on foot."

The men shouldered their rifles and fanned out in combat intervals.

After clearing the triplex, the team gathered in the backyard.

"You guys ready?" Hernández asked.

Three nods from the marines, and a delayed nod from Pierce.

"Keep quiet, watch your buddies' six, and don't do anything stupid," Hernández said. "That means no firing unless I tell you or we're fired on first."

"Copy, boss," Ronaldo said.

"I'll take point," Hernández said.

Under the glow of the rising moon, the big lieutenant trotted off toward a wall of California junipers that blocked the view of the base.

Hernández led them to the other side, scanned, and started across a field to the perimeter of the base. Tracks separated them from a chain-link fence topped with razor wire.

Ronaldo looked for sentries or patrols they might have missed, but the base was dark, and nothing moved in the green field of his NVGs.

After crossing the tracks, Tooth took a pair of bolt

cutters out of Bettis's pack and went to work cutting a doorway.

Hernández went first. He squeezed through and held security while the rest of the team went through.

Then they headed for the first warehouse in a row of three. If hostiles were hiding out, they would be in this area since the other half of the base had been destroyed during the war.

The team skirted a crater in the parking lot, made by a bomb meant for the warehouses they were running toward. The blast had knocked over three semitrailers and burned them to their metal bones.

Ronaldo crossed the parking lot, keeping low and scanning for hostiles. Not far from the first warehouse, he found another body hanging from a light pole. The other men saw it, too, and halted.

"Jesus," Ronaldo whispered.

This one was different from the ones they had seen on the road last night. It was a dead marine, still in most of his uniform. The barbarians who killed him had removed every organ from his chest. His rib cage had been cracked outward, as if a grenade had exploded inside him.

More Spanish was written on the side of the warehouse ahead.

"Those who don't give their heart and soul will lose both," Hernández said.

"This is some evil shit," Tooth whispered.

Another chill passed through Ronaldo, and not much spooked him. Marines were not responsible. They would never do this, especially to one of their own. This stank of the cartel.

The hunt continued. The first two warehouses

were filled with racks of supplies but showed no sign of recent activity.

The third structure was likewise empty—nothing but a run-down truck parked inside.

When the team went back outside, headlights speared the horizon.

Hernández motioned for the rest of the group to take cover behind the carcass of a flatbed trailer. The beams turned off Highway 40 and came down the road along the front of the base. Ronaldo got up and zoomed in on what he hoped was a black Humvee.

But it was a pickup truck. A second dark shape drove behind it, using the lights from the first to see the road. That was suspicious because it was smart.

Both vehicles headed for the warehouses obliterated by bombs. An administration building separated the team from that area. Hernández gave the order to advance.

In the short run across a parking lot to the building, they came across three more corpses strung up on poles. All were marines. Spray paint marked the concrete in Spanish.

This time, they didn't bother stopping for Hernández to translate. Their mission was simple: end the fucks responsible for killing Devil Dogs.

Hernández cut through a plot surrounded by a fence of ironwood trees. From here, they had a better look at the two rows of destroyed warehouses.

They were out there somewhere, hiding amid the destruction. It was smart. No one would think to search for them in a place that looked as though it had been blown to bits.

Ronaldo crept past the trees for a better view. The first two and the last two warehouses in each row were destroyed. But in both rows, the middle one was only damaged, still standing.

There the vehicles had parked, right in front of the warehouse nearest the tracks. Ronaldo finally identified the second truck: a black Humvee.

Ten men loitered outside the open doors of the warehouse. Two were smoking cigarettes.

Hernández motioned to continue to the last clump of trees. Electrical boxes and a concrete retaining wall also provided some cover. A voice shouted as the Desert Snakes took up position.

Ronaldo flipped up his night-vision optics to look with his own eyes. What he saw seized his breath.

In the open warehouse near the tracks, two men were wrestling a woman to the floor, and a child was sobbing nearby. It wasn't just the sight of kidnapped people that had him shocked. These men were wearing the same uniform Ronaldo once wore.

They were indeed marines.

He crouched next to the lieutenant. "We've got to take them down," Ronaldo said.

"Fuck no," Hernández said. "I count eleven of them, and there are five of us. Even with the drop, it would be dicey. And there could be more out there."

"Then we kill them, too," Ronaldo said.

"Salvatore, I said—"

A flashlight beam flickered across the parking lot, and Ronaldo backed behind the electrical boxes with Hernández. Pierce, Tooth, and Bettis ducked behind the trees.

Hernández put his optics on Ronaldo as if to say, *Don't you fucking try* anything.

"We can take 'em," Tooth said quietly.

Bettis patted his sniper rifle and nodded.

"*No*," Hernández grunted.

A low rumble grew louder, and Ronaldo peered above the electrical box to see a train coming toward the base. He leaned back down. It was a perfect distraction.

"You don't have to help," Ronaldo said to Hernández. "Tooth, Bettis, and I will do it."

The train's horn blared, and the flashlight beam flitted away. A panicked wail came in the respite after the air horn, as the men started tearing at the woman's clothes.

Ronaldo gave a nod to Tooth, then Bettis. They ran for firing positions across the road separating them from the destroyed warehouses.

"Salvatore!" Hernández growled.

Fuck him, Ronaldo thought, taking off after his teammates.

Gunfire cracked just as Ronaldo got to the mound of rubble and sheet metal that remained of the first warehouse. Rounds smacked into the trees and the electrical boxes they had left Hernández and Pierce hunched behind.

Tooth and Bettis moved into flanking positions while Ronaldo stayed put to lay down covering fire. He rose for a better view of three men running away from the warehouse, shoulder-firing automatic rifles as if they had unlimited ammo.

Hernández cried out and went down on his back

while Pierce took off running. Somehow, the young man made it away from the hail of gunfire without getting picked off.

Ronaldo looked back to the warehouse just as Bettis's sniper rifle cracked and one of the three runners went down.

The chaplain was no doubt saying another silent prayer right now as he acquired the next target.

The second man went down with another head shot.

Ronaldo seized the opportunity and got up to fire at the third man crossing the parking lot toward Hernández. A three-round burst brought him down.

With Tooth and Bettis out of view, Ronaldo bolted back across the street to the electrical boxes, where Hernández gripped his shoulder.

"Stay down, LT," he said.

More gunfire exploded from the warehouse. Ronaldo counted four muzzle flashes before bullets pounded their position, forcing him down.

"You okay?" he asked Hernández.

"Yeah, I think so."

Ronaldo turned back to the warehouse and fired a burst at an approaching man. He fell to his back, and Ronaldo moved back to cover as more rounds slammed into the electrical box.

Tooth and Bettis would be in a flanking position soon. All Ronaldo had to do was stay with Hernández. But the LT didn't seem to want to get down. He grabbed his rifle and scooted back to another box while Ronaldo fired again.

The sniper rifle cracked again, and then came the automatic chatter from Tooth's M4. Three more enemies went down. Ronaldo counted three more, all inside the garage now.

"Cover me when I tell you to," Ronaldo said.

"What?" Hernández said. "You fucking crazy?"

"Not always."

Ronaldo waited for Bettis to take down another guy in the warehouse before giving the order. "Now."

He got up and took off running.

A burst of gunfire came from behind him as Hernández rejoined the fight.

Ronaldo ran across the open lot, trying not to flinch as bullets zipped past from a shooter inside the garage. He could see the woman and her son inside the open bay now, and all he could think about was Elena and Monica.

He had to save these people and find out who their captors were.

Another hostile got up from behind the Humvee and aimed at Ronaldo. There was no time to get down, only to keep running.

A muzzle flash came from the left as Tooth dropped the guy behind the Humvee.

Ronaldo moved inside the building with Tooth. Bettis was out there, hidden, covering them.

A bullet from his rifle found the neck of a hostile Ronaldo hadn't even seen until he was already dead. The guy slumped behind fuel drums in the garage.

Ronaldo saw one more figure darting for a door in the distance. Aiming for the legs, he squeezed off a shot, then another when the first one missed. Tooth fired at the same time before Ronaldo could stop him.

The guy went down, and Tooth and Ronaldo ran over.

Behind them, Hernández and Bettis secured the area. Pierce was out of sight, probably hiding.

When Ronaldo got to the garage, he saw that the guy he shot wasn't going to be much help. Tooth had hit him in the back of the head.

Bettis ran inside and knelt with the woman and her child. Seeing they were safe, Ronaldo checked the downed enemies to see if any were still alive. He scanned the dark garage and found a guy choking on his own blood.

Ronaldo leaned down and put a hand under the man's shoulder, hoisting him up so his head was above his heart. The name tag over his breast pocket read "Clare." He had PFC insignia on his collars.

Wild eyes, full of fear, locked on Ronaldo as blood leaked from multiple bullet holes.

"It's okay," Ronaldo said. "We'll get you patched up and help you, but I need you to tell me something. Are you the Shepherds?"

Tooth crouched down with a medical kit.

Clare choked, and pink froth bubbled from his mouth.

"Come on, I can make the pain go away," Ronaldo said. "Tell me if you're the Shepherds or where they are."

Tooth held up a shot of morphine.

"Do something good with your life, kid," he said.

Clare looked at the two men in turn, then tried to speak, coughing.

"Not . . . Shepherds," he said.

"Do you know where they are?"

The kid managed a nod.

"Where?" Ronaldo asked. "Tell us where they are."

"More . . . in . . . Vega . . ." Clare said, choking.

"What?" Ronaldo said. "Come on, kid, tell us where they are!"

PFC Clare's lips moved like those of a fish out of water, but nothing came out.

His eyes rolled up, and then he was gone.

"God *damn*," Ronaldo said.

He looked around the scene, counting twelve dead bad guys. Most of them looked like former marines. But some were cartel affiliates.

Ronaldo had seen much over his career, especially during the past year. But nothing that rivaled this evil.

* * *

Antonio had a stomach full of pizza and was lusting for wine, but he wasn't going to break his cardinal rule of not indulging before or during business.

He sat on the torn couch of their apartment, waiting for the hunt to begin.

Christopher slept in the bedroom—out like a light, judging by his snoring. But Lino was at the window, stiff as a statue, keeping an eye on the courtyard and balconies for any sign of hostiles.

Open pizza boxes lay on the broken kitchen counter. A cockroach skittered across the cracked surface, and Antonio was glad he'd had his fill. They had cleaned the place up, but here in the slums there was little one could do about the vermin.

A knock came on the door. Lino scampered quietly over, pistol in hand.

Antonio grabbed his gun off the table and went to wake Christopher. By the time they got to the living room, Lino had opened the door to let Diamante into the apartment.

He was breathing heavily from running up the flight of stairs.

"We got to hurry," he said.

Christopher stroked his goatee. "Why?"

"The woman that I told you about, Violetta, the one that knows Roberto Canavaro—she is getting off work soon," Diamante said. "If you want to know where they sleep at night, she is your best bet."

Antonio already knew the story. Violetta, girlfriend of Diamante's cousin, worked at a café across from University of Naples Federico II, where Roberto Canavaro liked to stop in from time to time for an espresso and pastry and to fraternize with a few of the baristas or play chess with the college students.

From what Antonio could remember, Roberto was an educated man with a love for Italian history and philosophy. Apparently, he had studied the art of betrayal. Unfortunately for him, so had Antonio.

"Let's go," he said, talking over Christopher and Diamante.

Both Lino and Christopher concealed submachine guns under their coats. Antonio took an extra pistol, tucking it in the back of his waistband.

The moon was already glowing over the rooftops.

Diamante had his own vehicle, a blue Audi SUV, parked in the lot. Christopher got into the passenger seat, and Antonio got into the clunker BMW with Lino.

"Don Antonio," Lino said as they pulled out of the lot, "I have a question."

"What?"

Lino swiped at his scarred chin. "Was killing those old men necessary when we got here?"

Antonio looked over at the soldier. Unlike Frankie and Carmine, Lino had never once questioned him over the years.

"Because if it was, then what are we going to do about Diamante?" Lino continued. "I don't trust him, even if my sister does."

Antonio relaxed when he saw where Lino was going with this. "I don't trust anyone, and that's why Christopher is riding with him," he said. "Your sister has good instincts. She survived all these years over here on her own. And besides, we don't have any option except Diamante."

The rest of the drive to the southern part of the city was quiet, and Antonio spent the time thinking of the past and the future. Angela, Lino's sister, was one of the last relatives they had left in Naples after their other relatives moved to Rome or South America, as Vito had done after the ambush.

Now his family was spread out across the world again. In Mexico, his nephew was on a mission with several of his most trusted men to secure a new deal. And back at the compound, Lucia and Marco were waiting for Antonio.

If all went according to plan, he would be with them soon, and Vinny would return with a new supplier to continue building their empire. But a lot of stars had to align for that to happen, and for the first time on the trip, Antonio feared that something would go bad.

He shook away the thoughts.

Lino sped up to keep pace with Diamante. The Audi had pulled onto the freeway. There wasn't much traffic out tonight—the one similarity to Los Angeles. With fuel shortages worldwide, most people couldn't afford to drive. In Europe, gas was more expensive than rent.

Diamante pulled off about ten blocks from the bay and turned down a road lined with trees. Motorcycles and scooters were parked neatly along the curbs.

Antonio was so busy admiring the cobblestone streets that he almost missed the turnoff for a place he remembered better than any other.

Lino stared at the looming basilica. The facade and Roman columns were lit up. A police car was parked outside, and an officer spoke to a pedestrian on the sidewalk.

Antonio felt the sour drip of anxiety, and not because of the police. The memory of the massacre twisted in his gut. A wave of anger rushed through him, and his jaw flexed as they passed.

The Basilica di San Paolo Maggiore towered above the street—a shrine to death and betrayal. Scenes from that day replayed in his mind.

"We'll avenge them," Lino said. "You have my word, Don Antonio."

The drive took them through the ancient blocks of churches and other stone buildings over two centuries old. But it wasn't just the history Antonio could see that filled his thoughts. The BMW thumped over a street built on land settled by Greeks over 2,800 years ago.

It was hard to fathom the history beneath their tires. For most of his life, Antonio had been determined to make his mark in this city, but while it would always be his home, it would never be part of his empire again.

No, his destiny had taken him to Los Angeles for a reason, in a cruel twist of fate that had left so many of his family members dead in the Basilica di San Paolo Maggiore.

And soon he would get his revenge.

The historic university was on the next street.

Students strolled on the sidewalks. A group hung out smoking cigarettes near a statue. Unlike in the United States, most of the educational institutions in Italy had remained open despite the worldwide turmoil.

As Lino parked the car, Antonio wondered whether this might be a good place for Marco to come in a few years. After the Canavaros were nothing but bones.

A little squadron of Vespas sped by as Antonio got out. His hand darted to his waistband, then stopped when he saw they were just students, not the thugs he was used to seeing back at the Four Diamonds.

Christopher led the way across the road to the café, where Diamante pulled out a cigarette.

"I thought we were in a hurry," Christopher said.

Diamante frowned and tucked the cigarette behind an ear.

The café was bustling with students and locals enjoying pastries and espressos, reading textbooks, working on laptops. Lino stayed outside while Christopher followed Antonio in. The sprawling café had wood tables, and a marble bar around a gleaming bank of brass urns, valves, and levers.

"There," Diamante said, looking at a petite twenty-year-old girl behind the bar. The cappuccino machine hissed as she moved nimbly, making drinks for three waiting students.

"You're up," Antonio said to Diamante. They walked up to the bar while Christopher found a seat facing the windows.

"*Ciao, Violetta,*" Diamante said to get her attention.

The young girl looked up, smiled, and held up a finger. Then she finished making the drink and handed it to a young man.

Antonio went to the register and ordered an espresso for himself, and coffee for Christopher, before joining Diamante in the line of customers.

"I thought you were almost off," Diamante said to her.

"Shift is over, but the manager wants me a bit longer," Violetta replied. Her eyes shifted to Antonio. He held her gaze, sizing her up, trying to see how much she knew about what she was getting involved with.

The innocence and absence of fear told him she had no clue.

"Go ahead and go home," said a second barista with braided dark hair. She was a mature beauty in her thirties, maybe even forties.

Violetta nodded and took off her apron as the new woman stepped up to the machine.

"I'm going to have a cigarette," Diamante said.

Antonio nodded and turned to watch him go.

"Want an extra shot in this espresso?" said the new barista.

It took Antonio a moment to realize she was talking to him. He stepped up to the bar and noticed the silky black shirt that emphasized her eye-catching cleavage.

She cracked a half smile—cocky almost.

"I'm not supposed to," she said, "but I'd rather give this extra one to you than to one of those asshole students."

"No, two is fine," he said. "Otherwise, I'd be up all night, and this old man needs his sleep."

She looked up again, her dark brown eyes holding him. "You don't look old to me," she said. "You remind me of someone, actually."

Antonio scrutinized her, but he didn't recognize this girl.

A male student wearing black-rimmed eyeglasses and a ponytail stepped up to the bar, huddling a little too close to Antonio as he watched for his drink.

Antonio gave the young man a glare. That did the trick. He backed away and pulled out his phone, suddenly busy scrolling through text messages.

"I haven't seen you here before," said the barista.

"Just passing through—always wanted to try this place. How long's it been here?"

"About ten years. I've worked here for a few. It's my second job . . ." she smiled again. "Do you want some sugar?"

Antonio felt his cheeks heat up. Apparently, it showed.

"In your espresso," she clarified.

"Yes, a pinch."

"Where do I know you from?" she asked.

Antonio smiled politely at the woman, curious now. "I'm not sure."

"Do you mind?" said the kid with the ponytail. "I got shit to . . ."

Antonio turned and said, "Have a seat before I put you in one."

The young man's eyes narrowed behind the over-size glasses, but Antonio didn't move.

"Yeah, okay," he said, retreating to his friends. They all gawked at Antonio as the kid sat down and whispered something.

When Antonio turned back to the bar, the woman had put down a coffee and an espresso cup. Under the cup, she had placed a note with her name and a phone number.

Irene Canavaro.

Antonio nearly choked. No wonder Roberto came here.

The dumb shit Diamante thought the Canavaro underboss was coming to hit on Violetta when, in fact, he was just coming to see this woman, who had to be his sister.

Antonio slipped his hand in his pocket to hide his wedding ring, hoping she hadn't already seen it. If she had, it didn't seem to bother her.

"You want to get a drink tonight, after your shift?" he asked.

She blushed and looked to see whether anyone was listening. Violetta was outside with Diamante now, but Antonio didn't need her.

"I was hoping you'd get around to that," Irene said. "But actually, how about coffee tomorrow morning? I have plans tonight."

He thought on it for a moment just to make her wait, then smiled. "I'd like that."

"You going to tell me your name?" she asked.

He reached across the bar with his right hand. "I'm Riccardo Angaran," he said. "Pleasure to meet you, Irene."

"Oh, a northern Italian," she said. "The pleasure is most certainly mine."

-20-

Sweat trickled down Vinny's back and belly. He lifted his tank top and fanned his chest with his cap. The back of the enclosed truck was a sauna.

Sebastián had said the journey would be long, but much more of this, and Vinny was going to pass out. The Moretti crew had spent the past twenty-four hours on a long drive through the jungle, stopping only to piss and, in Yellowtail's case, shit and puke.

At least, their cartel captors had taken off the stifling hoods a few hours earlier, which suggested they may be getting close. It made breathing easier, and he could now see the driver and passenger of an SUV behind them, as well as the sicario driving their battered Jeep.

They were in the mountain jungles, on a dirt road that didn't seem to end.

Another horsefly made it through the open window and landed at once on Vinny's neck. He slapped it hard, crushing it before it could nail him.

The truck thumped up and down over the washboard

road, eliciting a groan from Yellowtail. He was in bad shape, probably dehydrated.

Raff remained quiet on the other side of the enclosed truck bed. Earlier, he had reassured Vinny that things would be okay, but Vinny was starting to second-guess the decision he had made in Sayulita. He didn't normally question his father's or uncle's orders. But if Sebastián had kidnapped them and was planning to use them for ransom, then they had just made the same mistake the Yamazakis made.

And look how that turned out.

Vinny rested his head against the forward bulkhead. Trying to sleep was pointless, but he could try to relax a bit and save the mental energy.

Any hope of that ended with the distant sound of gunfire.

Small, round lights appeared in the side of the truck, one of them right above Yellowtail's head. That snapped him alert.

"Down!" Raff yelled.

Vinny and his three companions dropped flat against the floor as the truck swerved. Another volley of automatic fire pounded the front as it veered.

Flailing, Vinny tried to hold on to something. Then they were slammed in the side. The impact sent him crashing against the wall. Both glass windows shattered, raining glass on the four men.

The truck careened on its left wheels and began to tilt over. Raff cried out in pain, and Doberman fell on top of Yellowtail.

"Hold on!" Vinny yelled.

He felt the world go sideways for what seemed like

a minute before the truck finally slammed down on its side. It skidded to a rest. Gunfire continued outside, intermixed with sporadic shouts and screams.

Vinny glimpsed movement through the broken windows and finally saw who had attacked the convoy: Mexican soldiers in camo fatigues, helmets, and black boots. Some carried old-school M16 rifles and M9 pistols; others had shotguns. A few had long bolt-action rifles. One pointed his at Vinny.

Someone pulled him away just as a gunshot rang out and a bright new hole appeared in the door where he had been sitting.

"We got to get out of here!" Vinny shouted.

Raff took his hand off Vinny, and Doberman rolled off Yellowtail.

"Once we get the door open, run for the Jeep!" Vinny said.

Yellowtail sat up and ran a hand over his sweaty head.

Scooting away from the bashed and bent doors, Vinny started kicking the one on the right. Doberman joined in on the left, and together they banged the doors open to a scene of battle on the narrow jungle track.

Down the road a hundred yards, several bodies lay on the ground around a military truck. Flames and smoke billowed from the hood. The surviving soldiers had taken cover in the trees and brush but were still firing their rifles at the cartel's convoy.

Vinny scrambled out, keeping low and darting toward the cartel pickup behind them. When he got to the bumper, he looked back at the truck they had just escaped from, where his friends were still hiding. It was at the edge of the road, practically hanging over the mountainside. A few feet farther, and it would have teetered over, into the valley below.

The green and brown camo-painted military pickup that had T-boned them was smoking. A Mexican soldier had gone through the windshield, half his body on the hood, the other half bent inside the cab.

Up the road, more soldiers had flanked the convoy. The cartel soldiers were pinned down behind two trucks and the Morettis' red Jeep.

Vinny turned and looked through the cracked windshield of the truck he was hiding behind. Both of Sebastián's men were slumped over, dead.

A bullet broke the side mirror loose, and Vinny hunched back down. Raff was beside him now and moving to the driver's door.

Yellowtail and Doberman crawled out of the toppled truck and joined them.

"Stay down," Vinny said.

Raff pulled one of the dead cartel soldiers out from the driver's door. Then he grabbed an M9 from the corpse and handed it to Vinny. He also unstrapped a submachine gun.

"What about me?" Yellowtail said.

Bullets threw dirt, and one hit the front right tire with a loud hiss.

Vinny ejected the magazine in his pistol to make sure it had ammo. Fifteen cartridges remained—not a single round fired.

The question now was whether to kill the Mexican soldiers or to run.

Vinny looked down the mountainside and saw nothing but the tropical canopy. The squawk of birds and chirp of bugs reminded him they weren't on some hike. This was straight-up jungle.

Without water, they wouldn't survive a day out there. They were already dehydrated and exhausted from the journey. The only option was to take their chances fighting, and the side to be on was Sebastián's.

Raff rose to fire the submachine gun, and Vinny crawled into position near the deflated tire. They both fired to give Yellowtail and Doberman a chance to make it to the truck that had blindsided them.

Both made it there without being hit, and Vinny rolled back behind cover. Bullets pounded their position, another tire hissing, glass shattering.

Vinny spotted men closing in on the Jeep where Sebastián was crouched with two men. Three soldiers advanced, weapons shouldered. He aimed his pistol and fired four bullets, hitting one of the soldiers twice. Yellowtail and Doberman opened fire with machine guns they had recovered, taking down the other two guys approaching Sebastián.

"I'll cover you," Raff said.

He didn't give Vinny a chance to protest.

Rising up, Raff fired a burst from the submachine gun and yelled, "RUN!"

Vinny took off for the smoking truck that had slammed them. He got behind the passenger side and fired at the soldiers down the road, giving Raff a chance to escape.

"Go!" Vinny shouted. He was cautious with the last of the bullets, firing them one at a time. Raff kept his head down as he ran and almost made it to Vinny when a bullet hit him in the neck. He crashed to the dirt not far from the bumper.

"Raff!" Vinny yelled. He darted away from the truck and grabbed Raff's hand, dragging him to safety as rounds whizzed past.

Sweat stung Vinny's eyes, and he wiped it away with his upper arm. Then he helped Raff sit up against the passenger door. Blood dripped from Raff's neck, and Vinny grabbed his hand and pushed it against the flap of torn skin.

"Hold this and don't let go, okay?" Vinny said.

Raff managed a nod, but he was going into shock. Vinny grabbed the submachine gun and got down on his belly to see six pairs of boots fast approaching the vehicle. He knew there was little ammo left, and his pistol was completely out.

He considered getting Raff up to run back toward the rest of the convoy, but there was no time, and he wasn't sure Raff could move.

Yellowtail and Doberman weren't in view, and Vinny knew he couldn't count on the cartel soldiers.

He must do this on his own.

Ejecting the submachine gun's magazine, he counted eight bullets of the original thirty.

Make each count.

He crouch-walked to the back of the truck, leaving Raff at the front. At the back bumper, Vinny took a deep breath and prepared for what would probably be the final moments of his life.

Getting down on his belly, he lined up the sights and fired into the first Mexican soldier he saw.

His shots, and the audible *thunks* they made hitting

the soldier's flesh, got the attention of the other soldiers, who aimed their rifles in his direction.

Holding his breath, he braced for the onslaught of rounds that would be the last thing he ever felt.

But before a single shot came, the Mexican soldiers all started to jerk and flail, slinging blood from their bodies.

Vinny watched them all slump in front of him. One guy twitched, but a sicario finished him with a point-blank shot to the head.

Vinny stayed on the ground, perhaps in shock himself.

A few moments later, he felt a hand on his back. He rolled over, expecting Doberman. Instead, the man helping him up had a weathered face, and a red bandanna around his sweaty hair.

It wasn't just any sicario. It was Sebastián, and he was aiming a sawed-off double-barrelled shotgun at Vinny.

A grin crossed his wrinkled face as he lowered the weapon and reached down with his other hand.

"Nice shootin', hombre," Sebastián said.

Vinny took the hand and got to his feet. Sebastián brushed the dust from Vinny's shoulder.

"You look like you could use some weed, amigo," he said. "*Y una cervecita, ¿no?*"

"I'd go for some water first."

Vinny turned and saw his comrades standing behind them, all safe. But they weren't alone. Another man, his hands bound and a hood over his head, was being led back to one of the cartel vehicles.

Vinny squinted, noticing the guy's gait. There was

something familiar about him, but he was gone before Vinny could figure out who he was.

Sebastián handed Vinny a water bottle from his duty belt. Vinny took it to Raff first, who was standing and gripping the flesh wound to his neck.

"You okay?" he asked.

Raff nodded and drank the water, his hand still on his neck.

"*¡Vámonos!*" Sebastián called out. He looked to the Moretti crew. "You can ride with me now, amigos."

* * *

A day after raiding the Marine Corps Logistics base at Barstow, the Desert Snakes were back on the road. Ronaldo thought back to the final words of Private First Class John Clare, the marine turned traitor who had died in his arms.

"*More . . . in . . . Vega,*" he had said.

That could have meant any of several things. The Shepherds could have been linked to the Vega family in Los Angeles, but Ronaldo was increasingly convinced Clare meant Las Vegas, the city.

More in Las Vegas. That had to be it. The Moretti family and the Vega family were operating only in Los Angeles, as far as he knew. But the only way to find out was to check.

Hernández had radioed the new intel to Sheriff Benson and Lieutenant Marks. Then they had dropped the woman and her son back in Barstow. She had insisted on staying there, believing that her husband was still making his way home from the Midwest.

The Desert Snakes had finished patching up Hernández, who had decided to press on. They were now heading east toward Vegas, with Pierce driving the M-ATV just ahead of Ronaldo, Tooth, and Bettis in the Humvee.

They knew that after losing another LA County Sheriff's APC unit in Palmdale, the journey ahead would be more dangerous than ever. And Ronaldo respected that Hernández had decided to push on after being shot.

Raiders, bandits, and desperate people trying to survive posed a threat in every direction. The entire territory north of LA County had fallen into anarchy. For that reason, they had not taken Interstate 15, selecting the longer route of Interstate 40. The sight of another charred minivan on the shoulder suggested that the road less traveled could be just as dangerous.

They had decided to take Highway 66 after that, but any road to Vegas was a bigger gamble than putting your money down once you arrived.

Ronaldo pulled into the left lane to avoid the charred vehicle.

He turned around to look at Tooth, who was reading an old skin magazine they had found in an office drawer of their hideout in Barstow.

Tooth handed the magazine to Bettis. "Wanna check it out?"

"That trash? No, thanks."

"Don't act like you never looked at porn, old man."

"Actually, I haven't," Bettis said. "Never been in a strip club, either. Women are not meat."

"Brother, I hate to break it to you, but some women like to show their goods."

"Tooth, give it a rest, yeah?" Ronaldo said.

Bettis turned back around and studied the skyline. "Looks like a real nasty storm," he said.

Heat lightning flashed out of a thick black storm front that had turned brick red as it rolled across the Mojave. And Ronaldo guessed some of that dust still contained fallout from the nuke in Sacramento.

They were about three miles from Fort Mojave Indian Reservation when Pierce pulled off on Highway 95 to head north. The M-ATV halted in the road, and Ronaldo eased off the gas.

"What the hell's he doing?" Ronaldo muttered.

The radio crackled again, and this time Hernández told them to keep heading east. Ronaldo did so, heading for the Colorado River and Fort Mojave.

It was a smart move, for the storm caught up with them not long after, pounding the armored vehicles with fifty-mile-per-hour winds.

Pierce followed the interstate toward the Mojave Reservation, and Ronaldo drove like hell to keep up. Both vehicles were built for this, but the visibility was terrible.

"Careful," Bettis said.

Tooth had tossed the skin mag aside and was leaning forward to watch.

"Jesus," he said.

Bettis normally would have shot the younger man a glare, but his eyes were glued to the map as he tried to figure out where they were.

Pierce and Hernández turned down another road.

"Looks like we're coming up on Palms Resort," Bettis said.

"Or what's left of it," Ronaldo said.

Through the storm, he could see the shells of buildings. Several burned semis were scattered across a parking lot.

Pierce drove past, then around a junkyard, and finally into a small community that looked almost as bad as the Palms Resort.

Ronaldo was more worried about people firing on their vehicles out here than about the storm, but apparently, Hernández had the opposite concern. Not long after passing through the abandoned housing complex, they pulled up to a warehouse with a closed roll-up door.

"Clear the building with him," Ronaldo said to Tooth. "And put your mask on first."

The two men hopped out and lifted the door manually. Ronaldo pulled into a garage full of tires and vehicle parts. Pierce then drove the M-ATV inside.

Tooth closed the door, wincing from his arm injury. After struggling a moment, he got it down, sealing out the screaming wind that had already covered the floor in fine sand.

"We'll wait it out here," Hernández said.

"You do realize these babies are made for this, right?" Ronaldo asked.

He heard his condescending tone and walked it back as Hernández pulled off his mask.

"But I get why you wouldn't want to drive with the visibility so poor," Ronaldo added.

Hernández went to the back of the M-ATV, leaving the other four men standing there.

"Someone's pissed off," Tooth said.

"Well, he did get shot last night," Bettis said.

"Hey, is it okay to take our masks off?" Pierce asked.

Ronaldo shrugged and went back to the Humvee to clean his weapon—something he hadn't had a chance to do since the battle last night.

The storm continued to pound the warehouse for the next hour, but it did seem to be letting up some. When Ronaldo had finished cleaning his rifle, he went back to the M-ATV and knocked on the back hatch.

"LT," he said.

"What," Hernández growled.

"Just seeing how that wound is."

"It stings like a motherfucker."

"Want me to take a look?"

Hernández winced as he touched his shoulder. Ronaldo really did respect the guy for pushing ahead. He had to be in some major pain.

"You about got me killed last night," Hernández muttered.

Ah, shit. Here it comes.

"But you didn't. You came back, saved my ass, and then lit those assholes up like I've never seen before."

Ronaldo couldn't help but grin.

"We're Devil Dogs, LT. It's what we do."

"Yeah, well, I feel I owe it to you to keep going as long as I can now," Hernández said. "For the record, I'm hoping we find your daughter."

Ronaldo was a bit taken back by the change of heart. But saving a man's life had a way of changing his opinion of you.

"Lemme take a look at your bandage."

Hernández took off his body armor and shirt, then

turned around. The gauze and dressing were brown with congealing blood.

"Bettis, bring the med kit," Ronaldo said.

He brought it over, and Ronaldo carefully lifted away the dressings. The skin around the sutures was inflamed, but the wound didn't look infected.

"Looks pretty damn good," Bettis said.

"Getting shot ain't so bad," Hernández said.

"I disagree," Tooth said, flexing his arm.

They all laughed. But the jocularity was short-lived.

"Uh, guys," Pierce said. "I think I hear an engine outside."

Ronaldo rushed to the garage door, placing his ear against the metal. Sure enough, over the wind he heard the rumble of an engine.

"Someone's definitely out there," he said quietly.

Ronaldo went to the window at the far end of the warehouse for a look. The filthy glass was cracked and covered with grime, but he could see a pickup truck with what looked like a buffalo skull mounted on the grill.

The truck was parked, motor running, with only one man inside.

Hernández walked over just as it drove away.

"We clear?" he asked.

"Someone knows we're here, but looked like only one guy in a truck."

"Which means his buddies are probably waiting," Tooth said. "All of a sudden, these walls seem about as tough as a used rubber."

"Used rubber . . ." Ronaldo said, looking at Tooth. "I don't even want to know."

Tooth shrugged. "At least I use 'em. Can't be bringin' no little ankle biters into this shitty world."

"I say we get back to the road," Bettis said, all business.

"Follow me," Hernández said. "Drive hard, and don't stop even if we're followed."

"How about letting Bettis drive?" Ronaldo asked.

Hernández gave a nod, and Bettis and Pierce got into the M-ATV with him.

Ronaldo climbed into the Humvee, and when both rigs were running, Tooth lifted the roll-up door.

Bettis pulled out and drove through the desolate neighborhood they had gone by on the way in. Ronaldo followed, eyes out for the truck, but saw nothing bigger than a creosote bush.

Now that the storm had passed, Ronaldo could see the Colorado River alongside them. Across the river, to the east, was Fort Mojave, and to the west, the Dead Mountains Wilderness Area.

Everything out here looked dead to Ronaldo.

He relaxed slightly as they left the city behind them and headed back into the desert. Then he saw the rooster tail of dust behind them.

Tooth saw it, too. "Shit, looks like two trucks ... No ..."

"Three," Ronaldo said.

A tan Toyota Tacoma, a black Nissan Frontier, and the Ford with the buffalo skull. Each pickup had at least one man in the bed, holding a rifle or shotgun.

"Bandits that want our gear and rigs," Tooth said. "And our gasoline."

"Wantin' ain't gettin'," Ronaldo said, accelerating to just behind the M-ATV.

It quickly became obvious that they weren't going to outrun these trucks. The pickup with the buffalo skull caught up and paralleled them on the shoulder, and the guy in the back leveled a shotgun at Tooth.

Ronaldo braked as the guy fired a blast, hitting the front bumper. The two trucks behind the Humvee swerved onto the shoulder, then back onto the road in pursuit of the M-ATV.

"You going to shoot these pricks, or what?" Ronaldo said to Tooth.

"Keep us steady." Tooth rolled down the window and aimed his M4, but dust from the pursuers on the shoulder filled the Humvee's cab.

Ronaldo slowed down as he passed through the cloud.

All three trucks were chasing the M-ATV now, and he floored the pedal to catch up. The Toyota pulled onto the shoulder to pass the armored vehicle but had to swerve back onto the road as the flat terrain turned into hills.

Ronaldo pulled out his pistol.

"Get me closer," Tooth said.

"Hold on."

The guy with the shotgun in the pickup fired again, taking off a side mirror. Another blast slammed into the roof of the M-ATV.

"Shit!" Tooth said.

Ronaldo swerved to avoid a second shot, and Tooth's burst went wide.

"Hold me steady, dude!" Tooth yelled.

Ronaldo moved back into position as the guy with the shotgun reloaded. Tooth's next burst caught him, and he slumped against the cab of the truck.

"Got him!" Tooth yelled.

The truck peeled off, heading out into the desert.

Ronaldo sped up to the other two pursuers and rolled his window down. The guy in the bed was busy firing at the M-ATV. He turned just as Ronaldo put a burst through the right rear tire. The vehicle jerked into the ditch, and the guy in the back cartwheeled out onto the highway behind them.

Ronaldo passed the truck as it slammed headlong into a rocky hillside.

That left the truck with the buffalo skull. The driver apparently decided to cut his losses and drove off the road, right into Tooth's field of fire.

Ronaldo felt a grim satisfaction as the bullets punched through the Ford's doors and shattered the glass. Dirt flew, and the pickup skidded to a stop.

Bettis slowed the M-ATV, allowing Ronaldo to pull up alongside and give a thumbs-up.

Any sense of victory faded at the crest of the next hill. The Humvee jolted and pulled to the right.

Tooth looked out the window. "Fuck. Right tire was hit," he said.

Ronaldo eased off the gas as he saw another surprise. Horsemen armed with rifles stood along the crest of the rolling hills.

The M-ATV stopped a quarter mile from a roadblock of rusted vehicles in the middle of the highway. Two SUVs and men on four-wheelers waited behind the wall.

"Holy crap, where'd they come from?" Tooth asked.

Ronaldo counted at least twenty men and a half-dozen vehicles. But these guys looked different from the bandits they had just disposed of, and they weren't firing.

Most of these people weren't even aiming their rifles and crossbows. They were a different group.

Not just any group, he realized.

These were Indians from the Mojave Reservation.

The radio crackled.

"Stand down," Hernández said. "And let me do the talking."

-21-

Marks sat in the living room of the Salvatore apartment with Dom while Elena worked on a delicious-smelling early dinner in the kitchen. Dom spoke quietly to his father's best friend, the former staff sergeant of the Desert Snakes.

In four hours, Dom would be heading back to the cage for the first time in years, to fight the Rattlesnake. All in the hope of catching Esteban Vega outside his castle.

"You don't have to do this, you know," Marks said. "It's dangerous, Dominic. You almost got yourself killed the other night."

"Softly," Dom said.

He looked to the kitchen. His mom had her back to them, and if she could hear anything, she wasn't letting on.

Over the past week, Dom had watched his mother sink deeper into depression. That was part of the reason he had asked Marks to come for dinner. Maybe he could help, although Dom wasn't sure how.

"I promised your dad I'd look after you," Marks said. "You go and get yourself killed in that cage, and he won't ever forgive me."

"I'm not going to get killed, sir."

"You don't need to call me 'sir' anymore. Call me Zed."

"How about 'Lieutenant'?"

"At work, but at home, Zed."

"Okay, Zed," Dom said. "If I win this fight, then I'll get the respect needed to keep fighting, and eventually I will lead us right to Esteban Vega."

Marks sighed.

"You saw yesterday what kind of army he's built," Dom said. "We'll never get to him in the Angel Pyramids. We have to get him when he's outside, and this is our best shot."

"Yeah, I know, but I don't like it. Who's to say he'll even be there?"

"He said if I win, he would put money on me in the next fight."

"Yeah, but if you lose . . ."

"Lose what?" Elena asked. She had sneaked up on them.

"My bet on how long Camilla will be in the hospital," Dom said. "Want me to set the table?"

She scrutinized him for a moment, probably sensing the lie, but then returned to the kitchen. Dom followed her and helped load up plates of spaghetti. It wasn't the normal type of noodles, but it was all they had. The homemade sauce with fresh tomatoes would make up for it, though, and tonight they also had some Parmesan to sprinkle on top.

They sat down, and Elena bowed her head in prayer. Dom shoved a forkful into his mouth.

"Mom, this is so-o-o-o good!" he said.

Elena looked up from her plate but didn't smile as she used to when he complimented her cooking.

"It's delicious," Marks said. "Thank you for having me."

She nodded briefly.

"So, Ronaldo mentioned you were thinking about volunteering once schools open," Marks said. "From what I heard, some will be starting again this spring."

"I . . . I'm not sure I want to do that now," Elena replied. "With Monica still gone . . ."

"I understand," Marks said. "But I do think you should find something. Sitting around inside these four walls all day isn't good for—"

"I'm fine," she said. "Once Monica is home, everything will go back to normal."

Dom exchanged a worried glance with Marks.

Everyone else had come to grips with his sister's kidnapping. But Elena still seemed to think Monica was just going to waltz right into the house, and life would pick up right where it left off a year ago.

Marks took another bite, then set his fork down.

"Elena, I think you need to talk to someone," he said, "especially with Ronaldo away and Dominic working so much. Someone you can talk things through with."

"I don't need someone to talk to," she said. "I need to find my daughter. Maybe that's what I should be doing: searching the streets instead of sitting here all day."

"Mom, we're doing everything we can," Dom said.

"Are you?"

The question took him aback. "I'm out there looking for her every day, Mom."

Elena wiped her mouth off with a napkin and shook her head.

"I should never have let you join the police," she said. "I still remember when Andre came over and gave you that pamphlet on your eighteenth birthday. I should have said no then."

"I'm not a kid anymore. I'm fighting to save this city, and I'm proud of that."

"What about fighting to save your *sister*? If you had been there that night at the school, she never would have been taken."

"Elena, all due respect," Marks said, "but Dominic probably would have died if he tried to stop those men that night."

"I would have proudly died trying to save Monica," Dom said. "But that's not how things went down, and I'm sorry for that. I've done everything I can to bring her home, and so has Dad. And we're not giving up."

Elena's sad gaze fell on the plate of food she had hardly touched.

She was wasting away right in front of Dom. Her cheeks were sunken and her hair frizzled. He barely even recognized her.

"I wish you would talk to someone, Mom," he said. "I agree that it would really help."

Elena stared down at the table.

"Let's talk about that later and just enjoy this lovely dinner," Marks suggested. "Shame to let it go to waste when so many people are hungry out there."

Elena looked up, and a tear raced down her cheek. She wiped it away.

"I'm sorry," she said. Then she got up and left the kitchen, heading through the living room to the bedrooms. A door closed.

Marks let out a long sigh and dabbed at his mustache with his napkin. "She's worse than I thought," he said.

"I know," Dom said, "and I'm not sure how to help her."

"Not getting yourself killed in the ring tonight would be a good start."

"I'm not going to get killed."

"I know, because I won't let that happen," Marks said. "Here's the plan."

They discussed what Dom would do later that evening at the fight. If Esteban Vega showed up, Moose was to send a text, and the police would storm the building.

"I'll have the team a few blocks away, ready to go," Marks said.

"Better have more than the team."

"I'll have enough bodies, don't worry." Marks finished his plate of spaghetti. "I better get going so we'll be ready. Thank your mom for me."

"I will."

"And, Dominic, be careful, okay?"

"I will."

Marks gave Dom a hug and then left.

Dom cleaned up and then walked back to his parents' bedroom. He opened the door to find his mom lying on her side, sobbing.

"I cleaned the kitchen and put your food in the fridge for later," he said. "Now I have to get going." She didn't respond, and he stepped inside the room.

"Mom?"

She moved but didn't turn.

"I'll be home in the morning," he said. "Are . . . are you going to be okay?"

"I'm fine."

Dom's heart cracked at the thought of his mom lying here all night by herself, crying. He stood there feeling the guilt set in. Leaving felt like abandoning her, and each second that passed, more guilt ate at his insides.

Guilt because he had broken his promise about bringing Monica home. Guilt because he couldn't help his parents. Guilt because he had let Camilla get shot in the cemetery.

And the only way to break through the paralyzing wave of guilt was to keep fighting.

* * *

It was a beautiful morning in Naples.

Antonio had risen before dawn in the crummy apartment. After his morning routine of sitting in silence to plan his day, he woke his brother.

"Today is one of the most important days of our life," he said.

Christopher dressed quickly, and by the time the first sunbeams spilled over the horizon, they were driving with Lino to the bay. When they got there, the fishing boats were motoring out to drop nets and lines into the water.

Antonio walked along the piers, taking in the view. But not everyone was enjoying the morning.

"You sure this is a good idea?" Christopher asked.

Antonio halted and turned to his younger brother. "Remember our conversation about trust?"

"Yes, but they have more men than we do here, and this could be—"

"A golden opportunity," Antonio said. He clasped his hands behind his long coat and kept walking, admiring the view.

Lino watched the streets for anyone who might have spotted them, but this morning, Antonio wasn't worried about being discovered by any Canavaro allies. His only concern was sitting down with a woman who wasn't his wife.

He stopped on the pier and looked down at his wedding ring. He tried to pull it off, but the gold band was too tight, and he had to spit on it and twist it back and forth to get it off.

For the first time in twenty-five years, he would have to go without it.

"Hold this for me," he said to Christopher. "And remember the plan."

They returned to the road, where Diamante sat in his Audi, smoking a cigarette. Christopher got in with him, and Antonio got in the BMW with Lino.

The drive up the coast took fifteen minutes, and the sun had popped up over the bay when Antonio arrived at the bar for his coffee date with Irene.

Sitting at a table with a view of the bay, she wore a white dress, with a denim jacket draped over her shoulders.

Seeing her profile, he felt the spark of lust. There was no denying her beauty, but she wasn't Lucia beautiful, and he suppressed the sinful thoughts.

Irene was a means to an end. A tool, nothing more. He would fuck her if it helped him kill the Canavaros.

"Irene," Antonio said.

She turned and started to get up.

"Please, sit," he said in Italian.

They exchanged a kiss on each cheek. He took the chair across from her, checking her out to convey that he was interested, then looking out at the water so he didn't make her uncomfortable.

Being married for a quarter century didn't mean he couldn't remember the mating dance. Marriage was like dating, but harder in that he must always look for new ways to keep Lucia happy.

"Gorgeous morning," she said.

"Like you," Antonio replied.

She smiled, and he noticed a scar on her dimpled cheek.

"You say that to all women, I presume," she said.

"No, just a few."

She glanced at his hand. "No wedding ring this morning?"

"You're beautiful *and* observant."

"I've been with enough Italian men to know the games, and I'm curious . . ." She leaned across the table. "What's yours, Riccardo Angaran?"

"Truthfully, I'm a widower," he lied. "My wife died of cancer five years ago. I still wear the ring but didn't think it was appropriate for this . . . whatever this is."

She scrutinized him for a moment, then shook her head. "I'm sorry, Riccardo. I didn't . . ."

He held up a hand. "It's fine, really. How would you have known?"

A waiter came over and waited politely until they had finished talking. Antonio ordered an espresso.

"Just two shots—he's an old man," Irene said, grinning.

Antonio dipped his head. "She's right."

The waiter walked back to the bar, and Irene took a sip of her coffee.

"You hungry?" he asked her.

"Not really. I'm not big on breakfast, but I adore coffee."

"I gathered that."

"So . . ." She set her cup down. "What do you do for a living?"

"I'm a businessman."

"What sort?"

"An investor."

"You don't like to talk about it?"

"What's there to say?" Antonio asked. "I build empires."

She smiled at that. "That sounds very impressive."

"Not really. I've got to be honest. I'm in town for only a few days. My office and home are in Rome."

Irene seemed to sulk a bit at that, which told Antonio she was even more interested than he had supposed.

"So what else do you do, besides serve fancy drinks to old men and entitled students?" he asked her.

"I'm a painter, kind of."

"Sounds impressive."

"Not really. Honestly, the only reason I get to do what I do is because of my brother."

"He's a famous painter?"

She snorted. "Not at all."

"Oh?"

Time seem to stand still as Antonio waited to see what she would reveal. After all, that was the entire point of their meeting.

"He's a businessman, too, I guess you'd say."

"So perhaps we're alike."

"I sure hope not," Irene said.

The waiter returned with Antonio's espresso. "Sure you wouldn't like anything to eat?" he asked.

"Why not?" she said, and ordered fresh fruit and a pastry.

"Same for me, please," Antonio said.

The waiter nodded and was off.

"I guess I am hungry," she said. "Probably good since I won't have time for lunch today." She raised her coffee cup, the jean jacket falling off to reveal her bare shoulder. "I've got a little art showing today at a place my brother arranged. Nothing big, just a little—"

"I'd love to see it," Antonio said almost too anxiously.

She raised the coffee cup to lips barely grazed with lipstick. It made Antonio think of his wife and the bright red lipstick she wore. The two women were so different, but he had a feeling that in some ways, they were much the same.

Irene stared at him the way Lucia used to stare when they first fell in love.

"What?" he asked.

She shook her head. "It's just that I don't even know anything about you, and here I am inviting you to an art show."

"I kind of invited myself."

"True." She touched her scar—some sort of nervous habit, he supposed.

"Ask me anything," he said. "I'm an open book, as they say."

Irene drank and looked out over the water, perhaps thinking of a question.

He decided to go first. "You live here your entire life?"

"Yes, and never left—one of my life's regrets."

"There's always time."

"That's true, but I'm not getting any younger."

Something about her seemed broken. Her soul had suffered, but there was no room for sympathy. He couldn't let those feelings distract him from what he had to do.

"Maybe you just haven't met the right person to share the world with," he suggested.

"Maybe."

The waiter brought their food over, and they ate slowly, talking more. He was gentle with her—not pushy, just trying to get her to open up. It worked. Over the next hour, he learned more about her past.

He had been mostly correct in his assumptions. Her soul hadn't merely suffered; it had been tortured.

A fiancé dead of a heart attack at thirty-five. Because of the heartbreak, she had never finished her university degree. Then came a period of drug use, which she was quite up front about.

Antonio sat and listened, taking it all in. "Life isn't supposed to be easy," he said when she had finished. "Heartbreak reminds us that we are alive and that we can again find love. I'm the perfect example of that."

"You found love after your wife?"

"No, but I have a feeling I will," he said with a warm smile.

Her cheeks flushed.

"So where and when is your art showing?" he asked.

Irene looked at him again, chewing on her lower lip. Then she pulled out a notepad from her purse and wrote down an address. She passed it over to him.

"Don't make me regret this," she said.

"Time to stop regretting things." Antonio slipped the note into his pocket. "With me, there is no regret. There is only the building of empires."

-22-

The jungle was alive with the noises of nature. Chirring insects, the fluting caws of birds, and the cry of some beast that Vinny couldn't see filtered through the open SUV windows. A slight breeze also drifted in, but it did little to bring relief from the humidity of the tropical terrain.

Vinny would have killed for a cold shower, ice water, and air conditioning—all of which probably existed at the place they had just pulled up to.

Packed between Yellowtail and Doberman, Vinny leaned closer to the window for a view of the two-story stone palace built on the mountainside. From what little he could see, the mansion consisted of interconnected buildings, hidden from above by the forest canopy enveloping it from all sides.

"Here we are," Sebastián said from behind the wheel.

Raff, sitting shotgun, woke from his nap. His hand went right to his bandaged neck.

A guard holding an AK-47 looked in the window and Raff nodded, but the guard did not return the gesture.

Sebastián laughed. "Most of us have never seen a guinea before," he said.

"Prepare to be amazed," Yellowtail said under his breath.

Sebastián either didn't hear or decided not to respond. He followed what was left of their convoy. It now included a Mexican military pickup with a cargo of three captured soldiers.

More sicarios waited in front of a steel gate and fences topped with razor wire. They opened the gate.

Vinny finally got a view of the compound. There were three connected two-story stone buildings, constructed in an H shape. Trees grew in the front and back, concealing the structure. Men with bandannas and baseball caps patrolled with automatic rifles. Others stood on balconies.

Sebastián put on his aviator glasses and turned around, smiling. "Home, sweet casa."

"Hope you guys got cold beer for real," Yellowtail said.

"Oh, we do, hombre."

A guard let Vinny and his comrades out. It was late afternoon, and the sun was high in the sky, but the canopy kept the sun off the exhausted men.

Vinny turned to look for their Jeep and saw it parked with the other vehicles in the convoy. The front window had cracked, and several bullets had punched through the side. He didn't care about the clunker, but he did care about the cargo underneath.

A group of cartel men helped unload the Mexican Army soldiers from the back of the truck. One guy fell out, curling up in a fetal position.

Sebastián laughed as the other men kicked the downed soldier.

"This way, amigos." He slung his AK-47 over his back and walked toward the front of the house. The other guards eyed the Morettis like hawks watching prey.

Vinny followed their guide down a stone path to a wide stairway with planters of tropical flowers. On the landing, an older woman with white hair and dress held a silver plate of small rolled-up towels. She offered them to Raff first.

"*Fría*," she said.

Raff took one and wiped his face. Yellowtail nearly pushed Vinny out of the way to grab not one but two. He put one between his lips and the other on his forehead, letting out a moan of relief.

"Wait here," Sebastián said. He opened a thick wooden door with a golden handle.

A few minutes later, the door was opened again, this time by a gorgeous brown-skinned woman wearing a short red skirt and a flowery blouse that exposed her shoulders and cleavage.

"Welcome," she said in nearly unaccented English. "Or should I say, *benvenuti*."

Vinny was surprised to be greeted in Italian.

"*Grazie*," he said. "Or should I say, *gracias*."

She gave him a dazzling white smile. "This way, please."

She led them to a marble entryway that opened into a large living area furnished with expensive leather couches and glossy wood tables.

The woman who had given them towels returned with ice water. They took the glasses, and she walked away.

"Damn, it's like we just got to heaven," Yellowtail said. He stared at the woman who seemed to be their hostess.

Sebastián returned, the bandanna gone and his sweaty hair spiked up. He grinned when he saw Yellowtail practically drooling over the woman.

"I see you've met Irma," he said. "She will show you to your rooms."

"Thank you, but would it be possible to get something for my neck?" Raff asked. He winced as he pushed on the bandage.

"Of course," Irma said. "I've already requested our doctor. He is on his way."

Vinny had let his guard down some, but he still didn't like this. It seemed like a big game, and he wondered what would have happened if he hadn't helped save Sebastián and his men back on the jungle road.

Sebastián took them to a hallway on the third floor. Irma opened the first closed door to reveal a room furnished with four beds.

"Please, make yourselves comfortable," she said. "There are showers with fresh towels and everything you need to clean up."

"I'll be right here," Sebastián said, fingering the strap of his AK-47.

Irma went to close the door, but he stopped her. Then he reached into his vest and pulled out a joint.

"A man is only as good as his word, and I promised you one back on the road," he said with a grin. "We'll bring you some beer, too."

Vinny took it. "*Gracias.*"

"Dinner is in an hour, and *el patrón* does not like it when people are late, so don't be, *putos.*"

Irma closed the door, and Yellowtail grunted.

"I really don't like that prick," he said as he walked to the bathroom. "First dibs on the shower."

Raff opened another door to a second bathroom.

Vinny was the last to shower. He scrubbed the dirt and blood from his body and let the cold water rinse away his anxiety. Once he was clean, he threw on a robe hanging from the door and collapsed on one of the mattresses. He could sleep for a day but would make do with the half hour he had before dinner.

Raff stirred him awake.

"Get up, Vin," he said.

Vinny rubbed his eyes and sat up.

They dressed in slacks and white shirts that were laid out for them.

"I guess this means they aren't going to kill us," Doberman said. "If they were, why go to all the trouble?"

"I still don't trust them," Yellowtail said.

"Rule number one that Don Antonio taught me is never to trust anyone," Raff said.

When they opened the door, two men in livery with silver belt buckles were waiting. Neither introduced himself; they just motioned to head down the hall.

Irma waited on the first floor. She had changed into a white skirt and top that again emphasized her spectacular breasts.

She gave a friendly smile that Vinny thought looked forced.

"This way," she said.

The journey through the house led them through a kitchen bustling with activity. A chef and his assistants were preparing a dinner that made Vinny's stomach growl. He hadn't eaten anything substantial since Puerto Vallarta, almost twenty-four hours ago.

Irma took them to a deck on the back side of the house, overlooking a partially cleared patch of forest with a view of the mountains. She seated them at a table with ten places, all empty. Vinny sat next to Doberman.

Irma left them for a moment, then returned with a bottle of tequila.

She leaned down close enough that Vinny could smell her perfume and the heavy cologne of a man. He kept his eyes forward, not risking a glance at someone else's property.

At six on the dot, the doors to the deck opened, and Sebastián walked out wearing an open black shirt. A silver-gripped handgun was holstered on his silver-buckled belt.

He stepped aside to let a tall man through the open doorway. The man had to duck slightly, exposing his shaved head.

Vinny was the first of his crew to stand. This had to be the *jefe*. He walked with purpose, and his sharp brown eyes were quick to size a man up. And right now they were on Vinny, scrutinizing him, taking his measure before moving on to Yellowtail, Raff, and finally, Doberman.

"My name is Eduardo Nina," he said in a deep voice. He stuck out his hand, and the cuff of his sleeve pulled back enough to reveal a tattoo of a cross with a skull surrounding it.

"Welcome to my home," he said.

Eduardo shook each man's hand, listening to their names with interest.

"My English is not the best," he said, "*pero no hablo Italiano*, so English it is."

"Very good," Vinny said.

Eduardo took a seat. "I hear you had a difficult journey," he said, glancing over at Raff. "And I heard you helped see that my cousin Sebastián and his men weren't slaughtered."

"We did what we had to do," Vinny said.

"I will make sure you are rewarded for your help, but first let's eat," Eduardo said. "Later, we can discuss the reason you came here."

They sat, and Sebastián joined them, along with Irma, whom Eduardo introduced as his second wife.

The other two wives came out with food. One was a freckled blonde woman about Vinny's age. The other, closer to Eduardo's age, was dark-skinned and thin.

Dinner started with a pork soup.

Eduardo did most of the talking, and it was almost immediately clear to Vinny why he was the boss. Like Antonio, he spoke well. Every move he made was calculated, down to picking up a fork.

Then there was his cousin, who ate like a caveman.

"The marrow is the best part," Sebastián said, sucking from a pork bone. "Try it."

Vinny had the feeling it wasn't a suggestion. He followed his host's lead, and it was indeed quite good.

"It's funny to me," Eduardo said, "that Americans are migrating to Mexico now that their country has fallen to shit. It makes selling them drugs a lot easier."

Irma laughed, and so did the other women. But it sounded nervous—the laughter of women who were not in love, but enslaved.

Eduardo took a drink of tequila and leaned back. "I hear you are immigrants yourselves," he said.

"Yes, we are," Vinny said. "We left Italia and came to Los Angeles to rebuild what was taken from us."

Eduardo stroked his shaved jawline but didn't ask any more questions. He didn't seem interested in talking about business around his wives. In this culture, as in Vinny's, the women did not participate in such discussions.

"Like you, I was almost wiped out by an acquaintance of yours," Eduardo said as he carefully cut a piece of meat.

Vinny raised a brow, eager to hear more.

"Esteban Vega," Eduardo said. He put a slice of pork into his mouth, chewed it, and swallowed. "Back when he and his brother were high-level narcos in the Gulf Cartel. They caused the Sinaloas *muchos problemas*."

Eduardo chuckled. "Never would I have thought so many enemies would join under his banner. MS-Thirteen, Eighteenth Street—those *pendejos* are all desperate. I would rather eat out of a dumpster again than join them."

He shook his head. "I once watched a posse of MS-Thirteen beat an Eighteenth-Street kid to death for stepping onto the wrong street corner. Now they fight together."

A second course was served—chicken with some sort of salsa glaze. Eduardo had come a long way from eating out of the garbage.

"This was my favorite dish growing up—something we ate only on Christmas," Eduardo said. "Nothing like comfort food to remind you where you came from."

Sebastián nodded as he ripped a leg off the chicken. Juice ran down his chin.

"I grew up in a small tourist town on the other

side of the country," Eduardo said. "Me and Sebastián used to sell Chiclets to tourists and scrounge metal and other treasures from the dump."

"I imagine you are quite proud of everything you have accomplished," Vinny said. "And you should be. You have quite the place here."

Eduardo looked at him and snapped his fingers.

"There are plenty of people who still want to take it from me," he said. "Rivals. And the military, which no longer tries to stop us, but they love to steal our product, our weapons, our money, and our women."

Vinny realized now more than ever why his uncle had chosen Eduardo Nina as an ally. They shared an enemy, and that was priceless.

The sun was starting to go down, and the forest sounds shifted to the eerie clicks and cries of insects, tree frogs, and nighthawks.

Vinny peered into the jungle for the creatures, but nothing moved. It was as if the trees themselves were making all the racket.

The women brought dessert and this time went inside, leaving the Morettis with Eduardo, Sebastián, and two guards on the deck as the tropical night descended like a curtain.

Irma returned only to light candles. She offered a polite smile to Vinny, who simply nodded, not wanting to disrespect the *jefe*.

"This is another of my favorite dishes," Eduardo said. "Pound cake—not what any tourist would order, but to us it's a delicacy."

"Very good," Raff said.

"Delicious," Vinny added.

"Glad you like it," Eduardo said. He looked to the guards on the deck and spoke to them in Spanish.

Vinny felt a chill as one of them walked over with a gold-plated AK-47.

Eduardo took the gun and stood with Sebastián.

Spotlights clicked on, illuminating the trees at the edge of the clear area, where four men stood with their mouths taped shut. Three were the Mexican Army prisoners, but the fourth man's face was hidden by a mask.

"Are you ready for dessert?" Eduardo asked.

"I thought this was dessert," Yellowtail said.

Eduardo smiled. He raised the AK-47 to his shoulder. The men all squirmed in their restraints.

Quick bursts from the gilded Kalashnikov ended two of the soldiers' struggles.

Eduardo lowered the rifle, leaving one soldier and the masked man.

"We'll save them for later," he said.

Several guards ran across the yard to take away the two corpses while Vinny stood watching, his heart thumping.

A pat to his shoulder snapped him back to the moment. It was Eduardo, and he still had a smile on his face.

"Get some rest, my young friend," he said. "Tomorrow, we talk business."

* * *

Almost five hours after Marks left the house, Dom walked to the same shopping center turned fighting ring with Moose by his side. Clouds blocked the moon.

This time, security was much tighter. Vega guards stood outside while others patrolled the parking lot.

Dom and Moose exchanged a glance as they got into the line of people waiting to enter. When they finally reached the front door, they were patted down. The bag Dom carried with his fighting gear was searched, then tossed to the floor at his feet.

Moose was allowed to keep his phone, but their guns were taken and stored in a weapons locker just inside the building. A group of burly, tattooed men with long beards and shaved heads guarded the room with sawed-off shotguns.

A Latino man about as tall as Dom, but with shoulders wider than Moose's, walked over. Body odor wafted from his muscular body.

"You here to fight, *ese*?" he rumbled.

"Yeah," Dom said.

"Follow me," the man said.

He led them through the open floor that was already packed full of spectators around one of the cages. But this time it wasn't men fighting inside.

Guttural barking and the sight of two pit bulls fighting in the ring made Dom pause. Watching humans fight didn't bother him, but seeing animals tear each other up hurt his heart.

He felt a visceral hatred for the excited spectators cheering on the violence while holding their bets in the air.

Other men hung back, drinking beers, probably waiting for the human fights.

It finally sank in that Dom was going to be in one of them. Walking past the other cage, he noticed the bloodstains on the mats.

Their escort took them to a door guarded by two more bouncers with handguns tucked into their pants.

"You his trainer?" one of them asked Moose.

"No, his friend."

"Then you stay here," the guy said.

Moose grunted and pulled Dom aside. They exchanged a shake and a pat on the back, but as Dom started away, Moose held his grip.

"Kick some ass, man, okay?"

"Yeah."

They parted, and Dom followed the bulky guard into the dark locker room. A few other fighters were getting ready separately from their opponents, who were in another room. A wiry white guy about thirty years old was jumping up and down in his boxing trunks.

About halfway down the locker area, a black guy cracked his neck from side to side and then exhaled as he put his hands in a pyramid. He was Jason, a mixed martial artist Dom had trained with in high school. Dom tensed, wondering whether Jason knew he was a cop, but there was no way. He hadn't seen the guy in years.

Jason spotted him and walked into the light.

"Dominic, that you?" he asked.

"Yo, what's good, Jason?" Dom said.

They embraced and exchanged a homie handshake.

"Good to see a friendly face," Jason said. "You fight here before?"

"Not really. You?"

"Twice. Got to earn that coin somehow, you know, brah?"

"That's why I'm here."

"What you been up to since school?" Jason asked.

Dom sat down on the bench with his bag, buying time to cook up a lie.

"Construction," he said. "Got hired on that Four Diamonds a few months ago, but work dried up, so here I am."

"I hear ya, man."

Dom started to change into his jock and trunks. The other fighters walked around the corner to a sitting area. Each time the locker-room door opened, the sounds of the crowd poured in, and with the shouts came the growls and barks of the dogs.

Not long after he got his shorts and gloves on, the crowd noises dwindled, and the same voice from last week announced the upcoming fights.

Dom was third on the card, and he had the bad luck of fighting Rattlesnake.

He put his bag in a locker and walked around the corner, where several fighters were hanging out with a trainer.

Jason was at the door, stretching.

"First one up," he said with a chipped grin.

"Good luck, bro."

"I got this, man. Ain't no thang."

Dom forced a smile as Jason was led outside. The shouts of the spectators filled the locker room, and Dom stepped up to see if he could glimpse any Vegas in the audience, but the door closed before he could get a look.

If they were here, then Moose would already have called in reinforcements, and Dom wouldn't have to step into the ring at all. With each passing moment, that became more unlikely.

A bell rang, kicking off the fight outside. The door opened again, and the same handler from earlier returned. This time, he propped the door open, and Dom moved for a better view.

He discreetly scanned the balconies for Esteban and Miguel, but the faces were all shadowed, and he turned back to the match.

Inside the cage, Jason fought an Asian man who was a good foot taller. It wasn't just the height difference that put Jason at a disadvantage, though. The guy had a long reach, and Jason was having a hard time getting close enough to swing or kick.

"Come on, bro," Dom said.

In the first round, the Asian fighter landed several solid punches and a kick to Jason's midsection. Even at this distance, Dom could see he had a cut above his eye and another on his lip.

The crowd booed as Jason limped back to his corner.

In the second round, he came out strong, scoring a kick to the back and a punch to the face that had his opponent stumbling.

"Hell yes!" Dom said, clenching his fist.

Jason raised his hands in the air and turned to the crowd, shouting, "How do you like that!"

He turned back to a flurry of punches and kicks, which he effectively blocked. But then the Asian fighter feinted with a snap kick, which he turned into a roundhouse that caught Jason in the face. Dom could hear the crack over the shouts as Jason fell on his side, landing at an unnatural angle.

The onlookers cheered, and some laughed.

Dom bowed his head as Jason was dragged out of the ring, unconscious and possibly dead from a broken neck. Normally, there should be a medical crew standing by, but not at this place. Jason was carried away without any spine-stabilizing precautions.

Life was cheap here.

For the next fight, Dom retreated back into the locker room for a few minutes, thinking about what Marks had said about not risking his life in the ring.

Dom took deep breaths and focused. A few minutes' silence was all he needed to get his mind in the right place. He remembered what his dad had taught him in the wilderness, when they were trying to make it back to Los Angeles during the war.

To beat evil, sometimes you have to become evil.

In other words, to fight an animal like Rattlesnake, Dom must become one.

A voice snapped him out of his trance.

"Let's go," said the handler.

Dom kept his head down as he walked out through the crowd. He did look up when Moose called out.

"You got this, bro!" he shouted.

Dom held his friend's gaze long enough to learn that the Vegas weren't here.

He clenched his jaw, cursing his luck. But he had known this was a possibility, just as losing his life was a possibility.

Rattlesnake was already in the cage when Dom got there. He watched Dom enter, staring at him with dark, emotionless eyes like those of his namesake animal.

As soon as Dom's bare feet hit the mat, the adrenaline surged. He stretched his muscular frame, then limbered up his wrists and hands, all while staring back at his opponent.

The announcer came out in a black suit. He raised a mike and introduced the fighters, with Dom getting mostly boos—except from Moose, who was shouting like a bad drunk at a strip club.

When his name was called, Rattlesnake raised a long arm covered in tattoos. Then he gave Dom a grin of black or missing teeth.

Dom put his mouth guard in and strode out to meet his opponent. But instead of touching gloves, the announcer said, "Not tonight, hombres."

Rattlesnake spat on the mat and stripped his gloves off, but Dom hesitated.

"You some sort of *pinche lilo*?" he asked Dom.

Dom pulled his off, too, and they went back to their corners.

The announcer left the ring. As soon as the gate clicked shut, the bell sounded, and the room erupted in applause.

Rattlesnake, still grinning, walked toward Dom. He suddenly spun and whipped a roundabout kick that Dom narrowly ducked.

By the time he turned, Rattlesnake was coming at him again, throwing a right hook that Dom barely had time to evade.

No question, this guy was fast. Dom would have to get creative to win this match. And he would probably have to get the guy down on the mat for a submission.

He faked a punch and then swept with his right foot. The trick worked, and he caught Rattlesnake in the calf, knocking the leg out from under him.

As soon as the man hit the mat, Dom surged forward, trying to get him in an arm bar or choke hold—any submission move.

But once again Rattlesnake was wicked fast and skittered away. A second later, he was back on his feet and kicking with those long snake-tattooed legs. One hit Dom's shoulder, which didn't really hurt; the next caught him in the ribs, which did.

He tried to counter with a punch combination, but he wasn't fast enough and a roundhouse kick nailed him in the side of the head. His mouth guard flew out and he stumbled away, stars breaking before his vision.

The crowd went wild. Rattlesnake basked in the applause, giving Dom a moment to get his bearings.

Chanting broke out in the audience. "Vega! Vega!"

That was just the reminder that Dom needed. He blinked away the stars as a wave of thoughts and memories raced through his mind's eye: Monica being taken . . . his dad killing the two lowlifes in the Angeles National Forest . . . the first AMP soldier Dom had killed during the war . . . Camilla getting shot in the cemetery.

The memories filled him with anger that tripped a switch inside him—something he had experienced only two or three times in his life. Fueled by rage, he charged Rattlesnake, who lowered his arms and tore his attention away from his adoring fans.

The man threw several punches and kicks, but Dom moved with calculated precision, avoiding each blow. Then, as Rattlesnake began to show signs of fatigue, he went on the offensive.

He threw a right hook to the spleen, then a left

uppercut under the chin, then a right one-knuckle punch to the side of the neck.

Reaching up, Rattlesnake stumbled backward as Dom hunched like a linebacker. He barreled into his opponent, knocking him onto his back, and the air from his lungs.

Dom wasted no time. Instead of wrapping the stunned fighter up in a choke hold, he went to work on the face: nose, right eye, base of jaw.

Blood spattered Dom as he pounded his opponent. Thoughts of murder, war, and the dread of the past year kept him battering away. In a fit of anger, he used his fists to drown out the noises of the crowd.

Hands tried to pull him off, but Dom fought free of them and kept hammering, even when Rattlesnake went limp and his eyes rolled up. Finally, more hands grabbed Dom and pulled him off.

His vision cleared enough to see the result of his rage. Hands covered in blood, chest heaving, he looked down at the bloody, swollen face of his opponent.

Voices sounded around him, but they were muffled.

He dragged his wrist across his face to wipe away blood.

A moment later, his hearing returned. Sort of.

The room was quiet. Stunned faces stared at the ring as Rattlesnake was dragged away, still breathing somehow, leaving a streak of blood in his wake.

"Yeah!" someone shouted from the audience.

Moose raised a fist in the air.

Dom raised his in response, shouting, "Vega!"

The crowd joined in, starting another chant as

Dom looked at the balconies to see if the man he had come to capture was here.

But this time, the narco king had remained in his castle keep. Dom would have to fight again to kill the real snake.

-23-

At midnight, Ronaldo found himself in about the last place he had expected to be: as a prisoner in a makeshift jail of outdoor basketball courts, across the street from the Mojave Reservation tribal offices.

Almost four hours ago, Hernández had ordered the Desert Snakes to stand down at the roadblock. Outnumbered, they couldn't win in a fight, even with their armored vehicles. And with a flat tire on the Humvee, outrunning them would have been impossible.

Ronaldo and the other deputies had been forced to give up their weapons and were then loaded into a truck and driven here.

Razor wire topped the basketball courts outside the tribal offices' white admin buildings. Ronaldo twisted his wrists against the rope, but the knots were so well constructed that he wouldn't be getting loose until they wanted him loose.

If *they want you loose*.

Six tribal guards watched over them from outside

the courts, while two more patrolled inside the perimeter. All were well armed.

So far, their captors hadn't raided the vehicles. The M-ATV and the Humvee were parked within view, and Ronaldo hadn't seen them touched, besides the tire, which was replaced earlier.

A coyote howled in the distance, prompting dogs to answer the call.

Tooth squirmed closer to Ronaldo. "We should have made a run for it," he muttered. "I got a bad feeling about these guys."

Ronaldo kept quiet as one of the two guards inside walked over. He had short hair, spiked up slightly, and a red-and-black-patterned scarf around his neck.

He held a torch in one hand, a pistol in the other. Slung over his back was a bolt-action rifle.

"Someone going to tell us what's going on?" Hernández asked. "You can't just hold us here."

The guard waved the torch from Tooth to the lieutenant.

"We can do whatever we want," said the man. "This is our land."

"We were just trying to pass through, and those bandits attacked us," Tooth said.

The guard nodded. "You did us a favor by getting rid of those assholes."

Ronaldo nudged Tooth with an elbow to shut up.

"So why not let us go, then?" Bettis asked.

The guard pulled his scarf down, exposing an angry snarl and a nose that had been broken more than once.

"All those that pass shall be judged," he said.

Bettis bowed his head, perhaps in prayer or perhaps to avoid any further conflict.

These guys were hostile, but Ronaldo couldn't exactly blame them for defending their territory after all that he had seen out here since leaving Los Angeles.

An hour later, a voice called out, "Get them up!"

Another Mojave man, with long hair pulled behind his head, opened the gate. He lit a torch and motioned for the other guards to surround the deputies.

For a moment, Ronaldo thought they were about to be shot where they stood, but then a guard came over and pushed him out of the basketball court. From there, the Desert Snakes were marched down a road and through a field of weeds, toward the Colorado River.

Again, Ronaldo feared they were going to be gunned down like dogs.

Pierce was shaking visibly in the glow of a lantern that another guard carried. The man with the torch took point, guiding them through a flat area covered in chaparral.

In the glow, Ronaldo made out what looked like a speedboat at the water's edge.

Pierce tripped and fell, crying out in pain. A guard yanked him to his feet and used a wooden club to push him forward. They stopped a hundred feet from the river that rolled by in the darkness.

The man with the torch went to the boat.

Just one man stood on the deck. He was dressed in black plants and a white shirt, and his face was shadowed, even as he stepped ashore.

"Which of you is the leader?" he asked.

"I am," Hernández replied.

The man walked into the glow of the torch. He had a kind face and graying black hair that the wind ruffled over his wrinkled brow. A holstered handgun hung at his hip.

Ronaldo put him in his early fifties. He was in great shape for his age. A white shirt clung to his muscular frame. On the breast was the same Fort Mojave Tribe logo as on the admin building, featuring a bow and arrow; a map of the Colorado River running through the tribe's corner of California, Nevada, and Arizona; and the face of an Indian man, half in shadow.

As he walked out into the darkness, he looked at each deputy in turn, stopping to scrutinize Hernández.

"You may be the leader in name, but you are not the leader of this group," he said.

Then he continued past Tooth and Pierce, slowed at Bettis, but ended up in front of Ronaldo.

"You are the leader," he said.

"No sir, I'm—"

"Those men you killed on the road weren't the only ones following you. I have been watching you since Barstow." The man drew in a breath. "You are the leader of this group, and there is no denying that. Now, come with me."

He turned and walked back to the boat. The guard with a wooden club poked Ronaldo in the back. He glared over his shoulder but kept walking until he was on the deck.

"Where are we going?" Ronaldo asked.

"Have a seat," said one of the guards.

The man with the torch handed it to another guard and got aboard, along with the guy carrying the club. They untied the boat and pushed off.

For the first few minutes, the boat drifted, but then the man with spiked hair got behind the wheel and started the engine. He steered them out toward the middle of the river and increased the speed.

Ronaldo sat on a leather seat, his heart kicking, though not from fear—certainly not of the man in the white shirt who sat across from him.

"My name is Tomson Mata, and I'm the chair of the Mojave Tribe—what once we might have called a chief."

"Ronaldo Salvatore, Los Angeles deputy sheriff and retired sergeant in the Marine Corps."

Ronaldo stood and put out his hand. His dad had always told him he could learn a lot about a man just by shaking his hand. Too hard, and the man was probably not confident, and lacking in areas that made a good leader. Too weak, and he probably was a weak man in strength and heart. An equally firm shake meant respect.

But it wasn't just the equal, firm shake that told Ronaldo what type of man Tomson was. The callused hands said he was a worker.

They both sat down as the boat cruised down the channel.

"*Pipa aha macav*," Tomson said. "The people by the river."

Ronaldo looked out over the water.

"The Mojave people have relied on this water a very long time," Tomson said, "from the life source it brings to our beans, seeds, and roots, to the fish and animals it supports. The river is our *blood*." He thumped his chest. "We have defended it with fierceness over the centuries and will until the day we die . . ." His words trailed off for a moment. "The war has brought our people closer to extinction than ever before. Today, we were prepared to fight a rival group that has been terrorizing my people for the past month."

"We had nothing to do with them," Ronaldo said. "I swear we are only trying to get to Las Vegas, to find my daughter and the men who took her."

Tomson was quiet a moment. Then he looked at the moon and, finally, off toward the far shore, which Ronaldo assumed was the same direction as Vegas.

"The road between here and Las Vegas is deadly," said Tomson, "but I'm sure you know that from your experience. It has already claimed many of my warriors."

Ronaldo held his tongue.

"That is why I wanted to speak with you," Tomson said. "My scouts told me you are a brave man with a compassionate heart. You saved a woman and her child in Barstow, and you also saved the man who claims to be your leader."

"I did my duty."

"There are very few who make such sacrifice and take such risk to do their duty," Tomson said. "The man with the glasses, Pierce, is like many men: scared of what must be done."

The boat swung around and started back to shore.

"And what must be done is not for cowards," Tomson said. "Especially now, at the end of the world. To survive, we need warriors."

He got up and gestured toward the shore. "Follow me," he said.

Ronaldo jumped out onto a muddy bank. Two

men were waiting at the top of the bank, in a stand of trees. He almost didn't see them until another torch was lit.

They turned and walked into the chaparral.

Ronaldo saw the bodies a few minutes later, but it took a moment for his brain to understand what his eyes were seeing. The corpses of six naked men were strung up on trees, their bodies nailed to the trunks and limbs. Their jaws were crushed and their scalps removed, leaving bright pink patches over their skulls.

"These were the men who tried to kill you on the road," Tomson said. "You may think what we did was cruel, but if you knew what they did to some of my people, you would understand that one must use evil in war."

Ronaldo looked at Tomson in the torchlight.

"We may come from different worlds," Tomson said, "but we are linked through the torture of our souls after losing a daughter. And while we might not be able to save them, we can at least avenge them."

"You lost a daughter, too?"

Tomson nodded. "These men were part of a larger group of bandits terrorizing our land and farther north. We do not have the numbers or weapons to go after them—it's hard enough defending what we have now."

Ronaldo understood where this was going. "You want justice, but you need someone to help you?"

"Yes."

"To help find the men who took my daughter," Tomson said. "I want you to take my son, Namid."

A young man with a spotty brown beard walked out of the shadows. He was slender but strong. A hatchet hung from the belt of his jeans, and a tan chest rig with armor plates held extra magazines for his rifle.

"Take him with you on your journey, and help us restore our honor," Tomson said. "He will help you fight the demons."

* * *

It was warm in Naples for this time of year, and most of the people walking on the side of the cobblestone streets were in shirtsleeves. For that reason, Antonio had taken off his coat and thrown it in the back seat of the BMW.

Not having the coat meant he couldn't bring his SIG Sauer P320, which was too big to conceal under his shirt, but the smaller P365 he had brought from home fit perfectly inside his waistband.

The small pistol held a magazine of ten bullets—more than enough to kill the man he hoped to find at Irene's art showing.

If not, Lino would be shadowing him the entire time, making sure Antonio wasn't stepping into a trap. The younger soldier sat behind the wheel, searching the street as he waited.

Diamante and Christopher were across town, waiting for Roberto's uncle Pietro, whom Christopher would handle on his own. They had found out where he was attending an afternoon Mass, and would gun him down outside—an ironic end to a man who had planned the ambush of the Morettis inside another church in the same town.

Antonio wished he could be there to see Christopher

finish off the old bastard, but the plan would work only if they split up.

"Good luck," he said to Antonio. "I've got your back."

Antonio did something he normally didn't do: he flipped the shade visor down and looked at himself in the mirror. It had been some time since he looked this closely at his own face. Crow's-feet surrounded his dark eyes, and three stress lines cut his forehead beneath his thick hairline. At least he had kept it, and the grays hadn't completely overtaken his head as they had his beard.

He had shaved when he woke early that morning, but a light shadow had already cropped up. There wasn't anything he could do about that now.

Flipping the sunshade up, Antonio grabbed his flat hat and tucked it over his head. Then he nodded at Lino and got out of the car, joining the stream of pedestrians on the sidewalk. He put on his sunglasses to help him blend in with the throng. The scent of fresh-baked bread and garlic filled the air.

He put his hands in his pockets, looking inside a bakery window as he passed. A baker set a fresh tray of pastries on the sill. A row of flaky cherry croissants caught his eye. But he kept walking, past the gated entrance to an ancient church with a steeple rising high into the sky.

A bell chimed, reminding him he was late.

He picked up his pace and stepped onto the street to avoid a pedestrian, when a horn bleated behind him. A man on a Vespa shot by, cursing at him and shaking his fist.

Antonio's heartbeat surged but quickly returned to normal.

Around the next block, he found himself at the

edge of a park with local artists displaying their paintings, pottery, and jewelry. At other booths, local vendors sold produce from the countryside.

The plaza was filled with customers shopping for food, crafts, and art.

In the center of the square stood a fountain that no longer worked. A pool of water still surrounded the base, and a group of men sat around stone tables playing chess.

Antonio remembered coming here as a kid and getting fresh-pressed pomegranate mixed with orange. But where that stand had been, there now stood a booth selling nuts.

And beside it stood something far sweeter than pomegranate juice.

Irene chatted with a customer in front of a white tent. She had her back slightly turned to him and was now wearing a brown dress that showed off the small of her back—the same place he was carrying his pistol.

She had a tattoo there, something he couldn't make out.

He lifted his hat slightly to scan the customers for her brother. Antonio didn't see him here. He did see a flower stand across the plaza, though. He crossed through the customers to buy a bouquet of roses.

Lino stood nearby in the shadows. He gave a subtle nod. Antonio went to the florist's booth and bought the only flowers he had ever gotten for a woman other than Lucia in his entire life.

Bouquet in hand, Antonio crossed the square, breathing in the scent of the fresh-cut roses, remembering the smell that would mark his revenge.

Irene still had her back turned when he arrived at

her stall. He pulled a flower out and handed it over her shoulder.

She turned with a smile. "You made it," she said.

He took off his sunglasses and raised his hat a little. "I had to see the next Artemisia."

"Ah, well, you know some Italian history, then, I see." She smelled the rose, her eyes brightening.

"I do, and I even know she was a baroque painter who lived and died in Naples."

"Everyone knows that, but do you know what type of art *this* is?" She gestured to the white tent, which had paintings that looked quite modern.

Antonio stepped in, genuinely impressed.

"Futurism," he said.

She smiled again. "Yes, good. My work was influenced by the second generation of Italian futurists, like Benedetta Cappa."

Antonio nodded as if he knew whom Irene were talking about. But he didn't hear a damn thing she said after that.

For out in the square, at the chess tables, sat Roberto Canavaro.

Antonio felt a hand on his shoulder.

"Riccardo," she said. "Are you okay?"

"Yeah, fine. Why?"

"You look like you just saw the devil in the flesh."

He turned away before she could follow his gaze.

"I'm sorry. I was just thinking about . . ."

"What? You can tell me."

He took a step closer to a painting that looked like something out of a sci-fi magazine. "My wife would have loved your work," he said.

For a moment, he worried that the lie would make her retreat, but instead she stepped closer to him.

"She would have liked you, too," Antonio said. "I'm sorry if that sounds weird."

"It doesn't." Irene smiled. "It's sweet, actually."

A customer ambled over, and Irene went to attend her. Antonio took a look at Roberto again. He was certain this was the new don of the Canavaro family, not only because of his rough profile and slicked-back hair, but also because of the two guys in shades and pin-striped suits standing near the fountain.

Lino had made his way over and was pretending to look at fruit. He glanced over at Antonio and scratched his scarred chin—a signal that he was ready to move in.

Antonio scratched his back. He began to walk out of the tent, when Irene called out to him.

"Riccardo, where are you going?" she asked.

Antonio turned toward her. The woman she was helping was looking at a painting.

"I'll be right back," he said. "Going to get a coffee. Would you like one?"

Irene nodded. "Yes, that would be great."

She gave Antonio a sad look as he walked away, as if she knew he was leaving her forever. He made his way over to a stand selling fresh-brewed coffee, using the opportunity to look for more guards. But as far as he could tell, it was just the two men and Roberto.

Roberto suddenly looked over from his match, and Antonio kept walking, face forward, hoping he hadn't been made. He got to the coffee stand and ordered.

If Roberto had made him, Lino would put a bullet

in his head and the heads of his guards before the coffees were in Antonio's hand.

When he got the two cups, he almost sighed with relief.

Revenge would be his.

Antonio turned, keeping his head down. Then he walked toward the tables with the two coffees in hand. Roberto was busy playing his opponent, a man at least two decades older who had a bald pate covered in liver spots.

As Antonio approached, time seemed to slow. All his family's pain and suffering flashed before his eyes. Everything they had endured led to this moment.

"Roberto Canavaro," he said in a deep voice.

Roberto looked up, tilting his head and narrowing his eyes before they widened with realization.

A gunshot sounded, then another.

Both bodyguards fell, one landing on his back in the fountain.

Lino pointed the gun at the old man sitting in front of Roberto as Antonio dropped the cups of coffee to the ground and pulled his pistol.

"Your sins have been forgiven," he said.

Roberto reached for his own gun, but Antonio put two bullets in his chest before he could touch it. Blood spurted out onto the chessboard. He gasped for air, his back arching and his eyes wild.

Screams rang out as customers ran for cover. Antonio walked over and gently pushed over the king on the chessboard.

"Checkmate, dog shit," Antonio said, spitting on Roberto.

Customers continued to run and shout in the distance, but not all of them were fleeing. Irene ran over, tears running down her face. She stopped and stared at Antonio.

"How . . . how could you?"

She walked over, but Lino blocked her.

Glaring at Antonio, she dropped next to Roberto's body, eyes down on her dead brother. His eyes stared at the heavens—a place he definitely wasn't going.

"I'm sorry, but your brother was a demon," Antonio said. "Let him burn in hell with the rest of your family."

She looked up through tears.

"Follow your dreams," Antonio said. "And get as far away from this place as you can."

And he was gone, running with Lino out of the market.

Sirens wailed, but they were in the BMW and a block down the street as the first cruiser arrived.

"Good job, Don Antonio," he said.

"You as well."

A few blocks later, Lino took out his cell phone and handed it to Antonio. Christopher was panting on the other end.

"It's done," Antonio said.

"Same."

Antonio felt like a man who had just left prison after a decade inside.

"And Diamante?" Christopher asked. "What should I do with him?"

"Pay him his money." Antonio was feeling generous today.

"Okay. See you soon."

He handed the phone back to Lino, and they drove straight to the airport.

On the drive, Antonio thought back on what he had done, and recalled the shock on Irene's face. Maybe someday she would come looking for him, and against that possibility, he would remember her face. He always remembered the faces of those he had betrayed, just as he never forgot the face of someone who had betrayed him.

At sunset, he met his brother at the airport, took his wedding ring back, and boarded the private jet waiting for them. Walking down the narrow aisle, Antonio twisted his ring back on, feeling a flood of relief. He looked out his window to say goodbye to his old home as the plane lifted off on the way back to their new one.

-24-

The next morning, Vinny woke to the smell of coffee. He sat up into sunlight streaming through the window.

Raff stood holding a drape open, watching something outside. He had a fresh bandage on his neck, and a mug of coffee.

"Want some?" he asked.

"I'll grab some in a bit," Vinny said. He looked over at Yellowtail and Doberman, both still in their beds and sleeping hard.

"Better get dressed," Raff said. "Looks like our hosts are going somewhere."

Vinny put on his shirt and made his way to the window. It was cracked open, letting in a breeze that was already warm. He saw what Raff was looking at.

At the border of the property, a green military-style troop truck idled. Workers wearing sun hats and long-sleeved shirts boarded in the back.

From the beds of two pickups, armed sicarios watched over them.

"Must be heading to the fields," Raff said.

"Shut those fucking drapes," Yellowtail grumbled, a pillow over his face.

Doberman was awake now and putting on his pants.

"Get up, man," he said.

"Shit . . ." Yellowtail threw off the sheets and sat up, exposing his muscular upper body and impressive gut. The bullet scars showed pink in the morning sunlight.

"Feeling better?" Raff asked him.

"Yeah, but I'm ready to get the hell out of this jungle," Yellowtail said. "Vin, can you make a deal already so we can go home?"

"When I get the chance, man."

Irma knocked on their door, accompanied by a woman holding a tray with coffee and bottled water.

"There is food downstairs," Irma said. "If you're ready, please come with me."

In the living room, the open windows let in a breeze laden with the scent of marijuana. Sitting on a leather couch was Eduardo, dressed in fatigues and smoking a joint.

He stood when he saw the Morettis.

"Ah, *buenos días*," he said.

"Good morning," Vinny replied.

Irma joined her husband.

"I trust you slept well?" he said.

"Very well, thank you."

"There's fresh fruit, bread, and eggs if you're hungry," Irma said. "Help yourself."

"Thank you, but—"

"I'll have a look," Yellowtail said, cutting Vinny off. He went to the kitchen and returned a few minutes later carrying several sugar donuts, and one in his mouth.

While Yellowtail ate, Vinny joined Eduardo on the balcony. Eduardo handed him a joint.

"Have a try," he said.

Vinny sucked the smoke into his lungs, held it a few moments, and coughed.

Eduardo laughed and clapped him on the back. "*¡Muy bien!*"

"Very good," Vinny said, smiling.

In fact, it was some of the best bud he had ever smoked.

"I was about your age when I first started to 'rise through the ranks,' as you might say in English." Eduardo took the joint back and looked at it. "Hard to believe that a common plant can create such wealth."

"You have built something great here," Vinny said. "On behalf of Don Antonio Moretti, I would like to create a successful business venture that will endure for years to come."

Eduardo sucked in a long drag and held it. After exhaling the fragrant cloud, he said, "Perhaps, but time will tell. I'm all that's left of the Sinaloa Cartel, and I will only make deals with those who will help us regain our former power, lost because of the war across the border."

Flicking the joint off the balcony, he then motioned for Vinny to follow him back into the living room. From there, they went outside to join a small entourage of heavily armed soldiers.

The old army truck was already driving away, and the pickups followed, kicking up a thick trail of dust.

Sebastián led the way around the mansion to a big garage. The Morettis' red Jeep was parked beside a black muscle car and two Mercedes G wagons.

Vinny noticed something under the Jeep, and swallowed when he realized it was a mechanic's creeper that someone had rolled underneath to have a look.

And to remove whatever had been stored there.

Raff glanced over at Vinny but didn't say anything.

At the garage, Eduardo and Vinny got into a Mercedes with Sebastián behind the wheel. He followed the thinning cloud of dust from the first caravan, down the same road they had come in on.

This time, Vinny wasn't given a mask, and this time, he had refrigerated air blowing in his face.

"I respect you coming here to talk business," Eduardo said. "I know how dangerous the journey has been for you, but there is one more thing we must do before we discuss a partnership. Two, actually."

After another hour and a half on the twisting roads, Vinny saw the fields.

Marijuana plants taller than a man covered two jungle clearings. The trucks drove past acres and acres of them, then turned onto another road, up a steep mountainside covered in thick vegetation.

More fields, mostly coca plants.

Long wood buildings waited at the next turnoff. Workers stood outside with masks around their necks. As soon as they saw the vehicles, they put the masks on and went back inside the buildings.

"Lazy *cabrones*," Sebastián grumbled.

He pulled up outside and turned off the engine. Eduardo and Vinny got out as the other black Mercedes kept driving up another road, deeper into the hills, with the rest of his crew.

"Don't worry," Sebastián said. "Your friends are safe."

Vinny took a mask from another guard and pulled it over his face. The group went inside the first long building, which was shaded by banana plants and a canopy of trees.

Inside, it felt like a steam room. Men and women were busy soaking coca leaves in drums of gasoline.

Next, he saw the metal drums where the gasoline was drained. Other workers performed the task of filtering the liquid from the base. After that, they dissolved the base in a solvent.

A group of shirtless men wearing masks had the dangerous job of adding solvents to the mixture, then introducing a concentrated solution of hydrochloric acid.

Vinny found the process fascinating. The workers glanced up as he passed them by. Some of them seemed high from the solvents; others just looked tired from the grueling long days in torturous conditions.

Finally, he saw the end product, wrapped and sealed in brown plastic.

Eduardo picked up a brick and handed it to Vinny.

"Best blow in the world, amigo," he said.

Vinny held the brick. With Vito's expertise, they could make millions cutting this before it hit the streets. He placed the brick back down and followed the group outside.

Sebastián got back into the Mercedes and drove them to another laboratory, inside a brick building.

"What I'm about to show you is something new,"

Eduardo said. "Something that many of my enemies have tried to obtain, and the reason the Mexican military ambushed your convoy."

Sebastián opened a steel door into a two-story room with balconies. Guards patrolled the platforms overlooking rows of tables and masked workers.

Eduardo held up the final product—a pill the size of a pinto bean.

"Try it," he said.

Vinny put the white pill on his tongue and swallowed it with a pint bottle of water.

"You're about to feel very good, brother," Sebastián said with a grin.

They got back into the SUV and drove to the top of the mountain.

By the time Vinny got out and saw his crew, he was already feeling the effects. His legs and feet felt light, as if he were walking on thick, puffy clouds. He hardly had any sensation of breathing, and his entire body felt as though he had just finished working out and was resting.

"Walk with me, Vinny Moretti," Eduardo said. He started down a dirt road at the crest of the bluff, which gave a panoramic view of the jungles.

"So what do you think?" he asked. "You've tried my weed and my pills."

"*Me gustan*," Vinny said, hearing the slur in his own words. It was all he could think to say. His mind had calmed, every worry and fear rising away like mist under a bright sun.

Eduardo stopped and grinned. "I'm glad, amigo. So now we talk payment."

"I think you found our down payment," Vinny said, suddenly feeling confident. Invincible even. "Gold is how we will be paying if we come to an agreement here."

Looking out over the gorgeous view, Vinny was filled with a sense of the divine. Here he was, standing on a mountaintop, beside a notorious cartel boss, doing business with gold he had obtained by killing a Japanese gangster.

It seemed like a dream—or a nightmare, if he thought about the things he had done to get here.

"I like gold," Eduardo said, running a hand over his shaved head. "Who doesn't? The question is, How much of my product do you want to buy now that you have seen it and gotten a taste?"

"All of it," Vinny said. "We will take everything you have."

Eduardo arched a thick, dark brow.

"We want to be your only customer," Vinny said.

Bringing his finger to his lips, Eduardo whistled.

Sebastián went to the black Mercedes where the rest of the Moretti crew was standing. A sicario helped Sebastián pull from the back a bound man whose his face was covered with a mask—the same man Vinny kept seeing without knowing who he was.

Sebastián brought the guy over and then kicked out his leg. He fell to his knees in front of Vinny and Eduardo.

The *jefe* wasted no time ripping off the mask.

Long dark hair stuck up from a battered and bloody face, but there was no mistaking those bruised features.

"Chuy," Vinny gasped.

Sebastián ripped a piece of duct tape from his mouth, prompting a cry of pain.

"¡*Por Dios!*" Chuy said. "Please, please, don't kill me."

"Oh, I won't," Eduardo said. Then he looked to Vinny. "But my Italian friend will—if he wants to make a deal, that is."

Sebastián reached into his vest and took out a vial. He handed it to Vinny.

"If you want to be our only customer, then prove I will be your only supplier," Eduardo said.

"No, please, what is that?" Chuy said, shaking his head. He looked at the vial, then tried to squirm away.

He made it a few feet before Eduardo stomped on his leg.

Chuy cried in pain and looked at Vinny with wild eyes. "Don't do it, man, please. You're my—"

Eduardo kicked Chuy in the gut, making him recoil. He went back down on his stomach, whimpering.

"What about the González brothers?" Vinny said. "This could start a war." He glanced over at his crew.

"The González brothers are on their way out," Eduardo said. "That's why you're here, is it not? They can't produce enough for you. And unlike me, they can't deal with their enemies."

Vinny nodded, but it almost seemed as if an invisible hand were moving his head. His body still felt euphoric, yet his heart was thumping away—partly from the drugs and also from the task he had just been given.

He took the vial in his hand, again thinking of the events that had led him here.

"Please, Vin," Chuy begged. He sat up, his hands still behind his back, drooling blood as he sobbed. "Please don't hurt me."

Vinny looked back at Raff, who gave a nod so subtle that Vinny might not even have caught it if he weren't high. His senses seemed sharper than normal.

"Hold him down," Eduardo said.

Sebastián and several other guards grabbed Chuy and pinned him to the ground. He screamed and screamed as Vinny twisted the cap off the vial.

He tried to keep his hand steady, to keep from spilling the liquid and looking like a frightened kid. If not for the opiates in his system, he might not have been able to do it.

As he bent down, Chuy bit one of his captors and kicked at them. Vinny pulled the vial away, but not before a few drops spilled.

Chuy gave an anguished scream as the acid sizzled into his leg.

The men held him down and Vinny dumped the rest of the vial into Chuy's face and forced-open mouth. The long banshee howl made Vinny shiver as Chuy's face bubbled and melted like chocolate in a hot skillet.

"Jesus," Sebastián said, chuckling nervously.

Eduardo and his men watched, emotionless.

It was another minute before Chuy finally stopped struggling and went still. He kicked a few times, making Sebastián flinch.

Eduardo did laugh at that.

Vinny stepped back, still gripping the vial as if it were a hand grenade with the pin out.

By taking a life, he had secured for the Morettis a

pipeline that would flood Los Angeles with high-quality drugs and help the family expand along the West Coast. Eventually, no one would be able to stop them. And like many business deals in this world, it came with a heavy price.

Eduardo reached out to Vinny, and they shook, sealing the deal like any other businessmen. But Eduardo wasn't a businessman. He was a monster in tailored suits and Gucci loafers. And now Vinny was a monster, too.

He walked back to his crew, bile rising in his throat as the reality of what he had done to another man—a *friend*—suddenly hit him.

A deep sense of dread coursed through him like ice water. He stepped away to vomit coffee and stomach acid onto the forest floor.

* * *

Dom still hadn't heard anything about his dad, and his mom continued to deteriorate. Coming home with a broken nose, split lip, and swollen eyes didn't help things. Seeing him like this had driven a further wedge between his mother and him.

He looked in the mirror of the bathroom he had shared with Monica, hoping this was the last time he had to see his face looking like this, even though he knew it wouldn't be.

Turning on the sink, he splashed cool water over his skin.

When he went back into the living room, his mom was still gone. She had left a note that she went shopping for groceries, but he had found it two hours ago, and it was going to be dark soon.

"Where are you?" he whispered.

Concerned thoughts whirled through his mind. Had she gone off to search for Monica? Had something happened to her out there? But he buried those fears, trusting that his mom could handle herself.

She was still strong, and she would come home.

He pushed all the worries aside to focus on the fight.

Tonight could be the night they took down Esteban Vega.

He took a pen and wrote on the note that his mom had left on the counter while he slept.

Sorry I missed you. I love you, Mom. See you in the morning.

—Dominic

He grabbed his bag and left the apartment, locking it before he took off down the sidewalk.

A voice called out from behind him. Dom turned and found his mom walking down the sidewalk, carrying two bags.

"There you are," he said. He slung his bag and took her groceries inside. "Fruit, vegetables, and fresh bread—nice work, Mom!"

She nodded but didn't smile.

"I'm going to make some soup tonight," she said. "I'll leave you some in the fridge."

Elena finished putting away the other groceries as Dom arranged the fruit in a decorative wooden bowl.

She put a hand on his chin and gently turned his face toward her.

"My boy," she whispered. "Is this where the extra money you are bringing me comes from?"

Dom still hadn't told her about the fights. For all she knew, he was attacked on the job—which wasn't all that far from the truth.

"I've had a few bad nights on the job," he said. "I'm sorry. I'll be more careful."

She shook her head and sighed. "I never thought life would be like this."

Dom watched her retreat to the living room and sit on the couch. He hated being yet another source of her anxiety, but he didn't know what else to do.

"Are you going to be okay tonight?" he asked.

"Yes, I just need to rest my eyes."

Dom went over and gave her a kiss on the forehead.

"I love you."

"I love you, too," she murmured.

He left her again, feeling guiltier than ever. He tried not to dwell on her sitting in the darkness at home, waiting for her family to return, and instead focused on winning his fight.

Two hours later, Dom was back in the ring on the roof of a ten-story building, beating the crap out of a white guy with a blue Mohawk. The fighter had a hell of a punch, but Dom avoided every blow, knowing that if one did land, he was done.

All around the rooftop ring, torches burned, lighting up their glistening musculatures. The warrior with the Mohawk strode forward, throwing punch after punch that Dom backed away from or ducked.

His opponent started to tire, and Dom went to work.

He aimed a roundhouse kick to the solar plexus as the man went in for another punch. The kick was high, but he had already landed several body shots, and the guy's ribs had to be hurting.

The guy threw an ill-timed right hook, and Dom got him with a crescent kick along the diaphragm, knocking the air from his lungs. He doubled over, his Mohawk sticking out like the teeth of a power saw. Dom wasted no time taking him to the mat and wrapping him in a choke hold.

A minute later, the announcer was raising Dom's hand into the air for his sixth victory. This time he hadn't even gotten a bruise, and the crowd chanted something new.

"¡Sementaliano! ¡Sementaliano!"

Dom almost laughed at the nickname. The mostly Latino audience seemed to be splicing together the words for "Italian stallion."

He walked away, happy that he hadn't taken any real hits.

But the night was still young, and he had another fight to go—the main event, which he prayed that Esteban and Miguel would show up for.

Moose was in the audience, watching and cheering as always.

And a few blocks away, Marks and his teams waited to move in and take out the brothers.

It had been decided. They wouldn't be taken alive like Mariana—the cops couldn't risk the Vega brothers escaping.

Dom left the ring, looking for them in the crowd and then in the windows of the adjacent building, where more people were watching, but he didn't see them yet. And anyway, if they were here, Moose would have called it in. That was to be expected—it wasn't the main event.

Dom went inside to a bathroom of the offices on the tenth floor. He drank half a bottle of water and mopped his face dry. Then he stepped up to a urinal to relieve himself.

Another fighter stepped up right beside Dom. He cleared his throat and spat in the trough.

"The Italian Stallion," the man said, then chuckled.

Dom kept his eyes forward. He didn't need to look over to see who it was, but he did anyway. Rattlesnake's face was still bruised blue and yellow. It seemed a miracle that he could even stand.

"You're good, I'll give you that," said the warrior.

Dom finished pissing, and as he started away, Rattlesnake reached out and grabbed him by the arm. Dom braced for a fight, but the guy didn't attack.

"You win this next one, and you'll see the real money, hombre," he said. "The kind of money people like us only dream of—something I almost had before you came along and fucked my face up."

"You'll get there," Dom said. "You're a good fighter."

Rattlesnake hawked and spat again. "You're a better one. *Suerte*, Sementaliano. Good luck, amigo. You'll need it."

Dom walked away, not wanting to linger, yet still a little worried that Rattlesnake might kick him in the back. But the kick never came.

The tall warrior followed the code of honor that respected the better fighter.

When Dom was finally called up for the main event, he saw why Rattlesnake had told him he would need luck.

The guy inside the cage was called the Apache. Dom had heard all about the tall, thick American Indian with a fauxhawk that was slicked back into a long ponytail. Tribal tattoos covered his lean muscles.

Unlike Rattlesnake, this guy seemed to have no respect for anyone.

He sported some sort of horns through his earlobes. It was odd, and damn cocky, to wear something like that in the ring. In MMA, they would never have been allowed. But this wasn't MMA. Even MMA had rules.

Dom walked to the center, feeling sick to his stomach. Apache was a stronger, bigger, better fighter, and to beat him, Dom needed to make some magic happen. Chances were good that Dom would go home tonight in worse shape than ever. But if it got him a chance at the Vegas, then so be it.

Apache walked up to the center of the ring, his muscles glistening under his sweaty tattooed flesh. He showed off his front teeth. The top incisors were chipped.

No, *sharpened*, Dom realized. This guy was a beast.

Dom swallowed hard, trying not to show his fear. He must transform into a beast, too.

The announcer made the introductions, the crowd went wild, and Dom raised his fists, which were still bleeding from the last match.

Instead of a bell, this time, a starter pistol cracked.

But as Dom strode toward his opponent, the gunfire continued. This wasn't the bell.

People screamed and scattered away from the ring. Dom hunched down, and so did Apache. Apparently, he was afraid of something after all.

The gunfire was coming from a nearby rooftop, but it didn't seem to be directed at the crowd. Dom didn't see anyone injured yet, either.

A few more shots rang out, then faded away. Dom got slowly to his feet and looked at Apache.

The announcer and the two people working the ring had taken off with most of the audience, leaving just the two of them and a few people hunkered down behind tables. Moose was one of them.

"Let's go, man," he said to Dom, waving.

Apache stared. "Next time," he said, showing his teeth again.

"Next time," Dom replied.

He left the ring and went back into the building with Moose. The jig was up, and they both knew it, although Dom had no idea what had happened—until he got onto the sidewalk with Moose.

"He was here," Moose whispered. "I think that's why the shooting broke out. Maybe an assassination attempt or something."

Dom stopped in the dark street, which was lit by only a few lamps. The rest were either out or shattered by vandals.

"Esteban Vega was here?" he said quietly.

"I think so," Moose said.

"And you didn't call it in?"

"Dude, we have to be sure before . . ."

They heard a voice and footsteps.

They were about six blocks from the Angel Pyramids—not an ideal place for two undercover cops.

He turned down the empty sidewalk and spotted several people hanging out around burning barrels.

On the walk to the fight, Dom had passed an old skate park that was being used for dogfights. There were still people there, but he didn't hear any barking.

"Come on," Moose said.

They picked up their pace.

Down the street, a car sat with the engine running. That was odd. Who would waste even a second's worth of precious gasoline?

Dom and Moose kept walking, then bolted around the next corner. Coming up on some abandoned buildings, they hid behind a dumpster overflowing with trash.

A minute later, the car he had seen earlier passed them by, as he knew it would.

They tossed something out, then sped away.

Dom heard whimpering and got up from his position.

"Hold up," Moose said.

The whimpering wasn't human, and Dom ran when he saw the body of a dog in the street. He knelt beside a beautiful female pit bull with a mangled hind leg. She looked up at him, but despite her injuries, she didn't bite or even growl.

"It's okay, girl," he said. "I'm going to help you."

Moose hurried over. "Jesus," he said. "She's in bad shape, man."

"Go get the car," Dom said.

"Dude, we should just put her out of her—"

Dom glared at his friend. "Get the car, man. I'm taking her to get help."

-25-

A week had passed since Ronaldo and the Desert Snakes left the Mojave reservation. They had continued their journey to Las Vegas slowly and carefully. Not using the main roads. Tracking and scouting on foot at times.

Chief Tomson was right about the road to Vegas being a path to hell.

As Ronaldo drove down a desert road under a mauve and crimson sunset, he couldn't help thinking of his days in Afghanistan, when the natural beauty often disguised threats. He found himself scanning the edges of the highway for IEDs, as well as snipers posted on rock bluffs or behind the burned-out shells of abandoned vehicles.

But all across the United States, worse things were happening. The new Executive Council, which had taken the reins of government after the peace treaty with the former leaders of AMP, had lost all control in some cities, which were falling deeper into anarchy with every passing day. Ronaldo couldn't believe what had happened to his country, and it was going to get worse before it got better.

If it ever gets better.

"Almost there," said Bettis from the passenger seat. "Take a right on the next dirt road."

He was studying a map that Namid had marked up for them.

The twenty-five-year-old Mojave sat in the back seat next to Tooth, reading a physics book while Tooth thumbed through the same porn magazine he'd been reading since Barstow.

The two young men couldn't be more different.

Namid was quiet, and sharp and concise when he did speak. Tooth, by contrast, never shut up and usually had the most banal things to say.

"Where'd you go to school again?" Ronaldo asked Namid.

His hazel eyes glanced to the front seat. "I was at Caltech when everything went to shit."

"Damn, that's, like, a computer school for brainiacs, right?" Tooth asked.

Namid glanced at him as if he were dumb.

"What? Tooth said with a shrug.

"Nothing."

Bettis pulled out his binoculars as Ronaldo drove. They were on the outskirts of Border City, a few miles from the Hoover Dam and Las Vegas, checking out all the major roadways into the city.

For the past week, the Desert Snakes had stopped a few trucks and searched them but found nothing. They had raided multiple houses that locals tipped them off to, finding nothing there, either. Ronaldo felt they were chasing ghosts, but they had to be getting closer.

It was Namid who provided them with the most

intel. His people had defended the roads north of the rez for the past six months. And just as at the borders of Los Angeles, they had faced bandits, scavengers, and refugees looking for a safe haven. He knew the most dangerous roads and the areas that still had electrical power, which meant there was still some sort of municipality in charge.

Namid told them that his father, Tomson, had taken in some families from the nearby cities onto the reservation when things got really bad during the war, but afterward, food had dwindled and the government had abandoned the town and the rez. Once again life had not been kind to Native America.

Ronaldo had always empathized with their plight, especially after fighting alongside so many of them overseas. He was grateful to have Namid along for the journey.

The young man went back to reading, while Ronaldo scanned the road.

On the left side, hundreds of solar panels absorbed the day's last rays. Ronaldo looked away from the road for a moment to check out the field. White pickup trucks were parked here and there among the rows, where maintenance workers checked the panels.

Much of this area was powered by the solar farms, and Los Angeles would soon be building the same massive fields.

"Turn here," Bettis said. He put the map away and grabbed his rifle as they hit the junction of Highway 95 and Interstate 11.

A few cars drove down the other lanes, and Ronaldo kept an eye on all of them for anything suspicious.

By the time they pulled up at the truck stop, the sun had vanished behind the mountains, shadowing the valley and the semis parked in the long spaces. Ronaldo counted ten rigs—a surprising number. They also had armed escorts with them—cars and pickups to improve their odds of safe passage. The semis hauled all sorts of cargo, from aid sent by other countries, to slaves.

Ronaldo grabbed his rifle and got out of the vehicle, his heart quickening at the thought of finding kids in the trucks.

Hernández walked over to give orders to everyone but Namid, who hung back. He carried an AR-15 with a vertical grip. A vest stuffed with full magazines and gear hung over his olive-drab fatigue shirt.

"Pierce, you go inside and talk to the clerk," Hernández said. "See if they've seen anything unusual. Don't ask about the Shepherds, though. Rest of us will ask to search the trucks."

"Got it," Ronaldo said. "Let's do it."

"Namid—"

"Is with me," Ronaldo interrupted. "Cool?"

Hernández motioned Ronaldo behind the M-ATV. The lieutenant was still not happy about bringing the guy along after their captivity. He had wanted to make Namid give up his weapons, but Ronaldo had made the case that he was more useful armed.

"You want to babysit Namid, that's fine, Salvatore, but that means making sure he doesn't shoot anyone or get us all killed. Got it?"

"Understood, Lieutenant."

Hernández grunted and glanced back at the young man.

"We need every man we can get, sir," Ronaldo said. "And Namid isn't evil. I know evil, and he isn't."

"Did you see what his people did to those raiders?"

"Do you mean raiders who would have done even worse to us if they caught us?" Ronaldo asked.

Hernández snorted. "Let's get this done and then find a place to camp," he said.

Ronaldo walked around the truck and started off into the parking lot. Several people had gotten out of their vehicles, armed with rifles, shotguns, even a crossbow. Even with the armored vehicles sporting the Los Angeles County Sheriff Department logo, people didn't trust them.

It was no wonder, looking at the Desert Snakes logo that Tooth had scrawled onto the side of the M-ATV.

Ronaldo might have laughed if his heart weren't pounding at the thought of what they might find here. The first few armed people weren't happy about having their loads searched, but they let Hernández and Tooth look without putting up a fight.

As Ronaldo advanced into the lot, one truck seemed suspicious. Two escort cars, both sporting several bullet holes, were parked next to it.

Ronaldo motioned toward them with his chin. Namid moved around the other side while Bettis, Hernández, and Tooth finished checking other trucks.

"Los Angeles County Sheriff," Ronaldo said. "You mind opening the back of your truck?"

The driver, a big man with a gut and a beard, had hopped out. The guards were either inside the rest stop or lurking in the shadows.

"Why you want to search my truck?" the driver bellowed.

"We're searching all the vehicles in this area," Ronaldo said.

"For what?"

"Please open the back."

The driver folded his arms over his chest. "Or what?"

"Or we will," Namid said.

That got a chuckle from the driver. "Good luck with that, Tonto."

"So that's how it's going to be?" Ronaldo asked.

Namid clenched his jaw and said nothing.

"That's how it's going to be," replied the driver.

His armed escorts finally made their presence known. Four of them stepped around the semi with shotguns and rifles.

"This is property of the State of Arizona, and we've been instructed not to let anyone near it," said the driver.

"We're asking you nicely to open those doors," Hernández called out.

"And we're saying *no* nicely," said one of the armed guards. "You ain't the law. There ain't no law out here."

Ronaldo knew they were trying to hide something, but what? If it was people, then there had to be a way that he couldn't see to get air in there.

Namid unbuckled the sheath on his hatchet, and all four guards swung their guns his way.

"Whoa, easy," Ronaldo said, raising his hand.

Namid moved his hand from the hatchet but the men kept their rifles pointed.

"You know what, go ahead and show them," said the driver. "We got nothin' to hide."

One of the guards looked over, then shrugged.

They all lowered their guns, and Ronaldo exhaled discreetly.

"Namid, get back to the truck, please," Ronaldo said.

Namid backed away, and Hernández strode up, glaring at him as they passed. Then he stepped up to the back of the trailer with Ronaldo. The driver fished in his pockets for the key.

His guards hovered around, eyeing Bettis and Tooth, who watched from a distance.

"Here you go, gentlemen," said the driver.

He opened the back to reveal a nearly empty box trailer. Only a few crates were strapped down inside.

Ronaldo climbed up into the back. He flipped on the tactical beam on his M4 and shined it on the crates. The boxes were all marked in Chinese.

"Rice," the driver called out.

"Rice," Ronaldo whispered. Why the hell did they need armed escorts for rice?

He played his light into the corners, finding nothing but a single shoe and a few stains on the floor. As he walked to the back, he caught a whiff of urine. That made him pause.

"You done yet?" the driver asked.

"Just about."

Hernández had climbed inside. "Let's go, Salvatore."

Ronaldo picked up the shoe. It was small and female. Holding it in his hand gave him a chill.

Rice, my ass.

With his back turned, he pulled out a tracking device. Then he turned off his light, and in the darkness, he stuck it onto one of the crates on the way out.

"Someone lost a shoe," he said, tossing it to the driver.

The beefy driver fumbled it, dropping it to the asphalt.

Ronaldo walked away with Hernández just as Pierce came running away from the station. He was breathing heavily.

"LT," he said. "LT, I think—"

"Tell me at the truck," Hernández said.

They got there a moment later, but Hernández was more interested in the shoe than in whatever Pierce had to say.

"You thinkin' what I am, Salvatore?"

"Exactly, sir. I dropped one of our trackers."

"Good." Hernández looked to Pierce. "So what's got you all in a lather?"

"The clerk didn't know shit, but when I was taking a dump, I overhead some guys talking at the pissers," he said, eyes flitting nervously. "I think I know where they're taking people."

* * *

While the country continued to burn even when it seemed there was nothing left but ashes, Antonio had returned home from Naples and was enjoying time with Lucia and Marco.

Killing Roberto Canavaro had given him a sense of peace that he hadn't felt since the day Marco entered the world, when he had held the precious new life in his arms.

It was ironic that taking a life could bring the same feeling.

Antonio stood in his apartment as darkness carpeted

the City of Angels. He looked out the window, hands clasped behind his back, while Marco played video games and Lucia finished cooking dinner.

The familiar flash of red and blue police strobes illuminated the city blocks beyond the wall of his compound. Seeing extra guards patrolling the ground added another layer of peace to his mind.

The extra muscle and firepower that Rush had hired after consulting with Frankie and Carmine would come in handy during the next phase of his plan.

But for the plan to continue, he must first make sure they had the drugs to support their growing business. Soon he would know.

Vinny and his small crew were due back from Puerto Vallarta on a boat tonight. If they had completed their mission and secured a deal with Eduardo, then Antonio was closer to his goal than ever before.

He went from the window to the table as Lucia pulled out a tray of baked lasagna—one of his favorites. Boiled egg and carrots helped give the dish some extra flare.

"Marco, come here," Antonio said.

He continued playing his game with his headphones on.

A flash of anger threatened to disrupt Antonio's sense of peace. He got up and walked over to his son, then flipped the headphones off the boy's ears.

"Hey!" Marco protested.

"Dinner is ready."

"I'll be right there."

"No, you'll come now." Antonio picked up the remote and shut off the TV.

"Hey!" Marco yelled.

"Get to the table, or you won't be playing that game again."

"I never get to do shit," he groaned.

Antonio grabbed his son by the arm, but he yanked free.

"Watch your mouth around your mom," he said.

"Yeah, okay." Marco walked around Antonio and went to the table.

Lucia set out a fresh loaf of garlic bread, eyeing Marco. Then she sat and held out her hands for the blessing. They all three joined hands.

"Lord, thank you for giving us so much in a time when so many have nothing," Antonio said. He looked over at Marco to make sure he was listening.

"Thank you for watching over us and giving us nourishment to continue on the path you have paved for us to walk. Amen."

"Amen," Marco and Lucia said simultaneously.

When Lucia started to pour, Antonio put a hand over his wineglass.

"You have to work tonight?"

"Yes."

"Can I come?" Marco asked.

Antonio shook his head.

"I never get to do anything," Marco whined.

Ignoring his son, Antonio dug into his meal. He ate several bites while Marco pushed his food around.

"Are you not hungry, my love?" Lucia asked him.

"I don't like carrots," Marco groaned.

"Next time, I'll leave them out."

"No, you won't leave them out," Antonio said. "You will eat them and not complain."

"But—" Marco started to say.

Antonio slapped the table hard. Both Marco and Lucia flinched.

"You haven't listened to anything I've taught you, have you?" Antonio said. "Or maybe it's that you don't understand the things I've shown you."

Lucia looked across the table, clearly a bit rattled. But their son needed to hear this. He needed to be disciplined.

"You still don't know how lucky you are, because you have everything given to you," Antonio continued. "And it's our fault."

He returned his wife's gaze.

"Soon we will correct that," Antonio said. He got up and put on his suit jacket, then holstered his pistol.

Marco was still at the table, lip quivering, eyes glazed.

"It's okay, Marco, your father is just worried about work," Lucia said.

But it wasn't okay, and Antonio wasn't worried about work. He was worried about their spoiled son.

"Raff is coming home tonight," Antonio said. "But he will no longer be looking after you."

"What?" Lucia said.

Marco wiped a tear away. "Why not?"

"I'm sending Marco away," Antonio said. "To school in another country, where he will study and be around kids his age."

Antonio looked to Marco. "To get away from this 'prison,' as you called it, and be with kids your age. Isn't that what you want?"

"I . . ." Marco stammered. "I just want to be with my friends and be able to go outside."

It was a reasonable thing for a child, Antonio knew, but the problem was much deeper than having a spoiled son. It was having a son with no life or world experience.

Antonio had gained his experience on the streets because that was the only way. It wasn't Marco's fault things were different, and Antonio finally realized that his son was right.

This was a prison, and it would only end up getting Marco killed if Antonio didn't find a way for him to learn how to survive in this new world.

"We will finish this conversation later," Antonio said. "I have to go."

Lucia glared at him, and he felt her eyes on him even as he left.

But this had been a long time coming, and going to Italy had helped him understand what he must do for their son.

He made his way to the lobby, where Frankie and Christopher were waiting.

"Don Antonio," Frankie said.

Christopher pulled out a cigar and jammed it between his lips.

"Let's go," Antonio replied.

Frankie opened the door, and they went outside to the two black Suburbans waiting for them. Rush was standing beside one, a comm piece in his ear.

"Security is in position at the port, Don Antonio," he said as he opened the door.

Antonio slid into the back seat with Christopher.

The front doors opened, Rush got behind the wheel, and Frankie took shotgun.

The two SUVs sped away from the compound in the dark city. There was much anticipation for this moment, especially with no one knowing how the trip to Mexico had gone, other than that all four men were coming home alive.

From what Carmine had told Antonio, they were down to 10 percent of their product from the González brothers, and the last building at the Four Diamonds was due to open in a week. All their other dealing spots were doing such a brisk trade that their store of drugs was dwindling fast.

Antonio looked out the window at his expanding empire. The pieces were almost all in place now. And the war against the Vegas was about to ignite once again.

The drive to the port was quiet and uneventful—just what Antonio needed to calm his mind and heart. Anger had ripped away his earlier sense of peace.

His temper had always been his Achilles' heel, something he had never found a way to control. But it wasn't all bad. Anger had also helped his rise to power.

The port glowed in the distance, lights illuminating the ships moored along the wharf. It was the busiest he had seen this place since before the war—partly because more countries were sending aid, and Los Angeles was one of the main ports of entry.

Another reason he continued to thrive while, all across the country, other places continued eroding into anarchy.

Mayor Buren, Chief of Police Stone, and all the

people keeping the city running needed him, and soon they would need him more than ever. Soon he would make a play for something more important than the selling grounds.

The utilities. Wind. Solar. Water. He would own it all.

Rush drove through a back entrance to the port. He stopped at a freighter out of France. Hundreds of containers were stacked on board. Cranes slowly unloaded them onto flatbed trailers waiting in a line.

"Area is secure," Rush said. "Follow me, Don Antonio."

The Moretti soldiers and associates hopped out of the vehicles and set off down the wharf. Workers paid them no attention, except for a guy on a forklift who stopped to let them by. He nodded at Rush, and Rush nodded back.

He led them to a ship at the end of the next pier.

"Hey, dick bird—I mean Trentino!" came a voice from above.

Several figures looked down from the gunwale.

"God damn it," Frankie muttered.

Yellowtail laughed from above.

The group continued up a platform to the ship's lowest deck. Vinny walked over and reached out to his dad, who grabbed him and gave him a hug.

"Damn glad to see you, Vin," he said.

Antonio felt the hint of jealousy. Not because of how close they were, but because of how strong Vinny was—thanks, in part, to his father.

Marco was Antonio's biggest failing—something he had to correct before it was too late.

"Don Antonio," Raff said. He had a bandage on his neck and looked as if he had lost weight. Antonio patted him on the cheek.

"Welcome home," he said. "Are you good?"

"Fine," Raff said. "And you?"

"I'll find out in a moment."

They exchanged pleasantries and handshakes, but when it was Vinny's turn to greet Antonio, he could tell that something was off about his nephew.

He was acting differently.

Antonio wasn't sure how, but Vinny had the gaze of a man harboring guilt and regrets.

"Where's Carmine?" Yellowtail asked.

"Lino and Carmine are at the Four Diamonds," Frankie said. "Waiting for what we hope is a new supply of food."

"Come with me," Vinny said.

Raff and Doberman led the way down into the bowels of the ship. Rusted bulkheads framed a narrow passageway that stank of mildew.

Doberman opened a hatch and ducked into a long space with secured wooden crates stacked two high. Red paint marked them "Perishable."

Yellowtail went to one that was open. He pulled out an orange and tossed it to Frankie. The lights switched on, spreading a glow over five rows, three wide, of the stacked crates.

"This can't all be . . ." Christopher said.

"This is the future," Antonio said with a wide smile. He joined Yellowtail at the open crate.

Reaching inside, Antonio worked his fingers between oranges until he felt plastic. He grabbed a sealed bag of pills. There had to be a hundred thousand in this crate alone.

"Try one," Yellowtail said.

Antonio opened the bag and handed a pill to Frankie, who spat out the match he was chewing on and popped it in his mouth.

"I want this unloaded fast," Antonio said. "The truce with the Vegas is still alive, but not for long, and we need this shipment secure before we strike."

Vinny nodded to Doberman, who pulled out a burner phone and went topside to make a call.

"We have all the drugs we can buy, now," Raff said. "Thanks to Vin."

"I'm guessing you brought back a few stories," Antonio said, eyeing the bandage on Raff's neck.

"Yeah," Raff said. "I bet you have some of your own from Naples."

Antonio clapped his friend on the shoulder. "Indeed, my friend, and we will share them soon, but first we will celebrate your marriage to Crystal. Then we end the truce with the Vegas and go back to war."

-26-

Two days after Vinny arrived home from Mexico, the Moretti compound was alive with activity. While staff and family members decorated the ballroom for Raff and Crystal's wedding ceremony, Vinny guzzled coffee to prepare for his first mission since his return.

He was dog tired. He had thought having his own bed back would help him rest, but the only sleep he got was infested with nightmares of Chuy's agonized screams as his face melted into the leaf litter alongside a jungle road.

It wasn't just Chuy haunting him now. The people he had killed were visiting him more frequently at night. And soon he would be adding more bodies to the death count.

He finished off his coffee and drove with Doberman across town to the RV park at Dockweiler Beach. Some RVs were still parked here, abandoned and long since raided for any usable thing.

Vinny parked behind one and sat on the hood of his car to watch the waves while Doberman made a call.

A brilliant sunrise had blessed the city this morning, and there wasn't a cloud in the sky. It was the first time in a long while that Vinny hadn't needed his mask. If the weather held, it was going to be a perfect day for a wedding.

Vinny hoped so. Raff deserved the best. After so much heartbreak in his life, the kind, brave, loyal man was due some luck. Vinny just hoped to finish whatever he was supposed to do today, so he could get to the wedding on time.

The roar of a plane taking off distracted him, and he turned from the ocean to watch a 747 lift into the sky, heading east with a belly full of passengers.

Vinny wondered where those people were going. To get a ride out of here, you had to have major coin. Only a few flights were still running out of LAX on the two airlines, which were now owned and operated by the city.

"He's on his way," Doberman said, returning from the beach. "But he wants us to meet him at a new location."

Vinny jumped off the hood and got back into the car. Doberman pulled out onto Vista Del Mar. They passed the Hyperion Water Reclamation Plant, where the city had installed the energy-efficient desalination technology that Japan had given to America after the civil war.

A caravan of city trucks was leaving one of the gates with a police escort on the other side of the road. Security at the facility was impressive, with a small army of masked officers patrolling along the fences and looking down from watchtowers.

Mayor Buren had the facility on lockdown, but Vinny knew that his uncle had his eye on this place, along with the other utilities keeping Los Angeles alive.

The meeting location wasn't far from the plant. Doberman pulled off the road and drove behind the Boeing Satellite Systems building, now abandoned. In the back parking lot, Detective Ray Clarke leaned against his black Audi, arms folded across his leather coat.

He gave his million-dollar, panty-dropping smile as Vinny got out and walked over. It was the first time Ray had seen Doberman since the Yamazaki attack, and he didn't hold back.

"Ho-lee shit! I heard you got messed up, but *day-umn*, boy," Ray said, lowering his sunglasses. "You got *seriously* messed up, dog."

Doberman spat on the ground.

"What you got for us, Detective?" Vinny asked.

Ray pushed his glasses back up, then shrugged.

"You called us out here for *nothin'*?" Doberman asked.

Ray beamed another radiant smile. "Oh, I got somethin'. Depends on how much you want to pay for it, though. I met a lady, and unfortunately, I didn't wrap my wang, if you know what I mean."

"So you just added two more hungry mouths to your tab?" Vinny said.

He reached into his pocket and fished out a small disk of gold they had melted down. He held it out for Ray to see.

"Yeah, bro, that'll do it," Ray said, reaching out.

Vinny pulled it back. "Info first, Detective."

SONS OF WAR 2: SAINTS

"Info, eh? How about the location of the Vega brothers?"

"We already know where they are," Doberman said. "No way we'll be able to—"

"I mean, I know when they are leaving their pyramid castle," Ray interrupted. "A time window that's worth that gold you got."

"I'm listening," Vinny said.

Ray gave the information and reached out again, but Vinny slipped the gold back into his pocket.

"What the fuck, homie!" Ray said.

"You get the gold *after*," Vinny said. "Just in case this intel is bullshit."

Ray glared at him, all jocularity erased from his face. Then he grunted. "A'ight, man, but if you can't get the job done, I still get paid, got it?"

"Deal," Vinny said.

They shook and returned to their cars. The next stop was the warehouse hub by the Long Beach Freeway and the Los Angeles River. The shipment from Mexico was already being unpackaged and prepped for sale inside the sultry open room.

Carmine was barking orders at the workers on the factory floor. Vito was working a blender, mixing cocaine and showing some new hires how it was done.

"Out back," came a voice.

Vinny and Doberman turned to a side door, where Frankie was waving. He led them to an adjacent building that served as a garage for a black passenger van with tinted windows and two dusty SUVs. Christopher and Yellowtail sat on metal chairs in front of the van, playing cards.

The sight of his dad in jeans and a black hoodie instead of his normal suit told Vinny that something big was going down before the ceremony.

"Vin's here," Frankie said.

Christopher stood and turned. His cheeks were flushed—something else Vinny wasn't used to seeing. His dad actually looked nervous.

Christopher opened the van door, and Vinny saw why.

Inside sat three bruised and bloody Latino teenagers with their hands tied behind their backs and tape covering their mouths.

Vinny stepped closer.

One wasn't even a teenager—the boy looked no older than eight. But the other two were fourteen or a bit older.

He didn't recognize any of them, but he had a feeling they were spotters for the Vegas—kids who looked out for enemies and helped the dealers find new customers.

"We plucked them off the streets last night," Christopher said. "And soon we will be returning them, with a message."

The younger kid squirmed in his restraints, but the older boys remained docile—beaten so badly, they knew what would happen if they tried anything.

Christopher massaged his hand, and Vinny saw bloody knuckles. He had done this. It was one thing to go after the teenagers and use them in the soon-to-be-reignited war, but an eight-year-old?

The boy's right eye was swollen shut. But at least he had an eye. The image of Chuy's melting face surfaced again in Vinny's mind. He blinked it away—for the moment, anyway.

You wanted to be made.

And this was the life of a made man: to do *whatever* it took to make money and protect the family against threats of any kind.

The Nevskys and Vegas were the only two threats left in Los Angeles. Soon there would be none, and Vinny prayed things would get better then.

"Can I talk to you a minute?" Vinny said.

Christopher walked away. They went outside and stood in the glaring sun.

"We met with Detective Clarke," Vinny said. "He gave us a location where the Vega brothers are going to be tonight, and it's outside the Pyramids."

"What time tonight?"

"Ten o'clock."

Christopher grunted and pulled out a cigar. Sniffing it, he said, "Not great timing, but at least the ceremony will be over."

"Guess this means no wine," Vinny said.

"Maybe a glass to take the edge off." Christopher patted Vinny on the shoulder. "Tonight we have an opening to kill the Vega brothers."

He started to walk away, but Vinny called out, "What are you going to do with the kids?"

Christopher looked through the open door into the garage. "I was going to use them as a message that the war is back on, but that might not be necessary if your pig friend is right."

He reached into his pocket and pulled out a plastic bag of pills. "But if he isn't, then I'm going to have to do something very unpleasant."

"What are those?"

"Death," Christopher said. He put the pills back in his pocket. "This is what it takes to survive in our world, Vin."

They were probably laced with something. It was a brilliant but evil plan: hit the Angel Pyramids with drugs that would kill customers. That was one way to stop the drug trade for the Vegas and poach their customers if the assassination attempt failed.

Either way, a lot of people were going to die tonight. The question was *who*: the Vega brothers and their main crew, or kids and innocent civilians?

If Vinny could kill Esteban and Miguel Vega, he could save a lot of lives.

* * *

Ronaldo had promised his son that he would take him camping again. That they would sit by a crackling campfire under a jeweled sky, drinking beers and roasting hotdogs.

But that wasn't going to happen anytime soon. Maybe not at all.

He sat with his back to the Humvee tire, gazing up at the moon. For the first time, the Desert Snakes had split up, with Hernández, Pierce, and Bettis taking the M-ATV to follow the truck Ronaldo had hidden a tracking device in. He had stayed behind in the desert outside Boulder City with Tooth and Namid.

In a few hours, they were going to raid the storage units that the truck stop clerk had told Pierce about. Probably a dead end, but Hernández asked, and Ronaldo had agreed.

Loud snoring came from the Humvee—Tooth, grabbing some z's before the mission.

Ronaldo walked away from the noise and found Namid hanging out by a rock outcropping, reading a book in the glow of a candle set in a jar to protect it from the breeze.

"Mind if I join you?" Ronaldo asked.

Namid looked up and said, "Please."

"What are you reading?" he asked.

"Some B-rated science fiction—my guilty pleasure."

"My daughter loved science fiction—*loves* it," Ronaldo corrected himself.

Namid closed the book. "When did she get taken?"

"Seven months ago."

Ronaldo sat down with his back against the rock, folding his arms over his chest. "How about your sister?"

"Three." Namid put his book away. "She's out there somewhere, taken by the demons and probably sold away like many of her ancestors once were."

Ronaldo shook his head wearily. "We could still find her and my daughter," he said. "Don't give up hope."

Namid stood and slung his backpack over a shoulder. "Hope has been ripped away one too many times for me to put much stock in it. Besides, you have no idea what it's like in Vegas, if that is where they are."

He paused, looking in that direction. "I'm sorry, you seem like a good man," Namid said. "But if I were to hope for anything, it would be that they are both dead rather than prisoners in that hell."

Namid walked away and left Ronaldo to ponder his words.

The moon laid a soft carpet of light over the rocky desert landscape. Ronaldo closed his eyes to block out the painful thoughts of Monica, out there somewhere. Instead, he landed in a memory of Afghanistan, when the Taliban had crept up on his encampment in a desert landscape not so different from this.

His eyelids popped open. There was no escaping the evil—not in waking life, not even in his dreams. No matter where he was, Ronaldo couldn't avoid the misery and horror of war.

Taking in a deep breath, he let anger replace the dread and returned to the Humvee.

He opened the back door and gently shook Tooth's boot.

"Time to get ready," Ronaldo said.

Tooth rubbed his face and mumbled, "I don't want to go to school today, Mom."

Namid looked over from prepping his gear. "Did he say 'Mom'?"

"He talks in his sleep," Ronaldo said.

They shared a much-needed laugh, and Ronaldo shook Tooth harder. He shot up, eyes open.

"The fuck, man!" he said.

"Get ready," Ronaldo said. "We're going to check out those storage units."

The drive took thirty minutes. Before reaching the location, they put on their night-vision goggles and turned off the Humvee's lights. Ronaldo parked a block away from the storage units.

Tooth looked to Namid in the back seat. "Since you don't have night-vision goggles, you better stay here and watch the Humvee."

"I learned to hunt at night when I was a kid," Namid said. "I can see just fine."

"Stay here and watch our backs," Ronaldo said.

Tooth flipped up his night vision to look at the other young man. "Can we trust you?"

"Can *I* trust *you*?" Namid asked.

"Yeah, man, I'm a marine."

Namid didn't reply.

"If you hear gunshots, then help," Ronaldo said. "Otherwise, stay here, okay?"

"Understood."

They set off for the storage units, cutting through a block of abandoned houses with boarded-up windows. When they reached the street, Ronaldo knelt and looked for contacts inside the fenced-off compound.

Several cars were parked inside, but not a single person or guard dog was in sight. A concrete wall bounded the far side.

As he made his way around, he smelled cigarette smoke and glimpsed motion inside. He heard a voice.

Tooth held up two fingers. Two contacts, both armed. It seemed they were guarding something, after all.

Ronaldo flashed a hand signal.

Tooth got up and crouch-ran across the street, rifle up. Ronaldo followed. When they got to the concrete wall, Ronaldo nodded at Tooth. He hopped up and climbed over, dropping silently to the other side. Ronaldo slithered over after him. The two contacts were all the way across the compound, but that didn't mean there weren't more.

Tooth got up and walked through a passage

between units, then knelt to look right and left. Seeing no one, he motioned for Ronaldo.

The first row of units was unguarded. Instead of checking them, Ronaldo pressed on, knowing that the traffickers would be guarding the units with something valuable inside.

Tooth went right, and Ronaldo went left, setting off through the middle of the open space, toward the voices. They had five rows of units to check before they reached the other side of the compound.

Ronaldo cleared each passage between them, with Tooth moving at the same pace.

As they neared the two men, a new voice spoke—a woman, and she sounded in distress.

Ronaldo and Tooth exchanged a nod and then swept the final row of units.

Ronaldo got down behind a pickup, the first vehicle in a neatly parked row. He could see one of the men.

Tooth suddenly showed up at his shoulder.

"Got a female prisoner," he said quietly. "Two men with shotguns."

Ronaldo moved low around the truck with his rifle shouldered. Tooth followed, and they moved out into the open.

"On the ground!" Ronaldo shouted.

Both men turned with their shotgun muzzles out, and both took rounds to the chest. They dropped, but one managed to get off a round of double-aught, punching a dozen small holes in the door of a parked car.

Ronaldo went over, kicked the shotgun away, and ended the man's squirming with a shot to the head. He swept the area for more hostiles but saw only a woman.

She was backing away, hands up, features shadowed in the darkness.

"We're not going to hurt you," Ronaldo said.

Tooth disarmed the two bodies and joined Ronaldo.

"It's okay," he said. "We're here to help."

The woman kept backing away toward the wall of units. In the green hue of his night vision, Ronaldo saw that several were open.

The woman stared wild-eyed, breathing heavily.

Ronaldo lowered his rifle, and Tooth followed his lead.

As soon as they did, she reached behind her back and pulled out a pistol.

"You killed them, you bastards!" she wailed.

Ronaldo didn't even have time to bring his gun up. She fired one shot and pitched forward with something attached to the back of her head.

Another figure had emerged on top of one of the storage units. Namid jumped down and ran over to retrieve his hatchet from her skull.

Ronaldo nudged her body over with his foot. He saw then that the wild eyes were not from fear, but from drugs. Zits marred her sallow flesh, and half her teeth were missing.

She wasn't a prisoner; she was one of them.

"Area's secure," Namid said, wiping the hatchet on her clothing and sheathing it back on his belt. He went to the open storage units and clicked a lighter. Ronaldo flipped up his NVGs and joined him.

Empty plastic buckets and jars of water littered the floor. In one corner were small piles of dried feces. Whoever had been kept here was long gone.

So what were these people guarding?

Ronaldo searched the other units for the next hour and discovered nothing.

His radio crackled, and he cursed as he pulled it out.

"Snake Two, go ahead, over," he said.

"Snake Two, this is Snake One," Hernández said. "That truck is headed away from Vegas and toward Arizona. Guess it's just rice after all."

"Fuck," Ronaldo said, kicking a metal door so hard it hurt his ankle. They had been too late, both here and with the truck.

Tonight wasn't just a disappointment for him; it would be one for Elena and Dom as well, when he called them. But he couldn't delay any longer.

They needed to know the truth—and to know he was still alive.

"Guess it's on to Vegas we go," Tooth said.

Namid looked at Ronaldo and Tooth in turn. "I hope you're ready to enter the lions' den."

-27-

The call that night was unexpected.

"It's your dad," Elena said.

She handed the cell phone to Dom, and he stepped into the living room of their apartment, holding it close to his ear. Almost in disbelief.

"Dad?" he said.

"Dom, how are you?" His father's voice crackled. The reception was bad, wherever he was.

"I'm . . . good. I've been worried sick about you. How are you?"

"Fine, but I'm afraid I still have no news on your sister."

Dom had already surmised as much from the dour look on his mom's face. She wasn't crying. Yet.

Dom turned his back slightly and whispered. "Mom isn't doing so good. When will you be home?"

"I'm not sure, but soon, I hope. Watch over her until I get home, okay?"

Dom looked back at his mom, but she had returned to the bedroom, where the dog Dom had rescued was resting.

"I can't talk long, but your mom will fill you in on some of the other stuff we talked about," Ronaldo said. His voice crackled in and out.

"Dad," Dom said. "Dad, I can't hear you."

"I love you."

He heard that. "I love you, too, Dad."

"Take care of your mom and yourself. I'll see you both really—"

And that was it. Dom waited for a call back, but it didn't come. After gearing up for work, he went to his parents' bedroom to check on his mom and the pit bull.

He opened the door quietly. Elena sat on the bed, next to the dog.

"Hey," she whispered.

"Hey," Dom said. "How's she doing?"

"Good."

Dom checked the bandage on the stump where her right hind leg had been amputated. The vet had no other choice but to chop it off.

Looking up, the pit bull wagged her tail. She pushed herself up and hopped to the floor before Dom could stop her. Crouching, he stroked her head as she licked his face.

"I always wanted a pittie," Dom said.

Elena smiled. It was the first smile Dom had seen on her face in a very long time.

"Dad said you'll fill me on some of the stuff," Dom said.

She went back to petting the dog, clearly not wanting to talk.

He decided to let it rest. He was just glad to have talked to his father. Knowing he was alive and unhurt filled him with relief.

Dom hung out there for a few minutes, even though he was late for work. But they both needed this.

Elena leaned down and hugged the dog. "We still need to name her," she said.

"I know. Got any ideas? I was thinking Cayenne," Dom said. "Like the pepper."

"I like that. She's kind of a firecracker."

"Do you like 'Cayenne'?" Dom asked the dog. "Is that a good name for you?"

She wagged her tail. He hugged her, feeling the thick, lean muscles. She was a fighter for sure, but she had a kind heart.

Dom kissed the big square head. "Look after my mom, okay?"

The dog licked his hand, and Dom got up. She hopped after him to the door. At first, she had been frightened of her own shadow, but she was already starting to trust him.

He felt a lot better about leaving Cayenne with his mom. It seemed to help her mood, and the dog would keep her safe. Even a tripod pit bull was a formidable adversary and a good alarm system.

By the time Dom got to the warehouse where the task force had gathered, he was energized and feeling good about his mom, the dog, his dad, and what he must do tonight.

He and Moose watched for the text revealing the top secret location of his next fight. The other officers waited around with Marks. He had moved them to a central location so they could be ready to drive anywhere at a moment's notice.

The wait before a mission was never good, but

seeing these loyal, uncorrupted men and women who stood with Marks against the crime families filled Dom with determination.

Seeing Camilla here also helped. Out of the hospital for only a day, she had insisted on coming on the raid. And truth was, they needed her. Not many people could be trusted.

Moose pulled out his phone and nodded at Dom. "Got it."

They went over to Marks, who kicked off the briefing.

"Gather round, everyone," he said. "Mission's a go."

The officers huddled around. Marks wouldn't divulge the location yet, just in case one of these people was a rat.

"Tonight, we take two kingpins off the street," Marks said. "Remember, we don't take them alive."

"I got no problem with that," Camilla said.

This got a couple of laughs; one sounded nervous.

Marks pointed at Dom. "Officer Salvatore has put his life on the line to get us close to the Vega brothers," he said. "Tonight, his hard work pays off."

"Hell yeah," Moose said.

The other officers grunted and nodded.

"Make no mistake," Marks said, "the brothers will be guarded with some major firepower. But we will have the advantage with a surprise attack. Questions?"

The warehouse was dead silent.

"Get ready to move out, and good hunting," Marks said.

He pulled Dom aside from the rest of the group as they finished gear prep.

"If something happens, look after my mom and my new dog," Dom said before Marks could say anything.

"You're going to be fine."

"I know, but just in case."

"We've got your back, and I know you can beat this guy."

"He's better than I am."

Marks held Dom's gaze. "If you believe that, then you have already lost."

"Sir . . ."

"You can win. Get him on the mat and use your jujitsu skills."

"I'll . . . I will."

"Good." Marks put a hand on his shoulder. "Good luck."

"You too."

The officers in armor, black masks, and helmets piled into four black SUVs. Camilla ran over, wincing as she stopped in front of Dom.

"Kick his ass, Dominic," she said. Then she leaned in and kissed him on the cheek.

Moose grinned.

Dom and Moose climbed aboard their ride, and the convoy pulled out of the garage. An hour later, they were at the former Chevron Oil refinery.

Moose parked on the east side, along with other vehicles that had already arrived. Almost all the silos on the other side of the razor-wire fence had been obliterated by bombs dropped during the Second Civil War.

Dom felt his heart rate accelerating. He had a bad feeling about this.

The invitation-only fight had a bigger crowd than Dom had thought when they got inside. A crowd of fifty had gathered outside one of the two silos still standing. Most of them looked like narcos, wearing fancy belt buckles, western shirts, and cowboy boots.

Men with machine pistols patrolled the grounds. The tight security confirmed what Dom had hoped: the Vega brothers would be here, although he didn't see them at the moment.

Dom hoped the risk would be worth the reward. Cops were going to die tonight. The question was how many, and whether they would take down the Vega brothers with them.

"Sementaliano."

Dom turned toward a smiling dark-skinned Latino not much older than he. He wore his checkered shirt open to expose gold chains.

"I'm Pedro Vega, but my friends call me Negro," he said.

Dom couldn't believe it. He was talking to the nephew of Esteban Vega. A guy with a reputation as a playboy and a killer.

Pedro glanced to Moose, then back to Dom. "I've seen you fight, and I hope you have some surprises tonight, amigo, because I've got a lot of money on you against Apache."

"I've come to win," Dom said.

"*Muy bien*," Pedro said. He nodded and walked away. Two of the guards who had accompanied him followed, but a third remained.

"Let's go," he said.

Moose started to follow, but the man shook his head. "You stay here until the fight starts."

"Good luck, man," Moose said.

Dom was led to a stairwell that wound up the silo

that would serve as the fight venue. Coming out on the rooftop, he was greeted with the glow of candles burning around human skulls decorated with paint. It looked like some sort of satanic ritual display. A fresh red circle had been painted to mark the ring.

But it wasn't the weird candles or skulls that made him pause. It was the two wooden baseball bats lying outside the ring. His gut dropped at the sight. He took off his coat and started stretching to keep his mind off the fight.

Fifteen minutes later, the crowd started to come up. When he saw Esteban and Miguel Vega, his fear vanished, replaced with sheer determination.

The crowd spread out around the rooftop. Moose was here, and he gave Dom a nod. The call had been made.

Marks and team would be here soon, moving on foot through the other side of the refinery.

All Dom had to do was put on a show. And stay alive.

Seeing Apache emerge from the crowd reminded him that this was not going to be easy, especially with the bats.

"You got lucky last time," Apache shouted. "This time, only a war can stop me from killing you!"

The same announcer from the earlier fights stepped out into the ring. He was already talking in Spanish to the crowd, getting them riled up.

Dom tried not to look at the Vega brothers, but Esteban was staring at him with a golden grin. He tipped his cowboy hat at Dom.

The announcer switched to English. "And now, what you all have been waiting for!" he shouted. "Apache against Sementaliano, the Italian Stallion."

Apache removed his shirt and dropped it to the

deck. Every inch of his body seemed to be lean, ropy muscle, all covered in tattoos. He ran a hand over the freshly buzzed sides of his scalp and then his slicked-back fauxhawk that seemed to shimmer in the moonlight.

"Let's GO!" yelled the announcer.

Dom walked to pick up a bat, but Apache beat him there and kicked it away. It hit one of the skulls and knocked over a candle.

Apache swung his bat, and Dom jumped back twice to avoid the blows. With each stroke, he came closer.

"You need a weapon to beat me, huh?" Dom asked.

Apache hawked and spat a yellow glob on the floor. Then he dropped the bat and strode toward Dom, throwing a flurry of long kicks and punches.

Dom blocked and parried, but his opponent was fast, and a kick got through. The foot cracked against Dom's shoulder and glanced off the top of his head.

He stumbled backward, then deflected another kick meant for his ribs. His forearm throbbed from the impact.

The crowd shouted and cheered as Dom winced in pain.

Vision blurred on the right side, and he moved away from Apache to catch his breath and prepare a ground strike.

Come on, Marks, he thought.

Apache kept coming, giving Dom only seconds to prepare. He threw a snap kick, and Dom hammered down just above the thigh, stuffing the kick before catching Apache in the ribs with his knee.

The spectators roared. It caught Apache off guard, and Dom seized the opportunity.

He lowered his shoulders and rammed Apache to take him down. But all Dom managed to do was wrap him up.

Dom tried to sweep a leg, but Apache brought his elbow down into Dom's back once, twice, three times, forcing him to release.

He staggered back, fists up.

A crooked grin crossed the warrior's face. He said something in his native language and then came at Dom again with another barrage of punches.

And again Dom deflected the blows, managing to land a fist on Apache's left cheek. Even the man's face was rock hard, and Dom felt a knuckle pop.

He pulled back his throbbing right hand.

Everything seemed to blur around him as the fight continued.

Apache jumped into the air and whipped out a crescent kick, narrowly missing his chin. Dom fell backward into the crowd, taking several people down with him.

"Get up, pussy!" Apache yelled. "Let's go!"

Dom pushed against the floor as people moved away from him. On his knees, he looked out and saw muzzle flashes like fireflies in the eastern part of the compound.

Hell yeah.

He got up, feeling the flush of adrenaline, and returned to the ring, hoping to buy Marks and his team a few more precious seconds.

"You want more?" Dom shouted.

Apache's smile vanished.

He ran at Dom, and Dom walked toward him. As Apache jumped into the air for a kick, Dom went low, slipping under him. He got up and turned as Apache touched down.

Dom kicked his right knee as hard as he could, and Apache crumpled to the side, screeching in pain.

At first the crowd didn't react, but then came the screams.

And the gunfire.

These weren't suppressed shots, but loud automatic fire.

The crowd scattered, almost everyone pulling out a gun as they ran for the stairwell. Dom looked for the Vega brothers, but they were lost in the chaos or already gone.

He rushed to the edge of the silo to look down at what was happening.

A convoy of SUVs screeched to a stop below, and men in masks jumped out. But they didn't look like part of the task force.

Dom suddenly realized what was happening. The masked men weren't cops or Vegas. They were someone else who had come to kill the Vega brothers. They opened fire on everyone, including the police officers rushing the silo.

Dom stared in horror until something hit him in the back. He crashed to the floor.

He already knew it was going to be the Apache. The tall warrior stood awkwardly, favoring his jacked-up knee, a bat in one hand.

"You won't get away this time, pussy," Apache snarled.

He raised the bat in both hands, above his head, and Dom could do nothing but hold up his arm to protect his head.

Someone suddenly slammed into Apache, and in

the blur of bodies, Dom glimpsed a hairstyle even more distinctive than Apache's fauxhawk. He pushed himself up, staggering.

A few feet away, Moose had Apache on the ground. He slammed the warrior's head on the metal deck over and over until it crackled like a watermelon.

Panting, Moose rolled off and motioned for Dom. "Come . . . on . . . man," he said.

Dom heard his friend, but he couldn't pull his eyes away from the sight below.

A dozen officers lay on the broken asphalt, and the masked men were still firing on the downed men and women and on those retreating.

Cops weren't just dying. They were being slaughtered.

* * *

Antonio sat at the long head table set up on the terrace. He had enjoyed the beautiful ceremony between Crystal and Raffaello for the past three hours, but he was growing tired and a bit bored.

The bride and groom were having their first dance on the stone terrace inside the walled-off compound. The DJ booth flashed like a police car. The bass line from a rap song Antonio had never heard before boomed loud enough to rattle the fillings in his teeth.

He took a drink of coffee just for the caffeine.

On the dance floor, Raff's redheaded bride looked stunning in her traditional white dress. Raff, dashing in his white tuxedo with a red rose, leaned in for a kiss after the song ended. Family surrounding the dance floor laughed and cheered. Raff held Crystal's hand in the air.

Antonio had never seen his old friend so happy. He raised his glass of champagne and yelled in Italian, "To the beautiful bride and her handsome groom!"

Raff looked to Antonio, radiating a smile of pure bliss and joy.

Another song came on, and the couple danced near a table covered in a white cloth. On it, a tower of cake waited to be carved up. Drawn onto the side with frosting were the home countries of the bride and groom: Ireland and Italy.

Soon they would take a bite of the most expensive cake Antonio had ever paid for in his life. It was worth it, of course, but it put things into perspective.

Outside the compound walls, most people in the city were suffering. Going to bed hungry, cold, or sick.

And somewhere out there, his men were killing those who stood in his way of making this city his kingdom. Vinny, Christopher, Doberman, and Frankie were out there with Moretti associates, doing his bidding. The rest of the family was here, clapping and having fun, oblivious to what was happening at the former oil plant.

Raff motioned for people to join, and they flooded out onto the terrace. Lino took his sister Angela out there, both of them laughing.

"You just going to sit there? Or are you going to dance with me?" Lucia said, her tone kinder.

"You know I don't dance."

"You used to," she said. "Now, come on."

She put a hand over his shoulder, and he took it with a sigh. Then he followed her to the improvised dance floor. Lino wiped the sweat from his shaved head and then nodded when he saw Antonio.

Yellowtail was getting down. Surprisingly agile considering all the bullets he had taken over the past year, he had shucked off his suit jacket and the white shirt underneath and was busting moves in his suit pants, white tank top, and gold cross.

Showing off his scars as usual, Antonio thought.

An excited crowd circled Yellowtail as he twirled and contorted in an impromptu break dance.

Antonio led Lucia out to the middle of the floor as the music switched to a smoother, more romantic beat. He gently but also firmly took her by the waist, his eyes meeting hers.

Lucia was still mad at him for his severe manner with their son, but that was her way. She held grudges, and she would not let it go until he apologized.

This was one thing he couldn't back down on, though. The fate of their son was hanging in the balance. Antonio had to stick to his guns, but he could still lighten the blow.

She seemed to soften as they started to dance. More family members joined them, laughing and having fun. A faster song came on, and Antonio picked up the pace. He twirled her just as he used to when they were younger.

Marco, sitting at a table with his friends, looked up when one of them pointed. He shrugged and went back to playing on a new tablet.

"I know you're not happy with me," Antonio said to Lucia, "but we can't baby Marco anymore. It's time he learned to be a man."

"I don't want this life for him."

"Neither do I, my love. And that's why I'm sending

him to a school where he can get a good education and be around kids his age."

He twirled her again, and she cracked a hint of a smile.

Antonio found his groove and started to settle into his old dance moves. Lino and Yellowtail cheered him on, and applause broke out all around. Raff and Crystal watched, laughing, from the edge of the dance floor.

Lucia smiled wider.

"Antonio," she said, blushing.

"What? Is this not what you wanted?"

She reached out, and he took her hands again, falling back into sync with her as they danced. All around them, the family relaxed and enjoyed the celebration. For the first time in as long as he could remember, Antonio was having fun.

Another song came on, but before this one ended, Antonio saw Christopher across the terrace, near the circle drive, waving. All sense of fun and celebration left him, and he remembered why he rarely felt so carefree.

"I'll be right back," he said.

"Is everything okay?" Lucia asked.

"Yes, fine. If I'm not back, cut the cake without me."

She nodded.

Antonio hurried off to meet with Christopher. Vinny was with him. They were both flushed, but uninjured from what he could tell at first glance. Frankie and Doberman were standing by the garage across the grounds, where their vehicles were parked.

Antonio had been enjoying himself so much, he hadn't even seen or heard them come in.

"What happened?" he asked.

"The Vegas were there, but so were the cops," Vinny said, still out of breath.

"I know," Antonio said.

"You do?" Christopher asked.

Antonio had kept his plans a secret again, not even telling his brother this time. But if things had gone south, then they needed to know.

"The night after we got back from Naples, I met with Chief Stone and made a new deal with him to get rid of a task force that has been causing us problems."

"*What!*" Vinny gasped. "So it wasn't Detective Clarke that sold out those cops—it was Chief Stone?"

"Why didn't you tell me?" Christopher asked, just as shocked as his son.

"The deal wasn't broken. A new one has been made," Antonio said. "Stone promised me the Vegas. I couldn't let the cops get him first."

"Well, Esteban and Miguel got away," Christopher said. "Was that part of the plan?"

Antonio clenched his jaw. This was an unforeseen and unfortunate development.

"We'll get them," he said with a grunt. "Soon."

Antonio looked at his brother. Saw the blood on his face, and the anger in his eyes.

"Go get cleaned up," he said. "The night is still young, brother. There is still much to celebrate. The Canavaros are gone, the task force we couldn't tap is gone, and Raff is married."

Christopher hesitated, then turned and stormed off.

Vinny remained behind.

"We lost two men, Don Antonio," he said. "And not all the cops are dead."

Then he, too, walked away, leaving Antonio to ponder what had happened.

A cool breeze ruffled his tuxedo as he stood there. Despite the cool air, his flesh was hot with anger.

He turned back to the terrace. The wedding couple were at the table with the cake now. Raff sliced into it with a knife and pulled out a piece.

Antonio looked out at his family, all of them still oblivious to what had happened. His son had put the tablet away and was laughing with some of his friends. Lino was talking to Yellowtail and knocking back glasses of wine. Carmine was kissing his wife on the neck, making her laugh and swat him.

In this moment, Antonio wished he didn't have the burden of being the boss. But he wouldn't have it any other way. Fun was a young man's pursuit.

His was war. And he was damn good at it.

He had finally avenged his family by killing the Canavaros. The image of gunning down Roberto in front of his sister surfaced in his mind, but he buried it. There was no need to relive vengeance. He was finally at peace after restoring the family's honor. They might never return to Naples, but they had a home here now, and the beginnings of an empire.

Antonio started walking toward his family as Raff stuffed a piece of cake in Crystal's mouth. Frosting stuck to her chin, and she backed away, taken by surprise. Then she laughed and grabbed a piece to feed to her husband.

The crowd clapped around them. But over the noise came a humming sound that Antonio couldn't quite place.

He looked to the sky. Now he remembered the noise. It was the sound of war.

Antonio started running. "Everyone, get down!" he shouted.

He spotted a shadow crossing the moon. The shadow dipped, and the shape of a drone came into focus. The remote-controlled machine dived toward the terrace.

Raff looked up and grabbed Crystal, shielding her body with his just before they both vanished in a fireball.

The impact shook the ground, and shrapnel whizzed in all directions. Even from a hundred feet away, Antonio could feel the heat of the blast.

He raised an arm to shield his face and ran toward the screams on the burning terrace. Several simmering bodies, most of them still moving, were scattered around the flaming pile of rubble that had been a table, chairs, and the newlyweds.

"Lucia, Marco!" Antonio shouted.

He searched the smoke for his family as people ran, shrieking in horror.

Eyes burning from the smoke, he yelled for his family again. Then he saw them near the head table. Lucia clutched Marco against her. Both appeared unharmed.

Antonio ran to them.

Morretti associates flocked to help the wounded and evacuate the terrace.

"Antonio!" Lucia yelled, crying.

"Dad, what happened?" Marco shouted.

Antonio put his arm around both of them and herded them away. Christopher and Vinny were running toward the terrace now, only partially dressed in their suits, hair waving in the wind and smoke.

"Help the others!" Antonio yelled.

He glanced over his shoulder to see Lino and Angela fleeing the devastation. But one person was still there. Yellowtail stood at the edge of the flaming wreckage of the drone and table, shielding his face from the glow.

There wasn't much left of Raff or his wife—just blood and scraps of meat and bone and clothing in the smoldering crater.

Antonio checked Lucia and Marco again to make sure they weren't hurt. But the shock wouldn't go away. No stranger to death and gore, Antonio couldn't seem to shake the sight of his dead friend and his wife of less than four hours.

Of all his soldiers, Raff had been the most loyal. And on what should have been the happiest day of his life, he had been killed.

No. He was murdered.

Rage gripped Antonio as he led his family to the safety of their castle. He would find whoever had done this and kill them slowly, savoring every second.

But as he walked, he had a feeling—no, he *knew*— exactly who had done this.

The brothers he failed to kill tonight had already struck back.

He should have been there instead of celebrating here. Next time, he wouldn't make the same mistake. Sometimes, one must do things oneself. And next time, he would.

-28-

Three months had passed since Ronaldo left Los Angeles, and he still hadn't made it home to see his wife and son. The journey with the Desert Snakes and their guide Namid had taken them south, east, north, and even into the heart of Las Vegas.

And there was still no sign of Monica or the Shepherds.

Ronaldo had held doggedly on to hope and had even encouraged Namid to hold on to hope about his sister. But that hope had flaked away like an old scab.

In two days, the team would start the journey back to Los Angeles. It was time for Ronaldo to see Elena and Dom. Going home empty handed, with no leads, was heartbreaking, but he needed to see them.

Marks had been the one to persuade him to give up the hunt for now. Things were getting worse in Los Angeles. From what little Ronaldo knew, the strike team working under Marks had been ambushed at an oil plant while trying to take down the Vega brothers.

Driving the Humvee, Ronaldo thought of his

promise to his wife, who would never forgive him for the night their baby was taken. She hadn't forgiven Dom, either, but Ronaldo didn't blame his son. He blamed himself. But while he hated giving up, this wasn't the end.

The radio crackled with a message from Hernández. They were going to pull off and rest a bit, eat something.

Ronaldo followed the M-ATV and parked. But he didn't get out and join the other men for a break. He took his rifle and a pair of binoculars and started toward a low bluff.

"Wait up," Namid said. "I'll come."

Ronaldo didn't want company, but he wasn't going to say no. The young Mojave tracker had proved his loyalty and support over the past two months. And he had saved both Ronaldo and Tooth from the crazy woman in Boulder City.

"So you're going back to Los Angeles in two days?" Namid asked.

"Yes, to see my wife and son. How about you?"

"I'll go back to the rez, see what my father wants me to do."

Ronaldo stopped and pulled out his water bottle. Sweat beaded on his forehead. Spring had finally arrived, and temperatures were rising every day.

"The mission doesn't end," Ronaldo said. "You're welcome to stay out here with us, to search for the men that took your sister."

Namid nodded.

"You know, my father was right about you," he said.

"Right how?"

"He said you're a great warrior, and from what I've seen these past few months, I couldn't agree more."

"Not sure that's a compliment," Ronaldo said. "Killing people doesn't seem like something I should be proud of."

"You should if they are evil."

Fight evil with evil. It was how he had eradicated so much of it over the past year and a half. And it was what he would go right on doing to bring to justice the men who had taken his Monica.

Namid squinted and then raised his binos.

"You see something?" Ronaldo asked.

"Yeah, I think so."

Namid started up the side of a hill and suddenly crouched down at the top. Ronaldo joined him there and glassed the horizon. What he saw made him pause.

A caravan inched across a stretch of desert in the distance. Trails of alkaline dust followed a dozen plodding horses trying to keep up with the old pickups and panel trucks.

The brownish plume must be how Namid had spotted the convoy.

Ronaldo pushed up his goggles and looked through the binos again. The view transported him back almost a century and a half, to a time when settlers with ox-drawn wagons risked the perilous journey west in search of a place to call home.

But this caravan wasn't carrying people seeking a better life—it was carrying slaves. He would bet a year's salary on it. Most of them were probably young, like Monica, from a generation that would never have the opportunities he had as a kid.

Ronaldo checked the bearing on his compass. Sure enough, the traffickers—or slavers, as they were also called now—were headed northeast, to Las Vegas.

The Second Civil War had changed a lot of things, but Vegas, spared by the nuclear fires and radiation, remained Sin City. You could fulfill your most depraved fantasies there.

Their choice of the desert over the highway confirmed his suspicions. Anyone who took the dangerous overland route through the desert had something to hide.

The question Ronaldo always asked ran its endless loop in his mind. *Have you finally found Monica?*

Had they finally found the Shepherds?

Ronaldo zoomed in on the convoy, checking the small arms they carried. They had a lot of weapons, but they didn't have an M240. He did.

He noticed black smoke on the southern horizon. Another settlement that survived the war had fallen to raiders. In the new American Wild West, it was survival of the cruelest.

Ronaldo placed the goggles back over his eyes and hurried back down the sand dune with Namid.

Hernández waited in the shade of the Humvee with Pierce while Tooth and Bettis hung out near the M-ATV. They all looked relaxed until they saw Ronaldo and Namid running over.

"What's up?" Bettis asked.

"Got a caravan to the east," Ronaldo said. "Ten men on horseback. Another dozen in the back of four pickups. A black SUV and three enclosed trucks. Didn't see anything but small arms on them."

"Even if it's just M16s, that's still a lot of fire-power," said Hernández.

"You think it's the Shepherds?" Tooth asked.

"Mount up," Hernández said. "I want to take a look."

The men piled into the vehicles, with Tooth taking the wheel of the Humvee, and Pierce in the M-ATV.

"Salvatore, up top," Bettis said.

Ronaldo climbed into the modified turret of the Humvee and grabbed their new M240. Scratches and rust ran along the barrel of the weapon they had recovered on a raid a month ago. Like much of their gear, the gun was at least a decade old.

Despite the dated equipment, scorching sun, and danger, time in the desert continued to get the team a steady check with hazard pay that went to their families back home. It was far more than the average citizen got.

Ronaldo pulled his tan shemagh scarf over his nose and made sure his goggles were secure. Pierce drove around the dune and tore out onto the open stretch of sand, trailing the caravan.

The two vehicles quickly closed in, and Ronaldo used the time to pick out targets. He counted four pickups, three enclosed trucks, an Escalade, and the mounted men.

Leading the convoy was a boat of a car with over-size off-road tires.

"I'll cut 'em off," Hernández said over the radio. "Salvatore, send a few rounds across their path to show 'em we're serious."

Pierce pulled up alongside and tried to cut them off, but the vehicles and horses weren't stopping.

Ronaldo waited for the Humvee to level out after a

jolt and then pulled the trigger. Tracer rounds streaked through the air, punching into the sand in front of the car.

That did the trick.

The vehicles rolled to a stop, and the horsemen worked to calm their mounts. Ronaldo spotted more armed men inside the pickups and estimated another half dozen inside the Escalade and the car with the monster tires.

His heart quickened. These could be the Shepherds.

All his earlier sense of despair vanished, replaced with hope that these were the lowlifes they were searching for. One thing was certain: they had a lot of firepower.

So far, none of the hard-looking men had pointed a weapon at the Humvee. But this was the Wild West, and things could change fast.

Most of the escorts wore goggles, face masks, and camo fatigues. A few had light coats to protect against the wind and dust.

"Drop your weapons and get out of the vehicles!" Hernández yelled in his deep, gravelly voice.

Ronaldo slowly played the barrel back and forth while his squad mates fanned out with their rifles on the armed slavers.

The Escalade's front and left-rear passenger doors opened, and two men stepped out. The one on the left looked like the muscle. A glistening bald head, tattooed with a crown, suggested that this was no ordinary trafficker.

Nor was the man in the fancy silk shirt and cowboy hat. He removed a pair of gold aviator sunglasses and propped them on his short-cropped hairline.

This man was a narco and, judging from his appearance, a well-connected one.

"What seems to be the problem here?" the man said in a thick Mexican accent.

Hernández stepped forward, his rifle cradled. "No problem at the moment. We just want to know what you got in those trucks."

The man grinned, revealing two gold crowns on his front teeth. A thin mustache curled around his lips as he reached into his vest.

"Careful, there, *mi amigo*," Hernández said, raising his rifle slightly.

This wiped the smile off the guy's face. Apparently, he didn't view the lieutenant in the same regard.

"Not your amigo, *puto*. I'm Paco Vega." He pulled his bandanna down from his chin to show off his neck tattoo: a dagger with a ruby in the hilt. The equivalent of showing off his gun—or dick size, for that matter.

Ronaldo slid his finger along the trigger, his gut tight in anticipation of the inevitable fight. His mind recalled the final words of the marine turned raider back at the logistics base in Barstow.

It made sense now. "The Shepherds" wasn't just a code name for the Vega family's trafficking businesses—the *Vegas* took their slaves to *Vegas* the city.

The bodyguard on Paco's left approached. That got him the M240 pointed at his face.

"Take another step, and your tattoo will be a decal on that fancy truck," Ronaldo said.

Paco Vega's eyes flitted to him and then back to Hernández. "I got papers for these trucks in my suit jacket, if you'd let me pull them out."

"I betcha do, and I don't much care," Hernández said. "Open the trucks."

Paco licked his thin lips, then nodded at one of his men, who walked over to a gray truck with the faded letters "U-Haul" on the side. It had air grates, but the inside had to be hot as a blast furnace.

Moving to get a better look at the interior, Ronaldo could see several people in shackles.

"I bet them girls are all here of their own accord, right?" Hernández said.

Paco smiled again. "That's what my paperwork says."

"Pierce, go check it out."

Ronaldo managed to keep his eyes on the men, though he had to fight the urge to look in the back of the truck. From his vantage point, he could see a few boys. None appeared old enough to grow a beard. From what Ronaldo had heard and seen over the past few months, the sex traders in Vegas loved the boys for clients with certain tastes.

"Open those, too," Pierce said.

The man who had opened the first truck moved to open another, and Ronaldo leaned left for a better view. His scarf fell away from his nose and mouth.

Pierce, Tooth, Bettis, and Namid moved in, and as soon as they did, gunfire cracked over the whistling of the wind.

Blood suddenly exploded out of the back of Pierce's head from a bullet through the mouth that knocked him backward. Two more shots to the face, and his legs folded under him.

Hernández was the second to go down. He fell to his knees as several bullets punched into his chest armor. Somehow, he still managed to bring up his rifle and fire.

It all happened so fast, Ronaldo didn't have a chance to fire before a flurry of shots pinged off the turret's armor plating, forcing him down.

Heart pounding, he rose back up and pulled the trigger, unleashing a barrage of fire into the pickup truck where three slavers had taken cover on the other side.

Automatic gunfire erupted from all directions, pinging against the Humvee. Another roar of pain came from behind the turret. Hernández fired like a madman, screaming as he squeezed off burst after burst.

Screams from the prisoners rose over the din.

Ronaldo raked the big gun back and forth at any slaver foolish enough to expose himself. Once he had forced them down, he fired with precision, taking down anyone that dared to show their face with bursts of fire.

Hernández went down and crawled across the sand. Bullets slammed into his back, and he jerked from each impact. For a fleeting moment, he locked eyes with Ronaldo, pain and terror on his face.

A bullet to the base of his jaw ended the big man's suffering.

Ronaldo screamed as he took down a slaver. Two others jumped up to fire at the same time, and he sent both sprawling backward.

In front of the Humvee, Paco had pushed himself up to his knees. He fired a gold-plated .45 pistol, catching Ronaldo in the shoulder. The impact knocked Ronaldo backward, but he managed to pivot back into position and train the barrel on the gangster.

The rounds erased his gold crowns, along with the rest of his face, in a spray of blood and bone. His bodyguard, hiding behind the Escalade, let out a roar and fired his Kalashnikov.

Ronaldo swung the gun over and fired. The rounds destroyed the man's left arm below the elbow, forcing him to release his weapon. He looked at his shredded flesh, then tried to raise the AK-47 in his other hand.

"Fight evil with evil," Ronaldo said. He pulled the trigger again. It clicked on a jammed round. He watched the man struggle to aim his weapon while blood from his arm trickled off his fingertips.

"Come on, come on," Ronaldo said, working the charging handle. He abandoned the gun and used his M4 instead. But Namid beat him to it. The young warrior had flanked and gotten behind the guy. Two hatchet blows to the head finished the job.

He ducked away, and Ronaldo went back to looking for targets with his M4.

One of the slavers popped up and aimed at Namid. Ronaldo lined up the sights and fired, blowing out the side of his head.

Namid got behind a car and then nodded at Ronaldo.

Several more shots rang out before the wind again took over, whistling through the eerie silence after the battle.

When the ringing in his ears faded, Ronaldo heard other noises: the cries of frightened prisoners, and moans of wounded fighters. Stars broke before his vision, and he felt the warmth of his blood seeping down his chest as he scanned a battlefield littered with corpses.

He shot a man crawling across the ground. The slaver fell limp not far from Pierce.

Ronaldo searched for Bettis and Tooth but didn't see them.

"Bettis! Tooth! Where are you?" he shouted.

"I'm good," Bettis yelled back.

Ronaldo turned toward the voice and saw Bettis hunched beside Tooth, who was down.

"You okay, Salvatore?" Bettis asked.

Ronaldo ducked back into the Humvee, pressing his hand to his shoulder. He forced his rifle up as he got out, his shoulder throbbing in great waves of pain.

Tooth tried to smile as he approached. "This one hurts worse than the last."

"Mine too," Ronaldo replied. He swung his rifle toward movement under a truck, where a prisoner came crawling out.

"Help us!" shouted a voice.

Ronaldo snapped into action. "Namid, stay with Tooth. Bettis, with me."

They ran over to the caravan, and Bettis went to open the other trucks while Ronaldo helped pull prisoners out of the first. It was full of young girls and boys. He scanned the dusty faces quickly. Monica's was not among them.

"Bettis, stay with them," Ronaldo said.

He traded places with Bettis and went to the next truck, which was filled with women—girls, really. Most were still in their teens. He scanned their faces one by one, stopping on a girl slumped with her back to the metal wall, brown hair covering most of her face.

"Monica," he whispered.

The girl pulled the curtain of brown hair from her face and tried to focus her catatonic brown eyes.

Not his daughter—just some other poor child stolen from her family.

Her eyes suddenly widened, and when Ronaldo held up a hand to calm her, she let out a scream. A gunshot cracked, and realization set in when a fiery needle punched into his lower back, and another through his neck.

Ronaldo dropped to the ground, sending the world upside down. He saw Tooth come stumbling and screaming across the sand, firing a pistol at the slaver who had shot Ronaldo in the back. Namid was right behind him, his rifle sweeping for more contacts.

"Ronaldo!" Bettis cried. He rushed over and dropped to the sand. Tooth finished off the slaver who had shot Ronaldo, then fired three more rounds just to be sure.

"Oh, shit, no," Tooth said as he hunched down. The pain in his voice confirmed what Ronaldo already knew. There was no coming back from this.

Bettis tried to stop the bleeding, pressing his palm against the wound in his neck, but Ronaldo could feel his life force draining from the three holes in his body.

"Don't speak," Bettis said when Ronaldo tried. He swallowed, choking on blood. The world went dark for a moment before he fought his way back to the light.

Namid put a hand on Ronaldo but didn't say anything.

Both Bettis and Tooth were staring at him and talking, but Ronaldo couldn't hear their voices. He reached in his vest pocket and fished out the note he had written.

"Give . . ." He coughed, blood bubbling from his lips. "Dom."

Bettis made the sign of the cross and gripped Ronaldo's hand while Tooth took over applying pressure to the neck wound. A tear fell from Tooth's eyes—the first Ronaldo had seen since they met. Namid, too, had glazed eyes.

They all knew there was no coming back from this.

Ronaldo tried to smile at his friends, knowing they were here for him at the end, and wishing Marks were here, too, and his family. With the last bit of energy in him, Ronaldo pulled out the bloodstained note he had written to Dom and Elena.

Bettis took it and nodded. "We got you, brother," he said. "We'll look after your family."

"I'm so sorry, bro," Tooth said, bowing his head and sobbing.

"May you pass into the next life safely, my friend," Namid said. "It was an honor fighting with you."

Closing his eyes, Ronaldo allowed the soft darkness to envelop him like a swarm of butterflies. His fight ended here. It was finally time to rest and pass the torch to his son. The fate of their family was on his shoulders now, and Ronaldo died knowing that if anyone could save them, it was Dominic.

-29-

The Four Diamonds were all up and running, and business was booming. Vinny had helped ensure that by securing the new drug supply from former Sinaloa cartel boss Eduardo Nina.

The profits from their expanding operation had filled the Moretti coffers to the point that Don Antonio was starting to move into new businesses.

For that, Vinny was thankful. The more legit money they made, the fewer people died.

After a long shift of overseeing operations at the Four Diamonds, Vinny and Doberman drove across town to a new Moretti project, a casino that Don Antonio was having built in old Hollywood.

The family had salvaged many of the machines, card tables, and other games from the Commerce Hotel, storing them for later.

Later had become now.

Vinny parked on a famous street where tourists had once spotted actors, athletes, and celebrities driving Ferraris and Lamborghinis. Storefronts that were once part of the expensive shopping district stood boarded up or lay in rubble.

But soon that would change. Vinny's uncle wasn't the only entrepreneur with his eye on this area.

"What's your uncle going to call this place?" Doberman asked.

"I'm not sure yet." Vinny straightened his silver tie and buttoned one button on his black Armani suit jacket. He walked toward the collapsed awning over the front drive of the abandoned building. Letters from the former sign were scattered amid a scree of rubble. A bulldozer had already started clearing the debris.

With all the damage from the war and the squatters who had moved in afterward, it was hard to imagine what this debris pile might look like again.

Rush and a crew of Moretti associates had chased off the last of the homeless a week earlier, setting one of them on fire to make sure everyone got the message.

Vinny scrutinized the building in the waning sunlight. His uncle had grand plans for this place, and knowing his uncle, it was going to be a world-class casino.

Two cars parked and flicked off their lights. Yellowtail and Lino got out, leading Don Antonio across the street. Christopher joined them a moment later from another vehicle.

"Good evening, Don Antonio," Doberman said.

"Yes, it is," Antonio said. Tonight he wore a black hat, which he tipped to his men.

Vinny gave him a polite nod in return.

The group walked to a metal trailer that the contractor had furnished with tables and chairs.

Carmine and Frankie were already inside, looking over some of the blueprints.

"Hard to believe you're going to turn that dump into this," Carmine said, holding up a drawing. "I just hope it's worth the price."

"It will be," Antonio said. He went to the window of the trailer, rubbing the thick beard he had grown over the past few weeks. He turned back to the table. "You will see, in time."

Vinny had heard the men privately question the new venture—especially how they were going to make any money in a city where almost everyone was poor and struggling to find work and make a living.

But one of the things Vinny had learned over the past year was that addicts always found money for drugs. And there were still plenty of fat cats out there making a killing off construction projects. Many of them were from other countries. There were also plenty of gangsters making money off the drug trade, who had to spend it somewhere. His uncle seemed to be reading his mind.

"It's not just us trying to make a dime; remember that," Antonio said. "Where one shark feeds, so do others."

Yellowtail fingered his gold cross as he looked at the drawings.

"This place is going to be fucking sick when it's done," he said. "I can't wait to see the clubs and bars, man."

The door to the trailer opened, and Vinny took a long look at the men who entered. Chief Stone climbed into the trailer, followed by Mayor Buren. The head of the LAPD wore street clothes and a baseball cap, but the mayor was in a three-piece suit.

He was fit and cocky, but what made dealing with

him even more unpleasant was the Vandyke beard that was way too dark to be natural color.

"Don Antonio," Buren said, flashing his business smile.

Antonio shook his hand and then shook the chief's hand. The chief kept his hat on. He clearly didn't like being seen with the Morettis.

Vinny didn't especially like being seen with cops, either, but their deal was working out damn well for both parties.

"Have a seat, gentlemen," Antonio said.

Everyone pulled up chairs around the table, but he remained standing.

"I called you here tonight at the site of the casino to discuss far more than gambling," Antonio said. "I called you to discuss the very future of this city—a future in which its citizens will once again flourish."

"That's the same future I'm working toward," Buren said.

Chief Stone didn't reply.

"With the rise of radiation-related illnesses and diseases from the toxins in the air, it's now more important to ensure that medicine is readily available," Antonio said. "It's also important for clean drinking water, as well as power, to be available for all."

"We are doing our best," Buren said.

"And with my help, you can do better," Antonio said. "I'll be donating three million dollars in gold to provide medicine to the citizens of Los Angeles, and another three million for construction projects to expand the network of pipes distributing clean water."

Buren stood and put a hand over his chest. "Thank you, Don Antonio. That is very generous of you."

Antonio nodded and looked to Chief Stone. "And how are you coming with bringing my enemies to justice?"

Stone shifted uncomfortably in his seat. He finally took off his hat and placed it on the table, exposing his natural tonsure.

"Outside threats are going to keep getting worse," he said, "and I've had to send five hundred officers to the border to help Sherriff Benson protect the walls. The Vegas are hunkered down in the Angel Pyramids, and I simply don't have the manpower to go in and get them out."

Antonio scratched his beard.

This was the first time in months that Vinny had seen his uncle meet with the mayor and the chief of police, but he knew that it happened more often than that. There had to be more to tonight's meeting than telling them about his charitable donations.

"One thing I failed to mention is that the money isn't the only thing contingent on my receiving the heads of my enemies," Antonio said. His eyes flitted to the mayor and then the chief. "Your *jobs* are contingent."

Mayor Buren reached for his tie, then placed his hands in his lap.

"We can bring this city back from the brink together," Antonio said, "or I can find someone else to work with. Make no mistake, Los Angeles is no longer ruled by a democratic process. The voters do not get a say, nor do you."

Antonio clasped his hands behind his back.

"There can only be one king," Christopher said. "And his name will be Moretti."

Buren and Stone looked ahead, not responding.

"Figure out a way to get the Vegas, or I will figure

out a way to replace you," Antonio said. "They must pay for what they did during my friend Raffaello's wedding, profaning a sacred night."

"Where is Mariana López?" Christopher asked.

"She's in prison and is well guarded," Stone replied. "Rest assured, she isn't going anywhere. However, if you'd prefer that she hang herself in a cell, that can be arranged."

Christopher looked to his brother.

"No," Antonio said. "She could be valuable in the future."

Stone nodded.

Vinny wasn't sure what his uncle or his dad wanted with Mariana at this point, but he had a feeling it had to do with Miguel Vega. He was known to have a relationship with Mariana and had already tried to break her out of prison once.

"Bring me Esteban and Miguel," Antonio said.

Stone nodded. He remained sitting with Buren until Antonio unclasped his hands and pounded the table.

"Now, get the fuck out of my sight," he said.

Both men got up and left the trailer.

Antonio acted as if nothing had happened, and pulled over an elevation drawing. The door had just shut when he started talking about the casino with the Moretti men.

An hour later, the meeting ended, and Vinny was walking back to the car with Doberman. A voice called out. It was his uncle.

"Ride with me," Antonio said.

Vinny got into a Mercedes with him, and Christopher took the wheel. Vinny knew that something was up when Christopher reached into his pocket and pulled out a hip flask. He handed it back to Vinny.

This wasn't just any old flask. It was made of sterling silver. He could tell by the weight.

"A gift," Antonio said. "From your father and me, for your hard work this year."

"Thank you," Vinny said.

"Take a drink," Christopher said.

Vinny brought it to his lips. There was no mistaking the smell of tequila. Not the traditional spirit, but he understood the irony.

"The best we could find," Antonio said. "Figured you should acquire a taste for it since you might be seeing Eduardo Nina again."

Vinny took a drink. It was smooth and warm.

"Your future is bright, Vin," Antonio said. "Someday, you will be a captain with your own crew, perhaps even the head of the family."

"The king of Los Angeles," Christopher said.

Vinny passed the flask around on the drive back to the compound. He thanked his uncle and father. Then, instead of going inside, he took the flask and walked into the gardens, now replanted after the drone attack.

The stone path and terrace had also been replaced. But Vinny paused to look at the area where Raff and his wife had died. The only evidence of the explosion was a few broken tiles that had yet to be replaced.

Vinny took a sip of the tequila. Then a gulp. The liquor burned his throat and warmed his gut. He took a second gulp, hoping to blur the memory of that night and many other nights. Nights of cruelty, violence, and death.

He was on a fast track to becoming a captain, but

was it worth what he must become? Did he really want to be king?

He walked to the eastern section of the Moretti compound, where the new mausoleum stood between two jacaranda trees. Raff was entombed here with Crystal.

Before it was over, more Moretti soldiers and their family members would be dead. And Vinny knew he could very well end up being one of them. He might never be king, or even a captain, for that matter. But this was his family, and this was the life he had chosen.

In war, sacrifices were made. He was a soldier now. There was no turning back.

* * *

The solar farm shimmered under a scorching sun. Dom stood in the tower overlooking it. Wind turbines slashed the horizon as cotton-puff clouds scudded across an ocean of blue sky.

It was a beautiful day in Los Angeles County, but he wasn't here to enjoy the weather or admire all the clean energy. Months after his father died in the desert while looking for Monica, Dom had met Marks at the nearly complete site, which was already feeding energy to a sizable chunk of the county.

They had seen each other only a few times in the months after the task force was slaughtered at the oil plant.

Marks shut the door to the tower and took off his goggles.

"You look . . . I don't know, *younger*," Dom said.

Marks grinned. "You mean I don't look like a doddering old man with one foot in the grave?"

They embraced, and Marks clapped him on the back.

"How you holding up, Dominic?"

"I'm okay."

"It's okay not to be okay." Marks sighed. "I miss your dad more than ever, and I wish I'd been out there with him. But we made a pact that I would stay here and look for your sister and look after you."

"I know," Dom said. He held back his emotions. He was getting better at that now. Losing his sister and then his father over the past year had hardened his heart, and he had a feeling Marks could see it.

"How's your mom?" Marks asked.

"She's hanging in there. Having a dog around helps. She's really taken a liking to Cayenne, but she still blames me for Monica."

Marks shook his head. "I'm sorry. That's not fair. What happened is not your fault. It was the Vegas who took your dad, and probably who took your sister."

"And I will get my revenge," Dom said. He turned to the window. "So, are you going to tell me why we're here?"

They both looked out over the solar farm gleaming in the sun like a vast, square lake. The city-owned utilities were a big part of why Los Angeles was still on the map. Many other major cities across the country were falling into ruin in the wake of the Second Civil War because they lacked power and clean water.

"We're here because, now that the Morettis and the Vegas have taken over the public housing, they have their eyes on what you're looking at."

"So?" Dom said. "They won the war. The task force is dead, and there doesn't seem to be any way to stop them."

A necessary lie because Dom didn't want Marks to know about his plan.

The lieutenant eyed him. This could all be a test to find out what Dom had been up to with Moose these past few months. They had taken the law into their own hands on several occasions, stealing medicine and dropping it off at hospitals, killing gangsters, and hunting the narco bastards who had taken everything from Dom. But he didn't think Marks knew about all that.

"Follow me," Marks said. "Time to see why I *really* brought you here."

Dom pulled his face mask back up and followed him to their pickup truck, parked outside the observation tower. They took it down a dirt road, cutting through the solar farm. Thousands of panels shone, absorbing the precious rays that helped power the city on days when the dust storms didn't force them to retract.

Dom hated wearing his mask on a gorgeous day like this, but the dust and chemical toxins in the air were bad out here.

Marks drove them to the fences surrounding the precious desalination plants. Sheriff's deputies in guard towers watched over the terrain. Their orange goggles seemed to glow in the sun.

Guards at the gate waved the truck through after Marks showed his badge. He drove through a compound of a dozen buildings and stopped beside a warehouse.

"This way," Marks said.

They got out, and Dom followed him around a three-story brick building with a placard that read "Los Angeles County Seawater Desalination Plant. Founded by the Executive Council of the United Cities of America."

A sobering reminder hung from a pole. The Stars and Stripes. Only fifteen stars stood on the blue field, representing the remaining capital cities not destroyed in the war or in the aftermath.

Marks took a path toward a cluster of domed buildings. It was the first time Dom had ever been to the newest desalination plant. He had seen the one the Japanese gave to the city after the war, but not this one.

"Monica would have loved this place and the science behind the reverse osmosis process," Dom said.

Marks nodded. "You know, your dad always bragged about you two. Saying you were the smartest kids he had never known. He was pretty damn proud of that."

"Monica's the smart one," Dom said.

Marks opened the door and waved Dom inside. He stepped into a sprawling room of pools and metal platforms. Clear water sparkled under the glow of bright lights. Halfway across the room sat a man in a wheelchair, his back to them.

The man swiveled his chair around.

"Tom, it's good to see you, my friend," Marks said.

Years had passed since Dom had last seen his father's former marine commander.

"Dominic, meet Councilman Tom Castle."

"I've heard a lot of stories about you, sir," Dom said, walking forward with his hand outstretched.

"'Sir,'" Castle said with a snort. "I've heard a lot of stories about you, too, Dominic." He reached up and shook Dom's hand. "To start, call me 'Councilman,' 'Tom,' or just 'Castle,' but not 'sir,' if you don't mind."

"Councilman," Dom said.

"I suppose you're wondering why you're here."

"The thought crossed my mind."

"I'm thinking about running for mayor, but we need help," Castle said. "As you know damn well, the police department is poisoned by corruption."

Dom nodded.

"We already know that Chief Stone has sold off the public housing to the highest bidder," Marks said, "but we can't let the crime families get hold of this place, too. We can't let them control this entire city, or we will lose everything."

Castle turned his chair and wheeled away. The men followed.

"I didn't fight overseas and come back home to fight a corrupt government, only to see this country handed over to the mobsters and what's left of the cartels."

"Me, neither," Marks said.

"I agree," said Dom, "but how can we fight against them?"

"I've heard some stories about you and your partner, Andre Clarke," Castle said. "Marks has told me you guys have quite the reputation on the force. And he says that besides taking down gangsters, you're responsible for stealing shipments of medicine and dropping them off at hospitals and refugee camps."

Dom glanced at Marks.

"What, you thought I didn't know?" Marks said. He clapped Dom on the back. "Son, I've got eyes in the back of my head."

"I assure you, none of it links back to me or Moose."

"I know," Marks said. "If it did, you'd both be dead already."

"We're just doing what Chief Stone and Mayor

Buren refuse to do," Dom said. "Taking down the men responsible for abducting my sister and killing my dad. For that cause, I will happily give my life."

Castle's brow went up. "A word of advice about revenge, son. Don't let it consume you, or you'll end up no better than the men you hunt."

Marks remained silent, but Dom could feel his eyes on him. They had already talked about what happened to Ronaldo before his death, and his motto: *Sometimes, you have to use evil to fight evil.* Dom agreed wholeheartedly with the idea, but it was something Marks and his father had split on during the last year of Ronaldo's life.

"So, back to why I wanted to meet you," Castle said. "These two newest desalination plants won't be up and running for a while, and as you know, the water lines outside the city limits are compromised with heavy metals. How many refugees are out there?"

Marks scratched his mustache. "Depending on the month, fifty thousand to a hundred thousand people enter our borders."

"That's a lot of people without access to clean water, and that's why I've started a program that will spend city coin to shuttle extra water tankers to the camps while our engineers get these plants up and running. That's where I could use help."

He wheeled down the platform.

"You're not the only one fighting out there. I'm in contact with civilians who have started safe houses and stockpiled weapons and supplies to fight the crime organizations. But we're missing a key ingredient."

Castle stopped at the entry to another room, his blue eyes flitting to Dom. "We need soldiers. Men like you."

Marks opened the door to a space filled with chemical containers and barrels. Two men in city uniforms stood in the shadows, arms folded, masks covering their faces.

The men pulled down their masks.

"*Tooth?*" Dom said. "*Bettis?*"

"How you doin', Dom?" Tooth asked.

Bettis gave him a hug.

"Good to see you, kid," Tooth said.

Dom hadn't seen either man since his father's funeral, and he could tell by their tanned, weathered features that they had spent much of that time out in the desert.

They looked different. Bettis had grown a ponytail, and Tooth had a buzz cut. He sported new ink, too. Both forearms were covered.

There was another man with them, a Native American scout named Namid, whom Dom had met at Ronaldo's funeral.

He reached out and Dom shook his hand.

"You knew my dad, huh?"

"Not long, but he was a good man, a *great* warrior," Namid said. "I was proud to fight at his side."

"I'm putting together a new team," Marks said. "And I want all of you on it."

Bettis and Tooth nodded. So did Namid.

"And I want your partner and anyone else you trust," Marks said. "I know you have good intuition. We build a team that fights the crime organizations but can't be connected to the LAPD."

"We take back this city," Castle said. "It's the only way, and I will do everything in my power to support this team."

"We followed your father," Bettis said, "Now we will follow you."

"*Me?*" Dom gave them a puzzled look.

Marks nodded. "You're young, but you've got the intuition of a man twice your age, and the experience we need. Bettis and Tooth don't know the streets, or the crime families, like you."

"Moose would definitely be down for this. Camilla, too. There are a few other cops I trust. Rocky, and Pete, but I don't know . . ."

"This would all be undercover work," Marks said. "And for it to work, you would need to transfer to the Sheriff's Department, to work with Tooth and Bettis. I'll pay you out of a back-channel fund from the LAPD."

"Make no mistake, you won't be playing by the same rules you followed as cops," Castle said. "You'll be judge, jury, and executioner. Vigilantes."

"A modern-day Robin Hood," Marks said with a grin.

Dom looked at each of them. Bettis and Tooth looked eager but also anxious. They were his dad's brothers, and Dom trusted them with his life. Namid stood proudly, waiting for an answer.

"Well?" Castle said.

"You in?" Marks asked.

Dom smiled. "Yeah, I'm in, but does this team have a name?"

Bettis ran a hand through his long hair and then smiled back at Dom.

"How about 'the Saints'?"

Don't miss the next installment in
the Sons of War series!